DARK BEACON

The sky blazed with stars, singly, in clusters, and in great swirling eddies. So dense was the star field that it was difficult to find even a tiny part of the heavens that was completely dark. Except, that was, for the area high overhead where there hung an enormous, black, featureless mass which absorbed the light around it like a gigantic shadow.

Martin slowly became aware of his pulse hammering in his ears. He had been looking at the sky with such an intensity of wonder that he had forgotten to breathe.

"Is...is it some kind of black hole?" he asked.

NEGATIVE, came the examiner's reply on the terminal screen. THIS IS THE FEDERATION WORLD!

By James White
Published by Ballantine Books:

AMBULANCE SHIP

ALL JUDGMENT FLED

CODE BLUE—EMERGENCY!

THE DREAM MILLENNIUM

FEDERATION WORLD

FUTURES PAST

HOSPITAL STATION

MAJOR OPERATION

SECTOR GENERAL

STAR HEALER

STAR SURGEON

FEDERATION WORLD

James White

A Del Rey Book

BALLANTINE BOOKS • NEW YORK

To Walter Willis

whose example some forty years ago, and on many occasions since, made a young fan artist realize that words can say more than pictures

in Appreciation

A Del Rey Book
Published by Ballantine Books

Library of Congress Catalog Card Number: 87-91847

ISBN 0-345-35263-7

Manufactured in the United States of America

First Edition: June 1988

Cover Art by David B. Mattingly

Chapter 1

THE building was a white cube twenty stories high with a broad flight of white stairs leading up to the quietly impressive entrance on the second floor. From past experience Martin knew that the stairs retained their perfect whiteness no matter how many hundreds of people climbed them and that the sign above the entrance, which read FEDERATION OF GALACTIC SENTIENTS EXAMINATION AND INDUCTION CENTER, projected the same message regardless of the language or degree of literacy of the person viewing it.

He had not had the opportunity of speaking to a blind candidate for Galactic citizenship, but presumably he or she would have received the message in some other fashion.

As he began to climb, Martin saw that there were just three other people on the stairs—a young couple, working students judging by their age and dress, and an old man who was obviously much too frail to work. The oldster's face had the anxious, stubborn look of one whose life on Earth had become untenable for a variety of reasons which forced him to try for something better, or at least different. The young couple climbed briskly and confidently, as if they knew what to expect at the top. Like Martin they had probably been here before and had had second thoughts. Unlike Martin they now seemed to have made up their minds.

Not wishing to get into a discussion with any of them, Martin held back to allow the others to precede him.

Going through that entrance was still a shock, he thought, and always would be no matter how often he did it. There was no physical sensation, just the shattering realization that one had arrived in the center of an

1

enormous reception area with a transparent roof, and
that it was not on the second floor but the twentieth.
Like the perpetually white stairs and the omnilingual
signs, instantaneous matter transmission was just another piece of technological intimidation aimed at making the backward Earth people more amenable.

The reception area was carpeted and furnished in
warm, relaxing shades of gold and green and brown, and
covered with random groupings of chairs and reading
desks. All but a few of the chairs were empty, and the
desks were heaped with Federation literature. Three of
the distant walls were covered by large pictures, each of
which showed a stylized, almost heraldic, representation
of one of the member races of the Federation of Galactic
Sentients. There were close to two hundred of the pictures ranged around the three walls and, so far as Martin
could see, none of them was duplicated.

Along the wall facing him, like a row of unmanned
reservation desks at an air terminal, were the examination computers.

By the time he reached them the old man had been
passed through, and he could hear the young couple
talking quietly to the visual display unit of the examiner.
But they were several desks away and Martin could not
tell whether they were asking or answering questions.
Then suddenly they lifted their hands from the top surface of the unit and moved around the desk to disappear
through one of the two doors beyond it, the door bearing
the symbol which appeared on all of the Federation's
literature and equipment. He had been watching the successful candidates so closely that he walked into the
outer edge of another desk.

The display unit lit up, and the words which appeared
on it shone white against a field of deep green.

GOOD AFTERNOON, SIR. PLACE ONE HAND ON
THE UPPER SURFACE OF THIS UNIT AND STATE
YOUR REASONS FOR WISHING TO BECOME A CIT-
IZEN OF THE FEDERATION OF GALACTIC SEN-
TIENTS. PLEASE RELAX AND TAKE ALL THE TIME
YOU REQUIRE.

Martin looked at the examiner, at the large, smooth
cube whose only features were its display screen and the

everpresent Federation symbol centered on top, and kept his hands by his sides.

He said, "I have studied the brochure and have asked questions not covered by it on two previous occasions. I do not want to waste your time."

THANK YOU, SIR. PLEASE PASS THROUGH ON THE RIGHT AND USE THE UNMARKED DOOR.

For a moment he thought about passing on the left and going through the other door, the one bearing the symbol of a black diamond with rounded sides set in a circle of silver, and which looked so much like a single, alien eye, then he discarded the idea. During his last visit he had tried to do just that and found himself without warning at the foot of the entrance steps, with prospective candidates looking anxiously at him in case they, like himself, might be expelled as temporarily or permanently Undesirable.

The induction centers had attracted a large number of Undesirables in the early days. There were stories told of individuals and groups who had tried to exert physical or psychological pressure of various kinds with a view to organizing private armies on the new planet. And there had been the more simple, direct types who had wished merely to dismantle, remove, and study the Federation equipment for its weapons potential. The response in all cases had been nonviolent, but salutary.

At the first sign of tinkering, either with the minds of the candidates or the induction center equipment, the offenders were moved—teleported—a distance of a few miles. The more persistent or aggressive ones found themselves suddenly on the other side of the planet, without their weapons, equipment, or clothing.

Martin considered himself at worst a borderline Undesirable, so he went through the unmarked door.

He found himself in a small room which, judging by the view from the window, was on a much lower level of the building. The room was bare except for the desk containing the examiner at its center, and the display screen was partially hidden by a female candidate standing before it. She turned her head briefly to look at him, then returned her attention to the screen.

She was tall, slim, dark-haired, with a firm and mature face and skin so smooth and unblemished that her age could have been anywhere between twenty-five and forty. Like the heavy, dark-rimmed spectacles she wore, her clothing was functional rather than decorative. Nevertheless, and in spite of what the examiner might decide about her as a candidate, Martin would not have described her as Undesirable.

"No, I am not frightened by your advanced technology," she said quietly in answer to a question Martin could not see, "nor do I consider it to be magic. Your miracles are superscientific, not supernatural, in spite of the symbolism of the entrance stairs and the near Heaven you are offering us. But I keep wondering why you try so hard and often to impress us with this technology."

Martin edged sideways until he had a clear view of the screen, upon which appeared,

IT IS OUR POLICY TO TAKE EVERY OPPORTUNITY TO DRIVE HOME THE FACT THAT THE ADVANCED TECHNOLOGY EXISTS, WHETHER OR NOT YOU HAVE OCCASION TO USE IT, OR HAVE IT USED AGAINST YOU IN THE FUTURE. DISTANCE WITHIN THE GALAXY MEANS NOTHING TO US. NEITHER ARE THERE ANY PROBLEMS OF TRANSPORTATION, SUPPLY, ACCOMMODATION, OR LIVING SPACE ON YOUR NEW HOME. WE ARE CAPABLE OF TRANSPORTING YOUR ENTIRE SPECIES, ALL OF ITS ARTIFACTS, DOMESTIC ANIMALS, LARGE NUMBERS OF NATURAL FAUNA, VEGETATION, AND EVEN THE ENTIRE GAS ENVELOPE OF YOUR PLANET WERE IT NOT SO POLLUTED AS TO BE SCARCELY BREATHABLE.

THAT TECHNOLOGY ENSURES THAT NO FEDERATION CITIZEN LACKS FOR ANYTHING IN THE PHYSICAL SENSE. WHAT THEY DO WITH THEIR MINDS IS THEIR OWN BUSINESS PROVIDED THE END RESULT OF THEIR THINKING DOES NOT INTERFERE WITH THE FREEDOM OF OTHER CITIZENS, EARTH-HUMAN OR OTHERWISE.

"I know, I've studied the brochure," she replied sharply. "But I'm concerned about the long-term effects of such mollycoddling. Surely there is the danger that the whole race will vegetate, stagnate?"

YOU HAVE NOT STUDIED IT CLOSELY ENOUGH, OBVIOUSLY. THE INTENTION IS NOT TO FORCE YOU INTO IDLENESS BUT TO ENABLE YOU TO ACHIEVE YOUR FULL POTENTIAL. ALL INTELLIGENT SPECIES FEEL IMPELLED TO WORK AND BUILD AND THINK CONSTRUCTIVELY. HOBBYISTS, FOR EXAMPLE, FREQUENTLY DEVOTE MORE TIME AND EFFORT TO THE WORK WHICH INTERESTS THEM THAN TO THEIR SO-CALLED PROPER JOBS. BUT FEDERATION CITIZENS DO NOT WORK BECAUSE ANOTHER INDIVIDUAL TELLS THEM TO DO SO. NOR WILL THEY BE OVERPROTECTED. YOUR PEOPLE WILL STILL DIE BECAUSE OF OLD AGE, ACCIDENT, OR DISEASE, AND IF ANYTHING IS DONE TO CHECK THESE PROCESSES, IT WILL BE YOUR DOCTORS AND RESEARCHERS WHO DO IT. YOU MAY REQUEST FEDERATION ASSISTANCE WHENEVER YOU NEED IT, BUT THE REAL WORK WILL STILL BE DONE BY YOU.

IS IT STILL YOUR WISH TO BECOME A MEMBER OF THE FEDERATION?

"I—Yes," she said.

THERE IS HESITATION. HAVE YOU MORE QUESTIONS?

She nodded, then said, "Two, perhaps unimportant ones. You communicate with us pictorially or by projecting written language. Why do you use written rather than oral language? Also, it was twenty-two below zero and snowing heavily at my local induction center half an hour ago, and I left my protective clothing with the—"

THE QUESTIONS ARE UNIMPORTANT BUT THEY WILL BE ANSWERED. WE ARE CAPABLE OF PROVIDING AURAL TRANSLATIONS OF OUR COMMUNICATIONS, BUT THE TRANSLATION PROCESS ROBS THE WORDS OF MUCH OF THEIR EMOTIONAL CONTENT AND MAKES THEM SOUND, TO YOUR EARS, HARSH AND UNFEELING. THERE IS THE PROBABILITY THAT YOU WOULD BE LISTENING FOR EMOTIONAL TONES AND NUANCES, OR

HIDDEN MEANINGS, WHICH MIGHT CONFUSE YOU AND DISTORT THE MESSAGE. VISUAL PRESENTATION OF THE WORDS REDUCES THIS PROBABILITY.

REGARDING YOUR PROTECTIVE CLOTHING, IF YOUR APPLICATION FOR CITIZENSHIP IS UNSUCCESSFUL YOU WILL BE RETURNED TO YOUR LOCAL INDUCTION CENTER. IF YOU ARE ACCEPTED FOR CITIZENSHIP YOU WILL NOT NEED THEM.

PASS THROUGH ON THE RIGHT AND USE THE UNMARKED DOOR.

Martin saw her shoulders droop with disappointment, but otherwise she remained motionless. She said, "What would happen if I were to be directed through the other door?"

ALL OF THE MARKED DOORS OPEN INTO THE FEDERATION WORLD WHICH WILL BE YOUR NEW HOME, SPECIFICALLY INTO ONE OF THE REORIENTATION CENTERS. THEY ARE THE DOORS USED BY SUCCESSFUL CANDIDATES. THE UNMARKED DOORS ARE FOR THE NON-CITIZENS.

"Dammit, what's the difference?"

NON-CITIZENS DO AS THEY ARE TOLD.

She opened her mouth to ask another question, but the examiner's screen had gone dark. She looked at Martin, tried to smile and said, "Good luck." The unmarked door closed behind her before he could reply.

QUESTIONS? The word appeared on the screen as soon as his palm made contact with the sensor plate.

The letters were white on bright red, he noted. The first examiner's screen had been a restful shade of green and its conversation polite, even friendly, while the words he had seen projected onto this screen had been curt and downright critical at times. Perhaps the examiners were becoming impatient.

Martin wet his lips and thought, *So non-Citizens do as they are told?* . . . This datum suggested that the Federation was something less than a perfect social organization since it contained lower grade or second-class citizens.

"The previous candidate asked some of the questions

I had intended asking," he said to give himself time to think and, he realized suddenly, because he was honestly curious. "Is it permitted to know her name and background?"

ONLY IF YOU ARE BOTH ACCEPTED AS CITIZENS OR NON-CITIZENS INTENDING TO WORK ON THE SAME PROJECTS. MY SENSOR INPUT SUGGESTS THAT THE QUESTION YOU WANT TO ASK IS NOT THE ONE BEING VERBALIZED. THIS IS A FORM OF DISHONESTY AND IS WASTEFUL OF EXAMINATION TIME. IF YOU REQUIRE MORE TIME FOR CONSIDERATION, YOU MAY RETURN LATER.

The green screen had told him to take all the time he needed, but this one was rushing things to say the least. Did the red screen imply a warning of some kind? Was he about to be failed?

POLITENESS AS WELL AS INDECISIVENESS IS ALSO A WASTE OF TIME. YOUR MANNER IS UNIMPORTANT. SPEAK HONESTLY. THE SENSOR PLATE IS NOT A TELEPATHIC DEVICE, BUT IT WILL REGISTER THE SLIGHTEST DEVIATION BETWEEN YOUR INTENTIONS AND YOUR WORDS.

IF YOU CANNOT ASK QUESTIONS, THEN VERBALIZE YOUR FEARS OR SUSPICIONS. AND REMEMBER THAT I CAN OFFER YOU NO VIOLENCE, SO DO NOT BE AFRAID. THE MOST I CAN DO IS DECLARE YOU UNSUITABLE FOR CITIZENSHIP.

Martin felt himself begin to sweat. Why could he not simply accept everything he had been told and *ask* to be a Citizen? The standards for acceptance were unclear but, judging by the large numbers and types of individuals who made it, they could not be so high. Unless there was something inherent in his personality which rendered him unsuitable, something which was registering on the examiner's sensor plate?

"Why do so many others qualify?" he asked suddenly. "Oldsters, children, people of average intelligence and below, or those with no particular skills or training? Some of them were accepted at first examination in less than fifteen minutes. I saw it myself."

DO YOU CONSIDER YOURSELF SUPERIOR TO THEM?

He felt his hand sweating on the sensor plate and he thought, *Be honest.* Truthfully, he replied, "Superior to some of them. But why are they accepted?"

THEY ANSWER QUESTIONS. YOUR TYPE, INDIRECTLY OR OTHERWISE, ASK QUESTIONS. YOU ARE ABOUT TO ASK ANOTHER.

"Very well," Martin said angrily. "Considering your advanced technology and its potential for giving virtually unlimited assistance, why must we leave Earth to join the Federation?"

THIS IS COVERED IN DETAIL ON PAGES 7 THROUGH 18 OF THE BROCHURE.

"I know, I know," Martin said, wondering why a mere device, no matter how sophisticated its design, should make him feel like taking a sledgehammer to it. Was the examiner merely a terminal of an advanced computer as the brochure said it was, or was he taking their word for that, just as the unquestioning, unsuspicious, ordinary, and successful candidates for citizenship had taken it? More calmly, he went on, "I fully realize that our solar system is very far removed spatially from the center of galactic science and culture and that, because of your advanced transportation systems, this separation is more important psychologically than physically. But surely if we were to remain on Earth, our contacts with other Federation cultures would be more gradual, and natural?"

REFER TO PAGES 21 THROUGH 25.

Perhaps there was not a multi-tentacled Federation Citizen controlling the examiner as Martin had begun to suspect. It was behaving like a computer now, one which had been programmed by a bunch of extraterrestrial bureaucrats.

"I have studied those pages closely," Martin said patiently. "Earth is a very sick planet. Polluted, overpopulated, and denuded of natural resources to such an extent that in a few decades starvation and war will result in virtual genocide, according to your people. You are probably right. But why, with the incredibly high level of technology which you are so fond of demonstrating to us, don't you simply cure our sick planet? Forcing our people into premature contact with alien cultures could be dangerous."

DOES THE PROSPECT OF MEETING EXTRA-TERRESTRIAL INTELLIGENCES FRIGHTEN YOU?

The sensor plate was clammy against his palm. Give an honest answer, he reminded himself, because if you do not, then this damn thing, whether it is a device or a front for a Citizen examiner, would be aware of it.

"I don't know," he said.

Chapter 2

THE screen remained blank, projecting an angry red rectangle on which he expected the words of rejection to appear. Not only was his palm on the sensor plate sweating, but he could feel sweat beading his forehead and trickling down from his armpits. And still the screen remained blank.

He continued staring into it, and, because those events were so much on his mind, he began to form mental images on the blank red surface of the arrival of the stupendous Federation ships...

They had made no secret of their arrival. Upward of two hundred mighty vessels, ranging in size from three hundred yards to three miles in diameter, had taken up positions in synchronous orbit above the equator to hang like a blazing necklace of diamonds in Earth's night sky. Within the hour, they had identified themselves and given the reason for their presence.

The people of Earth were being given the opportunity of becoming Citizens of the Federation of Galactic Sentients. Examination and induction centers would be set up forthwith, and it was expected that the majority of the planet's inhabitants would pass these examinations and move to a world which had no pollution, power, population, or food supply problems, where there were no deserts or arctic wastes, and where every square mile of the new world's land surface was or could be made fruitful. To cushion the shock of first contact and to avoid the initial, and natural, feelings of xenophobia all communication between the Federation people and Earth candidates for citizenship would be by printed word only.

The invitation had appeared at hourly intervals on every TV screen in the world, and there was no way, short of switching off the set, of blocking the message. And when the big, white cubes which were the twenty-story induction centers appeared on pieces of empty ground convenient to the most populous areas, they could not be stopped either.

Many of Earth's most powerful governments and their armed forces tried very hard to stop them, but neither political argument nor military force had any effect. Armored columns, massed artillery, tactical nukes, and various other forms of frightfulness were tried and just did not work—the conventional weaponry malfunctioned and the nukes were teleported far, far away to be sealed in vast, subterranean caverns beyond the possibility of recovery by the limited technology of those remaining on Earth who might try to use them.

It was pointed out very firmly that the invitation to join the Federation was open to all responsible members of the Earth-human race, but it did *not* apply to certain of the world's political systems or any of its military organizations.

It was also pointed out that trust between the various species which made up the Federation was important, and that the earlier an Earth-human was able to trust the Galactic emissaries, the greater were his or her chances of being accepted as a Citizen. However, it was natural for a newly contacted race to feel suspicious of the Federation's motives and worried about their own reactions to the new world. To reassure these people, two-way travel would be permitted between Earth and the new world for a limited period, by observers nominated by the Earth's population, so that they could be satisfied in every respect regarding the desirability of the move from

Earth. After this period, for administrative and logistic reasons, travel would be one-way.

Except for the very small proportion of Undesirables and non-Citizens who would remain, it was intended to complete the evacuation of Earth in ten years . . .

"What happens to the people who are left?" Martin asked suddenly. But the screen remained blank except for the imagined images which came like the pictures seen in the flames of an old-time fire.

Many millions of Earth-people had passed the examinations and moved to the new world on trust, sight unseen—although to be fair, most of them came from areas where subsistence level conditions left them with very little to lose. Then there were the people who worried in case these first Citizens were not capable of looking after themselves, and they wanted to go along to organize things for them. The would-be organizers had a much harder time satisfying the examiners regarding their suitability for citizenship. They had to make it clear, by word and past deeds and sensor plate readings, that they were the type of person who had the ability and the need to care for other people, and not just the kind who wanted power.

Despite the early influx of the more simple and trusting Earth-people, the Federation saw to it that nobody went hungry or unsheltered. But for psychological reasons it wanted the new Citizens to become self-supporting as soon as possible—too much help from Federation technology could, at this early stage, set up an inferiority complex which might stunt future cultural and scientific development. So the appropriate public buildings, educational establishments, dwellings ranging from mud huts to skyscraper blocks, and whole factory complexes, were transfered with the minimum of physical and emotional dislocation.

One of the first and most pleasant discoveries made by the new arrivals was that the flora and fauna of Earth had been transplanted many centuries earlier and required only cultivation and domestication. Apart from the bright, stratospheric haze in the otherwise cloudless sky and the thirty-five hour day, the new world was very much like home. There was no moon, and the only way to see the sun was from a space observatory, but Earth's space hardware was not on the list for transfer.

It seemed that the human race was not to be given interstellar travel, matter transmitters, or other technological marvels of Federation science, but they would be given a little guidance in discovering these things for themselves. There was plenty of time, after all, and no pressure of any kind would be exerted on them. The Federation was deeply concerned that the Earth culture should not suffer from forced growth.

Surely, Martin thought angrily, these were the actions of a sensitive, altruistic, highly ethical group of entities. Why could he not accept what they were offering at face value? What stupid defect in his personality was making him uneasy?

Martin wiped his palm with a handkerchief. The screen remained lighted but blank. He put the hand back again.

He remembered how the early reports and then the Earth observers had come back, the former in an increasing flood and the latter in a reluctant trickle. It was a beautiful world, its climate semitropical throughout because of the heat-retaining stratospheric haze, and the Earth vegetation and animal life were flourishing. In short, it was the kind of world his grandparents had insisted that Earth had been back in the good old days when there was room to breathe and air which was breathable.

But that had been nearly eight years ago, Martin thought as he stared into the blank red screen. The transfer of Earth's population was virtually complete. Soon there would be nobody left but the people who, for personal or psychopathological reasons, were unsuitable for citizenship. There was nothing or nobody to hold him on Earth, and when he thought of the things he had heard and seen of the new world...

"I want to become a Citizen of the Federation," he said in quiet desperation.

But he was all too aware of his palm on the sensor plate saying, not in words but in the electrochemical changes in his skin and the equally tiny variations in muscle tensions and pulse-rate, something different. Unlike his voice, those psychophysiological reactions were saying that all this was too good to be true, that there had to be a catch in it somewhere, and that there was something the minds behind the robot examiners were not telling him.

The words PASS THROUGH ON THE RIGHT AND USE THE UNMARKED DOOR appeared on the screen suddenly.

The door opened into a room in another building. Outside the window there was a vista of pine trees poking like green spearheads through a blanket of sunlit, melting snow. He felt irritated because they still felt the need to impress him with their instantaneous transport system—had they never heard of the law of diminishing returns? But as he placed his hand on yet another sensor plate and looked beyond it his irritation changed abruptly to bitter disappointment.

Behind the examiner there was only one door, and it was unmarked.

QUESTIONS?

This time the word shone white on a field of icy blue, giving it an aura of cool, clinical detachment. But Martin did not feel anything at all like that.

"Am I being refused citizenship?" he asked angrily. "Am I an Undesirable? Am I wasting my time here?"

YOU ARE CURRENTLY A NON-CITIZEN, NOT AN UNDESIRABLE.

"What the blazes is the difference?"

THE STATUS OF NON-CITIZEN CAN BE A TEMPORARY CONDITION. UNDESIRABLES REMAIN SO.

Martin looked at the unmarked door again, remembering the girl candidate who had briefly shared an examiner with him before going ... somewhere else. She had been told that the unmarked doors were for non-Citizens and that non-Citizens did as they were told. No matter what was decided in this room he would go through that door. There was no alternative, and suddenly he was frightened.

"I would like to return to my own locality," he said as calmly as he could manage, "so that I can have more time to think."

I STRONGLY ADVISE AGAINST IT.

He took his palm off the sensor plate and rubbed it against his thigh. He did not replace it.

YOUR CASE SHOULD BE DECIDED NOW.

The examiner, the room, and the view outside the window became very sharp and clear to him, as if he might be seeing them for the last time, and his mind was holding onto the present moment because very shortly something awful was going to happen. When he spoke his tone was too high-pitched and harsh, a stranger's voice.

"What—what's the hurry?"

NOTIFICATION OF PROCEDURAL CHANGE. UNTIL TOLD OTHERWISE YOU WILL ANSWER, NOT ASK, QUESTIONS. PLACE YOUR PALM ON THE SENSOR PLATE.

Martin swallowed and did as he was told. As soon as his hand touched the plate the questions began.

DO YOU WISH TO BECOME A CITIZEN OF THE FEDERATION OF GALACTIC SENTIENTS?

"Yes," Martin said firmly.

SENSOR READING SUGGESTS RESERVATIONS. DO YOU WISH TO MOVE TO THE FEDERATION PLANET?

"Yes."

YOUR ANSWER IS NOT FULLY SUPPORTED BY THE SENSOR. DO YOU NOT WISH TO LEAVE EARTH BECAUSE OF EXPECTED HOMESICKNESS, PATRIOTIC FEELINGS FOR YOUR BIRTHPLACE, OR OTHER EMOTIONAL REASONS?

"No!" Martin said vehemently. He was thinking of what the Earth had been even before the eight years of the Exodus had left it with little more than a skeleton crew of Undesirables and people like himself who could not make up their minds or trust even themselves. Since his parents had died in a food riot twelve years ago, there had been nothing to hold him to any part of this sick and hopeless planet. He said again, "No."

IS IT A MATTER OF TRUST?

"Yes."

YOU ARE SUSPICIOUS OF OUR MOTIVES? DO YOU THINK WE ARE TELLING LIES?

"I'm—I'm not sure."

BRIEFLY OUTLINE THE NATURE OF YOUR FEARS, SUSPICIONS, FEELINGS, OR GRIEVANCES REGARDING THE FEDERATION'S ACTIVITIES SINCE COMING TO YOUR PLANET.

Martin could not think of anything to say, but he knew that his palm on the sensor plate was saying far too much.

THE FOLLOWING IS A LIST OF THE MOST COMMON FEARS AND SUSPICIONS ENCOUNTERED DURING THE EXAMINATION OF CANDIDATES FOR CITIZENSHIP. INDICATE VERBALLY THE ONE WHICH MOST CLOSELY APPROXIMATES YOUR CURRENT FEELINGS.

ONE: THE GALACTIC FEDERATION IS EVIL, IN-HERENTLY VICIOUS AND UTTERLY INIMICABLE TO MANKIND AND IS LULLING YOU INTO A FALSE SENSE OF SECURITY BY OFFERING THE EQUIVALENT OF HEAVEN ON THE NEW EARTH, WHERE YOUR RACE CAN BE EXTERMINATED PIECEMEAL WHILE BEING BEMUSED BY A COM-PLEX AND TECHNOLOGY-SUPPORTED CONFI-DENCE TRICK.

TWO: EARTH-PEOPLE ARE NOT DEMATERIA-LIZED AND TRANSPORTED TO THE NEW WORLD, THEY ARE REMATERIALIZED WITHOUT PROTEC-TION IN SPACE WHERE THEY DIE.

THREE: THE EARTH-PEOPLE ARE USED SIMPLY AS FOOD FOR THE FRIGHTFUL AND INSATIABLY HUNGRY POPULATION OF THE FEDERATION.

FOUR: THE FEDERATION IS A FIGMENT OF THE IMAGINATION OF AN ALIEN RACE, SO VISUALLY HORRIFYING AND REPELLANT THAT IT COMMUNI-CATES THROUGH DEVICES LIKE THE EXAMINERS WHICH SUBTLY CONTROL THE MINDS OF THE CANDIDATES SO THAT THEY BELIEVE EVERY-THING THEY SEE AND HEAR.

FIVE: THE FEDERATION IS SO ADVANCED IN THE NONPHYSICAL SCIENCES THAT THE PIC-TURES AND OTHER EVIDENCE OF THE NEW WORLD, THE VAST FLEET OF SHIPS IN SYNCHRO-NOUS ORBIT, THE RADAR AND VISUAL IMAGES,

AND THE REPORTS OF VISITORS TO THE NEW WORLD ARE THE RESULT OF DIRECT MENTAL CONTROL AND NONE OF IT HAS ANY PHYSICAL ACTUALITY.

SIX: YOUR PEOPLE ARE NOT BEING TRANS- PORTED ANYWHERE BUT ARÉ DYING ON THE OTHER SIDE OF THE DOORS MARKED WITH THE FEDERATION SYMBOL.

SEVEN: WE ARE SO COMPLETELY ALIEN AND INCOMPREHENSIBLE TO YOU THAT YOU COULD NOT EVEN CONCEIVE OF THE KIND OF PURPOSES FOR WHICH YOU WILL BE USED OR THE—

"But you understand *us!*" Martin broke in. "Surely understanding between intelligent races is a two-way process. That is a ridiculous suggestion."

THE SENSOR REGISTERS AN OVERREACTION TO FEELINGS OF DOUBT AND INFERIORITY. UN- DERSTANDABLE. ARE THE OTHER SUGGESTIONS RIDICULOUS?

"Yes."

BUT?

"Some of them are, well, worrying. The people who are being accepted for citizenship, while they are in many cases good, responsible, and sometimes highly in- telligent people, are not the type who will make trouble if things aren't what they expected. You're taking away the sheep and..."

THE SHEPHERDS.

"...leaving the wolves on Earth. What right have you to do this to us?"

THE RIGHT OF A RESCUER TO SAVE A BEING INTENT ON COMMITTING SUICIDE. A BASIC QUES- TION. DO YOU BELIEVE THAT WE MEAN YOU HARM?

"No."

SENSOR INDICATES PARTIAL UNTRUTH.

"Not intentionally."

EXPLAIN.

"You don't intend to harm us," Martin said firmly, "either as individuals or as a race. We would be hope- lessly paranoid not to believe that you are trying to help us, even though your reasons for evacuating Earth seem a bit high-handed and, considering the resources available to you, not wholly convincing.

"As well," he went on, "the brochure tells us that the Undesirables and non-Citizens who remain here will not suffer physical hardship unless they cause it themselves, but that the Earth will not be a pleasant place for them. On the other hand, the new planet will be a very pleasant place. So much so that there will be little for the Citizens to do for physical and mental exercise. They won't even be able to run away from the wolves. In spite of the brochure's reassurances, they may be opting for a cultural dead end, a world on which they will do as they like and risk degeneration and death as a species. Whereas on Earth you say that Undesirables and non-Citizens have to obey instructions. I wonder if they aren't the lucky ones."

INSTRUCTIONS FOR THE IRRESPONSIBLE AND UNDESIRABLE ELEMENT ARE SIMPLE. THEY WILL NOT CAUSE PHYSICAL OR MENTAL HARM TO NON-CITIZENS REMAINING PERMANENTLY OR TEMPORARILY ON EARTH. THIS INSTRUCTION WILL BE ENFORCED NON-VIOLENTLY UNTIL THE POST-EXODUS SITUATION STABILIZES ITSELF. NON-CITIZENS, DEPENDING ON THEIR ABILITIES AND PSYCHOLOGICAL PROFILES, WILL RECEIVE MORE COMPLEX INSTRUCTIONS. INSTRUCTIONS TO RESPONSIBLE NON-CITIZENS WILL NOT BE ENFORCED.

Earth would not be a pleasant place, Martin thought, but it would not be actively unpleasant if the responsible non-Citizens did as they were told. And the examiner seemed to be suggesting that they would do as they were told willingly because they would realize that it was for their own good. Whereas on the new world . . .

He said, "I can't quite believe . . . Is there something you're not telling me about the new planet?"

IS FEAR OF ULTIMATE BOREDOM THE PRINCIPAL REASON FOR YOUR INABILITY TO ACCEPT THE NEW LIFE WE ARE OFFERING YOU?

"I—I suppose so."

SENSOR CORROBORATES. CANDIDATE IS UN-SUITABLE FOR CITIZENSHIP. PASS EITHER SIDE AND GO THROUGH THE DOOR FACING YOU.

Chapter 3

HE stumbled as he went through the door. There was a sudden feeling of vertigo, and he instinctively put out his arms to keep his balance. It was a small room for the number of people in it, and for a moment he wondered if he was in a descending elevator.

"You'll get used to it in a moment," said the woman he had met earlier. Her face was pale, as if she had recently received some kind of shock, but her smile was reassuring and sympathetic. Apart from her there were six other people in the room, three women and three men of different ages and nationalities, and some of them smiled as well. They were all standing in front of the window, but they moved aside to let Martin see the view.

At first glance the stretch of harshly-lit, stony, and obviously airless ground made him think that he was on the moon—the low gravity would have explained his difficulty in keeping balance. But it was not *the* moon, he saw as soon as he raised his eyes above the horizon.

The sky blazed with stars—singly, in clusters, and in great, swirling, jeweled eddies—and so dense was the star field that it was difficult to find even a tiny part of the sky which was completely dark. Except, that was, in one area high overhead where there hung an enormous, black, featureless shape which looked at least twenty times larger than the disk of the full moon seen from Earth.

It was the shape of the Federation symbol.

Martin became aware slowly that his pulse was ham-

mering loudly in his ears, and that he had been looking at
the sky with such an intensity of wonder that he had
forgotten to breathe. He took a ragged breath and said,
"Is—is it some kind of black hole?"

NEGATIVE.

Because the room was lit only by that glorious star-
light, he had not noticed the examiner until the word
appeared white on a black screen. There was no sensor
plate on top, and this examiner, Martin thought, was not
fooling around with colored screens and subtle psychological pressures. He knew that his questions here would
be answered simply and directly.

Unless they were forestalled...

THIS IS THE FEDERATION WORLD.

... or he began to see the answers for himself.

IT IS A HOLLOW BODY FABRICATED FROM MA-
TERIAL WHICH COMPRISED THE PLANETS OF
THIS AND MANY OTHER STAR SYSTEMS. IT CON-
TAINS THE INTELLIGENT BEINGS OF NEARLY TWO
HUNDRED DIFFERENT SPECIES WHO ARE THE
CITIZENS OF THE FEDERATION OF GALACTIC
SENTIENTS. THIS WORLD, WHICH AMONG EARTH
SCIENTISTS WOULD BE CALLED A MODIFIED
DYSON SPHERE, ENCLOSES THE SYSTEM'S SUN
AND USES ITS OUTPUT FOR LIGHT, HEAT, AND
POWER FOR ITS SOIL SYNTHESIZERS, ATMO-
SPHERE PRODUCTION AND WEATHER CONTROL
MACHINERY, GENERAL FABRICATION, AND FOOD
SUPPLY.

THE DIAMETER OF THE FEDERATION WORLD IS
IN EXCESS OF TWO HUNDRED AND EIGHTY MIL-
LION MILES AND IT HAS A USABLE SURFACE
AREA, INCLUDING THE CONICAL EXTENSIONS AT
THE POLES, OF NEARLY TWO HUNDRED AND
FIFTY QUADRILLION SQUARE MILES, OR WELL
OVER ONE BILLION TIMES THE SURFACE AREA OF
EARTH.

THE PROJECTED FUTURE POPULATIONS OF
ALL THE PRESENT MEMBERS OF THE FEDERA-
TION, TOGETHER WITH THOSE OF THE
HUNDREDS OF AS YET UNDISCOVERED INTELLI-
GENT SPECIES WHO HAVE NOT YET BEEN IN-

VITED TO JOIN, WILL NEVER BE ABLE TO FULLY
POPULATE THIS WORLD.

The words, diagrams, and sharply detailed pictures
flashed onto the screen, describing the Federation
World, its topography, atmospheres, temperature and
weather control machinery, and the light neutralizer
fields which provided night and day for those species
which needed them. It rotated ponderously and with
seeming slowness, furnishing maximum gravity in the
equatorial areas for those Citizens who had come from
high-gee planets, and a diminishing artificial gravity approaching the poles where the surface was stepped and
terraced so that the centrifugal force would be at right
angles to the ground.

Citizens wishing to make contact with those of another species used ultralong-range aircraft or intra-plane-
tary spaceships. Such contacts were encouraged, but
only if they did not involve the risk of individual or species invasion of privacy. So touchy were some of the
cultures that the stratosphere of the entire Federation
World had been rendered opaque so that Citizens would
not be able to watch each other through telescopes by
looking upward and across their hollow superplanet.

The vast structure was a superthin eggshell of metal
which was ultra-hard and fantastically dense, and the
soils and atmospheres covering its inner surface were
synthetic and produced when population additions required them. Where the atmospheres of adjoining species were mutually toxic, one-hundred-mile-high walls,
transparent in the higher altitudes so as not to interfere
with the sunlight, separated the two areas. These were
similar to the walls which encircled the five-hundred-
mile entry ports, positioned at the points of the conical
polar extensions, to keep the atmosphere from being lost
into extraplanetary space.

In the gravity-free polar areas were the great, thou-
sand-mile-square tracts of bare metal on which were
built the atmosphere and soil synthesizers, the matter
transmitter units, searchship building and maintenance
docks, and the power sources for the long-range projectors which could turn aside or destroy any astronomical

body large enough to endanger the giant sphere by collision.

All at once the awful immensity of the Federation World, the incredibly high level of knowledge which had created and maintained it, and the inutterable pettiness of his suspicions made Martin want to run away and hide himself. He felt like an aboriginal grasshut dweller suddenly confronted with a block of skyscraper offices and rush-hour traffic.

"You are inviting us to join you," he said numbly, "and you built *that*!"

WE DID NOT BUILD THE FEDERATION WORLD, NOR WOULD WE BE CAPABLE OF DOING SO IN THE FORESEEABLE FUTURE. PLEASE TURN AROUND AND REGARD ME.

He turned quickly. The others, no doubt because they had already had this experience, turned more slowly. The wall on his right had become transparent, or maybe it was a wall-sized television screen showing a creature lying or perhaps standing surrounded by a complex control desk. It was vaguely crablike, with too many legs and appendages; the body was covered by warty excrescences and fleshy, frondlike growths. The single eye was wide and bulging, like a transparent sausage with two independently moving pupils. He had seen a pictorial representation of one of these beings in the reception area of the induction center, but this entity bore about as much resemblance to the picture as a real animal did to a cute cartoon treatment by Disney.

NO DOUBT YOU FIND ME AS VISUALLY REPULSIVE AS I DO YOU. THE FEELING DIMINISHES WITH REPEATED CONTACT. BUT TO ANSWER THE QUESTION YOU WERE ABOUT TO ASK, THE FEDERATION WORLD WAS THE ULTIMATE PROJECT, IN PURELY PHYSICAL TERMS, OF AN INCREDIBLY ANCIENT RACE WHICH NO LONGER DWELLS THERE, ALTHOUGH THEY STILL MAKE NON-PHYSICAL CONTACT EVERY FEW CENTURIES IN CASE WE NEED ASSISTANCE OR ADVICE. THE PROBABILITY IS THAT THEY HAVE EVOLVED TO A STAGE WHERE PHYSICAL EXISTENCE IS NO

LONGER A REQUIREMENT. THEY ARE THE BUILDERS.

MY RACE, WHICH WAS THEN AND STILL REMAINS THE MOST HIGHLY ADVANCED OF THOSE ENCOUNTERED IN THE GALAXY, WAS AMONG THE FIRST TO BE INVITED TO JOIN THE FEDERATION WORLD. WE ALSO HAD OUR SHARE OF RESTLESS AND IMPATIENT ENTITIES WHO WERE NOT SURE THAT THE SAFE, PROTECTED, AND INFINITELY SPACIOUS FEDERATION WORLD WAS FOR THEM. THESE PEOPLE WERE SELECTED AND TRAINED BY THE BUILDERS TO DO THE RELATIVELY MENIAL TASKS. ON EARTH YOU WOULD CALL US ERRAND BOYS, ODD-JOB MEN, SERVANTS. WE WERE TAUGHT HOW TO USE AND MAINTAIN THIS WORLD'S EQUIPMENT, OTHER-SPECIES COMMUNICATION AND ASSESSMENT TECHNIQUES, AND THE CONSTRUCTION AND OPERATION OF HYPERSHIPS FOR THE CONTINUING SEARCH PROGRAM.

WE FOUND THAT IN EVERY SPECIES SO FAR INVITED TO JOIN THE FEDERATION THERE WERE INVARIABLY A SMALL NUMBER WHO, INTELLECTUALLY OR EMOTIONALLY, COULD NOT ACCEPT THE INVITATION. THESE ENTITIES, THE NON-CITIZENS, CONTINUE TO JOIN US AND ASSIST IN PERFORMING THE TASKS SET BY THE BUILDERS.

One of the being's appendages rose ponderously to indicate the dense, shining star field and the pointed, ovoid silhouette that was the great, single world of the Federation of Galactic Sentients, and it went on,   OUR PRINCIPAL TASK IS TO SEEK OUT THE INTELLIGENT RACES OF THE GALAXY AND BRING THEM INTO THE SECURITY AND FREEDOM OF THE WORLD THAT THE BUILDERS HAVE PROVIDED FOR THEM, BEFORE THEY PERISH IN THEIR OWN PLANETARY EFFULVIA OR SOME OTHER CATASTROPHE BEFALLS THEM.

AFTER SUITABLE TRAINING, YOUR TASKS WILL INCLUDE ASSISTING US WITH SEARCHSHIP OPERATIONS AND CANDIDATE ASSESSMENT, WORK WHICH, CONSIDERING YOUR PRESENT

STAGE OF DEVELOPMENT, WILL TAX YOUR ABILI-
TIES TO THE FULL. TO AID YOU THERE ARE THE
FACILITIES OF THE FEDERATION MEDICAL ESTAB-
LISHMENTS WHICH WILL EXTEND YOUR LIFE
SPAN AND PHYSICAL CAPABILITIES SO THAT
YOUR LENGTHY TRAINING CAN BE PUT TO EF-
FECTIVE USE. IF AT ANY TIME YOUR WORK AS A
NON-CITIZEN BECOMES TOO ONEROUS, YOU
WILL BE GRANTED FEDERATION CITIZENSHIP AS
A RIGHT.

LIFE IN THE FEDERATION WORLD IS MORE LEI-
SURELY. ITS PURPOSE WAS AND IS TO BRING TO-
GETHER ALL THE INTELLIGENT RACES OF THE
GALAXY AND LET THEM INTERMINGLE AND
GROW SO THAT, IN THE FAR FUTURE, THE
PURPOSE OF THE BUILDERS WILL COME TO
FRUITION. THIS PURPOSE IS PRESENTLY IN-
COMPREHENSIBLE TO US, BUT WE HAVE BEEN
TOLD THAT THE COMBINED INTELLIGENCE AND
POTENTIAL OF THESE FUTURE FEDERATION CITI-
ZENS WILL FAR SURPASS ANYTHING ACHIEV-
ABLE BY EVEN THE BUILDERS. IT WILL BE A
SLOW, NATURAL PROCESS, HOWEVER, KEPT
FREE OF ANY KIND OF FORCE OR COERCION.

IN THE MEANTIME WE SHALL BE BUSY SEEK-
ING OUT AND ADDING RACES TO THE FEDERA-
TION, ENSURING ITS SAFETY FROM NATURAL
THREATS FROM WITHOUT AND THE POISON OF
UNDESIRABLES FROM WITHIN. YOUR LIFE FROM
NOW ON WILL BE VERY BUSY, PERHAPS EXACT-
ING, BUT NOT LONELY. AS THE SERVANTS AND
PROTECTORS OF THE FEDERATION, YOU WILL
COOPERATE CLOSELY WITH AND LEARN TO UN-
DERSTAND ENTITIES OF MANY DIFFERENT SPE-
CIES, LONG BEFORE THE CITIZENS ARE READY
TO DO SO, BECAUSE WE HAVE A VERY IMPOR-
TANT QUALITY IN COMMON—THE QUALITY
WHICH OUR SYSTEM OF EXAMINERS WAS PRI-
MARILY DESIGNED TO UNCOVER.

For a few moments the screen remained blank, and
Martin looked quickly at the other people in the room.
The woman he had met earlier smiled faintly and said,

"They do say that it is better to start a job at the bottom..." The others seemed to be looking somewhere deep within themselves and were silent.

He returned his attention to the monstrous, crablike being. Was it his imagination or was there really a glint of amusement in that great, bulging sausage of an eye as once more the non-Citizen's words were projected onto the screen.

CONGRATULATIONS. YOU HAVE BEEN EXAMINED AND HAVE BEEN FOUND UNSUITABLE FOR CITIZENSHIP IN THE FEDERATION OF GALACTIC SENTIENTS. PREPARE YOURSELVES FOR IMMEDIATE TRANSFER TO THE EARTH-HUMAN PRELIMINARY TRAINING SCHOOL ON FOMALHAUT THREE.

Chapter 4

By the time they had reached the final stages of their training on Fomalhaut Three they were eleven Earth-years older and, thanks to the advanced medical science available, they looked and felt at least that much younger. Several times Martin had asked by how much their life spans had been extended, but that was one of the questions which their supervisor refused to answer, saying that if they did not complete their training to its satisfaction they were likely to end their lives prematurely in some stupid and avoidable accident, so that giving them information regarding their probable life expectancies would serve no useful purpose.

They were now in possession of the knowledge and ability to control and direct mechanisms of a complexity and power undreamed of by the people they had been on Earth—although they had still, their superior insisted, to acquire the experience and wisdom to use this power effectively. So they had waited and trained to an even finer pitch, wondering when, if ever, their first assignment would come.

Due to training commitments, their original classmates and one-time friends had gradually drawn away from them to disappear, two by two, in the directions of their chosen specialties. But there were compensations. As the training programs of Martin and Beth, the woman he had seen during that final visit to the examination and induction center back on Earth, began increasingly to overlap, and their friends to move away, Beth and he had drawn—or had they been forced?—closer.

It was a disturbing thought, particularly when, as now, it returned to trouble both of them at the same time. Martin slipped his arm around Beth's shoulders and drew her back into the relaxer which, as well as being sinfully soft, was set for one-quarter gee. But her arm and neck muscles were stiff with tension, and she was wearing her totally unnecessary spectacles, which was not a good sign.

"How much does that slimy, supercilious supervisor know about us?" she asked, so softly that she might have been speaking to herself. "Was a few hours with the interrogation robots at the induction center enough to tell it *everything*? And if it knows everything, how accurately can it predict our behavior? Have we any free will, any choices? More importantly, have you, had you, any choice at all?"

"We can always choose to fail the next test," Martin said, in an attempt to change the subject. "But it might well be that, in our situation, teacher knows best."

"It knows us well enough to know that we wouldn't deliberately fail a test," Beth said impatiently. "And you know what I mean. We had no choice, no competition, no chance to make comparisons. I know that you were, well, impressed by Kathy. She impressed hell out of all the men, she's gorgeous, dammit. If things had been different you might have preferred . . ."

Looking miserable, she left the sentence hanging.

Martin gave her shoulders another sympathetic squeeze, trying to draw her closer. But the warm, yielding, and normally responsive body had become that of a cold, fleshy mannequin with tension-frozen joints. He sighed, remembering that during their first meeting in the induction center so long ago, before he had even learned her name, he had decided that she was a lovely and highly intelligent young woman who took things much too seriously.

He had found no reason to change his mind about her when they met in the spacious living module occupied by the school's Earth-humans, or during recreation periods in the forests and lakes overlying that tremendous underground training complex. Fomalhaut Three provided an environment suited to the needs of many of the Galaxy's warm-blooded, oxygen-breathing races, and much of its training and large-scale simulation equipment was in common use. But none of the trainees, including Martin, were allowed to make contact with a member of another species until they had graduated from the school.

He and Beth had met more and more frequently as their chosen specialties required them to share training simulations of increasing complexity, duration, and degrees of risk. She, who once had been responsible for the computer control of traffic in a small Earth city, and who was now able to direct energies and engines capable of changing the topography of a continent; and he, a cynical, discontented, one-time lecturer in zoology who, it seemed, was destined to do little else but talk. He shook his head and brought his mind back to the present time and problem.

"You're forgetting," he said quietly, "that the only one of us to impress Kathy was George. George with the muscles, and mustache, and the teeth. Did *you* fancy—"

"No," she said firmly. "Kathy is welcome to him."

"Besides," he went on, "they're both specializing in multi-environmental plant and animal husbandry. Fine, demanding, vitally important work, no doubt, especially if they want to stay inside the World, but it is still only farming. Teaming up with a ship handler, the class's only trainee hypership captain, no less, is much more fun. For personal as well as professional reasons."

Beth did not smile as she turned her head to look at him, and her eyes were hidden by light reflection in her spectacles.

He went on. "It is quite possible that the supervisor knows our minds much better than we do, and that would include being able to predict what we are likely to do in any given situation. But what of it? That creature is hyperintelligent, not omniscient, and I think that its thought processes are just too alien for it to be able to influence us against our wills where anything so subtle as Earth-human emotional relationships are concerned. The decisions we made, and will make, are still our own, regardless of the fact that it probably knows about them in advance. The point I'm trying to make is that, had the supervisor given you more female competition by confronting me with a dozen, or a hundred, tall, dark-eyed, lovely women who know what I'm thinking almost before I do, the process would have taken much longer, and wasted a lot of our supervisor's precious training time, but ultimately I would have made the same choice."

He felt her relax, but not completely, as she allowed herself to settle into the backrest beside him.

"If I had been confronted with a hundred men . . ." she began.

"I was lucky you weren't," he said.

Irritably, she said, "How can I argue with you when you always say the right thing? But I keep forgetting that you're training as one of those devious-minded, smooth-talking specialists in First Contact who never stops practicing . . ."

"This," he reminded her gently, "is not the first contact."

There was a small movement of her shoulder, and he felt her hand creep gently into his and grip the fingers tightly, and he knew that she, too, was remembering that first contact and all the tension and terror of the protracted, technological nightmare that had preceded it.

It had happened during one of their early shared training exercises, when they were still trying to familiarize themselves with what the supervisor, a being renowned for the magnitude of its understatements, referred to as the basic tools of the trade.

The tools of their trade . . .

Tool One, the hypership: the largest general-purpose

vessel operated by the Galactics; just under half a mile in
length, one-third that at its widest point, bristling with
such an angular, metallic outgrowth of hyper-drive generator assemblies, normal-space drivers, tractor and
pressor beam projectors, weather control machinery, and
long- and short-range sensors that it was incapable of
making anything but the most catastrophic of crash land-
ings on a planetary surface. Internally it was packed with
enough power generation equipment to satisfy the demands of one of the Galactic's most energy-hungry
cities, as well as a small army of monitor and self-repair
robots, fabrication modules capable of producing anything from a pair of boots to a medium-sized interplane-
tary space vessel, synthesizers for the crew's organic
consumables, and, in executive charge of all these systems, a computer which, to describe it as superhuman
would have been to damn it with faint praise indeed. In
spite of its virtual omniscience, the main computer was
subservient to the wishes of its organic crew, although
not always without argument.

This was one of the Galactics' standard-issue tools,
varying from ship to ship only in the control interfaces,
living quarters, medical support, and food and translation systems required by its organic occupants at the
time.

Tool Two, the lander: a small, fast, low-level recon-
naissance vessel and surface lander, with crew positions
for two but capable of being controlled remotely by the
mother ship. Designed as a secure base for the First
Contact specialist, it carried the full spectrum of communications equipment and, in the event of the contact
going sour, its meteorite screen was also capable of protecting the occupant from ground or air attack by anything short of nuclear weapons.

Tool Three, the protector: a small, surface observation vehicle capable of operating within the most hostile
of environments while enabling its crew to communicate
with any intelligent inhabitants who might be present.
For defense it relied principally on high mobility, but in
the event of it encountering a threat from which it could
not run away and which threatened the life of an organic
occupant, it had power sufficient for a short-range mat-

ter transmission link with either the lander or the hypership.

The other tools were much smaller, more specialized,
and tailored to the needs of the Earth-human life-form.
These included mobile, self-powered protective enve-
lopes, proof against any hostile environment they were
likely to encounter; a variety of nonlethal or psychological weaponry; and a two-way translator terminal so
small that it could be disguised as a piece of ear or neck
jewelry, and possessing a silent voice-bypass facility
which enabled the contacter to hold simultaneous conversation with the mother ship without the risk of giving
offense to an alien contactee.

But in that first major test, given without prior warning during the start of an otherwise routine training exercise to power-up a cold lander, the majority of those
increasingly familiar tools were deliberately withdrawn
from use.

It was a simulated, near-catastrophic malfunction
which had opened the hypership to space and taken out
the on-board power generation and all of the systems
controlled by the main computer. They protested, reminding the supervisor that they had been taught that the
hypership's design philosophy made such an event impossible. But they were told that it was a simulated and
not a real event, that it was designed to test, under conditions of extreme stress, their suitability for their chosen specialties, and that if they put into practice
everything they had been taught up until that time, they
should be able to survive the test without serious damage
or life termination.

Within seconds of the first malfunction alarm, the
lander's hull sensors reacted automatically to the loss of
external pressure and simulated radiation build-up by
sealing all entry and inspection ports, effectively trapping them in a ship within a ship.

Considering their level of technological ignorance at
the time, it was obvious that they could not do anything
about the condition of the distressed hypership, so that
the most that was expected of them was to act as they

would have done had the situation been real, and call for help.

But the distress beacon was mounted outside the hypership's hull, and they were trapped inside a lander whose power cells and consumables were all but depleted. A hurried inventory showed that they had enough energy to maintain an air supply for two people of thirty-six hours, provided they remained at rest and did not use the available power for light, heat, artificial gravity, or communication with anyone or anything outside the lander.

Plainly they had to breathe less, but communication was vital.

The main computer was down, and with it all of the mother ship's remote control systems. Through the crackle of simulated radiation interference, Beth was able to make intermittent contact with the three, self-powered repair robots assigned to the lander dock area. The robots were capable of performing a variety of delicate, precise, and quite complex tasks, she told Martin, provided they were given equally precise and complex instructions. Being in-organic and capable of operating in an airless, radioactive environment, it was possible for them to be given directions for finding and operating the manual release for the distress beacon—if she could remember the complicated internal geography of the mother ship and none of the different paths she programmed them to follow were blocked by simulated wreckage. But the first two robots died on her long before reaching their objective.

Beth complained angrily that the stupid things had done what they were told, not what she wanted them to do, and began the even more precise and careful instruction of the third and last one.

While she was working, Martin opened the seal between the flight deck and lock chamber to allow maximum circulation of their remaining air. Then he detached the wide, one-piece padding from their control couches and tied the attachment straps together to form a makeshift sleeping bag which he anchored loosely beside the direct vision port. Since the heating had been turned off, it was becoming colder by the minute—doubtless the rate of heat dissipation into space was being accelerated for the purposes of the test. He checked the food storage locker again, finding only two water bulbs and the characteristic shape of a self-warming food container, but the glow coming from their only working communicator screen was too dim to let him read the label.

Martin had succeeded in detaching one of the cabinet's short, metal shelves when the communicator began producing louder and more regular hissing sounds overlaying the background interference—the distress beacon was functioning. A few minutes later the communicator screen went dark as Beth directed what little power remained to air production.

Hastily they shared the hot food and fumbled their way into the makeshift sleeping bag. Then they put their arms around each other, the first time they had done so, and breathed slowly and economically and remained otherwise motionless. There was nothing they could do but try to conserve the remaining air, pool their body heat, and await rescue.

They had no way of knowing how long that would take, or if it would come in time. Their supervisor would not deliberately let them die, they thought, but it was a completely alien lifeform with a metabolism utterly unlike their own, and a misjudgment might occur.

It was also possible that their rescuers had arrived, and were trying vainly to raise them on the dead communicator before beginning a long, time-wasting search of the entire hypership. That was why Martin, at what he thought were reasonable intervals, reached outside their cocoon of relative warmth to hammer his piece of shelving against the nearest bulkhead, to signal their presence and position to rescuers who were probably not there yet.

A subjective eternity passed as they drifted weightless in the utter darkness, staring out of an unseen viewport at an equally dark lander dock. The temperature continued to fall, the air-maker's status light had dimmed to extinction, the air was thick and stale and painfully cold in the lungs. The sweat on Martin's face felt like a film of ice and there was a pounding ache in his head that seemed louder than the noise he was making with the shelf. Through their thin coveralls he was aware of every curve and contour and movement of Beth's body, which had begun to shake with a motion that was slower but more violent than shivering. It was the uncontrollable tremor of fear.

"If you're as cold as all that," he whispered between deep, unsatisfying gulps of stale air, "I've just thought of a nice way of generating more body heat..."

"L-liar," she said through chattering teeth. "I've felt you thinking it since we got into this bloody, two-person straight-jacket. No. A-apart from... from other considerations, dammit, it would be too wasteful of energy and oxygen, and it would let in the cold."

She was still shaking, and holding him more tightly than before.

"Don't worry," he whispered reassuringly. "It's only a matter of time before we're rescued. And I'd say you passed this test, no doubt about that. The way you directed that last repair robot to the beacon, with the ship in darkness and relying on memory alone for internal navigation, that was really fine work.

"As for me," he went on, taking another deep, gasping breath, "I've done nothing at all but talk and make noise. If you want to worry about something, worry about me flunking this test."

She had stopped trembling, and now it was her turn to be reassuring. He felt her cold, damp forehead rest against his equally clammy cheek as she said, "Moral support is important at a time like this. It's the only kind that doesn't waste energy. Besides, the sleeping bag idea was yours. I would have put us into the unpowered spacesuits, where we would have frozen to death by —*Look!*"

Bright, greenish-yellow light was streaming through the direct vision port and reflecting from the dead screens and control console. It was coming from a large vehicle with the unmistakable outlines of a manned rescue pod which was drifting through the unlit dock and toward their lander. But as it moved closer, and he heard it dock with their entry port, he saw that some of the structural details were unfamiliar. Frantically he began battering at the viewport surround with his length of shelving.

"Take it easy, they know we're here," Beth said, grabbing his arm. "What's the *matter* with you?"

"That isn't the rescue pod we trained on," he said urgently. "The configuration is slightly different. And look at that, that yellow fog inside the canopy, and their interior lighting. Dammit, our simulated bloody rescuers aren't even human! I've got to make them understand that we belong to a different species, and work out a way of telling them so before they open our lock and poison us with their air. Let go of my arm!"

"Hammering won't tell them anything," Beth said. "They'll think we're naturally excited at being rescued. But—but I'm sure you'll think of something."

Neither of them mentioned the fact that he was supposed to be the specialist in other-species communication, that the problem was all his, and that it was now his turn to be tested. Beth's face looked white even in that yellow light, and frightened, but the concern in her eyes seemed to be only for him.

He had to communicate urgently, send detailed physiological and metabolic data to an alien and intelligent lifeform, from a dead ship whose only channel of communication was a piece of metal shelving.

Or *was* that the only channel? . . .

"Close the bag after me and stay inside," he told Beth, and wriggled out into the biting, breath-stopping cold.

He was already searching the control deck with his eyes, but his head was enveloped in clouds of condensation, and objects in the weightless condition had the habit of drifting into dark corners. He wasted several precious minutes before he found them, then he dived into the lock chamber and checked himself against the airlock's outer seal, which was already beginning to open.

Fighting desperately not to inhale, he watched the crescent of yellow, foggy light widen as the seal opened. Some of the yellow fog eddied through, stinging his eyes so badly that he had to feel rather than see when the seal had opened wide enough for him to throw the objects into the alien rescue pod. Then he backed quickly out of the lock chamber and closed the inner seal behind him, dogging it shut so that it could only be opened from the inside.

Shivering uncontrollably and with his eyes streaming from the effect of the alien air, and coughing because some of it was still adhering to his hair and clothing, Martin groped his way back to the sleeping bag.

He felt Beth's hands on his body, helping him in and then holding him tightly in an effort to stop his shivering. He felt her fingers moving gently against his eyelids, as if he were a small, hurt child and she his mother brushing away the tears. He blinked several times and found that he was able to see her, and the way she was looking at him. But all she said was, "The rescue pod is moving away. What the blazes did you do back there?"

"Good," Martin said, smiling for the first time in many hours. "I think we've cracked it. I threw them a water bulb with a few drops still in it, and the empty food container, and made it clear that we did not want them to get any farther into the ship. If they put those samples into their analyzer, they should be able to learn enough about our metabolism to mount a proper rescue. It's just a matter of waiting a little longer."

But he was wrong.

As Martin finished speaking the control deck lights and heating came on; the cold, stale fog they had been breathing was being replaced by air that was warm and fresh. With the return of artificial gravity their makeshift sleeping bag settled gently to the deck, and the communicator screen lit with a message.

EXERCISE TERMINATED. TEST RESULTS EXCELLENT BOTH SUBJECTS. EXTERNAL ENVIRONMENT RESTORED TO EARTH-HUMAN OPTIMUM. YOU MAY RETURN TO TRAINEE QUARTERS.

They did not return to quarters, or leave the lander or the sleeping bag, for a very long time. It was during this period that what they came to think of as their First Contact took place. It was a contact which deepened and broadened and made the remaining long years of their training seem short, and it would, they believed, be maintained and strengthened during the rest of their lives.

Chapter 5

THEY were settling themselves for the first study session of what promised to be another not very exciting day, when it happened.

GOOD MORNING, read their desk displays. AS-SIGNMENT INSTRUCTIONS FOLLOW. PLEASE RECORD FOR LATER STUDY.

With the appearance of the words, the wall facing them became a screen depicting in unpleasantly fine detail their supervisor and the large, low-ceilinged, and dimly lit compartment in which it lived—or perhaps only taught. It was surrounded by two small consoles and eight untidy heaps of garishly colored material which Martin had thought at first were art objects or furniture but had later decided, after seeing the creature holding one of them close to a body orifice, were more likely to be food or collections of aromatic vegetation.

SUMMARY OF ASSIGNMENT. PROCEED TO THE SYSTEM LISTED AS TRD/5/23768/G3 AND TAKE UP ORBIT ABOUT FOURTH PLANET. STUDY IT, IN-TERVIEW A MEMBER OR MEMBERS OF ITS DOMI-NANT LIFEFORM, AND CARRY OUT PRELIMINARY ASSESSMENT OF THIS SPECIES' SUITABILITY OR OTHERWISE FOR CITIZENSHIP.

QUESTIONS?

Martin swallowed. He knew that the feeling was purely psychosomatic, but it felt as if his stomach were experiencing zero-gee independently of the rest of his body. At the adjoining desk, Beth was putting on her spectacles. She did not need them, or any other sensory aid for that matter, because all of the Earth trainees had received the benefits of the Federation's advanced medical and regenerative procedures so that they were as perfect physiologically as it was possible for a member of their species to be. But in times of stress, Beth wore her glasses because, she insisted, they made her feel more intelligent.

"No questions," she said quietly, glancing at Martin for corroboration. "Until more assignment data is available, questions would consist of requests for more information."

VERY WELL, THE PLANET IS CALLED TELDI IN THE LANGUAGE MOST WIDELY USED ON THAT WORLD. IT IS A DANGEROUS PLANET AND IS CONSIDERED SO EVEN BY ITS INHABITANTS, WHO LIVE ON A LARGE EQUATORIAL CONTINENT AND A CHAIN OF ISLANDS LINKING IT TO THE NORTH POLAR LAND MASS. TECHNOLOGICALLY THE CULTURE IS NOT ADVANCED. TELDI WAS DISCOVERED BY A FEDERATION SEARCHSHIP TWENTY-SEVEN OF YOUR YEARS AGO. BECAUSE OF GROSS PHYSICAL DIFFERENCES BETWEEN THE TELDINS AND THE SPECIES MANNING THE VESSEL, NO OVERT CONTACT WAS MADE.

QUESTIONS?

There was a very obvious question, and Martin asked it. "If direct contact could not be made because the searchship personnel were too visually horrendous so far as the Teldins were concerned, why wasn't indirect contact tried by translated visual word displays only, as was done on Earth?"

TELDINS WILL NOT DISCUSS MATTERS OF IMPORTANCE OR MAKE MAJOR DECISIONS THROUGH INTERMEDIARIES LIVING OR MECHANICAL. DISCOVERING THE REASON FOR THIS BEHAVIOR IS PART OF YOUR ASSIGNMENT.

"Then we shall be meeting them face to face," Martin said, wondering where all his saliva had gone. "May we see one of the faces concerned?"

OBSERVE.

"No doubt," Beth commented in a shaky voice, following a three-second glimpse of the lifeform, "they have beautiful minds."

THE MATTER TRANSMITTER NETWORK WILL NOT INCLUDE TELDI UNTIL A FAVORABLE ASSESSMENT HAS BEEN MADE. YOUR TRANSPORTATION WILL BE BY HYPERSHIP. DURING SURFACE INVESTIGATIONS BY THE ENTITY MARTIN, THE ENTITY BETH WILL REMAIN WITH THE SHIP IN A SURVEILLANCE AND SUPPORT ROLE.

QUESTIONS?

Martin lifted his eyes to stare at the monstrosity beyond the desk screen, feeling himself beginning to sweat. He said, "This . . . this is a very important assignment."

THAT IS A SELF-EVIDENTLY TRUE STATEMENT. IT IS NOT A QUESTION.

Beside him Beth laughed nervously. "What he is trying to say, Tutor, is why us?"

THREE REASONS. ONE: YOU HAVE BOTH SHOWN ABILITY ABOVE THE AVERAGE BOTH AS INDIVIDUALS AND AS A TEAM. TWO: AS MEMBERS OF THE SPECIES MOST RECENTLY OFFERED FEDERATION MEMBERSHIP, YOUR KNOWLEDGE AND UNDERSTANDING OF WHAT IS INVOLVED IN MAKING THIS ASSESSMENT WILL BE GREATER THAN THAT OF LONG-TERM MEMBERS. THREE: THERE ARE MANY SIMILARITIES BETWEEN THE TELDINS AND THE EARTH-HUMAN SPECIES WHICH SHOULD EASE YOUR COMMUNICATIONS PROBLEMS.

"Apart from breathing a similar atmosphere," Beth protested, "there is no resemblance at all. They are ungainly, completely lacking in aesthetic appeal, visually repellant, and—"

YOUR PARDON. I HAD THOUGHT THAT THE DIFFERENCES WERE SUPERFICIAL.

To you, Martin thought, they probably are.

YOU WILL ALREADY HAVE REALIZED THAT YOU ARE BOTH TO UNDERGO IMPORTANT FITNESS TESTS. THE VALUE OF THESE TESTS WOULD BE

DIMINISHED IF I ASSISTED YOU OTHER THAN BY
PROVIDING THE BASIC INFORMATION.

QUESTIONS?

"Can you give us advice?" he asked.

OBVIOUSLY. YOU HAVE BEEN RECEIVING AD-
VICE, GUIDANCE, AND INSTRUCTION SINCE YOU
CAME HERE. MY ADVICE IS TO REMEMBER
EVERYTHING YOU HAVE BEEN TAUGHT AND PUT
IT INTO PRACTICE. THE ASSIGNMENT NEED NOT
BE A LENGTHY ONE PROVIDED THE ENTITY BETH
USES ITS BRAIN AND THE SHIP'S SENSOR AND
COMPUTER FACILITIES EFFECTIVELY, AND THE
ENTITY MARTIN IS CAREFUL IN ITS CHOICE AND
SUBSEQUENT INTERROGATION OF THE FIRST
CONTACTEE.

IT IS POSSIBLE TO ARRIVE AT A COMPLETE UN-
DERSTANDING OF A CULTURE FROM THE INTER-
ROGATION OF ONE OF ITS MEMBERS. ALL THE
NECESSARY EQUIPMENT IS AVAILABLE TO YOU,
AND YOU HAVE BEEN FULLY TRAINED IN ITS USE.
WHILE YOU ARE DECIDING ON THE SUITABILITY
OR OTHERWISE OF TELDI FOR FEDERATION MEM-
BERSHIP, WE SHALL BE DECIDING ON YOUR
SUITABILITY AS A HYPERSHIP CAPTAIN AND AN
OTHER-SPECIES CONTACT SPECIALIST.

THE RESPONSIBILITY IS ENTIRELY YOURS.

The system had seven planets, and its only inhabited
world, Teldi, was encircled by the broken remnants of a
satellite which apparently had approached within the
Roche limit and been pulled apart by the gravity of its
primary. The planet had no axial tilt, and the orbit of the
moon had coincided with the equator. The constantly
colliding orbital debris had not yet formed into a stable
ring system, so that the equatorial land mass of Teldi was
regularly swept by a light, meteorite drizzle which was
seeded with enough heavier pieces to make life very uncertain for anyone who remained for long periods in the
open.

"It wasn't always like this," Martin said, pointing at
one of the sensor displays they had been studying. "That

gray strip with the old impact craters all over it was an airport runway, those heaps of masonry and corroded metal could only be industrial complexes, and the rubble of what's left of their residential area stretches for miles around. This culture must have been as advanced at least as that of pre-Exodus Earth before their moon broke up."

"It may have been more than one moon," Beth said thoughtfully. "The orbit and unusual clumping of the debris indicates a—"

"The difference is academic," Martin broke in. "What we have here is a once advanced culture which has been hammered flat by meteorite bombardment to the extent that they have regressed to a primitive farming and fishing society. Except for that polar settlement, which is virtually free of meteorites, their past technology seems to have been destroyed. The question is, where do I land?"

Beth displayed a blown-up photograph of the polar settlement along with the relevant sensor data. It was a scientific establishment of some kind, with a small observatory, a non-nuclear power source, and a well-built road which was obviously a supply route. Communicating with the inhabitants would be relatively easy, Martin thought, because the astronomers among them would be mentally prepared for the possibility of off-world visitors. But they would not be typical of the population as a whole.

An assessment should not be based on a species' intellectuals alone. Ideally he should talk to the Teldi equivalent of a well-educated man in the street.

The landing site finally chosen was by a roadside some ten miles from a "city" which lay on and under the floor and walls of a deep, fertile valley on the equatorial continent.

"And now," Beth said, "what about protection?"

For several minutes they discussed the advisability of using the ship's special protection systems while he was on the surface, then decided against them. He had to make contact with a technologically backward alien, and he would do himself no good at all by frightening it with gratuitous demonstrations of superscience.

"All right, then," he said finally. "My only protection will be the lander's force shield. I won't carry anything in my hands, and will wear uniform coveralls and an open helmet with image-enhancing visor, and a Teldin-type backpack with a med kit and the usual supplies. The Teldins seem pretty flexible in the matter of clothing, so I would be displaying my physiological differences as well as showing them that I was unarmed.

"The translator will be in my collar insignia," he went on, "and the helmet will contain the standard sensor and monitoring equipment, lighting, and the translator bypass.

"Have I forgotten anything?"

She shook her head.

"Don't worry about me," he said awkwardly. "Everything will be just fine."

But still she did not speak. Martin reached toward her and carefully removed her glasses, folded them, and placed them on top of the control console.

"I'm ready to go," he said, then added gently, "sometime tomorrow. . ."

Martin made no secret of his landing. He arrived at night with all the lander's external lights ablaze, and came in slowly so as not to be mistaken for one of the larger meteors. Then he waited anxiously for the reaction of the inhabitants and authorities of the nearby city.

With diminished anxiety and growing impatience, he was still waiting more than a full Teldin day later.

"I expected crowds around me by now," Martin said in bewilderment. "But they just look at me as they pass on by. I have to make one of them stop ignoring me and *talk*. I'm leaving the lander now and beginning to move toward the road."

"I see you," Beth said from the hypership, then added warningly, "the chances of you being hit during the few minutes it takes you to reach the protection of the road are small, but even the computer cannot predict the impact point of every meteorite."

Especially the rogues which were the result of collisions in low orbit, Martin thought, and which dropped in at a steep angle instead of slanting in from the west at the normal angle of thirty degrees or less. But the odd behavior of the satellite debris which fell around and onto Teldi, and which so offended Beth's orderly mind, faded from his mind at the thought of meeting his first Teldin.

It would be a member of a species which had advanced perhaps only to the verge of achieving spaceflight, and which still practiced astronomy in their dark, polar settlement. Such a species would have considered the possibility of off-planet intelligent life. Perhaps the idea might now exist only in the Teldin history books, but an ordinary Teldin should be aware of it and not be panicked into hostile activity by the sight of a puny and obviously defenseless off-worlder like Martin.

It was a nice, comforting theory which had made a lot of sense when they had discussed it back on the ship. Now he was not so sure.

"Can you see anyone on the road?"

"Yes," Beth said. "Just over a mile to the north of you, heading your way and toward the city. One person riding a tricycle and towing a two-wheeled trailer. It should be visible to you in six minutes."

While he was waiting, Martin tried to calm himself by examining at close range a stretch of the banked rock wall which ran along the side of the road. Like the majority of the roads on Teldi, this one ran roughly north and south, and the wall protected travelers from the meteorites which came slanting in from the west.

The banked walls were on average four meters high and built from rocks gathered in the vicinity. The roads were rarely straight, but curved frequently to take advantage of the protection furnished by natural features such as deep gullies or outcroppings of rock. When east-west travel was necessary, the roads proceeded in a series of wide zig-zags, like the track of a sailing ship tacking to windward.

Suddenly there was the sound of a short, sharp hiss and thud, and midway between his lander and the roadside there was a small, glowing patch of ground with a cloud of rock dust settling around it. A meteorite strike. When he looked back to the roadway, the Teldin was already in sight, peddling rapidly toward him and hugging the protective wall.

Martin walked to the outer edge of the roadway to get out of its path. He did not know anything about the oncoming vehicle's braking system, and it was possible that he was in greater danger of being run over by a Teldin tricycle than being hit by a meteorite. His action could also, he hoped, be construed as one of politeness. When the vehicle slowed and came to a halt abreast of him, Martin extended both hands palms outward, then let them fall to his side again.

"I wish you well," he said softly. Loudly and clearly and taking a fraction of a second longer, his translator expressed the same sentiment in Teldin.

The cyclist looked like a cross between an overgrown, four-armed kangaroo and a frog which was covered with sparse, sickly yellow fur. Because of the being's size and his own lack of defensive armament, Martin was acutely aware of the other's long, well-muscled legs which terminated in huge, clawed feet, and of the enormous teeth which showed clearly within the wide, open mouth. Its four, six-fingered hands also had bony terminations which had been filed short and painted bright blue, presumably to aid the manipulation of small objects and for decoration. It was wearing a dark brown cloak of some coarse, fibrous material, and the garment was fastened at the neck and thrown back over the shoulders where it was attached in some fashion to the being's backpack, probably to leave the other's limbs free for peddling and steering its vehicle. There was no doubt that this was a civilized entity, and that the open mouth with its fearsome display of teeth was simply a gape of surprise and curiosity, not a snarl of fury presaging an attack.

Perhaps there was a little bit of doubt, Martin thought nervously, and spoke again.

"If you are not engaged in urgent and important business," he said slowly while the translator rattled out the guttural gruntings and gobblings which were the Teldin equivalent, "I would be grateful if you could spare some of your time talking to me."

The Teldin made a harsh, barking sound which did not

translate, followed by other noises which did. They sounded in Martin's earpiece as "The conversation is likely to be a short one, stranger, if you do not move over here to the protection of the wall. Naturally I would be delighted to talk to you about yourself, the mechanism yonder in which you arrived, and any other subject which mutually interests us. But first there is a question..."

The being paused for a moment. There was no way that Martin could read its facial expression on such short acquaintance, but from a certain tension and awkwardness in the way the Teldin was holding its limbs and body, he had a strong impression that the question was an important one. Finally it came.

"Who owns you, stranger?"

Chapter 6

BE careful, Martin thought. The alien's understanding of the word "own" might be different from his. Could the question involve patriotism, or loyalty owed to its country, tribe, or employer? Was the Teldin using some kind of local slang which the translator was reproducing literally? He dare not answer until he was completely sure of the meaning of the question.

"I'm sorry," he said. "Your question is unclear to me."

Before the Teldin could reply, Martin introduced himself and began describing his planet of origin. He spoke of the Earth as it had been before the coming of the Federation, not the denuded and well-nigh depopulated planet that it had since become. Then he quickly went on to talk about the lander and the much larger hypership in orbit above them and, when the Teldin expressed sudden concern, he assured it that neither had anything to fear from the meteorites. He added that he, himself, did not carry such protection nor, for that matter, any other means of defense or offense.

When he finished speaking the Teldin was silent for a moment. Then it said, "Thank you for this information which, in spite of being hearsay, could be of great importance. Does the being in the orbiting vessel own you?"

In the earpiece he could hear Beth, who was monitoring the conversation, suppressing laughter.

"No," he said.

"Do you own it?"

"No," he said again.

"You only act that way sometimes," Beth said. "But be alert. Another pedal vehicle is heading out of the city toward you. It is painted brown and bright yellow, towing an enclosed trailer and flying some kind of pennant, with two people on board pedaling fast. It should reach you in about twenty minutes."

Martin bypassed the translator momentarily to say, "The local constabulary, do you think? I can't react until they come into sight, when it would be natural for me to ask who and what they are. But our friend here worries me with its constant harping on ownership. And what does it mean by hearsay? I can't give it a straight answer until I know why it thinks the question is so important."

He cut in the translator and went on to explain the relationship between Beth and himself. He was nonspecific regarding the division of their work, but he had to go into considerable detail on Earth-human social anthropology, cultural mores, and reproduction. But suddenly the Teldin was holding up two of its four hands.

"Thank you once again for this interesting hearsay," it said slowly, as if uncertain that the true meaning of the words was getting through to Martin. "You are answering questions which have not been asked, and not answering those which must be asked."

The brown and yellow tricycle came into sight just then. Martin said quickly, "The vehicle which approaches us at speed and flying a flag, and the beings propelling it. Is their mission important?"

The Teldin glanced at it in a manner suggesting impatience. "It flies the pennant of the Master of Sea and

Landborne Communications. Their mission has nothing to do with us and is of no importance compared with the visit of an off-planet being who avoids answering the most important question about itself..."

"Just a couple of mailmen," Beth said in a relieved voice.

"... Your status is not clear," the Teldin went on. "Do you or your life-mate own the vessels which brought you here?"

My *status*!... Martin thought. A little light was beginning to dawn. Aloud, he said, "The vessels are not our personal property, but we are responsible for their operation."

"But they are owned, presumably, by someone who directs you in their use?" the Teldin said quickly, and added, "You must obey this being's directions?"

"Yes," Martin said.

The Teldin made a loud, gurgling sound which did not translate, then it said, "You are a slave, Martin. Highly placed, no doubt, considering the nature of the equipment you are allowed to use, but still a slave..."

Instinctively Martin stepped back as one of the being's enormous hands swung toward him. But it stopped a few inches from his chin with one digit pointing at the Federation symbol on his collar.

"... Is that the emblem of your Master?"

His first thought was to strenuously deny that he was any kind of slave, and his second was to wonder what new complication would be the result of that denial. But the Federation was, in real terms, his master, as it was the master of all of its non-Citizens.

"Yes," he said again.

The Teldin turned its hand, which was still only a few inches from Martin's face, to display a bracelet on its thick, furry wrist. The bracelet supported a flat oval of metal on which an intricate design had been worked in several colors.

"Like mine," the Teldin said, "your mark of ownership is small, tasteful, inconspicuous as befits a slave in a position of trust and responsibility. But why did you ignore or evade the questions which would quickly have established your status?"

"I was unsure of your own status," Martin replied truthfully.

He remembered their tutor telling them again and again that in an alien contact situation they must always tell the truth, although not necessarily all of it at once. Measured doses of the truth gave rise to much fewer complications than well-meant diplomatic lies.

"I don't like what I'm hearing," Beth said. "The Federation does not approve of slavery or any form of—"

"Now I understand," the Teldin said before she could go on. "You thought I might be a Master and were being circumspect. Like the other passers by, I thought you were a Master and could not, therefore, speak first. But contact between ourselves and an other-world species would seem to be a project too important to be entrusted to a slave, regardless of its level of ability. My position forbids me saying anything which is directly critical of your Master, or any Master, but it seems to me that it would be more fitting if—if . . ."

"My Master did the work itself?" Martin asked.

"That was my thought exactly," the Teldin said.

Martin thought about their tutor and its enormous, sprawling body, and of the sheer size and complexity of any mobile life-support system capable of accommodating it, and he thought of that species' immense lifespan. Carefully, and truthfully, he said, "My remarks should not be considered in any way critical or disloyal, but my Master is grossly overweight, very old, and has other projects demanding of its time and available energy."

"Since we are speaking face to face I can accept this information as factual until I have been instructed otherwise by my Master," the Teldin said, and the sudden change in its manner was unmistakable. It added, "But my Master will not accept anything you say."

"For this reason," Martin persisted, "I have been instructed to land on this world and gather information about your species and its culture so that my Master will know whom to approach with the initial offers of friendship and exchanges of knowledge."

"Your Master seems lacking in sensitivity and intelligence," the Teldin said, this time without any apology.

"Your Master might just as well have sent a radio transmitting and receiving device."

"That has already been tried," Martin said, "without success."

"Naturally," the Teldin said.

The situation had gone sour, there could be no doubt about that. The impression given by the Teldin was that it belonged to an intensely status-conscious slave culture in which the Masters spoke only to other Masters or to God, and when a Master spoke to a slave, the slave had to believe everything it was told and, presumably, disbelieve everything it had been told earlier by a lowlier being.

This is crazy, thought Martin. "What would have been your reaction if I'd been a Master?"

"Had you been a Master," the Teldin replied, "I would not have been able to give you any information until it had been vetted for content and accuracy by my own or another Master. Knowledge which is not passed down from a Master is, as you know, untrustworthy. The only assistance I could have given you would have been to arrange a meeting with another Master. Had you been a Master we could not have exchanged hearsay as freely as we have been doing."

"May this exchange continue?" Martin asked eagerly. "I have many questions. And answers."

"Yes, Martin," the Teldin said. "It may continue until I have reported your presence and everything that has transpired between us to my Master, who will assess the value of the material and instruct me accordingly.

"My curiosity is such that I am in no great hurry to make my report," the being added. "And my name is Skorta."

"Thank you, Skorta," Martin said, relieved. The atmosphere seemed friendly once more, but he still needed clarification on the Master-slave relationship. He said, "Will you make your report in person, and where?"

"Careful," Beth warned.

"Thankfully, no," Skorta said. "I must make a hearsay report by radio. The device is in my Master's education complex in the city."

"Are you a *teacher*?"

Martin could hardly believe his luck. It would not matter which subject Skorta taught, because it was sure to have a grounding in many subjects, and it was quite probable that the Teldin would be able to furnish them with all of the information necessary for the completion of their assignment, possibly within a few hours.

"Properly speaking, only a Master can teach," it replied. "That is the law. I relay the approved information, suitably simplified for the age-groups concerned, to unruly little beings who only rarely think of questioning the validity of the information they receive. Even the words of a Master, as you know, may be doubted when they have been passed down through too many slaves."

"I should like to see your students," Martin said, "and other people in the city. Would I be able to meet a Master? . . ."

Martin felt like biting off his tongue. Without thinking he had blundered into that highly sensitive area again, and he could almost feel the atmosphere congeal. The Teldin made a soft, untranslatable sound which might have been a sigh.

"Stranger," it said slowly, "your presence here is an insult and an affront to our Masters, since it is plain that your own Master thinks so little of this world and its people that it sent a slave to us as an emissary. To my knowledge there has never been a greater insult, and I cannot even guess at what the Masters' reaction will be.

"But I am willing to take you to the city," Skorta went on. "In fact, I am anxious to do so in order to prolong this contact with you, and to discover as much about your people and their civilization as I can before I am required officially to forget it. But I must warn you that the visit to the city could place you in great personal danger."

"From the slaves or the Masters?" Martin asked. He was beginning to like this visually ferocious, four-armed nightmare that was glaring down at him. He could be certain of very little in the present situation, but he was sure that this being was honest and had a measure of concern for his safety.

"The slaves may restrain you if instructed to do so by the Masters," the Teldin replied slowly, "but only the

Masters bear weapons and only they may kill. Now, if you will climb into my carrier I shall transport you to the city."

"Don't go," Beth said, and gave reasons.

"I have received information," Martin said when she had finished talking, "that very shortly meteorite activity will increase in this area by a factor of three. I cannot be more specific because of ignorance regarding your units of time. According to the instruments in the orbiting vessel—"

"This is hearsay," Skorta broke in.

"True," Martin said quickly. "But the instruments are being read by my life-mate who is, naturally, anxious that no harm befalls me."

"Then I understand why you attach so much importance to this information," the Teldin said, "but I cannot. It comes through a device of your life-mate, through another device to you and then to myself. There are too many possibilities for cumulative error between the fact and the reported fact for me to accept this information as other than hearsay.

"Since you believe that the Scourge from the sky will be heavier soon," Skorta went on, "do you wish to return to the safety of your vessel now?"

In his other ear Beth was saying much the same thing in more forthright language, adding that there would be another time and another Teldin to talk to. But Martin wanted to go on talking to this one, and the intensity of the feeling surprised him.

"If I returned to my vessel," he said, choosing his words with care, "I could leave you a device which would enable us to continue our conversation. But this would be unsatisfactory for two reasons. I would not be able to visit your city, and you would consider any such conversation as untrustworthy hearsay. If, however, you can assure me from your own personal experience that this road is adequately protected, I would go with you to the city and continue to converse with you face to face."

The Teldin exhaled loudly and said, "Stranger, at last you are thinking like a Teldin." Martin boarded the tricycle and the Teldin began to pedal. Soon the protective

wall was slipping past at a respectable rate of speed.
Without taking its attention from the road, Skorta added,
"I can also assure you that you can speak to me face to
face while addressing the back of my neck."

Chapter 7

ON only two occasions did the Teldin move
briefly to the unprotected side of the road to let oncoming vehicles through on the inside. Right of way, it
seemed, depended on the pennant flying on the approaching vehicle and on the size and position of the
ownership badges being worn by the occupants.

A flag and distinctively colored vehicle driven by a
Teldin wearing a large emblem on a shoulder sash indicated that it was a slave of the lower order, a public
utility worker or such. Badges worn on armbands signified a much higher grade of slave, and emblems worn on
the wrist indicated a person in the highest level of the
hierarchy of Teldin slavehood.

Their road had detoured to utilize the natural protection provided by a small hill when there was a sharp,
crashing detonation followed by a diminishing, hissing
roar. Martin's eyes jerked upward in time to see a large
meteor trace an incandescent line across the sky below
the cloud base, and a moment later he felt the shock of
impact transmitted through the solid, upsprung structure
of the tricycle as it struck ground somewhere behind a
nearby rise. Then suddenly the stony landscape beyond
the outer edge of the road was covered by tiny explosions of rock dust.

"This must be the heavier Scourge you spoke of,"
Skorta said. "The Masters warn of such events, but even
they cannot be accurate in their predictions."

"Why do they refer to the meteorites as the Scourge?"

Beth asked. "Do they equate all forms of danger and pain with strokes from a Master's whip?"

Martin waited until a large vehicle flying what he now knew to be the pennant of the Master of Agriculture squeezed past on the outside, then asked the question.

"The Masters say," the Teldin replied, turning its head briefly to look at him, "that it is a continuing reminder that we cannot fully trust anything that is not experienced directly except, of course, the words of a Master."

"Are slaves, particularly high-ranking slaves like yourself, ever rewarded with your freedom?" Martin asked.

"We have freedom," the Teldin replied.

"But the Masters tell you what to do and think," Martin protested. "They alone have weapons. They alone administer punishment and have the power of life and death."

"Naturally, they are the Masters."

Martin knew that he was getting into a sensitive area, but he needed the answers. "Is the death penalty administered often? And which crimes merit it?"

"Sometimes the Masters execute each other for Masters' reasons," the Teldin said, slowing as the road curved sharply and continued into a deep ravine. "With slaves it rarely happens, and only if there is destruction of valuable living property. For less serious crimes slaves may be reduced in status or forced to work in unprotected areas of the surface for a time, or if the offense is venial, the peacekeeping slaves deal with it.

"An alert Master served by trusted and observant slaves," the Teldin added, "is able to stop trouble before it develops to the point where damage to property occurs."

For a few seconds Martin tried to control his revulsion at the picture of the Teldin culture which was emerging. If Skorta's Master received a full report of everything he had said to its slave, then his next question was foolhardy indeed, but it had to be asked.

"Do you ever feel dissatisfied with your status, Skorta, and wish you were a Master?"

"Have you gone *mad*?" Beth began, and broke off because the Teldin was speaking.

"There have been times when I would have liked to be a Master," it replied, and made another one of its untranslatable noises, "but good sense prevailed."

The floor of the ravine had begun to rise, and as it pedaled up the grade, Skorta had no breath to spare for speech, giving Beth the chance to express herself at length.

"You're taking too many risks," she said angrily. "My advice is to pull out as soon as you can. Some of the things you've said to Skorta could be construed as attempted subversion of a highly-placed slave, and the Masters won't like that. Besides, with all the surface sensor material we've collected that is still awaiting processing, plus your interview with Skorta, we should have enough information for our assessment . . ."

The picture which was emerging was clear but not at all pleasant, she continued. Teldi was essentially a slave culture, with the vast majority of the planetary population serving an elitist group of Masters who might be numbered in the thousands, or perhaps even hundreds. Their control of the slave population was such that the slaves themselves, with their minor graduations of responsibility and status, were, as a group, happy with the situation, although individuals like Skorta might occasionally have their doubts. So happy were they with their role that the slaves did not want to become Masters and helped maintain themselves in slavery by betraying any fellow slaves who looked like making trouble, while at the same time believing implicitly everything told to them by the Masters, even when this information contradicted first-hand knowledge. History was also vetted by the Masters so that the slaves had no way of knowing if there had been better times.

But the worst aspect of all was that the Masters held the power of life and death over their slaves and were the only people on Teldi allowed to bear weapons.

Beth went on, "You know how the Federation feels about slavery, or any other form of physical or psychological coercion in government. They will not be favorably impressed with this culture. But it's still possible that the slaves could qualify for cititzenship if we could find a way of separating them from their Masters."

"It isn't as simple as that," Martin said, instinctively lowering his voice even though the translator was switched off. "This fanatical distrust they display toward everyone and everything that is not experienced first-hand worries me. Trust between intelligent species is one of the most important requirements for Federation citizenship."

"That could change if the influence of the Masters was removed," Beth said. "But do you agree that the slaves must have the opportunity of deciding for themselves whether to leave this terrible world and join the Federation, or remain with their Masters? Our assessment, remember, should include recommended solutions to the problem here."

"Let's ask one of them now," Martin said. Through the translator he went on. "Skorta, would you like to live on a world free of the Scourge, and where you could farm and build houses and travel on the surface without danger?"

"Stranger..." the Teldin began, and then fell silent for nearly a minute before it went on, "It is senseless and painful to consider such possibilities. The Masters disapprove of mental bad habits of this kind. They say that the Scourge *is*, and must be accepted."

"Brainwashed!" Beth said disgustedly.

A few minutes later the ravine widened to become the head of a deep, fertile valley. Skorta pulled off the road and stopped to give Martin his first close look at a Teldin city.

The valley ran in a north-south direction and its heavily cultivated western slopes and bottomland were protected from the worst of the Scourge. Only when the meteorites slanted in from an angle of forty-five degrees or more, which they did very occasionally, was the city at risk. The city's structures hugged the ground and varied in size from tiny, private dwellings with extensions underground to large buildings which spread themselves outward rather than upward. Regardless of size, every one of them had a thick, earth-banked west-facing wall, and what appeared to be important machinery and vehicles were housed inside deep slit trenches. Suddenly the

Teldin pointed toward a high cliff further along the valley.

"That is my school," it said.

There was a flat apron of crusted rock around the base of the cliff and a wide, cavernous opening which was obviously a vehicle entrance. His magnifier showed about fifty smaller openings, regular in shape, scattered across the cliff face.

"I would like to see inside," Martin said.

The tricycle lurched across the verge and began picking up speed again.

"There aren't many children about," Martin said. "Are they at school? And the Masters, where do they live?"

Skorta overtook a structurally complex vehicle powered by four furiously pedaling Teldins before it replied. "If the children are to survive to adulthood they have much to learn from parents and teachers. And there are no Masters here. They live in the polar city, which is free from the worst of the Scourge, and only rarely do they visit our cities. We prefer it that way because the presence of a Master means grief for some and serious inconvenience for others. Believe me, stranger, while we are obliged to honor and obey our Masters, and we do, we much prefer them to leave us alone."

"Why?" Martin asked. The other's words had a distinctly insubordinate sound to them.

"They come only in response to reports of serious trouble," the Teldin explained, breathing deeply between sentences because the road up to the school had steepened. "Not just to administer punishment but to extend or amend existing instructions regarding virtually everything. When a Master comes, the visit must not be wasted.

"It is a long, difficult, and dangerous journey for them," the Teldin concluded, "and their lives are much too valuable to be risked without good reason."

Martin had heard of absentee landlords in Earth's history, but the concept of an absentee slavemaster was difficult to grasp, as was the idea of a slave society which seemed to be self-policing and largely self-governing. He could not understand why they remained slaves, why they did not rebel and start thinking as well as doing for themselves, or why they held their Masters, whose absence was infinitely preferable to their presence, in such high esteem.

The Masters, he thought, must be very potent individuals indeed. To complete the assessment he had to know more about them.

"Would the visit of a person from another world," he said carefully, "be considered important enough to warrant the attention of a Master?"

"Watch it!" Beth said warningly.

"The visit of a *slave* from another world," the Teldin corrected—without, however, answering the question.

The tricycle rumbled across the stony apron at the base of the cliff toward the vehicle entrance, and Martin saw that the tiny pupils of Skorta's eyes had enlarged to four or five times their normal size. The dilation mechanism had to be a voluntary one because they were still several seconds away from the tunnel mouth. Plainly the Teldins had no trouble seeing in the dark. He adjusted his image enhancer.

Patches of luminous vegetation coated the tunnel walls, and at frequent intervals he could see short tunnels opening into artificial caves containing machinery whose purpose was not clear to him. Skorta told him that important and irreplaceable machines were housed in these caves to protect them from the Scourge, and that metal was scarce on Teldi.

The Teldi guided its tricycle into one of the caves and they dismounted.

"I realize that to a stranger like yourself this is hearsay," Skorta said, "but it is widely held to be a fact that this school is the most efficient teaching establishment on the whole planet. The Masters of Transport, Agriculture, Communications, Education, and other associated Masterships send their slaves here, often from prepuberty, and when they leave they are most valuable pieces of property indeed."

Martin hastily revised his estimate of the Teldin's status. It was closer to being a university lecturer than a schoolteacher, he thought, and asked, "What is your position in the establishment?"

"The position is largely administrative," Skorta replied as it led Martin into a narrow tunnel which climbed steeply. "I am the senior teaching slave in charge. We are going to my quarters..."

He made another revision, from lecturer to Dean of Studies.

"Later, if you are agreeable," it went on, "I would like you to meet some of the students. But there is a serious risk involved—"

"The students are unruly?"

"No, stranger," the Teldin said. "The risk is mine in that the slave of another Master might report your presence before I did so. There is also the matter of your accommodation, should you wish to remain here for a time."

"Thank you, I would like to—" Martin began, when Beth's voice broke in.

"You can't just move in like a visiting lecturer," she said. "There are problems."

"There are problems," Skorta repeated unknowingly, "regarding your life processes, particularly food intake and waste elimination. It is a unique problem for us. There is no knowledge nor even the wildest or most speculative hearsay regarding the possible effects of off-planet diseases on the Teldin species, or the effectiveness of our disinfectants on your wastes. This aspect of your visit has only just occurred to me. It is a serious matter which requires consultation with our senior medical slaves. So serious, in fact, that they will be dutybound to refer the matter to the Master of Medicine."

The Teldin guided him into a large, cliff-face cave containing an enormous, high desk, chairs on the same massive scale, and walls covered by the luminous vegetation between gaps in the bookshelves. Martin had time to notice that the books were retained in place by heavy wooden bars padlocked at both ends.

Since the discussion about alien diseases, Skorta had been keeping its distance while still asking an awful lot of questions. Plainly the risk of a possible off-world infection was evenly balanced by its curiosity, and it was time he put the Teldin's mind at rest.

He said, "Your offer of accommodation is appreciated, but rather than cause discomfort to both of us I would prefer to spend some time every day in my own vessel. May I have permission to move it to the flat area in front of the school so that I can spend as much time here as possible?

"And the Master of Medicine has no cause for concern," he went on before the other could reply, "since off-world pathogens will not effect Teldins, nor will Teldin diseases be transmissible to the many hundreds of different species who inhabit the Galaxy. That is—"

"Hearsay!" the Teldin broke in.

"Naturally," Martin went on, "I have not visited all of these worlds, but I have lived for a time on three of them without contracting any other-species diseases."

He was bending the truth slightly because one of the three was Teldi itself. The others had been Formalhaut Three and the single, lifeless plant which circled the Black Diamond at the galactic center.

"It is still hearsay, but I am greatly reassured," the Teldin said. "And your vessel will arouse less comment outside our school than in any other part of the city."

"Thank you," Martin said. "If a problem arises suddenly, as it may have done today had I been a disease-carrier, how do the Masters learn of it?"

The Teldin pointed to a recess which contained a table, chair and shelves lined with what could only be Leyden cells. The batteries were wired in series to a collection of table-mounted radio equipment with which the legendary Marconi would have felt instantly at home. Skorta was giving him a rundown on the Teldin equivalent of the Morse code when Martin interrupted quietly.

"This is a mechanism. It transmits and receives information over a great distance, not face to face. Surely this is hearsay, and forbidden?"

The Teldin gestured toward the barred bookshelves and said, "That, too, is hearsay, but some of us are allowed to read it."

"You confuse me," Martin said.

"The volumes contain hearsay which is a transcription of much older hearsay," the Teldin explained, "selected by the Masters for study by only the highest-level slaves, slaves who are able to assimilate the material without mental suffering caused by disaffection with their present circumstances, or thoughts of what might have been had the Scourge not come upon us. Ignorance makes it easier to accept the inevitable."

"Are you saying," Martin asked harshly, "that the majority of the slaves are kept in ignorance?"

"I'm saying that they're happier in their ignorance," Skorta replied. "This hearsay material is not kept from them entirely. But it must be earned piece by piece, as a reward for physical and mental effort."

It was like some kind of freemasonry, Martin thought, with secrets of increasing importance being entrusted to the favored few who showed themselves able and willing to maintain the Teldin status quo. His sarcasm was probably lost in translation as he said, "And the Masters know everything?"

"Not everything," the Teldin said, showing more of its teeth. "As yet they don't know about you."

Chapter 8

ONCE again Martin got the impression that this particular Teldin was a potential rebel. "I have the feeling that you do not want my presence reported to the Masters," he said, "Is this so?"

"That is correct," Skorta said. "My reasons are, of course, selfish. Until official cognizance has been taken of your presence on Teldi, I am at liberty to learn as much as possible from you before the Masters rule on the factuality of your information. I expect that much of what I learn will have to be officially forgotten, not committed to writing, and will die with me. The Masters must consider the mental well-being of their slaves as the highest priority, and the simple fact of your presence here implies a way of life infinitely better than our existence on Teldi.

"Fortunately I can justify my delay in reporting you," it added, "because of initial confusion regarding your status and the necessity of educating you in our ways lest you inadvertently commit a crime, such as insulting a Master."

It was not lying, Martin thought admiringly, but it was certainly bending the truth into some fancy shapes.

"I had intended showing you the school now," Skorta went on, "but it would be better if I drove you back to your vessel so that you can bring it here."

"No problem," Martin said. "My vessel can be moved here without me being on board."

"There *is* a problem," Beth contradicted. "Not an urgent one, so you can let your friend show you its school. A cloud of denser meteorite material is due to arrive in about fifteen hours' time. According to the computer, the area for twenty miles around your city will be well and truly clobbered, so when I move the lander over there I suggest you excuse yourself politely and get the hell out."

"The lander's force shield will protect—" Martin began.

"It will be a very heavy bombardment," Beth said firmly, "and you will be safer in the hypership. There is something very odd about this Scourge, and the things the computer is telling me about it just don't make sense. I'd like to go over the data with you."

Martin did not reply at once because he had followed the Teldin into a tunnel whose walls and ceiling were smooth and completely unlike the roughly chiseled rock surfaces he had encountered earlier. He could see small areas of tiling still adhering to the walls, and many horizontal markings which were thin and pale green in color and which passed through small spots of dull red. He aimed the visual pickup in his helmet at them and paused for a moment so that Beth would receive a clear picture, then hurried after the Teldin.

"Copper wiring and ferrous metal staples holding it in position," he reported excitedly. "The insulation has rotted away and all that is left are the pale green and red corrosion traces. This is a much older section of the school, dating from the time when they had electrically generated rather than vegetation-produced lighting. That could have been hundreds of years ago."

Beth sighed. "So you intend staying there until the last possible moment?"

"At least," Martin said.

They came to an opening whose sides bore corrosion marks which suggested that it had once possessed a metal door. Inside, there was a large, square room rendered small by the presence of about thirty Teldins, who ranged in size from just over one meter to the full adult stature of three meters. The walls were hung with tapestries which were brightly colored, finely detailed, and dealt with various aspects of the Teldin anatomy.

His arrival caused an immediate cessation of work and a lot of untranslatable noises. He was introduced as an off-planet slave gathering information on Teldin teaching methods for its Master. Skorta told them to restrain their natural curiosity and resume work.

It was difficult to distinguish the teacher-in-charge from the adult pupils, Martin found, until he discovered that the more advanced students aided in the teaching process by instructing the less knowledgeable ones. He stopped beside two of the youngest, one of whom was immobilized and rendered speechless by practice splints and a tight, mandible bandage, and asked how long it took for a fractured forearm to heal.

"Thirty-two days on average, Senior," the young Teldin said promptly, staring at the Federation symbol on Martin's collar. "Longer if it is a compound or multiple fracture, or if it is sited at a joint or is complicated by severe wounding. If the accompanying wounds are improperly cleansed, putrefaction takes place and the affected limb must be removed."

Martin estimated the age of the Teldin medical student to be the equivalent of a ten- or eleven-year-old of Earth. "I thank you for this information," he said, and added, "How long will it be before you are a fully-qualified medical slave?"

Everyone had stopped working again and was making untranslatable noises. Anxiously he went over his question for implied criticisms or hidden insults and could not find any. In an attempt to retrieve the situation he said the first thing that came into his mind.

"I would like to answer some questions about myself and show you my vessel."

They were all staring at him in absolute silence. It was close on a minute before one young Teldin spoke.

"When, Senior?"

"I do not want to interrupt your study or rest periods," he said. "Would early tomorrow morning be convenient?"

When they were in the corridor a few minutes later, Martin asked, "Did I say something wrong?"

Skorta made an untranslatable sound, and said, "They would have observed your vessel at a distance, in any case. But now you have issued an invitation from your Master to view the machine closely and ask questions about it. The invitation extends, naturally, to the members of other classes. I trust, stranger, that your vessel is strongly built."

Martin was about to deny that his Master had issued the invitation through him, but then he realized that a mere slave like himself would never have been so presumptous as to issue it without permission.

"You misunderstand me," he said. "I was asking if I'd said something wrong when I questioned the medical student about the time needed to qualify. On my world such students spend one-sixth of their lifetimes in study before they are allowed to practice medicine on other people. Some of them continue to study and find new cures for the rest of their lives."

"What a strange idea," the Teldin said, stopping outside the next classroom's entrance. "You are correct, Martin, I did not understand you. Your question to the student was a nonsense question. Badges of ownership are not worn in school since the students are considered to be too ignorant to be good slaves, but the only medical student there was the teacher. The students will ultimately belong, if my memory serves me accurately, to the Masters of Agriculture, Communications, and Peacekeeping. Medical slaves are invariably teachers, and new medical knowledge must be sought only at the direction of the Master of Medicine.

"The incidence of injury and disease must be very small on your world," Skorta continued, "if students waste so much time studying medicine exclusively. On Teldi we study it as soon as we are able to read, write, and calculate. On Teldi injury and death are not rare. On Teldi everyone is a doctor."

They had completed the tour of the classrooms when Skorta turned into the entrance to a long, high-ceilinged chamber whose far wall was more than two hundred meters distant. Against the wall Martin could see, dimly by the light of the ever present luminous vegetation, a raised dais or altar with a cloth draped across it.

"This is the Hall of Honor," Skorta said, and began a slow march toward the opposite wall. "Here the slaves renew their promises of service and obedience to our Masters every day, or assemble for punishment or censure and, once a year, to graduate to higher levels."

It had not always been the slaves' Hall of Honor, Martin thought excitedly as he looked up at the great, curving ceiling and along the regularly spaced tunnel mouths where it arched down to meet the floor on both sides. He asked for and obtained Skorta's permission to use his helmet spotlight.

It showed lines and patterns of corrosion running along the floor and into the tunnels. The marks were widely spaced and suggested heavy metal rail supports rather than wiring conduits. The walls and ceiling were also covered by strips and patches of corrosion, and as they walked toward the dais they passed shallow trenches in the floor which were filled with powdered rust. Suddenly, Martin's mouth felt so dry that it was difficult to speak.

"This . . . this place is *old*," he said. "What was its purpose before it became the Hall of Honor?"

He already knew the answer.

"It is recorded only as hearsay." the Teldin replied, "But the hearsay is unapproved, forbidden as a matter for discussion by all levels of slaves. I know nothing other than that it was our first protection against the Scourge."

Suddenly Beth's voice was in his other ear.

"It was probably one of the causes of the Scourge in the first place," she said angrily. "That hall was once a storage and distribution facility which supplied missiles via the tunnels to less deeply buried launching silos. But you must have spotted that yourself. It certainly answers a lot of my questions."

"I spotted it," Martin said. "But causing the Scourge . . . I don't understand you."

"That's because you haven't been trying to make sense of the things the computer is saying about this ring system."

Normally such a system was formed as a result of a satellite or satellites approaching too closely to the primary and being pulled apart by gravitational stresses, she went on, and the debris being strewn along the plane of the moon's original orbit. Continuing collisions would eventually cause the pieces to grind themselves into a uniformly small size. But at the present stage of the process many large pieces should have survived the collisions with the small stuff, since the probability of the relatively few large chunks of the moon colliding with each other was small.

The material orbiting Teldi contained no large pieces of debris.

"Then the ring has been forming for a long time," Martin said, "and the process is far advanced."

"No," Beth said firmly. "The Scourge has been in existence for an extremely short time, astronomically speaking. The process began one thousand one hundred and seventeen years and thirty-three days ago, and was completed forty-seven years and one hundred and two days later."

"Are you *sure*?"

Beth laughed. "For a moment I thought you were accusing me of using hearsay. The computer is sure and I'm sure, and you know which one of us is omniscient."

"Are there any missiles left?" Martin asked. "Any traces of radioactivity in a forgotten silo somewhere?"

"None," she replied. "The sensors would have detected them. They must have used them all."

She resumed talking as the slow march toward the

dais continued, but Martin's thoughts were leaping ahead of her words as piece after piece of the Teldin jigsaw puzzle fitted into place. The reason for the Scourge and the fatalistic acceptance of it was now plain, as was the cause of the pathological distrust of everything which was not experienced first-hand, the rigid stratification of the slaves, and the thinking done from the top which was so characteristic of the military mind. Finally there was the planet-wide catastrophe which had driven the surviving population to shelter in such installations as this, and brought about a situation which was in essence a military dictatorship.

The Hall of Honor and one-time missile arsenal was certainly a key piece of the puzzle, but the picture was not complete.

"I must speak with a Master," Martin said.

"But there's no need!" Beth protested. "Sensor probes have been dropped on this and other cities. We have more than enough data on the ordinary people of this frightful planet. They are resourceful, ethical, hard-working, long-suffering, and, to my mind, wholly admirable. We should say so without delay. Our assessment can be based on an interview with one Teldin, remember, and we were not expected to spend a long time on this assignment. I say that the slave levels are in all respects suitable and should be offered Citizenship following reorientation training to neutralize the conditioning of the Masters.

"The slave owners, from what we've learned of them, don't stand a snowball's chance. Our Masters, the Federation, will not abide dictators who—"

"Wait," Martin said.

They had stopped before the dais which, now that he could see it clearly, consisted of a single cube of polished rock measuring just under two meters a side, with a large flag apparently covering the top and hanging down in front. The section of the flag visible to him was dark blue and bore the same design as that which appeared on Skorta's bracelet. The stone was too high for him to see the top surface, until he was suddenly grasped above the knees and under the elbows by four large hands and hoisted into the air...

. . . And saw the symbol of ultimate authority.

Unlike the richly embroidered flag, the sword looked excessively plain and functional. Simply and beautifully proportioned, it measured nearly two meters long and had a broad, double-edged blade which came to a fine point. Its only decoration was a small, engraved plate on the guard, which reproduced the design on the flag. Martin stared at it until the Teldin's arms began to quiver with the strain of holding him aloft, then he gestured to be put down.

"It is the sword of the Master of Education," Skorta said very quietly. "My Master died recently and a new one has yet to be chosen."

Martin was remembering the long, sharp blade of the weapon and the staining he had seen at its tip. He wet his lips and said, "Has it ever been . . . used?"

"The sword of a Master," it replied in a voice Martin could barely hear, "must draw blood at least once."

"Is it possible," Martin asked once again, "to speak with a Master?"

"You are an off-world slave," the Teldin replied, emphasizing the last word.

It was the last word, in fact, because neither of them spoke during the long walk back to the base of the cliff where Beth had already moved the lander. Martin had a lot on his mind.

Chapter 9

He had programmed the force shield to interdict inanimate objects and remain pervious to living beings. As a result, it was not the timer which awakened him but the excited voices of more than two hundred young Teldins who were surrounding the lander. The cliff-face and city were still shrouded in pre-dawn darkness, except for the intermittent illumination provided by the Scourge as it drew incandescent lines across the sky. He increased the intensity of the exterior lighting and went outside.

"I can't answer all of your questions at once," he said as his translator signaled overload, "so I will tell you about my vessel and some of the worlds it has visited..."

Except for a few of the older ones who muttered "Hearsay" they became very quiet and attentive. He began talking about planetary environments which were beautiful, terrifying, weird but always wonderful, and on the subject of the Federation he said only that it was a collection of people of many different shapes and sizes and degrees of intelligence who helped each other and who wanted to help Teldi.

When these youngsters grew up, Martin thought, it was likely that they would never again be able to regard their Teldin way of life with complete acceptance. And if the Teldins were not judged suitable for Federation citizenship and were left to fend for themselves, it seemed a particularly lousy trick he was playing on them by talking like this.

"I can't predict where exactly they will hit," Beth broke in urgently, "but that area is in for a bad time. Cut it short!"

"I'll answer a few questions, then send them to shelter," he told her. "The mountain on this side of the valley will protect us, so there's no immediate—"

The sky was lit by a sudden flare of bright orange, the sound of muffled thunder and the ground seemed to twitch under Martin's feet. He broke off and looked around wildly, then up at the cliff. Everything seemed normal.

"That was a big one," Beth said, her voice rising in pitch. "It hit close to the summit directly above you and started a rockslide. You can't see it past the shoulder of the cliff. Tell them to..."

But Martin was already shouting for them to run for the shelter of the school. Nobody moved, and he had to explain quickly, so quickly that he was close to being incoherent, about Beth and the orbiting ship and its instruments which had given advance warning of the rock-fall which they could not yet see.

Still they did not move—they were dismissing his warning as hearsay. He angled one of the lander's lights upward to show the top of the cliff and the first few rocks bouncing into sight over the edge.

They began to run then, too late.

"No, come back!" he shouted desperately. "There's safety here. Get back to the lander!"

Some of them hesitated. Without thinking about it Martin sprinted after the others and managed to get ahead of them—they were young and their legs were slightly shorter than his—and wave them back. There were about twenty of them outside the protection of the lander's force shield now, but they were slowing down, stopping. He did not know whether they were simply frightened or confused or, since his recent demonstration of foreknowledge of the rockfall, they believed him when he said that the area around the lander was safe.

The first rocks struck the ground between the lander and the school entrance, bounced outward and rolled toward them. Three of the Teldins were knocked over and another was down hopping and crawling on four hands and a foot, dragging an injured limb behind it. Martin pointed at the glowing line on the ground which marked the edge of the force shield.

"Quickly, move them to the other side of that line. They'll be safe there, believe me!"

He grabbed one of the fallen Teldins by the feet and began dragging it toward the line. The rolling and bouncing rocks were being stopped by the invisible shield, and the other students had realized that the protection was not hearsay. But more than half of them were down, and the uninjured were trying to drag them to safety. Martin pulled his Teldin across the line and went after another.

"Get back, dammit!" Beth shouted. "Half the bloody mountain is falling on you . . . !"

A rain of fine dust and stones struck his back as he bent over the Teldin casualty, and suddenly a bouncing rock hit him in the back of the leg. He sat down abruptly, tears as well as dust blinding him. The rumbling sound from high up on the cliff was growing louder, and large rocks were thumping into the ground all around him with increasing frequency. The force shield and safety were only a few meters away, but he did not know in which direction.

He was grasped suddenly by four large hands which lifted him and hurled him backward. He tumbled through the shield interface closely followed by the Teldin who had saved him. Martin blinked, trying to clear his vision as expert hands felt along his limbs and body.

"Nothing broken, stranger," the young Teldin said. "Some minor lacerations and bruising on the leg. You should use your own medication to treat the injury."

"Thank you," Martin said. He climbed to his feet and limped toward the lander.

The sound of the rockfall had become muffled because the hemisphere of the force shield was completely covered by loose rocks and soil. Several of the casualties lay looking up at the smooth dome of rubble which had inexplicably refused to fall on them, with expressions which were still unreadable to Martin, while the others had obviously accepted the invisible protection as a fact and were busying themselves with the injured.

When each and every victim and survivor was a trained medic, he thought admiringly, the aftermath of even a major disaster lost much of its horror.

Another young Teldin intercepted him at the lander's entry port. It said, "Thank you, stranger. All of the students who were trying to reach the school have returned or have been returned. There are no fatalities."

Not yet, thought Martin.

He was concerned about the tremendous weight of rock pressing down on the force shield. That shield could handle the heaviest of meteor showers or projectile-firing weapons without difficulty, but it had not been designed to support the weight of an avalanche. The drain on the small ship's power reserves did not bear thinking about.

He looked at the hemisphere of rocks above and around him, knowing that Beth's repeaters were showing her everything he saw, and asked, "How long can I keep it up?"

"Not long," she said grimly. "But long enough for

your air to run out first. There are over two hundred people in there. I'm coming down."

He started to protest, then realized that Beth knew as well as he did that she could not land the great, ungainly bulk of the hypership—its configuration suited it only for deep space and orbital maneuvering. The ship could, in an emergency be brought close to the ground, but it was not the kind of maneuver to be undertaken by a trainee on first assignment. Worrying out loud, however, would only undermine her confidence, so Martin remained silent while he applied a dressing to his damaged leg and watched the pictures she was sending down to him.

He saw the valley city grow large in his main screen, saw the fresh meteor crater on the mountainside above the school, and the gray scar left by the rockslide joining it with the great pile of rubble at the base of the cliff where the lander was buried. He saw four large, shallow depressions appear suddenly in unoccupied areas of the valley floor as the hypership's pressor beams were deployed to check the vessel's descent and hold her, braced and immobile, on four rigid, immaterial stilts. Her tremendous force shield covered the whole valley, and for the first time in over a thousand years the Scourge was impotent against the city.

A tractor beam speared out, came to a tight focus, and began to pull at the pile of rubble.

"Nice work," Martin said warmly. "Concentrate on digging us out and clearing a path to the school entrance. Some of these casualties will have to be moved there for proper treatment, and quickly."

Clearing the rocks above the lander was taking much longer than expected; every time Beth pulled out a mass of rubble, more slid down to fill the space. He decided to run a quick computation based on the volume of air trapped inside the shield and the rate at which it was being used by two hundred Teldins whose lung capacities were almost double that of a human being, and his anxiety gave way to mounting desperation.

He went out to talk to the younger students and try to reassure them, and discovered that three of them were the children of Masters.

Now I'm really in trouble, he thought.

All around him, the older Teldins were suggesting to each other, and by inference to Martin, that they should not waste air in needless conversation. He returned to the lander.

"You should seal yourself inside the lander," Beth said suddenly. "It's air-maker will easily produce enough to keep you alive while I'm digging you out, but the same amount of air distributed among two hundred Teldins wouldn't last ten minutes. The unit is not designed to support that many beings. Think about it."

For several minutes Martin thought very seriously about it. He thought about facing Skorta with the news that he alone was alive among two hundred asphixiated students. Briefly, he thought about playing God and squeezing a few of the Teldins into the lander—young ones, of course, and probably the children of the Masters. What would Skorta think of that compromise? For some reason that particular Teldin's good opinion of him had become very important to Martin.

Would it be better, he wondered in sudden self-disgust, simply to stay in the lander without speaking to any Teldin and—when he was able to take off—rejoin the hypership and return to Fomalhaut Three? He could tell the tutor that the problem had become too complicated, that the responsibility for assessing the Teldin species for citizenship was too much for him. In short, he should simply walk away from the whole sorry mess.

He was still thinking about it, and he had not closed the lander's entry port, when Beth spoke again.

"All right!" she said angrily. "Be noble and self-sacrificing and . . . and stupid! But I have another idea. It's tricky. I don't think the equipment is supposed to be used in this way, and it could be more dangerous so far as you're concerned . . ."

Her idea was to concentrate on clearing a small area at the exact top center of the shield, the point where it could be opened without the rest of the shield collapsing, and use wide focus pressors to stop the surrounding rocks from sliding into the opening for as long as possible—long enough, at least, for the stinking fog inside to be replaced with fresh outside air. The danger to Martin was that if the pressors slipped, the rocks which fell into the opening would smash through the canopy of the lander's control deck some thirty meters below, and he would no longer have to worry about his assignment or anything else.

Bitterly he cursed the design of the super-efficient meteor shield that allowed access to organic matter down to the size of the smallest microorganism, and forbade it to the even smaller but nonliving molecules of the air they so desperately needed. And there was no time for the complex reprogramming necessary to alter that possibly fatal error.

For the next twenty minutes he divided his attention between the rocks visible about him and Beth's outside viewpoint, which showed her doing things to the pile of rock with tractor and pressor beams which he had not thought possible. Then slowly, from both viewpoints, a gap appeared. It was about two meters wide and it was holding.

"*Now*," Beth said.

Very carefully he dilated the shield until the aperture was roughly a meter across. Stones and coarse gravel rattled down on the canopy, but nothing large enough to cause damage. The fine rock dust which had begun to fall was being blown out again as the hot, stale air rushed to escape. It held for one, two . . . nearly five minutes.

"It's beginning to . . ." Beth began.

He hit the stud which returned the shield to full coverage and cringed as several small rocks which had slipped through banged against the canopy. The gap above was again completely closed with rubble.

". . . slip," she ended.

Around the lander the uninjured students were on their feet, standing motionless and watching him in absolute silence. Martin gestured vaguely, not knowing what else to do, and they began sitting down again.

The next time they needed to freshen the air, enough rubble had been cleared to allow Martin to leave the aperture open. But the sun was close to setting before the lander and the school forecourt were completely uncovered and the students began moving in an orderly procession toward the entrance, carrying the injured with them.

Skorta came hurrying in the opposite direction.

It stopped in front of Martin and stood looking down at him for several seconds. The Teldin was trembling, whether from anger, relief, or fatigue Martin could not say.

"The students," it said, "would have been safe inside the school."

"There were no deaths," Martin said, by way of an apology. "And, ah, three of the students are the children of Masters."

The Teldin was still shaking as it said, "Those students are the property of their Master parent. They are loved and cherished, as are all children, but they are not yet Masters and may never be." It gestured with three of its arms, indicating the lander, the valley city, and the hypership, which still looked gigantic even through it had withdrawn to an altitude of three miles. "Your activities here have been reported to the Masters. Now I have been instructed to proceed at once to the polar city to undergo a Masters' interrogation regarding you. If you wish it you may accompany me."

"I would like that," Martin said. "I could explain to the Masters why I—"

"No, stranger," the Teldin said, no longer shaking. "At most we can speak together and be overheard by the Masters, but nothing you say to me has any value. To them it would be hearsay and irresponsible. Martin, can you send for . . . can you urgently request the presence of your Master?"

"No," Martin said. "My Master would not come."

"Then the Masters of Teldi will not accept your words," Skorta went on, "although I, personally, would like to speak with you at great length. But there could be grave danger for you here. I have no previous knowledge or hearsay which enables me to foretell what will happen when we meet the Masters.

"It would be safer," it ended, "if you left Teldi at once."

"That is good advice," Beth said.

Martin knew that, but at the same time he was feeling confused by a sudden warmth of feeling for this large, incredibly ugly, and strangely considerate extraterrestrial. There could be no doubt that the Masters were going to give Skorta a hard time, and that Martin was directly responsible for its problems. His presence during the interrogation would relieve the Teldin of a lot of the pressure—especially if Martin pleaded ignorance and took the blame for everything that had happened. It would not be right to leave this senior teaching slave to face them alone. Besides, giving moral support to the Teldin might give him a chance to complete the assignment.

"I want to meet the Masters," he said, to both Skorta and Beth. "Thank you for your concern. However, I can remove the danger of the long journey to the polar city. My lander can take us there very quickly, and a speedy response to their summons might favorably impress your Masters. Are you willing to travel in my vessel?"

"Yes, Martin," the Teldin replied with no hesitation at all, "and I am grateful indeed for this unique opportunity."

There was a feeling in Martin's stomach not unlike zero gee, a sensation composed of fear and excitement at the knowledge that, within a matter of hours, the empty spaces in the Teldin jigsaw puzzle would be filled in, and he would know the full extent of the trouble he had caused and, perhaps, the penalty to be paid for causing it.

Chapter 10

INITIALLY they flew only as far as the hypership, because the lander needed a systems check and power recharge after its argument with the avalanche. The Teldin was folded so awkwardly into the space available in the control cubicle that it could not see out and, much to its disappointment, the lander's dock in the

mother ship had no viewports, even though there was
enough headroom there for it to stand erect.

When it met Beth, Skorta made a bow which could
only be described as courtly. It told her that it had had a
life-mate who had perished in the Scourge many years
earlier, and it had not met another who had engaged its
intellect and its emotions to anything like the same extent, but that the fault was probably its own because
several of the teaching slaves had made overtures.

Martin left them talking while he went to the computer's Fabrications module. He did not intend going
down to meet the Masters either empty-handed or with
an empty backpack.

Beth joined him as he was listing and describing his
requirements to the Fabricator.

"I like your friend," she said, leaning over his
shoulder. "Right now it's in the observation blister and
looks as if it will stay there for a long time. You know, I
still don't agree with what you intend doing, but I can
understand why you don't want to let it face the Masters
alone . . . *No*! You can't take *that*!"

She was pointing at the image of the Fabricator's
drafting screen, and before he could respond she went on
vehemently, "You are not allowed to carry weapons. The
Federation absolutely forbids it in a first-contact situation. Maybe your only hope of surviving this meeting is
to go in unarmed as a demonstration that your intentions
are good even though you may have stirred up a hornets'
nest. Going down there is stupid enough!"

Her face was without color, and it was plain that she
was desperately afraid that she might never see Martin
alive again if he returned to Teldi and the Masters. She
wanted him to forget all about it, to return with their
assignment incomplete and to stay alive, but she knew
that he would not do that.

Reassuringly, he said, "I don't expect to use the
weapon on anyone. And I'm beginning to understand the
setup here at last. I'll be all right, you'll see . . ."

Because of their deep emotional involvement, it was
more than two hours before she was properly reassured
and fully satisfied in all respects, and Martin was able to
collect the Teldin from the observation blister.

He found that the teaching slave had not moved, seemingly, from the position in which Beth had placed it. Remembering the high acuity and light sensitivity of Teldin eyes, Martin could understand why. Not only could it see surface features on the planet below which Martin would have required high magnification to resolve, but from the now-orbiting hypership the number of stars it could see even in this sparsely populated region of the galaxy must have paralyzed it with wonder. He had to tell Skorta three times that the lander was ready to leave before it responded.

"Having looked upon all this splendor," it said, and its four arms rose and its head bowed in a gesture which was like an act of worship, "how can I go on living as a slave?"

Martin was not surprised to find that the polar city was bitingly cold, that the level of technology apparent was much higher than that of the valley they had recently left, and that Skorta, who had been born here, was able to direct the lander to within a few meters of the entrance to the Hall of the Masters. What did surprise him was that the Hall was ablaze with artificial light.

"A courtesy extended to a highly placed slave of a strange Master," the Teldin said, "a slave with imperfect vision. It means nothing more."

The Hall itself was surprisingly small. He thought that the debating chamber of the legendary Camelot might have looked a little like this, except that the Teldin table was horseshoe shaped rather than round, and partially bridging the open end was a small, square table and a chair. At a slow, measured pace, Skorta led him toward them and, when they arrived, motioned for him to stand at one side of the chair while it stood at the other.

"You are in the presence of the Masters of Teldi," it announced, and bowed its head briefly. Martin did the same.

There were several unoccupied spaces around the horseshoe. Before every Master's chair, whether it was occupied or not, the richly embroidered flags were spread so that their emblems hung down from the inside edge of the table. Lying on the flags were the swords of the Masters who were present. All of the Masters were adult, some of them looked very old and, so far as Martin could see, they showed no physical signs of the usual self-indulgence and excesses of beings with ultimate authority over a planet's entire population. And these omniscient and all-powerful rulers of Teldi numbered only seventeen.

He stood silently as the teaching slave was questioned regarding Martin's arrival and his subsequent words and actions by a Teldin whose flag bore the emblem of the Master of Sea- and Land-borne Communications. He thought that the Master of Education would have been more appropriate until he remembered that that Mastership was vacant and its authority shared by two other Masters on a caretaker basis. This particular Master was about to experience a lesson in communication that it would not soon forget.

They continued to ignore Martin's presence while Skorta described the rockslide and the strange vessel's protective device which had saved the students from certain death.

It's trying to make a hero of me, Martin thought gratefully. But the interrogator was not impressed.

The master wanted to know where the students would normally have been had the invitation to see its vessel not been issued. It added, obviously for Martin's benefit, that Skorta was no doubt aware that a slave was the property and sole responsibility of its Master, and that any serious wrongdoing on the slave's part should result in the punishment of that Master.

Martin smiled at the thought of these seventeen sword-carrying absolute rulers of Teldi trying to punish the Federation for negligence in his training. But the smile faded when he thought of the Federation's reaction to the news that Teldi held it culpable for his present misbehavior.

At times like these, he thought wryly, there was a lot to be said for the life of a happy and obedient slave.

Skorta was concluding its report. It said, "On being told of my instructions to report to the Hall of the Masters as quickly as possible, the stranger offered to bring me here in its ship. On the way we visited the larger vessel, which had been responsible for shielding the entire city from the Scourge while it was freeing the trapped students. There I spoke to the stranger's lifemate and looked down on Teldi, on all of Teldi, and at the stars."

"That experience," the interrogator said quietly, "we envy you. Do you feel friendship for this stranger?"

"I believe that we feel friendship for each other, Master," Skorta replied.

"Is this the reason why it accompanied you," the Master asked, "when you must have explained to it that the safer course would have been to leave this world and its Masters, whom it so grievously insulted?"

"It is," Skorta said. "This stranger also wanted to deliver a message to you from its Master and would not be dissuaded."

The interrogator made an untranslatable sound and said, "A staunch friend, perhaps, but undeniably a most presumptuous slave. Why is its Master not present?"

Quickly the teaching slave explained that the stranger's Master was of a different species which breathed an atmosphere noxious to Teldins, and could not speak face to face with any person not of its own species. Skorta ended, "This was the reason why the stranger was instructed to land on Teldi as an intermediary."

The interrogator recoiled, as if it had just heard a very dirty word, then went on, "Intermediaries are not to be trusted, ever. Their words are hearsay, untrustworthy, irresponsible, and cause misunderstanding and distress. Only a Master can be believed without doubt or question. That is the Prime Law."

Martin could remain silent no longer. "There were good reasons for the mistrust of hearsay, one thousand one hundred and seventeen of your years ago. But now the Prime Law has become a ritual and a means for enforcing—"

"You stupid, irresponsible slave!" Skorta broke in, shaking with what could only be anger. "Stranger, you

insult the Masters as your own Master has already done
by thrusting hearsay upon them. Be warned. You
may not speak to a Master, but if you must speak to
clarify some portion of my report you will do so only to
me and with the Master's permission."

"No insult was intended," Martin said.

"An insult can be given without intent," the teacher
replied more calmly, "because a slave, being a slave,
does not properly consider all the results of its words or
actions."

Martin let his breath out slowly and said, "There are
mechanisms on the larger ship which are capable of
measuring the individual movements of the pieces of
rock and dust which make up the Scourge. I do not know
the original reason for your Scourge, but these mechanisms tell me how and when it began, and from this information I have deduced—"

"Silence," the Master said quietly. It did not look at
Martin as it went on, "We have no wish to listen to a
slave's deductions from hearsay evidence. But I have in
mind to discuss with you, teacher, matters which will
instruct this stranger with complete accuracy..." It
paused and, grasping the hilt of its sword, looked all
around the table. "...regarding the Scourge. Since this
will involve discussion of the Ultimate Hearsay you, as a
slave, may refuse."

The teacher replied slowly, as if performing a spoken
ritual. It said, "No slave may know the Ultimate Hearsay. No slave, be it Teldin or other, may instruct a Master. The strange slave may not speak except to me,
therefore I shall remain. I do this willingly, and henceforth I accept full responsibility for the results of my
words and actions before the other Masters."

Martin almost lost the last few words, because suddenly everyone in the Hall was standing up and reaching
for their swords. he wondered sickly whether his short,
Earth-human legs could get him to the entrance before
the longer Teldin limbs—including the ones swinging
swords—could head him off. His own weapon was still
in the backpack, and pitifully inadequate anyway. But

the interrogator had swung round and was holding up all four hands palms outward.

"Hold!" it said. "This matter will be dealt with in proper form when its symbol has been brought to us. First must come the judgment and the ruling on this off-world slave."

"What's going *on*?" Beth said anxiously. "You said you knew what you were doing and now...I'm coming down."

"Wait," Martin said, switching out the translator. "The Masters can talk and listen to me through Skorta, and they will tell it things for my benefit which slaves are forbidden to know, because it is just as curious about me as they are. The punishment for learning this forbidden knowledge must be severe, yet Skorta seems unafraid. There's something very odd going on here, and I'm beginning to wonder if..."

Martin broke off because the interrogator was talking again. In calm, emotionless tones it was fleshing out, adding depth and a human, or at least Teldin, dimension to the catastrophe which had smashed their technologically advanced culture flat and returned its people to their equivalent of the dark ages.

Up until one thousand one hundred and seventeen years ago, Teldi had had a satellite, an airless body rich in the mineral resources which had become so depleted on the mother world. The moon had been colonized many centuries earlier and, because it had been given the best that the mother world could provide in the form of its keenest young minds and technical resources, the colony became much more technologically advanced than its parent. Its people remade their lifeless world, scattering its surface with domed cities and farms, and burrowing deeply toward the still-hot core. They became self-sufficient, justifiably proud and independent, and, finally, an armed threat.

But it was not a nuclear preemptive strike which destroyed Teldi's moon, the Master insisted. It had been a catastrophe deep inside the moon itself, associated with experiments on a new power source, which had detonated the satellite like a gigantic bomb.

On Teldi they watched their moon fly slowly apart, and they knew that if one of those larger pieces were to crash into the mother planet it would tear through the crust into the underlying core, and in the resulting planetary upheaval all life on Teldi would be wiped out. However, they had maintained in a state of instant readiness a tremendous arsenal of nuclear weapons capable of reaching their newly disintegrated moon, and the majority of these were hastily reprogrammed to intercept the larger masses of lunar material heading toward them and blast them into smaller and much less devastating pieces.

Many of these relatively small pieces fell on Teldi, and in the resulting devastation, more than a quarter of the planetary population lost their lives. But the threat had been neutralized, for the time being.

Computations made on the paths of the remaining large pieces of the satellite clearly indicated that the mother world was still in danger. There was a very high probability that world-wrecking collisions would take place on an average of three times every century. The planet's long-term survival depended on the Teldins reducing the size of these future world-wreckers in the same way as they had dealt with the first ones.

In spite of the highest priority that was given to missile production and the development of more effective warheads, and the manned missions which visited the larger bodies to planet charges designed to blow them virtually to dust, progress was desperately slow. Large meteors continued to fall: all too often they demolished key missile production or launching installations.

For this reason it required close on fifty years for the project to reach completion, completion in that there were no longer any bodies in Teldi's path capable of destroying the planet, and no missiles left to send against them if there had been. The moon had been reduced and scattered into a nearly homogenous cloud of meteorite material, most of which circled the planet and fell steadily onto its surface.

The Scourge had come.

No fabrication or person could live on or above the surface of Teldi for more than a few dozen revolutions without the certainty of damage, injury, or death. The remnants of the technology which had survived long enough to save them were eroded away or hammered flat by the Scourge. Their once-great civilization was reduced to ruins, its population decimated and driven slowly back toward the level of their savage, cave dwelling prehistory—but not all the way back.

They had been able to survive in their caves, deep valleys, mines, and underground missile installations and extend them into subsurface cities. They had farmed because the Scourge could not kill every plant and tree, and they had built protected road systems and kept as much as was useful of the old knowledge alive and stored the rest. But the chief reason for their continued survival as a culture had been that increasing numbers of the frightened and despairing population placed themselves under the protection and orders of the senior military officers.

It was the nature of things that saviors became Masters, and it had been all too easy for the system to perpetuate itself when the Masters had the respect as well as the obedience of their slaves, as well as a large measure of control over their thinking—including the habit of distrust which was instilled from birth.

For there had been a few minutes' warning of the destruction of their satellite, time enough for the mother world to be told that it was about to be obliterated because some technician had been too stupidly trusting— someone had accepted as fact something which should have been doubted and rechecked. For this error Teldi had been lashed by the Scourge for more than a thousand years. The reason for their fanatical distrust, Martin thought as the Master ended its grim history lesson, was now all too obvious.

If only the Masters had not enslaved the population while they were saving it, and made knowledge available only to a favored, high-ranking few...

"In every society there must be persons with authority and responsibility in charge," Skorta said suddenly, making Martin realize that he had been so affected by the Master's history lesson that he had been thinking aloud. "No mechanism should be overloaded by a responsible owner. But you have been to my school, Martin, and you know that in practice every person is given a little more knowledge than it needs, in the hope that it will evince a desire for even more. Naturally, it is not given more until it has shown that it is capable of responsibly using the knowledge it already possesses."

"I begin to understand," Martin said. "The instructions of my Master were that I—"

"Please inform this slave," the interrogator broke in, "that the instructions of its absent Master mean nothing to us. There are three instances of recorded hearsay describing the landing on Teldi of mechanisms which spoke our language and tried to show us great wonders projected into the empty air around them before they were destroyed. Our reply was that we would accept no communication unless it was delivered to us in person by a responsible Master. This slave is not a responsible person, its presence before us is an insult, and I cannot understand its Master's purpose in sending it here when that Master is fully aware of the situation on Teldi.

"We are not yet decided on what to do with this slave," the Master went on. "Should it be punished physically as is a child for persistent disobedience, or merely returned to its Master who will not act like a Master?"

Martin swallowed, thinking that a spanking from one of the overlarge Teldins would not be a pleasant experience either physically or mentally. He was also thinking about his tutor on Fomalhaut Three, who was most certainly aware of the problem, which Martin had been given full responsibility for solving. He could run away or try to solve this problem, the decision was his alone. Martin swore under his breath. He was beginning to view his tutor, the Teldin Masters, and even himself, in a new light.

"Before this decision is made," he said to the teacher, "is it permitted that I discuss with you, my friend and equal, my instruction regarding—"

"Martin," the Teldin said, "I am no longer your equal."

Chapter 11

His first feeling was of betrayal. He wondered if Skorta had been as honest with him as it had seemed. But then he remembered some of the things it had said on the way to the city, at the school, and on the hyper-ship. Skorta had come across as an intelligent, liberal-minded, responsible, and perhaps potentially rebellious slave who did not mind talking a little hearsay or think-ing for itself. To him, it had appeared to be a truly civi-lized and cultured being who was fighting its slavehood and beginning to win.

And now, Martin saw with a sudden flood of under-standing, the fight was over.

"Your bio-sensors are going mad!" Beth said, sound-ing both angry and frightened. "Pulse rate and blood pressure are way up and your . . . Dammit, are you get-ting ready to do something stupid?"

There was no need to answer her because she would hear and see everything he was going to do. Martin moistened his lips and for the first time he turned to ad-dress the assembled Masters of Teldi directly.

"I have considered this matter fully and the possible consequences of making my decision," he said, "and I wish to be once again the equal of my friend."

For several interminable seconds there was neither sound nor motion in the Hall. Then Skorta walked slowly to an empty place at the horseshoe table and turned to face him, leaving Martin alone beside the Table of Interrogation. All sound and motion ceased again, and even Beth seemed to be holding her breath. He thought of asking permission for what he was about to do, then decided against it.

Asking permission was for slaves.

He removed and opened his backpack and spread the Federation flag across the table so that the silver and black emblem hung over the outer edge in plain sight of the Masters. Then he withdrew the weapon, the scaled-down replica of the Master of Education's sword he had seen at the school, and laid it on top of the flag. The hilt, which also bore the Federation symbol, lay toward him. Then he folded his arms.

The Masters arose and seventeen hands went to the hilts of their swords, but this time the Master of Sea- and Land-borne Communications did not call a halt as it had done in the case of Skorta, the one-time teaching slave, because the interrogator was grasping its sword, too. Martin swallowed as seventeen swords were raised to Teldin shoulder height and held at full extension with their seventeen points directed unswervingly at his face.

"Will the new Master-Elect of Education," the interrogator said, "please join the off-world would-be Master and guide it in the traditional words and response."

Now I'm committed, thought Martin, but to what? The interrogator was speaking again.

"Do you accept sole and undivided responsibility for your words and actions, and omissions of words or actions, and the results thereof? Do you accept such responsibility for your property, whether animate or inanimate; its efficient working; its proper maintenance, training, feeding, and conduct toward the property of other Masters? Do you accept as your own responsibility the results of the conduct or misconduct of all such property, and will you reward, correct, or chastise the property committing such acts? Will you strive always to increase the efficiency, well-being, and intelligence of all your animate property in the hope that they will one day become capable of accepting the ultimate responsibility of a Master? As the bearer of ultimate responsibility, do you agree to defend with your life your person, property, and decisions and if, in the judgment of your fellow Masters, your actions and decisions threaten harm in large measure to your own or the property of others, that you will forfeit your life?"

Martin felt perspiration trickling from his armpits and he knew that if his arms had not been folded tightly across his chest, his hands would have been trembling.

"Consider carefully, off-world friend," said the new Master-Elect, who was again standing beside him. "An impulsive decision does not impress them, even though the impulse was of friendship and loyalty. If you withdraw now your punishment will probably be a token one, possibly banishment from Teldi society and removal of Masters' protection, neither of which will inconvenience you greatly."

Martin cleared his throat. He said, "The decision was carefully considered and is not based solely on sentiment. I am not stupid, but I have been confused by your Master-slave relationship on Teldi, and by the true nature and function of the Masters. I am confused no longer."

The swords were still pointed at him, so steadily that he could imagine that the scene was a still photograph, when Skorta spoke again.

"Raise your sword and hold it vertically with the base of the hilt resting on your flag," it said. "Support the sword in the vertical position by pressing the palm of your hand against the point. You will exert sufficient pressure for the point to draw blood. You will then speak the words 'I accept the duties and responsibilities of a Master,' after which you will replace the sword and self-administer the appropriate medication to the wounded hand and await the response of the Masters."

He nearly fumbled it, because the height of the Table of Interrogation made it necessary for him to stand on tiptoe to press downward against the point of the sword, so that the point slipped and jabbed him in the fleshy pad at the base of his thumb. But he was so relieved that the sword did not go skidding onto the floor that he scarcely felt the pain, even when the blood trickled slowly down the blade.

As steadily as he could, Martin said, "I accept the duties and responsibilities of a Master."

The swords were still pointing at him while he replaced his on the flag and slapped an adhesive dressing on his hand. Then one of the swords swept upward to point at the ceiling. Another followed suit, then another and another until all were raised, then all seventeen swords were lowered and replaced on their Masters' flags.

Skorta bowed gravely and said, "The election was unanimous, off-world Master. You may speak to us now, and everything you say will be accepted as factual if you say that it is, and any demonstrations by mechanisms operated by you will be given similar credence. If your words or actions prove false or inaccurate you will, of course, be answerable to your fellow Masters."

"I understand," Martin said, as he removed the tri-di projector from his pack. "What if the vote had not been unanimous? Would I have had to fight?"

"Only as a last resort," the Teldin replied, "and after many days debating other and nonviolent solutions. There are never enough Masters on Teldi, Martin. The senior slaves who become eligible for Mastership and are encouraged to apply are far too intelligent to want the heavy responsibility involved. But there are an occasional few who, like ourselves, are overtaken by a strange irrationality which makes us find rewards in performing thankless tasks and . . . You are ready to begin?"

"I'm ready," Martin said.

He waited until Skorta had returned to its place at the big table, then announced that he would describe and depict the events which had occurred on his home planet when Earth had been contacted by the Federation of Galactic Sentinents and its people offered citizenship. Indicating the entrance and wall facing their table, he started the projector. Several of the Masters made untranslatable noises as, in spite of the Hall lighting, there appeared a volume of blackness of apparently endless depth.

The show began.

He showed them the arrival of the gigantic matter transmitters in Earth orbit, and some of the feats of transportation of which they were capable. He showed them a few of the great, white cubical buildings which were the Federation's examination and induction centers, and described how the people of Earth went into them to be rejected as Undesirable, accepted as Citizens, or classified as non-Citizens requiring further examination and training.

"But you're telling them *everything*!" Beth's voice said anxiously in his earpiece. "Our tutor might not want that. Or don't you care anymore?"

"I care," Martin said. "But I'm not sure what our tutor expects of us. If it had wanted us to do or not do something, it should have been more specific, instead of simply telling us that the Teldi situation was entirely our responsibility. And I do care about these people, too, much to be dishonest with them."

"This Master business," Beth said quietly, "you're taking it very seriously."

"Yes," he said, then added quickly, "No more talking, the next bit could be tricky..."

Like every other planetary population offered citizenship, he explained, Earth's people had been screened and divided into three categories—the Citizens, the non-Citizens and the Undesirables. The majority of applicants were successful and became Citizens, to move to the Federation World to begin lives in which their potentialities could be fully realized free of all personal, political, and economic pressures. In the Federation, Citizens were not forced to do anything, because the type of people who would use such force were excluded as Undesirables.

But Martin could see that the Masters were becoming restless at the idea that they might be considered undesirable, and he went on quickly, "Unlike the Citizens, the non-Citizens obey orders and have to submit to training, but their work is vital to the functioning of the Federation. They have the option of becoming Citizens at any time, and they are—"

"Slaves," one of the Masters said.

"Why must these beings leave their home planets to become Citizens?" another asked. "And are the new worlds suited to their needs?"

What is a slave, Martin wondered. Aloud, he said, "There is only one world. Observe!"

The dark, tri-di projection blazed suddenly with the glorious, indescribable light that could be seen only amid the densely populated starfields of the galactic center. And hanging against that incredible, silvery field was a gigantic, black, and featureless shape, the shape reproduced on his Federation emblem.

"This," Martin said, trying to hold his voice steady, "is the Federation World."

It was a hollow body, he explained as simply as he could, fabricated from the material which had comprised this and many other star systems, and it contained the intelligent beings of over two hundred different species who were presently members of the Federation. The superworld enclosed its own sun, and its interior surface area was vast beyond imagining. The projected future populations of all the races in the galaxy would never overcrowd this world.

As the diagrams and detail pictures flashed into view, Martin tried to describe the awful immensity of the Federation World, its topology and environmental variations, its incredibly advanced supporting technology. But one of the Masters was waving for attention.

"Since the Scourge returned us to the dark ages, Teldi has nothing to offer," it said. "Yet you are considering us for citizenship of this—this— *Why*, stranger?"

Martin was silent, remembering his own reaction on first seeing the Federation World. The Masters had had enough superscience and frontal assaults on their feelings or superiority for one day. He softened his tone.

"The Federation accepts all levels of technical and cultural development," he said. "Its purpose is to seek out the intelligent races of the galaxy and bring them to a place of safety before some natural or unnatural catastrophe befalls them. On this world they will grow in knowledge and intermingle with other species, and, in the fullness of time, the combined intelligence of this future Federation will be capable of achievements unimaginable even to the most advanced minds among its present-day Citizens. And while all of its Citizens are climbing slowly to the scientific, philosophical, and cultural heights, they must be protected."

He canceled the projection, and for a long time nothing was said. They were all staring at his flag, at the black diamond on a silver field which was the Federation emblem, but still seeing the tremendous reality which it represented. Perhaps he had shown them too much too soon, and had succeeded only in giving them an inferiority complex from which they would never recover. But these were the top people on Teldi and they had earned their positions by rising through the ranks. They were tough, honest, and adaptable, and Martin thought they could take it.

It was the interrogator who found its voice first. "You came here to judge us on our suitability or otherwise for this...this Federation. We may not wish to join, stranger, but we would be interested in hearing your verdict."

To tough, honest, and adaptable, add proud and independent. Now Martin knew what he had to do.

But before he could speak, the Master-Elect of Education walked slowly to his side. Skorta was staring down at the Federation flag and not at Martin as it said, "Martin, this is important. If your pronouncement is open to discussion and subsequent modification, touch the hilt of your sword as you speak. If it is your own unalterable decision which you will defend, if necessary, with your life, then grasp the hilt firmly and hold the weapon in a defensive position."

"They're still in a state of shock," Beth said in the angry, despairing tone of one who knows that good advice will be ignored. "And there are no guards on the door. *Run!*"

"No," Martin said stubbornly. Through the translator he went on, "Before I deliver my judgment I must first draw analogies with the systems which govern Teldi and the Federation.

"Undesirables, troublemakers, the power seekers are excluded, rendered impotent, and ignored," he went on. "The Citizens are free and protected, and the non-Citizens do the hard but interesting work associated with the maintenance of the World's systems and ongoing projects. This work is not forced on them and the reason they do it is two-fold. They feel a self-imposed responsibility in the matter and they, regardless of their species or level of intelligence or competence, belong to that group of restless and adventurous entities who are not sure that the protected life of a Citizen is for them. They are the errand boys, the servants, the slaves of the Federation, save only in the area of personal responsibility."

Around the horseshoe table hands were twitching restively toward their swords, but Martin did not touch the hilt of his own. Not yet.

"On Teldi," he went on, "the system of government and the general display of mistrust were initially abhorrent to me, as was the tight mental control which apparently was being imposed by the Masters. But the reason for the mistrust and the insistence that hearsay be vouched for by a highly responsible person, a Master, became plain when I learned of the original cause of the Scourge. Regarding the control of imparted knowledge, I learned that much of the forbidden hearsay was available to low-level slaves trying for higher and more responsible positions. But few of them feel impelled to accept the ultimate responsibility. There are never enough Masters on Teldi.

"I also discovered," Martin continued, still keeping his hand well away from the sword, "that the slaves of Teldi are, in spite of its low-level technology, the most self-motivated, independent, self-reliant, and widely trained group of beings that I have ever experienced or learned of through hearsay.

"There is no reason for that level of technology to remain low if the Scourge is removed," he went on, hoping that the unsteadiness in his voice would not be apparent in translation. "I am not a Master of the mechanisms which can do this work, nor have I any direct knowledge of the length of time required, other than it will take many of your years. But the Scourge can be removed, allowing you to build again on the surface, and travel in safety, and grow..."

Martin broke off because he was talking to a three-dimensional picture again—there was absolute stillness in the room.

Slowly and deliberately he reached forward and gripped the hilt of his sword, then lifted it into a defensive position, diagonally across his chest.

Had he misjudged them? Was he about to misjudge them again?

He said gravely, "If the Federation was to set up examination and induction centers on Teldi at this time there would be very few beings judged Undesirable, and few also who would be accepted as Citizens. The great majority would be deemed unsuitable for the Federation World. I will explain."

The Masters were either touching or gripping the hilts of their swords now. Like the slave population of Teldi, they were proud, independent, self-reliant, and fantastically caring of the animate property from out of which they had risen to become Masters. Any criticism of that property was a personal insult to them.

"Teldi is a special case," Martin went on. "On Teldi there are never enough Masters, never enough people able and willing to accept the crushing responsibility that Mastership entails. In the Federation it is likewise said that there are never enough non-Citizens, and for a very similar reason: because the qualities required for the job are rare. It is my judgment that Teldins are not now and probably never will be suitable for Federation citizenship.

"It is my decision," he said, tightening his grip on the sword, "that the Scourge be removed and your world left alone for at least three of your generations. And it is my confident expectation that when the Federation next contacts you, it will make a unique and most valuable discovery—a planetary population composed entirely of non-Citizens ready to assume extra-planetary duties and responsibilities."

The Masters were sitting still and silent, and suddenly Martin knew why.

"My arrival on Teldi was not a secret one," he said, lowering his sword and placing it on the Federation flag. As he resumed speaking, he slowly rolled the weapon in the cloth. "As a result, much new hearsay will arise and more slaves will be impelled to try for Mastership when the Scourge is gone and they realize what was and what will again be possible for Teldins. There is something I would like to leave with you, with your permission..."

He walked slowly toward Skorta with the flag-wrapped sword held before him in both hands, then proffered it to the Teldin. Behind and around him he could hear the movements of Masters getting to their feet and the soft, rustling sound of metal scraping against fabric, but he did not look aside.

"Martin," the Teldin said, taking the sword from him, "I am honored to accept this additional responsibility of Master of Off-World Affairs and I, and my successors, will respect and promulgate the knowledge you have given us."

It did not say anything else, and neither did the other Masters, but as Martin turned and began walking toward the entrance, they remained standing, silent, motionless and with their swords held high in salute until he had passed from sight.

On Teldi, he had belatedly realized, silence was approval. It meant that there was no dissenting voice.

Chapter 12

EVEN though Martin was certain that he had done the right thing on Teldi, he knew that his actions and decisions had been high-handed to say the least, so that he spent the return trip worrying in case their supervisor, or the Galactics placed in authority above it, would show themselves less certain than he was. While insisting that it was silly to be so concerned about something which might never happen, Beth helped him worry.

But in the event, it was clear that there was nothing to worry about, because at the conclusion of the post-mission debriefing they were given another assignment.

YOUR PROCEDURES WERE UNORTHODOX AND SEVERAL RULES WERE CONTRAVENED REGARDING SHIP HANDLING AND FIRST-CONTACT DIRECTIVES, BUT TO GOOD EFFECT. THE REPORT, ASSESSMENT, AND RECOMMENDATIONS RE-

GARDING THE TELDIN SYSTEM HAVE BEEN AP-
PROVED.

WITH IMMEDIATE EFFECT, THE ENTITY MAR-
TIN, SERVICE IDENTITY MJC/221/5501 IS PRO-
MOTED NON-CITIZEN CONTACT SPECIALIST
LEVEL THREE. THE ENTITY BETH, ECM/221/4977
IS APPOINTED NON-CITIZEN SHIP HANDLER
LEVEL ONE. YOU ARE TO BE COMPLIMENTED.

SINCE YOUR FORMAL TRAINING IS NOW
COMPLETE, YOU WILL HENCEFORTH REGARD
ME AS YOUR SUPERVISOR AND NOT YOUR
TUTOR. YOU ARE NO LONGER TRAINEES, BUT
HOPEFULLY YOU WILL CONTINUE TO LEARN.

Martin did not know if their supervisor was capable of
audible speech, since it was the rule that all inter-species
communications were by the printed word. But he knew
sarcasm when he saw it, and remained silent.

SYSTEM TRL/5/11765/G3 AWAITS YOUR AT-
TENTION. THE DETAILS HAVE BEEN RECORDED
FOR LATER STUDY.

QUESTIONS?

"Is this planet's dominant life form to be contacted,"
Martin asked, "and its suitability or otherwise assessed
for membership in the Federation?"

CORRECT. BUT ONLY IF YOU FIND THE DOMI-
NANT LIFE FORM TO BE INTELLIGENT.

"Surely that was a job for the searchships," Martin
protested. "Ours is to decide whether or not they are
nice people. And why does this assignment follow so
closely on the Teldi job? Is it urgent?"

IT IS NOT URGENT. THE ASSIGNMENT IS TO
CONFIRM THE FINDINGS OF AN EARLY SEARCH-
SHIP INVESTIGATION WHICH DECLARED THE
PLANET FREE OF INDIGENOUS INTELLIGENT LIFE,
SO THAT TRL/5/11765/G3 CAN BE REMOVED
FROM OUR LISTS OF WORLDS REQUIRING AT-
TENTION.

THE ENVIRONMENT IS SUCH THAT THE EARTH-
HUMAN SENSORIUM WILL FIND IT RESTFUL,
QUIET, AND VISUALLY PLEASING. PROVIDING
BASIC PROTECTIVE MEASURES ARE TAKEN, THIS

ASSIGNMENT MAY BE REGARDED AS A VACATION
AND A REWARD FOR THE SUCCESSFUL COMPLE-
TION OF THE TELDI OPERATION.
  DEPART WHEN CONVENIENT.

On this planet it was a different kind of silence from
that on Teldi, the silence of fear rather than respect. The
insects did not hum, the birds did not sing, and the creatures that they could see, large and small alike, made
sounds which had to be amplified to be detectable at all.
Only the wind, which had no natural enemies to fear,
sighed quietly as it stirred the vegetation.

The silence was contagious.

Without speaking, Martin pointed toward two small,
lizardlike creatures who were tearing each other to
pieces with such quiet ferocity that it was difficult to tell
which limbs belonged to which. Beside him, Beth lowered her image enhancing visor to look at them more
closely.

"It's quiet," she whispered, "but there isn't much
peace."

Immediately the two combatants broke off hostilities
and moved rapidly and very quietly away—plainly startled by the sound of her whisper—to resume their battle
some fifty meters further up the hill Beth and Martin had
been climbing.

He sent their protector ahead to make sure that none
of the larger predators were waiting silently for them on
the other slope.

They had studied the surface of the planet from orbit
and during lower level atmospheric flights in the lander.
It was an Earthlike world seemingly devoid of indigenous intelligent life. The vegetation was varied, beautiful, and, unlike the fauna, nonaggressive. The largest life
form, although too heavily equipped with natural
weapons to be effective against members of their own
species, were fast enough on their six enormous feet to
ensure that their diet was not exclusively vegetarian.
Fortunately the species was not numerous, so that it was
unlikely that they would become a serious inconvenience
during a half-hour stroll.

"The whole planet is like this," he said, stooping to touch one of the gorgeous blooms. "We're wasting our time here."

They had climbed to the top of the hill before Beth replied. "We've been ordered to waste our time here, remember, so just relax and enjoy the scenery... Oh-oh."

He looked up to see that their protector, which had been hovering like an enormous metal insect about a quarter of a mile away, was rushing toward them flashing its warning lights. It was moving only slightly faster than one of the large predators which was coming at them from their right flank.

Running in any direction would simply have complicated the job of rescue by the robot, but it was incredibly difficult to stand still while that outsized predator was bearing down on them.

If anything, it resembled an Earth elephant, Martin thought, but with six padded feet and nearly twice the body mass. Two long trunks were mounted laterally above a mouth which could have been transplanted from an outsize shark. Although fast-moving, it had a jerky, hobbling gait caused by its peculiar leg motion. A fraction of a second before touching the ground, each foot hesitated so that three of the others were supporting the creature's weight and thrusting it forward while the remaining limbs were lifting to continue the cycle. Whether moving fast or slow, it had the ability to place each foot in turn with the minimum of sound and ground vibration.

While it was charging up the slope toward them, Martin found it difficult to believe that it represented a real threat—he had the ridiculous idea that it was simply a tri-di recording with the sound turned off, and at any moment an instructor's voice would draw their attention to the interesting anatomical details. Then sound and reality returned as the protection vehicle dropped to the ground with a most unsilent *thump* between them and their attacker, and they dived through the open entry hatch.

The charging predator struck the other side of the vehicle so hard that they were knocked off their feet. They picked themselves off the floor and tried vainly to strap in as the creature lashed at the upper hull with its twin trunks. The vehicle dropped to the ground, immobilized as its gravity cushion died, and the damage to the external sensors left half of the vision screens showing only white snow. Malfunction lights were winking all over the control console, and they could hear the creature climbing onto the top of the hull.

"What are you waiting for, dammit?" Martin yelled. "Blast it, before it beats you into a heap of scrap!"

One of the still operable screens lit with the reply.

I AM RELUCTANT TO DESTROY THIS CREATURE BECAUSE IT IS A MALE MEMBER OF A SUB-SPECIES WHICH IS CLOSE TO EXTINCTION. DAM-AGE SUSTAINED SO FAR IS WITHIN THE CAPACITY OF MY SELF-REPAIR SYSTEMS ONCE THE CREA-TURE REALIZES THAT I AM INEDIBLE AND WITH-DRAWS.

Why, Martin raged silently, were intelligent robots so stupid? But it was Beth who spoke first.

"We are edible," she said, clearly and simply as if speaking to a child. "The creature knows we are here and it has organic sensors which will confirm our continued presence within you. The creature will not, therefore, withdraw and we are seriously at risk unless you—"

"Get us out of here!" Martin broke in harshly as the floor heaved alarmingly and for a few seconds became a wall.

OF COURSE. MATTER TRANSMITTER EN-GAGED. DESTINATION?

"The lander, stupid."

They had been sprawled in an untidy heap inside the protector and that, following the split second of indescribable shock as their bodies were dispersed into their individual atoms and reassembled again, was how they arrived in the lander's control center. He helped Beth to her feet, wondering if there was a single square inch of his body which was not aching. Beth winced as she sat down at the console to set about protecting their lander.

The predator had lost interest in the damaged protection vehicle and was moving slowly in their direction. Martin hoped that it was simply curious about the large, unusual object occupying its territory and not aware, at a distance of nearly half a mile upwind, that they were inside.

Their view of the creature became hazy for an instant as Beth put up the lander's force shield. Then, with an expression which was distinctly maternal, she signaled the damaged protector for a status report.

EIGHTY PERCENT EXTERNAL SENSORS INOPERABLE. SEVERE DAMAGE SUSTAINED TO UPPER HULL. GRAVITY NEUTRALIZATION GRIDS INOPERABLE. POWER SUPPLY OPTIMUM. PRIORITY IS BEING GIVEN TO REPAIR OF THE GRIDS TO RESTORE MOBILITY. ESTIMATED TIME FOR GRID REPAIRS SEVENTEEN MINUTES. FOR RETURN TO LANDER NINETEEN MINUTES.

"There's no big hurry," Beth said. "Make a wide circle on your way back and keep the lander between you and the predator. You don't want to lose another argument with that thing."

REVISED ESTIMATE FOR RETURN TO LANDER TWENTY-SIX MINUTES.

But before she could acknowledge, the screen color changed from black to red.

EMERGENCY. MALFUNCTION IN SELF-REPAIR MANIPULATORS. SENSORY INPUT REDUCING. MOVEMENT IN ANY DIRECTION IMPOSSIBLE. THE VEHICLE IS TRAPPED IN A LOCAL LAND SUBSIDENCE. REQUEST ASSISTANCE.

"Maintain transmission of all sensory input, incomplete though it is," Beth said. "We'll pull you out of there as soon as possible." To Martin, she added worriedly, "My initial scan of the landing area did not show any subsurface pockets. I don't understand how—"

She broke off as the screen lit with the bright, crawling blankness indicative of a receiver which no longer had a signal to receive. The adjacent screen showed the already magnified image of the predator galloping rapidly into close-up.

Then for no apparent reason the creature slowed, veered to the right and came to a halt. It began to move slowly in a tight circle with its head held close to the ground. Then it stopped again and reared up with its forelimbs pawing the air and its twin trunks extended stiffly upward in a narrow V. For the first time since encountering the creature they heard it make a noise, a high-pitched hissing sound which wavered above and below the level of audibility.

"Some sort of courtship dance, I expect," Beth said doubtfully, "except that there isn't another one of the beasties within detection range— Now, what!"

Without warning the predator had dropped from sight. It looked as if the ground had opened up and swallowed it.

"I'm absolutely sure there were no subsurface caves this close to the landing area," she said, slipping into the control position and initiating the take off sequence. "We'll take a closer look at what happened to that creature on the way to rescuing our protector, and before a subsurface cave opens suddenly under us."

"Right," Martin agreed.

A few minutes later the lander was hovering above the fresh subsidence. The cave-in was about thirty feet across and roughly the same depth, and the predator was in the exact center of it. Part of a leg and one trunk lay loosely on the fallen soil, looking as if they had been freshly and very crudely amputated, and they did not need the sensors to tell them that the creature was dead.

When they moved to the subsidence covering the protector robot, Beth signaled it again on the off chance that it had been able to repair its communicator. There was no response.

"I'll work the tractor beam," Martin said. "Hold us steady while I uncover your sick friend."

"No," Beth said, indicating the sensor displays. She sounded as if she herself did not believe what she was saying. "You can't help my sick friend because it isn't there anymore. Apart from a few sections of plating, something or somebody has taken our protector robot apart and gone off with the pieces."

Martin looked over her shoulder, thinking that their lander could not be undermined and taken apart while it was five hundred feet in the air. But that did not mean that the agency which had dismantled their protector and killed one of the largest and most ferocious native predators had no other surprises up its sleeve.

Under emergency thrust, the lander was already climbing through the upper atmosphere when Martin said unnecessarily, "Let's get out of here."

Inside the orbiting mother ship they felt safe but very, very confused.

"At this range I can't detect anything less massive than a heavy screwdriver," Beth said, "that's why I'm losing sensor contact with the components of the robot. Even the parts which do not normally break down, such as the power and gravity nullification generators, are being concealed by increasing depth or intervening aggregations of ore-bearing rock. To get a clearer picture I'd have to soft-land a probe and do a proper sonic scan."

"I suppose we can afford to lose a probe," Martin said dryly, "as well as a protector robot."

"It will detect anything approaching from beneath the surface," she replied irritably, "in plenty of time for me to lift it clear."

Considering the virtually limitless resources of the hypership, the loss would be of little importance—except to Beth, who had a very tidy mind.

"Is it possible," he asked, "that the terrain conceals a life form large enough to ingest surface creatures at will? That predator was literally swallowed up and partially eaten. Maybe it thought our robot was edible, too."

Beth shook her head. "That's a bit fanciful. A single beast capable of opening mouths in any desired area of the surface would be large and extremely energy hungry, and the evidence of its presence would be hard to miss. Judging by the way that predator died, its killers are hunters and burrowers who operate as a team. For some reason they prefer to work below ground."

"On the surface they might be at a disadvantage against the predators," Martin said, "so they have to be sneaky."

Which was synonymous, they both knew, with the use of intelligence.

"I'm thinking," Beth said, "of the way the predator's

attack on the lander was diverted, and why. The presence of a large creature or object can be detected by its effect on the surface, but time is needed to undermine the target, during which it must not move away.

"The robot was easy," she went on, "because it was damaged and motionless. The predator had to be immobilised in a different fashion. The proper scent would do it, released a few hundred yards upwind. Strong, olfactory indications of a female nearby would make it lose interest in attacking the lander, and once it stopped moving, our friends trapped it in their freshly dug pit. But were they the same group who dismantled the protector, or a different one?"

"Does it matter?" Martin asked.

"It matters," Beth replied. "If there were two groups of hunters and burrowers who are used to trapping their prey in this fashion, the chances are significantly greater that we are dealing with another specialized form of predator. But if it was the same beings responsible for both attacks, they may have thought that our robot had not been able to defend itself against the predator and they may have diverted and destroyed the creature to save the lander from a similar fate. So it matters whether our friends were being guided by a highly evolved instinct pattern, or intelligence and, possibly, friendship."

Martin was silent for a moment, then he said apologetically, "I should have thought of that. But suppose our friends, realizing that the predator had wrecked our other vehicle, wanted to protect the lander so that they would have an undamaged machine to take apart?"

"That would mean," Beth replied worriedly, "that they were intelligent but not very friendly."

"Maybe we are misreading the indications," he said, switching sides in the argument. "Could there be a geological reason for the sudden appearance of those pits which—"

He broke off. Beth's disagreement was silent, but plainly evident.

"All right then," he went on. "We haven't seen these creatures or found any trace of their existence. We have no idea how they live except that it is underground. The reason why they don't show themselves is possibly because they are at a disadvantage on the surface. This suggests a small life form, a species of burrower which acts in concert to dismantle large predators and sophisticated robots alike. The latter capability suggests the possession of advanced technology, power sources and communications systems, none of which we have been able to detect. It is impossible to hide the radiation signature of a technologically advanced civilization unless they are hiding deliberately."

"Deliberately!" Beth said, and laughed. "Living underground as they do, their communication system could be very basic, simply modulated sonics transmitted through a solid medium. When we land the probe I'll have the answer to that one."

"Caution where strangers are concerned," Martin went on, feeling the hair at the back of his neck begin to prickle, "is also a sign of intelligence. The silence down there is complete, and the sound prints of indigenous life forms are already known to them, so that it would be easy to detect the presence of strangers.

"But they were hiding from us," he ended quietly, "while we were still in space."

For a long time Beth stared at the pastoral beauty which was pictured on the main screen, then she said, "I think it's time we reviewed this whole assignment."

Chapter 13

"SOME vacation!" Beth said when the data had been reviewed. Her tone was one of angry disbelief.

"If you remember," Martin said, trying to be objective, "the supervisor did not actually lie to us when we were assigned Teldi. It did not tell, because it did not know, the whole truth. Maybe it knows even less of the truth this time. Run the searchship data again, please?"

The third and only life bearing planet of a gee-type sun, the world had a near-perfect circular orbit, no axial tilt, no major topological features or temperature variations, all of which explained the absence of seasonal changes and the undramatic weather. The world had a predisposition toward silence and, Martin knew, the ability to hunt or graze quietly would be an important survival characteristic among its fauna. A species which could burrow underground and trap and smother their prey, regardless of size, would have a considerable advantage over the surface dwellers and might well have become the dominant, and intelligent, life form.

"The searchship carried out the usual surface scan," Martin said as the material was being presented. "They were looking for surface buildings, sea or airborne craft, power installations and radiation in the electromagnetic spectrum. They soft-landed probes to collect animal and vegetable specimens, then moved on to the next system on their list. The probes were not attacked while they were on the ground, so there was no way of knowing that intelligent subsurface life was present."

"*Possible* intelligent subsurface life," Beth said, stressing the first word. "Your conclusion is based on the fact that a robot protector was dismantled without causing its power cell to explode. But remember, our equipment is designed to cause minimum damage and pollution if a curious native tries to take something apart. It is more likely, although much less exciting to think about, that they are nonintelligent creatures with the magpie instinct, and that they were very lucky that the power cell did not blow up in their faces.

"Besides," she added, "if they're capable of taking apart a completely alien, to them, mechanism like the protector with safety, they would have to be very highly advanced scientifically, and the associated technology would leave a large and unmistakabale radiation signature. There was no such signature."

"They were hiding it," Martin said.

"From the searchship and now from us?" Beth asked quietly. "Aren't you becoming a trifle paranoid about this?"

As the hypership captain providing technical and

moral support to his first-contact specialty, she often took the devil's advocate position in an argument in order to clarify the situation for both of them.

"People usually hide because they are afraid," Martin said thoughtfully. "As yet we don't know why they are afraid. Maybe they had a very bad experience in the past as a result of a visitation from space. The searchship did not land and its investigations were carried out by long-range sensors and probes, which did little more than flatten a few square inches of grass. But there is no sign of the chemical and radioactive pollutants associated with a crash landing by a visiting ship, or other catastrophic malfunction which would have caused widespread damage or loss of life among the natives.

"Maybe they are simple xenophobes," he went on, "who are afraid of all strangers. I still think they are small, weak or have some other obvious disadvantage which would—"

"It isn't obvious to me," Beth said. "Look at what they did to our robot."

"If we saw one of them it might be," Martin replied. "I'm still convinced that they are intelligent, technologically advanced, and afraid; that is a tricky combination to deal with."

Beth was still regarding the data on the main screen as she said, "Suppose these as yet hypothetical people are hiding without realizing that they are hiding. They may be an omnivorous vegetable life form with a fast-growing, controllable system of roots capable of breaking up the soil under their prey and trapping—"

"And they had a sudden and urgent requirement," Martin broke in, "for mineral trace elements used in the metal of the protector?"

"It's a possibility," Beth said lamely.

"I prefer the idea of acute xenophobia," Martin replied. "That presupposes them having a knowledge of off-planet intelligent life, and methods of detecting the approach of such life from a great distance, and of concealing the detection system along with all the other traces of themselves. They must have something very important to hide, wouldn't you say?"

"Oh, come, now," Beth said, swinging round to face

him. "Surely a species with that capability would not want to hide, it would have more than enough technological muscle to defend itself."

"A good point," Martin said. "But suppose they can detect our ships only after they leave hyperspace, that would reduce the level of their technology by a few notches. And remember, a searchship doesn't start a planetary scan until it has taken up orbit, so there are several hours between emergence and close approach. Our friends would have time to power down their equipment and play possum."

"Switch off their entire civilization, you mean?" Beth said incredulously. "They would have to maintain some kind of communication channel, which we could detect, otherwise how would they know when we left their system if everything was switched off?"

"A receiver is very hard to detect compared with a transmitter," Martin said, "so they might know when we left without having to reveal themselves. And their internal communications, if they use sound conducted through subsurface rock strata with relays and boosters for the long-range traffic, would not be detectable from space.

"And I don't think they switch off everything everywhere," he went on. "Just in the areas we are likely to notice. On the hemisphere we cannot see, it may be business as usual.

"The problem," he added, "will be tricking them into showing themselves."

"The problem," Beth said seriously, "will be how you will feel if they don't show themselves because they aren't there. I can see you going all broody on me and needing lots of nontechnical support."

"You're trying to change the subject," Martin said.

"I'm trying to give myself time to think," she replied. A few seconds later she went on, "First, let's forget about complicated maneuvers like pretending to leave, waiting for an indeterminate time to lull them into a false sense of security, and then jumping out of hyperspace as close to the planet as we can manage. For operational reasons that would not be all that close, and the emergence itself makes an awful lot of radio frequency noise which our hypothetical friends would be sure to detect. Instead, let's use the present proximity to the planet to our own advantage, and act now."

Unresolved questions bothered her tidy, impatient mind.

Martin did not reply, and she continued. "Right now we are in synchronous orbit with one hemisphere constantly in view. Suppose we launch a couple of large probes toward the surface after dark, but programmed only to make the greatest possible noise in the visible and radio frequency spectra so that our friends will be blinded, confused, and distracted for several minutes. During that period we will apply maximum thrust on a course which will take us past the edge of the planetary disk as we now see it, with just enough altitude to avoid burning up in atmosphere.

"I haven't tried this idea on the main computer yet," she went on, a tinge of excitement creeping into her voice, "and a ship this size isn't supposed to go in for such melodramatic maneuvering, but with the gravity compensators at maximum and the drive on emergency overload, I think we could manage about eight gees. As we pass over the presently visible horizon to the hidden side, we kill the probe interference and switch off everything but our receptors. We should then get a picture of whatever is happening on the other side of the planet as we coast out and away, and it should happen too quickly for them to switch off everything and hide themselves.

"They will know what we are doing by then," she ended, "but even if they are expecting such a message, it must take a little time to warn an entire hemisphere to initiate an immediate radio silence."

"You're the Ship Handler One," Martin said, smiling. "And if the other hemisphere is silent, too, I shall reluctantly admit the possibility that there is nobody there."

They would not get a second chance to pull this particular trick and so the preparations took several hours. Most of the time was taken up programming the lander, unmanned for this mission, and the probes so that it would appear that a widespread and thorough investigation of the hemisphere below them was taking place during the hours of darkness. Success depended on whether or not their visible and radio frequency fireworks blinded the surface observers to what was really going on.

When the hypership finally began to move, all of the natives' attention, they hoped, was being focused on the darkside diversion.

From inside the control module, the power being expended to accelerate the tremendous ship was not apparent, because the gravity compensators were matching the acceleration so closely that the deck remained steady beneath their feet. The only motion visible was on the forward displays which showed the planet's edge expanding slowly, then not so slowly, until it was rushing up at them and all they could see was the pinkish gray sunrise line bisecting the screen.

A faint vibration against the soles of their feet told of the hypership encountering the soft vacuum that was the upper atmosphere, and a number of stress and temperature sensors winked red eyes at them. Beth insisted that they were merely polite warnings, not indications of an imminent catastrophic malfunction, and ignored them.

The sunrise line flashed past below them, the power was cut and the ship coasted spaceward again, the daylight side of the planet unrolling and shrinking rapidly in their rear screen. She reversed the image to black, the better to show up any points or areas of radiation which might be present.

For several minutes they studied the screen before Martin broke the silence.

"Well?"

Beth cleared her throat and said, "The natives display a very fast reaction time. Virtually everything was switched off within the first three minutes of their seeing us and realizing what we were doing. Some of the areas are still radiating, which could mean that their communications are at fault or that they now know that we know about them and further attempts at concealment are useless. We can study this material later, but right now I would say that these traces indicate power sources which are well below ground, and a few which are sharply defined and weaker, and are probably surface sensory equipment . . ."

The screen showed only a few widely scattered points

and smudges of light now, but Martin was remembering
how it had looked a few minutes earlier, when the reversed dayside image had been pockmarked as if by
some ghostly plague.

"... And I'm glad there is somebody down there,"
Beth went on, "because I hate it when you brood. Now I
won't have to be especially nice to you."

Martin laughed. "That was a terrific job you did just
then, and I want to be especially nice to you."

"Sometimes," Beth said, "I can't win."

It was some time later when she said, "I suppose we
should report back with the news that this planet contains indigenous intelligent life and that we are not, after
all, on vacation. But if we did that, the supervisor would
probably say that we know the situation here better than
anyone else, and we'd be sent straight back to carry out
the first contact and assessment procedures. We may as
well save ourselves the round trip."

She was hoping, Martin could see, for an argument.

The risks encountered while trying to establish communication with a completely alien race were major and
varied. For Martin especially it would be no vacation,
and Beth was beginning to show her concern.

"What can they be afraid of," she said in a baffled
voice, "to act this way?"

"When we know that," Martin said, "I have the feeling that, we'll know everything."

The recent game of hide and seek had proved that
there was a highly advanced culture on, or rather under
the surface of, this world beneath them—advanced
enough to detect and react to a ship operating in their
solar system. They had a knowledge of astronomy, at
least, and therefore the philosophical acceptance of the
idea that there might be other intelligent species among
the stars. In every advanced culture there were a few
beings who were actively interested in contact with off-
worlders, while the majority minded its own more mun-
dane business. But all of these people had hidden
themselves at the first approach of a visitor from space.

That was very bad. Xenophobia of the kind being displayed here, unless there was a very good reason for it,

would be an absolute bar to this culture achieving Federation citizenship.

"Let's return to our original station," Martin said. "The natives are used to us being there, and it might be more reassuring to them if we resumed contact where it was broken off, where they stole our protector."

Chapter 14

NOW that they knew what they were looking for and were going after it with sensors which penetrated the surface, they could see a number of underground tunnel systems, caverns, lakes, and rivers whose courses were far too straight to be natural. The complete absence of the outward signs of large-scale cultivation bothered them, until Beth noticed that certain areas of vegetation looked unhealthy, although not actually dying, while identical and adjacent plants were completely free of infection. Specimens retrieved showed the affected vegetation to be an edible root which was being cultivated and farmed from below the surface—but selectively, so as not to kill the plant by removing all of its roots. A combination of year-round growth and a chemical assist ensured that the plant would recover and its missing roots regrow.

One by one their questions were being answered, except for the really important one.

Why were these people hiding?

"When we see them," Martin said firmly, "we'll know whether or not their fear is based on physical weakness, and talking to them will tell us something about the way they think. All we have to do now is devise a safe method of letting me see and talk to them."

It was decided that the lander's touchdown would be overt but not noisy—the world was extremely quiet and the natives might prefer it that way. But even if the approach was well-mannered by Earth-human standards, there was no guarantee that the natives would regard it so, or react to it in human fashion. Martin would need protection.

Beth reminded him of the Prime Rule. "Weapons must not be taken into a first-contact situation, nor should defensive systems be used if, in operation, they appear to be offensive."

Martin nodded. "I was thinking of a modified protector vehicle," he said, "with a variable-speed digging or boring system forward so that I can maneuver underground. My best defense might be heating elements in the outer hull, precisely controlled so as to discourage would-be dismantlers without burning them to a crisp. In case of trouble there should be a quick-escape facility to the lander by matter transmitter. Can your fabrication module handle that?"

Beth looked doubtful. She said, "The space needed for those little items would mean trebling the size of the vehicle. But do you have to go burrowing around down there? Initially, couldn't we use an unmanned vehicle with—"

"How big," Martin broke in. She knew as well as he did that personal contact was necessary, and sooner rather than later.

She turned away and busied herself at the console. An image took shape in the center of her screen and began sprouting colored lines and symbols. A few seconds later she faced him again and said, "Approximately twenty-five meters long and eight at its widest cross section. Removing soil and rock from in front of a vehicle that size would be a slow job. Your top subsurface speed would be a medium walking pace. And if you were to enter one of their underground inhabited areas riding a monster like that, I don't think you'd make a good first impression."

"I agree," Martin said, laughing. "But if you reduced that cross section as much as possible by discarding the matter transmitter and antigravity systems, which are the biggest and most power hungry units in a protector, and stripped off unnecessary internal displays, how small could you make it then?"

"Without antigravity propulsers, mattran escape system, and with sensory equipment limited to sonic detectors, one vision input and two-way audio for external communication," she said, after a brief return to her console, "we are talking about a vehicle eight meters long and one-and-a-half meters at its widest point.

"But you would have to lie prone," she added worriedly, "and the specimen stowage space would double as your emergency exit. You would not be able to exit quickly."

"Hopefully," Martin said, "I won't need to. If I stay close to the lander and don't go too deep there shouldn't be any problems. What will you do about nonoffensively protecting the lander?"

"Subsurface sensors below the landing struts," she replied. "If anyone starts burrowing too close to it, yourself excepted, it will take off and land again wherever you need it."

"Fine," Martin said. "Is there anything I haven't covered?"

"I don't think so," she said, not looking at him.

Reassuringly, he said, "Don't worry. I'll be very, very careful. And after all, we've done this sort of thing before."

"I know," she said dryly, "just once before."

Beth took the lander down to the surface on remote control with the newly fabricated digger attached to its hull and with Martin already strapped inside, and placed the vehicle nose down in the shallow crater left when their protector was undermined. The lander's camera showed nothing moving on the utterly silent surface and the sonic probes were reporting negative movement underground.

"Here goes," he said, and watched from the lander's viewpoint as soil and shredded vegetation fountained up behind him. By the time the dust had settled he was at a depth of fifty feet.

In operation the digger produced so much noise and vibration that he was sonically as well as visually blind, so he switched off everything but the sound sensors, and waited. But all he could hear was an amplified, hissing silence broken occasionally by the rumble of soil falling into the tunnel he had made. Beth's voice in his headset sounded incredibly loud.

"Nothing from the lander's sensors, either," she said.

"I'm going to make a slow pass under the area where they took our protector," he said, "in case they left traces."

At reduced boring speed the noise was less but the vibration much greater, and Martin was wishing that his weight saving instructions to the fabricator had allowed him a little more padding on his couch. Suddenly there was a decrease in vibration and an increase in noise. The lander's sensors showed him passing through a small hollow which extended on both sides of the digger. He slowed the vehicle until the blades were pushing slowly through the densely packed soil instead of chopping it out and flinging it astern. When the hollow came level with his midship viewports he stopped and turned on the external lights.

"It's a tunnel," he reported, trying to control his excitement, "semicircular in section with maximum diameter at floor level of just over a meter. Vibration from the digger has caused a few minor cave-ins, but not enough to obstruct the view. On one side it angles upward in the direction of the pit where we lost the protector, on the other it curves to avoid what the sensors tell me is an area of solid rock. Are you getting this?"

"I see what you see," she replied.

"The tunnel walls are unsupported," he went on, "but there seems to be a difference in color between them and the floor, as if they had been smeared with something wet. There are short, shallow grooves at intervals on the tunnel walls and floor. They could have been caused by bits of the protector being dragged away. I want a specimen of that dark material on the tunnel walls, but I'll have to reposition the digger to be able to bring it into the hold."

"Go ahead," Beth said, "you're all alone."

Once again the cutting blades bit into the soil and the vehicle made a climbing U-turn which ended with the

tiny hold and its escape hatch level with the tunnel roof,
which partially collapsed because of the digger's weight.
He checked the air in the tunnel, opened the hatch and
deployed the telescoping collector to retrieve a sample of
discolored oil. Before placing it in the analyzer, he re-
sealed the hatch and had a precautionary look at his sensors.

"It appears to be some kind of organic glue," he said
after a few minutes. "I'd say that, given the small dimensions and semicircular configuration of the tunnel, it
would be strong enough to keep the roof from falling in
provided there were no major shocks. We'll have to be
careful, this vehicle could do serious damage to their
tunnel system. Now I'm returning to my original position
in . . . Did you see that?"

The vehicle had moved only a few meters when the
direct vision ports on both sides showed it intersecting
another opening in the soil, a small, near vertical fissure.
He cut power again to enable the sensors to feel it out,
and gradually a three-dimensional picture began to build
up on his screen.

"It can't be a natural fissure," he said, "because it
twists off the vertical, climbs, goes deeper, and finally
joins with the tunnel I just left. It is a flattened oval in
cross section, six inches deep, varying between four and
five times that in width. There are a few traces of glue on
the inner surfaces. The sensors are beginning to show
other fissures with similar dimensions and characteris-
tics, and they are either paralleling or joining the main
tunnel. Which is what I'm going to do right now."

"Computer analysis indicates a high probability,"
Beth said quietly, "that the fissures are made by individual burrowers who may not need to use these channels
again, or often. The patches of glue present in reduced
quantities suggests, our mastermind says, that it is an
organic discharge which, when a large number of the
creatures are acting together, is used to strengthen the
walls of the larger, permanent tunnels."

"Body discharges to support their tunnels," Martin
said. "Our friends aren't a physically attractive lot. Or
maybe as a first-contactor I shouldn't think like that."

"Just so long as you don't think out loud," she said

dryly. "But one thing about all this bothers me. Why, if they were so anxious to hide from us, did they advertise their presence by attacking the protector?"

"That bothers me, too," Martin said. "Maybe there is a bunch of rebels among them who are opposed to the idea of hiding. If so, they might be the kind of people we should contact first. Their scientific curiosity would—"

"Company," Beth interrupted.

His sensors registered no underground activity because of interference from the digger's equipment, so Beth was reading the lander's sensor data. But where were they?

"They aren't coming along the tunnel," she said, answering the unasked question. "They seem to be digging new ones."

Martin swore, not quite under his breath, and halted the digger. "I see them now," he said. "But if they burrow up against the digger through the soil, I *won't* be able to see them. We need to have a rough idea of their sensory equipment, at least, to program the translator."

Beth was sympathetically silent.

"Why don't they use the existing tunnel?" Martin went on. "It would get them here much faster. Do they have to be completely covered by soil to function effectively, or do they just not want us to see them?"

"If they maintain their present rate of approach," she replied, "you'll have some of the answers in just under seven minutes."

As he watched the trace on his screen move down the distance scale, Martin felt himself begin to sweat. He no longer felt sure that he was doing the right thing down here. His defenses might not be adequate to sustain an attack—or a serious investigation of the structure of his vehicle, which amounted to the same thing so far as the occupant was concerned—by creatures which in their behavior resembled subterranean piranha fish. And if their investigation was to prove successful . . .

"I'm getting out of here," he said.

When Beth replied, she did not mention his sudden decision, or the edge of panic apparent in his voice. She said calmly, "While you were speaking just now, they stopped moving. This supports our theory that they are highly sensitive to sound transmitted through the substrata, and probably use it as a medium for long-distance communication. They are three minutes from you now, and closing. Your vehicle isn't moving."

"I've had second thoughts," he said apologetically. "If they have a high tolerance for heat, they would be able to stay in contact with my hull long enough to start taking it apart. My only protection then would be to move away. But I can't do that without risk to the burrowers. Making mincemeat of a few of them with the digger blades would not be a friendly act. I think the best move now is to place the vehicle across a tunnel. That way I might be able to see some of them and better assess the risks on both sides.

"As well," he admitted, "I was having a touch of claustrophobia just then, and cold feet."

"Cold feet," she said, laughing, "are a prime survival characteristic in this job."

"I'm heading for the tunnel now," he said.

"They're moving quickly," Beth reported. "There are no indications that they are carrying metal objects, weapons, or tools. Their body temperature is high. Maybe they are ingesting and burning up the soil metabolically rather than compressing it. Your hull heating might not be much of a deterrent."

"I'm in position," Martin reported.

The sensor display showed the burrowers as bright, hot blobs trailing in their wakes the dull gray tails which were the tunnels they were making.

"I've had third thoughts," he said suddenly. "I don't want them to think they can trap me as easily as they did the protector, but I want to give them the idea that I want to meet, or investigate, them as much as they, me. If they are preparing a trap, I want to make it clear that I am walking into it of my own volition. So I'll move out again, to show that I can easily escape, then return to the tunnel a little closer to their present position. Does that make sense to you?"

"You mean," Beth said dryly, "will it make sense to them?"

The digger lurched forward and made a narrow U-turn which ended with his lateral vision ports looking out on the tunnel. He switched on the external lighting, at minimum power in case the burrowers had sensitive vision, and waited.

The over-amplified hissing and thumping of loose soil trickling onto the digger's hull and tunnel floor died away, and the silence closed in and became so all-pervasive that he found himself holding his breath. Beth's voice in his headset was deafening.

"They've stopped moving and are englobing you at a distance of about ten meters," she said. "I count seventeen of them close in, and another three who have stopped at about four times that distance. Maybe they are the directors of this operation, and consider themselves less expendable than the others. Now the closer ones are beginning to move in, but slowly. The other three are staying put."

"Careful people are the safest to talk to . . ." Martin began.

"Those three are moving in, now," she broke in. "But there's something odd here. When I'm talking on your headset there is no reaction from them, but they immediately stop moving when you speak. When the digger systems are shut down, they must be able to actually hear your voice."

Martin felt the tension in his shoulder and neck muscles begin to ease. Seemingly there was no immediate danger, either of the digger being taken to pieces around him or of the burrowers committing suicide on his cutter blades. He was being given time to think.

If the burrowers were not carrying tools, and he could not believe that they had taken the protector apart with their equivalent of fingernails, then it was possible that they knew that his vehicle, unlike the protector, had an occupant. It was also possible that they were not carrying metal objects for the same reason that Martin was not bearing weapons.

The picture on his screen flickered, then sharpened as Beth replaced it with the image being sent up from the lander's sensors. Unnecessarily, she said, "One of them is touching your hull now. Another two are moving into the tunnel on your right. Can you hear anything?"

She was hearing the same hissing silence as he was,

so he said nothing. The touch of a burrower, it seemed, could be incredibly light. Still dazzled by the light of the screen, he turned to peer into the tunnel.

It looked as if a large, thick piece of seaweed was growing out of the soil floor and was undulating slowly toward him. Another piece emerged, but not completely, from the roof and flapped slowly like a thick flag in a breeze. Loose soil brought down by the digger blades lay piled against the lower edge of the port, and the first burrower was climbing it. He moved forward for a closer look and his helmet tapped gently against the coaming.

The creature froze motionless for a few seconds, but otherwise ignored Martin's face, which was only inches away, and resumed its climb. He and the recorders had a perfect view of its underside as it moved up and over the port.

He was about to increase the external lighting, but thought better of it. He had no wish to frighten it off or hurt its eyes, and, in any case, he did not have to use his own eyes.

"Enhance," he said quietly.

The screen displayed pictures of a burrower viewed from above, below, and several lateral aspects. The main computer was capable of building up an accurate reconstruction from what, to human eyes, appeared to be a mass of confusing and incomplete detail. Outlined in ghostly blue and pink, so that they would contrast with the mottled gray and brown coloration of the skin and external features, were the main bone structure and organs.

In cross section the body was a narrow oval flattened slightly on the underside, circular in plan view and just over a meter in diameter. The upper and lower body surfaces were covered with short, organic stubble with swellings at the tips, which in the bad light Martin had mistaken for seaweed-like blisters. The stubble was equal in length but showed a wide diversity in thickness, the thicker bristles being on the underside.

The principal external features were a knife-edged, bony wedge flanked by two wide slit mouths on the forward section of the body, and a long, sharp sting or horn projecting rearward. Beth called for computer animation.

The mouths opened and closed rapidly as simulated soil was ingested and expelled through vents in the upper and lower rear body. Both mouths had large upper lips which could be curled down to seal the openings so that the creature was able to move forward without having to eat its way through the soil. When that option was chosen, the thicker stubble with enlarged tips retracted and extended rapidly to drive it forward; the sharp, wedge-shaped beak divided and compressed the soil in its path. When in motion, the finer stubble lay flat along the body, which was flexible enough to bend forward or backward on itself through nearly two hundred and seventy degrees.

With that horn or sting it could defend itself, Martin thought, from above, behind, and underneath and, with a small change in body position, from frontal attack.

"It couldn't have taken the protector apart with that beak and horn," Martin said, after he had studied the display for several minutes, "so the thinner stubble must act as digits specialized for fine work. But the stubble covers the entire body. Can you see any sensory organs?"

"Nothing," she replied. "But there are two patches, one positioned on top and the other directly opposite it on the underside. I'm highlighting them now. The material is organic but not alive, fibrous, and foreign to the underlying stubble, which is compressed by it severely enough to confuse the X-ray scan.

"I need a clearer picture of the internal structure," she went on. "Next time one of them is in clear sight, make a noise. For some reason those nearby freeze when you do that while the distant ones move about, perhaps in agitation or indecision. As soon as you can, stop a burrower and focus the X-ray scanner on it. The computer needs more physiological data for the translation program."

He did as she asked a few minutes later, then returned his attention to the screen.

The patches on the burrower's back and underside had an irregular, shredded look around the edges, Martin saw, and the individual threads were either tied or entangled with the underlying stubble securely enough for them to remain in position while the creature was burrowing.

"They might be decoration, or perform an identification function," he said thoughtfully. "But I've a feeling they are more important than that. If we could get one of them to remove its patch we—"

He broke off because Beth was laughing.

"A being with pieces of material attached firmly to its body suggests one thing to me," she said, "that it normally keeps parts of its body covered up. If I had a nudity taboo and some off-worlder asked me to take off my—"

"Point taken," Martin said, very quietly. "But I've had an idea. Increase your volume and I'll explain . . ."

It had been apparent for some time that when Beth spoke to him via the headset there was no reaction from any of the nearby burrowers, so presumably they could not or were not carrying the equipment to receive radio frequencies. However, when he replied to her, even though he was using the headset only with the helmet external speaker switched off, the nearer burrowers showed a mild reaction and stopped moving, while the distant ones displayed something like agitation. Plainly they were hearing his voice, loudly if not clearly.

The sound was being transmitted through the air of his life-support module, the heavily insulated metal structure of the digger, and outward via the densely packed soil to the distant burrowers. For his voice to travel through such diverse media over a distance, the beings receiving it would have to possess hypersensitive hearing.

". . . And I wouldn't mind betting," he ended, "that the distant burrowers are not wearing patches, and all of the nearby ones are."

"I don't follow you," Beth said.

"They aren't the burrower equivalent of a bikini," he replied softly, "just simple, old-fashioned earmuffs."

"You're right," she said excitedly, "and my omniscient computer friend here confirms it. The three distant burrowers are moving in, but at different rates of speed. A projection suggests that they will space themselves out into close, medium, and longer distances. The others haven't moved and are probably awaiting instructions from their unprotected superiors. What are you going to do now?"

"I'm going to be very, very quiet," Martin said, "and turn my external mikes to maximum sensitivity. I should be able to hear something while instructions are being passed. But I'll have to listen very hard because people with hypersensitive hearing will not have loud voices."

"While you are being very, very quiet," Beth asked, "what can I do?"

"You can keep on talking so I won't go psycho from sensory deprivation," he replied. "Keep showing me the overall picture from the lander's sensors; they are more accurate than mine and fiddling about at my console might cause noise. And get your friend working on a translator program for the burrower language, as soon as we hear them using it.

"After that," he added, "will come the difficult part."

Martin began his long wait in the triply distilled silence of this unnaturally quiet world. There was the subterranean silence all around him, the silence of his vehicle's inactive equipment, and his own personal silence which, to his straining ears, sounded positively noisy. His breathing was the biggest noise problem. Subjectively it had begun to sound like a gale blowing through high trees, but he experimented with it until he found that breathing very slowly through his nose was quietest. He increased the sensitivity of his external mikes once again, and listened.

But there was nothing to hear except an occasional trickle of soil falling from the tunnel roof with an over-amplified crash and rumble which made him wince. The sound of his suit rustling against the couch was even louder as he pointed to his ear.

"I can't hear anything either," Beth said. "But here is an update you'll want to see."

The picture on his screen was of a burrower viewed from the top and side, showing the positions of the being's internal organs, connective ducting, and musculature, with close approximations of the circulatory and nervous systems.

"According to our mastermind here," she went on,

"the creature's metabolism is not all that exotic. It is warm-blooded and oxygen-breathing, with the capability of metabolizing nutrient and oxidants from the soil and of breathing either water or air trapped in subsurface caves. The mouths have a triple valve arrangement which enables them to eat, drink, or breathe through the same orifices, and the longtitudinal flexibility of the body would allow it to undulate through water at a fairly high speed. In the hunting role it would be much more effective in water than on the ground, although the indications are that most of its evolutionary history was spent on or under the land."

The physiological details were sharp and solidly colored where the functions and positions were known with certainty, fainter and with varying intensities of shading when they were based on data stored in the main computer covering other and similar life forms encountered throughout the galaxy. But even then, the probabilities deemed worthy of display verged on certainties. Only in the area concerned with the nerve connections between the body surface and brain was there serious doubt.

The nerve linkages were so uniform and numerous that there was no way of telling where the organs of sight, hearing, smell, or touch were situated. The brain was housed behind and protected by a hollow in the wedge-shaped beak. For a creature which had less than one third the body mass of an Earth-human, the brain was exceptionally large. According to the computer, the possession of intelligence was a certainty.

Soon, Martin hoped, they would begin to show it.

As the computer had predicted, the three burrowers who were directing operations spaced themselves out so that any sounds emanating from the digger would be received by them in diminishing intensity. The nearest one had positioned itself inside the globe of subordinates, who had paired off and were taking turns to crawl onto each other's backs.

"What are they doing?" Beth asked, in a carefully neutral voice.

"Don't be alarmed," Martin whispered. "My guess is that they're helping each other remove their ear protectors."

Suddenly the burrowers were emerging from the walls and floor and swarming silently over his hull. The tunnel on both sides of the digger was full of them. With a feeling of self-satisfaction he noted that none of them were wearing earmuffs.

They were ready to talk.

Carefully, so as not to hit his hand accidentally against the console, Martin switched off the external lighting, then turned it on again for precisely one second. He waited for ten seconds then switched it on and off again twice, then three and finally four times. He repeated the one-two-three-four sequence several times, indicating his willingness to communicate in a fashion which would not painfully overload their hypersensitive hearing.

There was no response.

He turned up the external lighting to its full, eye-searing intensity and tried again. Still they ignored him. He looked away from the brilliantly illuminated cave to rest his eyes, and then it was that an even greater light dawned.

Incredulously, he whispered, "They're *blind*!"

Chapter 15

"ARE you sure?" Beth asked, matching his tone. "If you're right, it explains a lot."

It would certainly explain why the creatures preferred to remain under the surface. Above ground they would have little or no protection against the ultra-quiet predators and winged life forms who were guided to their victims by a sense the burrowers did not possess and might not even understand. Without sight, they would know only that on the surface there was death or serious injury, inflicted by beings who could not be evaded. As a result they had remained safely underground, developed their own peculiar culture, and ignored the beasts who roamed the surface and the atmosphere above it.

But not entirely.

They had dealt very effectively with the six-legged predator who had attacked the protector vehicle, with the vehicle itself, and they had successfully hidden themselves from a hypership orbiting their planet. A sudden, uncontrollable shiver made Martin's suit rub noisily against the couch.

What kind of people were they, and what additional or heightened faculties did they possess to compensate for their blindness? The question was unspoken, but Beth began answering it, anyway.

"Correlation of the latest X-ray scans together with the key datum that the life form is blind," she said excitedly, "explains certain physiological anomalies. Not only is this species blind, the indications are that it is deaf and dumb as well. There are no organs resembling functional ears or mechanisms for producing speech. The entire sensorium, virtually the whole surface of the body, is responsive to touch. Apparently it is the only sense they possess.

"According to the mastermind here," she went on, "this makes them highly sensitive to vibration transmitted through the soil or water and, to a lesser extent, air. Their equivalent of talking is to tap or rub specialized groups of stubble sited above and below the beak, whose shape gives the sounds a degree of directional focus. Properly speaking they do not talk and listen to each other so much as touch at long range.

"I've never called the main computer a liar before," she added, "but when I just did, it told me that if I disliked its conclusions I should have fed it a different set of data."

"So," Martin whispered, "they can hear, or rather feel me at a distance with the hypersensitive touch sensors we're calling their ears, but I can't hear them. Surely their tapping and rubbing sounds are detectable?"

The screen showed burrowers moving away from the tunnel. The movement was steady and purposeful, he thought, and not a panic reaction to the sound of his voice.

"They're leaving the area," Beth said, "and putting on their ear protectors as they go. For the next stage you're going to need very special equipment. Your tri-di projector and other visual aids to communication will be singularly ineffective with a species that is blind. Will you return to the lander now?"

"I'm not sure," Martin said. "I think we're making progress, and this isn't the time to break off contact. These are the only members of the species who did not hide from us, and we might not be able to find them again to resume where we left off. I can't see the details on this small screen, but they seem to be taking up some kind of formation."

"They've taken up a hollow cone formation with you at the center of its base," she reported. "The cone is pointed in a southwesterly direction and inclined downward by twenty-three degrees, and is moving forward slowly. I'd say that they are pointing the way and want you to follow."

"I'm following," Martin said quietly. "But what I need now is a method of attenuating the sound of my voice so they won't be deafened every time I try to say something."

Slowly he moved the digger out of the tunnel and lined it up with the direction indicated by the cone. The speed seemed to be comfortable for the burrowers because they matched his pace exactly and were not moving farther out to escape his noise.

"You are headed toward one of the small, permanent tunnels which must be their equivalent of a minor road," Beth reported. "Further ahead there is a subterranean river which flows, for no natural geological reason, in a straight line. It passes through a large cave, which is not entirely a natural feature either, containing small accumulations of metal which could be tools, machinery, or weapons. At this range the picture is unclear.

"I'm going to reposition the lander above that cavern," she ended, "because that is where the action is likely to be."

Operating from the orbiting hypership as easily as if she were in the lander's control module, Beth lifted the ship out of contact with the surface and set it down again directly above the cave. Had it been necessary, she could just as easily have remote-controlled the digger, which made Martin feel very safe but just a bit redundant.

For the few minutes that the lander was in the air, Martin was sonically blind, and when its probes were redeployed he had to act quickly to avoid a serious and almost certainly fatal accident. His vehicle had wandered from the indicated course and was edging dangerously close to one of his escorts, who was steadfastly, or stupidly, refusing to move away from his cutters. He turned away, swearing, then remembered that the burrowers had no way of knowing that, when his vehicle was in motion, he was nearly as blind as they were without the lander to shed its sonic light on the situation.

"This is interesting," Beth said suddenly. "Some of those metal objects are using power. Obviously the people in the cave aren't hiding from us anymore. But I'd like to know their purpose. Even the civilized, peace-loving races used weapons, both long- and short-range, at some period before they grew out of the habit. They could be getting ready to jump you."

"I can't imagine a long-range weapon being developed by a blind race," Martin said softly. "I wish they'd move faster."

He was impatient to reach that cave, now. But if he increased speed the noise would seriously inconvenience the burrowers and that, for the person wanting to establish contact with them, would not be a friendly thing to do. So he closed his eyes, forced patience on himself, and tried to think like a being who could only *feel* the world around it.

"The cone is changing direction," Beth said sharply. "Can't you see it?"

"I can now," Martin said, opening his eyes. "But wait a minute, they're pointing me nearly twenty degrees to the right of the cavern! That cavern is the place I want to see."

As he was speaking, Martin reduced speed until the burrowers forming the base of the cone had pulled more than thirty meters ahead, then he turned back on to the original course.

"What are you doing?" Beth asked. "No, dammit, what are *they* doing? . . ."

The cone formation was breaking up. Every burrower had changed direction and increased speed to head him off, and within a few minutes there was a tight screen of them blocking his path.

"Plainly they don't want you in that cavern," Beth said. "Probably they have delicate equipment there, or maybe some of their young. You should stay out."

"I realize that," Martin said irritably. "Driving in there would be like taking a bulldozer into a china shop. But I have to show them that that is where I want to go."

He fed a trickle of power to the cutting blades, just enough to inch the digger forward without endangering the burrowers ahead, then he brought the vehicle around until it was pointed in the direction they wanted him to go. Hopefully he was showing them that he was being a good little off-worlder and doing as he was told.

They were intelligent people and took only a few minutes to get the message. They reformed the cone and Martin and his escort were moving again.

Beth said, "They are leading you toward a tunnel which is one of several leading to their settlement. You should intersect it about one-eighty meters from the entrance.

"Your bio-sensors say that you are reasonably calm," she went on. "This suggests that you've already made up your mind about something, something which, knowing you, carries an element of risk. I wish you were a bit more worried. When you don't worry, I do."

"Don't worry," Martin said drily, "I'm worried."

On his screen, the shadowy, gray tube which was the tunnel was growing larger. His escort was slowing and beginning to break up again, but without the prior urgency. Obviously this was the end of the line. Martin guided the vehicle into the tunnel at right angles and cut the power when his ports gave a view in both directions along it and his cargo hatch was free to open. Then he waited.

His external lighting showed burrowers emerging from the tunnel roof and floor. They did not approach the vehicle closely, other than to remove the small heaps of soil his arrival had brought down. When the tunnel was smooth and unobstructed they, too, settled on the floor to wait.

"I think," Martin whispered, "they're ready to talk."

When she replied, Beth's voice sounded embarrassed, defensive, and angry—the tone one used when making excuses for a friend. She said, "The computer isn't getting anywhere with the translation. It's still working on a combination of amplification and filtration, trying to reproduce the process whereby Earth-people in noisy jobs, riveters, workers in sheet steel, and such, are able to carry on a quiet conversation while a boiler shop din is going on all around them. But all we can hear behind the background noise is more background noise. Listen."

Martin clenched his teeth as the hiss and static built up to what sounded like a continual barrage of sharp, irregular explosions. Then suddenly they were gone, converted into bursts of silence in a new and quieter background.

He was able to identify and isolate the regular, soft pulsing of the lander's sonic probes, but there was something more. It was a steady bubbling sound which rose and fell at frequent but irregular intervals, varying in pitch so that it sounded as if someone were playing a wind instrument under water. Beth stepped up the volume until there could be no doubt that the sound was not a natural phenomenon.

"If it is a language," Beth said, "then everyone is talking at once and the babble is untranslatable. If it isn't a language, then the sound is probably produced continually as an aid to fixing position and distance between individuals. The computer says there is a high probability that the sound performs both functions, but that doesn't help us with the translation."

"But that computer," Martin protested, "is supposed to be capable of instantly translating any intelligence-bearing sounds which—"

"This isn't a species like the Teldins," Beth said defensively, "whose words and the actions to which they referred were implicit in previously observed behavior patterns. These people are blind and the vibrations they produce are received as touches, which refer to the feel, not the sight, of objects and actions. We receive them as sounds, so translation is theoretically possible. But it may well be that in this case a successful contact will be just that, an actual physical contact."

When Martin did not reply, she went on, "We need a long, careful think about this one. You should return to the ship at once."

"No," Martin said firmly. "This bunch wants to make contact, and I don't want to have it all to do again with another group. They've gone to a lot of trouble and considerable personal discomfort to—"

"The computer," Beth said, just as firmly, "was not programmed with Braille."

"I want to give it another shot," Martin said stubbornly. "They've been whispering at me and I've been shouting at them, from inside a vehicle which has to be distorting the word sounds. Can I modify the digger's external address system to step down, attentuate, my voice instead of amplifying it?"

"No problem," she replied. "But the system is integral with the vehicle's structure, so you'll have to return here to have the . . . Oh, oh, they're moving out. I think *they* are breaking off contact, not you."

Bitterly disappointed, he watched them go. Obviously, the communication problem was presently insoluble, and hopefully they, too, were going back to have a long think about it. They were undulating rapidly along the tunnel, not burrowing through the soil, in the direction of their cavern—all except one, who stopped about ten meters from the digger.

"One of them still wants to talk," said Martin.

"Don't get too excited about it," said Beth, "they may simply have left a guard."

But she had to be wrong because the bubbling sounds in his headphones had become quieter, yet more distinct. Only one burrower was talking, the one outside who was tapping its forward stubble gently against its beak.

"My helmet!" said Martin suddenly. "Can I step down its external speaker?"

When she replied a few minutes later, her voice sounded far from enthusiastic. "There is an on-the-spot modification you can make to the helmet comm system.

If you wrap the mike and your lower jaw and mouth in sound absorbent material—some of your couch padding would do it—you should be able to talk quietly without the distortion caused by you pitching your voice unnaturally low.

"But it would mean you leaving the digger," she concluded warningly. "That suit you're wearing is little more than an overall, and your backpack has air for less than—"

"The air down here is breathable," Martin broke in, "and the backpack is too big and awkward to wear in that tunnel. I would be able to move more quietly and quickly without it. Don't worry, I won't move far from the digger."

To these people his voice must sound like a continuous, modulated explosion, Martin thought as he worked on the helmet, and unintelligible because of its sheer volume. He wondered how beings who had only the sense of touch would think of an explosion, how they had learned chemistry without being able to observe chemical reactions, and ultimately develop the other sources of energy which enabled them to detect starships entering their system.

It could not have been easy.

A boyhood memory came to him of reading a book on the early days of exploration and navigation on Earth. Instances had been mentioned of unsighted people who had been able to find their way among the widely scattered islands of the Pacific Ocean by sniffing the air for the almost imperceptible land smells, feeling the winds, and gauging direction by the warmth of the sunlight on their faces; in short, using the enhanced senses they had developed to compensate for the fact that they were blind.

There was growing in Martin a curiosity so intense, coupled with a feeling of such awe, that any risk he might have to take while getting to know and understand these blind burrowers seemed of secondary importance.

"The bio-sensors say you are less tense," Beth said hopefully. "Are you having second thoughts about coming back?"

"No," Martin said, "just thoughts."

Unavoidably there were a few clicks and thuds as he wriggled through the tiny hatch onto the tunnel floor. The noise must have bothered the being outside because, when he directed his helmet light along the tunnel, the burrower had backed away by nearly three meters.

He left the hatch open in case he needed to return in a hurry, knowing that if a burrower tried to enter, Beth could use the remotes to close it. Slowly, and as silently as possible, he began crawling toward what he hoped was the spokesperson.

The tunnel was just high enough for him to move on his hands and knees provided he kept his head down, which meant that only a small area of the floor in front of him was illuminated. To see where he was going he had to crawl on his stomach, using his elbows, forearms, and the inside edges of his boots to move himself forward.

Of necessity, his approach to the borrower was slow and, he hoped, reassuring. But when he had closed to within arm's reach it backed off to lie with its stubble rubbing gently against its beak three meters away. Martin tried again with the same result, although this time it halted a little closer to him. Once again he moved toward it, speaking quietly and noting by its reactions that it was hearing his attentuated voice with visible distress.

How would he have felt, Martin wondered, if an outsized extraterrestrial he could not see was crawling toward him. He could understand and sympathize with its timidity. Then suddenly the burrower was moving away at the same rate he was trying to approach it.

"Except for your timid friend," Beth said, "there are no other burrowers in the area. I think it wants you to follow it to the cavern. Maybe they have special communication equipment there that they want to use on you.

"You are twenty-eight meters from the digger," she added warningly.

Deliberately, Martin closed his eyes and crawled on. Not seeing where he was going for a while might put him more closely in tune with the burrowers, who could not see at all. But it also made it impossible for him to see the tunnel, which seemed to be growing lower and more constricting.

He tried to imagine that he was in reality crawling

along a narrow trench, keeping low because it was necessary for him not to be seen, while above him stretched a black, limitless sky and all the damp, earth-scented air that he could breathe. But his ability to delude himself had never been great, and so he knew with a dreadful certainty that a few inches above his head there were countless tons of the soil waiting to collapse and bury him alive.

"The bio-sensors report elevated pulse, respiration, blood pressure, and perspiration unaccompanied by a rise in ambient temperature," Beth said urgently. "Is the air becoming unbreathable?"

"It isn't the air," Martin said, trying to keep his voice down. It was impossible, he thought wildly, to have hysterics in a whisper. "This idea isn't working. I have to get back to the digger, at once."

"Right," she said briskly. "Stay put, relax, and I'll send it for you. You'll be back on the surface in no time."

Behind him the digger came noisily to life, and a sprinkling of loose, brightly lit soil fell like dry rain through his spotlight beam.

"No," he said with quiet desperation. "Don't move the digger! You'll bring down the roof wherever you come through, and I'd have to clear a way to the hatch with my hands. The tunnel isn't safe. It was made by people who eat dirt and don't mind being buried in it. I have to go back the way I came."

But moving backward along the tunnel was incredibly slow and awkward. He could not see where he was going and his boots kept digging into the walls, bringing down sizeable quantities of soil, raising the level of the floor, and making it harder to squeeze through.

The floor—! he thought suddenly.

If he dug downward, that would not affect the unstable condition of the walls and ceiling, and a hole just deep enough to take his legs and lower body would allow him to crouch down into it and turn himself around.

He knew that what he intended doing was dangerous, but he had to try it. He had to try it because he was not sure how long he could continue to function as a thinking and physically coordinated being. More and more of his mind was being swamped by the one all-pervading and irresistible urge.

To get *out*!

With fingers which were beginning to bleed inside the thin, tough membrane of his gloves, Martin tore at the loosely packed soil of the floor. As the hole slowly deepened he pushed the dirt to either side, packing it against the walls or throwing handfuls of it into the tunnel ahead. The burrower had edged a little closer, but the sweat running into Martin's eyes made it impossible to see what, if anything, it was doing.

Abruptly, he stifled a cry of pain as his fingers scraped against solid rock.

When Beth spoke she did not mention the gloves, which Martin had insisted on wearing because they would give him maximum touch sensitivity while dealing with the burrowers, or the shelf of rock he was uncovering, or even his bio-sensor readings which must have been worrying her badly. Her voice was calm and unhurried, as if by a process of sympathetic magic she could transfer those qualities to Martin. And even though they both knew what she was doing, it seemed to work.

"A suggestion," she said, "You have moved more than one-quarter of the distance between the digger and the cavern. Do you think it might be easier to go on instead of turning back? I can guide the digger to the cavern, which is protected by a rock overhang, without bringing the roof down on top of you . . ."

The bio-sensors were already telling her what he thought of that suggestion. He said, "The burrowers would try to stop you again and be chewed up by the digger. They seem to place a lot of value on that place. No. I'm going back, backward."

He had wriggled and pushed himself backward by less than two meters when it happened. One of his boot heels dug deeply into the tunnel wall and suddenly the leg, then both legs, were covered by what felt like a large, heavy cushion.

Martin made a sound halfway between a scream and a muffled grunt and tried to pull his legs free. They moved a little, but the pressure on them increased and began moving up to the back of his thighs, into the small of his back and toward his shoulders. Desperately he stretched forward, trying to grasp the edge of the hole he had dug to pull himself forward as the pressure from the falling soil rolled inexorably over his shoulders and head.

"The sensors show a cave-in! And the burrower is moving toward you. What can I *do*? . . ."

Chapter 16

NO longer calm, her voice was tinged with the helpless, hopeless desperation of one with control of a mechanism with the power to alter planetary orbits, and who was incapable of moving a few hundred pounds of soil off his back. Martin did not answer her for two reasons—there was nothing she could do, and his air had been drastically reduced to the tiny quantity trapped inside his helmet and between the floor and his chest and armpits. He could not afford to waste it by talking.

The very worst that he could imagine had happened. He was buried alive without hope of rescue, his tiny store of air would last only minutes, and the only movement possible to him was to clench his fists.

But there was a small, rebellious, stupid part of his mind which refused to accept the situation as hopeless. It reminded him that one of his fists was full of soil while the other was clenched on air, and it ignored with contempt the rest of the mind which was surrendering to fear and panic.

"Martin, oh, Martin . . ." Beth said helplessly.

The pounding in his head, whether it was due to lack of air or sheer exertion, was so loud that the burrowers in the cavern should have heard it. He pressed his free hand down against the floor and strained to lift his arm against the weight of soil pressing down on it. He was trying to create a tiny passage under the arm from the airhose spigot at the base of his helmet and the tunnel beyond the fall. But he did not know if he was doing anything at all. He could not see and his arm was becoming a single, excruciating mass of cramp.

Surely he had made an airway to the tunnel, he thought desperately, because his original tiny pocket of air must long since have been used up. But he did not *know.*

Something heavy moved across his hand, stabbing at it gently with what felt like blunt knitting needles. The sensation moved past his wrist, becoming duller as it continued along the area covered by the fabric of his suit.

The burrower had arrived.

An area of gentle, stabbing pressure was covering Martin's upper arm and shoulder, and he was aware of a weight pushing down on the back of his neck, then against the other shoulder. He tensed his neck muscles as it moved across the top of his helmet. The weight of soil had gone from his arm, he realized suddenly, and seconds later his visor and spotlight had been cleared and he could see again.

The burrower was only inches away, moving from side to side as it ingested and cleared the fallen soil from his other arm and the floor in front of his chest. Compared with his situation of a few minutes ago, Martin felt relief so intense that it verged on delirious happiness.

"You're seeing this?" he whispered.

"Of course," she replied, sheer relief at his escape making her angry. "Probably better than you are."

His head, shoulders, and arms were projecting from a shallow cave which the burrower had eaten out of the fallen soil, which was stabilized by the creature's organic cement, while his feet, legs, and hips were still pinned down. But he could see and breathe and his arms were free, and there was a chance that he could drag himself out. Scarcely feeling the pain of his fingers, he dug them into the soil of the floor and began to pull.

The burrower moved quickly on its under-stubble and landed heavily on top of both his hands.

"It doesn't want you to do that," Beth said.

She was right, he thought. But he did not want to

discuss it just then because he was getting an idea and, in any case, her thinking seemed to be duplicating his own.

"Probably it feels safer with you pinned down like that," she said. "I'd say that it is almost certainly non-hostile, but cautious."

"Is the translation computer on line?" Martin asked quietly. "I'm going to try talking to it."

Slowly he straightened and spread his fingers. The burrower immediately arched its body, taking most of its weight off the back of his hands. Very carefully he made loose fists, then rotated his wrists until the back of his hands lay against the floor, then he opened and closed his fingers. The burrower's stubble prodded gently all around them, and continued doing so as he brought his hands together and began taking off one of the thin gloves. The stubble concentrated on the glove for a few seconds, helping him remove it, then returned to the hand. Its touch became incredibly delicate, and one of the stubby digits went unerringly to the pulse in his wrist.

He bent and straightened his thumb and fingers in turn, then all together. He took a deep, silent breath, trying hard not to cough as the creature's pungent body odor invaded his helmet.

"Finger. Digit," he said in his quietest voice. "Fingers. Digits."

It jerked away from him at the first word. But the artificially attentuated voice emanating from the external speaker must have been bearable because it returned within a few seconds to re-cover his hands. He reminded himself again that its only sense was that of touch, but touch so delicate that it amounted to hypersensitive hearing. He rotated his wrists and opened and closed his hands while the stubble remained in contact without impeding the movements.

"Hand. Hands," he said. "Feelers. Touchers."

He laid the backs of his hands against the floor again and began speaking the language of mathematics using, as he had done when he was a very young child, his fingers.

"One," he said, bending up a finger. He bent it again and repeated "One." He brought up two fingers and said

"Two." Patiently, and with many repetitions, he demonstrated the permutations of additions up to ten.

"It seems to be repeating everything you say by touching the forward stubble against its beak," said Beth excitedly. "The computer says that it is a language similar to that used by the Kregsachi, who communicate by tapping and scraping medial limbs against their chitonous body armor, although they are a lot noisier about it. Taken in conjunction with earlier observations of burrower activity and the associated sounds we recorded, together with the biological and sensory data available, you are bringing us to the point where instantaneous two-way translation will be possible.

"Oh, man," she went on enthusiastically, "you don't appreciate what a truly beautiful hunk of machinery this computer is."

"It counts on its fingers," Martin said drily, "like me."

"We need a little more data," she continued. "A few more words, or an action and its associated verb that you both understand . . . Be careful!"

While she had been speaking he had withdrawn a hand from under the burrower and was extending it, very slowly, toward the mouth on the nearer side of its beak. The thick upper lip used in the soil ingestion process would, he hoped, be one of the least sensitive areas of its body. Gently he brought the tips of his fingers against the lip, which began to quiver.

"I touch you," he said. "I feel you."

He repeated the touch and the words several times, watching the stubble tapping against the beak. The lip was no longer quivering. Then he moved his hand to the beak and rested his bent fingers gently on the smooth, bony surface and he, too, began drumming just a few inches from where the stubble was doing the same. Hopefully he was indicating to the being that he understood that the beak was part of its system of speech production.

"I touch you gently," he said several times. Fractionally increasing the pressure on his fingertips and raising his voice slightly, he added, "I am touching you harder . . ."

"Got it!" Beth called.

And suddenly there was a new voice in his headset, speaking with the clear, accentless tones of the translation computer, which said, "You feel me talking! But even when you touch softly, stranger, you are much too violent for comfort."

"I'm sorry for causing you discomfort," Martin whispered into his helmet microphone. "My feelers lack fine control and my equipment is crude and insensitive. My name is Martin."

"Crude and insensitive, indeed..." Beth began.

"I must begin by thanking you," he went on, "for rescuing me from a very dangerous, perhaps lethal, situation."

"My personal touching is Cromonar," the burrower replied. "I could feel your distress, stranger. There was great physical agitation, and your general feel was that of a freshly trapped predator. But your situation is still fraught with danger. Am I right in assuming that you cannot live by eating alone, but must also breathe air to assist with the metabolizing of your food as do the surface dwellers?"

"That is correct," Martin said.

"Surely leaving your vehicle to crawl along this old and unstable pathway was not a sentient action," Cromonar said. "Or perhaps there are circumstances which render it so?"

"When we discovered that there was intelligent life on your planet," Martin replied, "we felt the need to investigate it and talk to you."

"I understand," the burrower said. "Curiosity can outweigh risk with some people. On this world such beings are in the minority, and a number of them are gathered in this area. Were there reasons other than curiosity for investigating us?"

"We wanted to know why you were hiding," Martin replied, "and to offer assistance if it was required."

"We need help," the burrower said, "even though the majority of us do not feel the need. But right now, stranger, your need for help is of greater urgency than ours. Can you remain absolutely still and refrain from violent touchings while I try to eat you out of there?"

The tunnel, Cromonar explained, enabled its people

to move between the cavern and an area of edible root crops without having to ingest the tasteless and nutrition-lacking soil of the locality. Due to the excessively heavy touchings of Martin's digger, the entire length of the tunnel was in danger of collapse. None of its colleagues were willing to risk physical contact with such a violent toucher, which meant that the rescue operation was likely to be a long one.

The soil had been removed from his back and the burrower's weight was centered on his buttocks when it happened—a sudden renewal of pressure on his shoulders and a fall which partially covered one arm. Martin's pulse rate skyrocketed again and sweat misted his visor so that the tunnel ahead became a bright, featureless blur.

"Do not move," Cromonar said, and it began patiently eating and clearing the new fall from his back. The process of ingestion did not affect its ability to talk.

It was talking, Martin realized suddenly, to reassure him and take his mind off his present predicament. If he panicked and tried to pull himself out before Cromonar was ready, the entire tunnel would fall in and he would certainly die, and so the burrower was talking furiously about itself, its species, their world, and everything under its unseen sun.

They had evolved from a species of small, sightless flat worm which had burrowed in the primal ooze of their world, paralyzing larger life forms with their sting and ingesting them piecemeal. As their physical size, numbers, and food requirements increased, they became blind hunters whose sense of touch became specialized to the point where they did not need any other sensory channel. They could feel the movements of their surface prey, identify its vibrations, and lie in wait for it just below ground until it came within reach of their stings. Or they could feel out and identify surface tracks and follow their victim to its lair, and either burrow underground and sting it from below or attack it when its internal vibrations indicated that it was asleep.

Because of the strange, extra sense possessed by the creatures who roamed the surface and the air above it, they had no success against conscious opponents aware of their presence, and very often they had become the prey rather than the hunters.

The surface animals, too, had become larger and stronger and less affected by the burrowers' stings. They were forced to act together in setting up more and more complex ambushes and cooperation in the matter of food-gathering, storage, and distribution led to the formation of subsurface villages and towns. They already educated their young by touch, and methods were devised for feeling each other over long distances.

Martin had his eyes closed, the better to see the incredible mind-pictures the burrower was painting with its history lesson. His pulse was still racing, but with excitement now, and the threat of an unknown tonnage of soil falling on him seemed to have lost some of its urgency.

Amplifiers and transformers enabled them to refine their sense of touch to the point where they could feel light and radio frequencies. Their attempts at powered flight were still in progress. These had claimed the lives of a great many burrowers who could only gauge their position and altitude by feeling the touchings of air currents on their flying surfaces and trusting to a sense of balance which was woefully inadequate in the alien environment of the sky. These inadequacies had been overcome in part by using long touchings of the irregularities in the ground below.

Blind flying, Martin thought incredulously, with Doppler radar indications in Braille! He wanted to compliment the burrower on its species' achievements in spite of the worst possible handicap. But the fallen soil had again been eaten clear of his back and Cromonar was still doing all the talking.

The increasing sophistication of their long-range touching systems made them aware of complex vibrations reaching them from beyond their own world. This knowledge had excited some people, but the majority had been made fearful and wanted to conceal themselves lest these faint touchings indicated the pressure of other beings with the strange extra sense, beings more powerful and dangerous than the predators of their own world.

All things considered, Martin thought, it was a good reason for hiding; good enough to satisfy a Federation

which normally had no time at all for people who treated
others with fear and distrust. More than any other race
in his experience, these burrowers needed Federation
help. He was not out of trouble himself yet, but already
he was considering methods of assessing their suitability
for citizenship.

"You have a most unusual and interesting feel," said
the burrower, who was working above his lower legs. "I
assume, from earlier touchings felt while you were on
the surface, that these are the limbs on which you balance when you move quickly over the ground. On that
occasion you were accompanied by a lighter being
whose presence I no longer feel."

Martin kept quiet so that Beth could speak for herself.

"I am the being whose presense you felt earlier," she
said, and went on to give a brief, simplified description
of the two-way translation system which was converting
the burrower's stubble touchings into sounds which the
visitors could understand, and the visitors' words into a
form which the burrower could feel. She went on, "I
thank you for your efforts to rescue my life-mate, and I
apologize for the irritation caused by the devices we
must use to touch you underground. Solid material is
impassible to our extra sense, and your own species'
highly developed sense of touch is truly unique."

"Uniquely unfortunate, I fear," Cromonar replied,
and even in translation the anger was apparent in its
voice. "It seems that every sentient and non-sentient
creature in existence has the ability to accurately navi-
gate over long or short distances without needing to feel
the touch of sun or wind or sea currents or vibrations
bouncing off distant objects. We are cripples, beings
lacking vital organs, and we know not what it is that we
lack.

"The sensitivity of our long-range touching systems,"
it went on more calmly, "made us aware of the many and
complex vibrations reaching us from beyond our world.
These touchings were not natural occurrences, and we
hoped that, some day, beings much more advanced than
ourselves would visit us and perhaps help us attain that
ability which we alone lack. Your presence and actions
here demonstrate that my people need no longer fear

everyone and everything above the surface. More, it proves to us that there are other planetary surfaces and subsurfaces warmed by countless numbers of suns whose touchings we can barely detect, but whose soil and creatures we may one day like to feel around us. Believe me, your gratitude is appreciated, but it is we who are in your debt."

Martin gave an involuntary shiver which caused the burrower to renew its warning against unnecessary movement. When Beth spoke she bypassed the translator so that only he could hear her.

"This Cromonar," she said, "is giving me goose-bumps. It's blind, dammit, and still it wants to go to the stars!"

"The ends of your rear limbs have awkward, angular projections," the burrower went on, "which were responsible for the original cave-in. My body is arched across these limbs to support the tunnel, which is about to collapse again. Move forward carefully, but with speed."

Straining to kept his toes pointed backward, Martin used his elbows and forearms to drag himself clear of the fall. But he had moved less than three yards when there was a sudden, heavy pressure on his feet. For a heart-stopping moment he imagined that the whole roof was collapsing on top of him, but he was able to pull his feet free without bringing down any more soil.

"Are you all right, Martin?" Cromonar said. Before he could reply it went on, "I can feel that you are. But there is instability in the whole tunnel. Keep moving."

Martin kept moving and the burrower kept on talking. Maybe it liked talking, or perhaps it was still trying to take his mind off his present predicament.

"The majority of my people are unwilling to take risks," it went on, "whether physical or philosophical. They tend to ignore challenges until the challenger has either died of old age or... Can you move faster, Martin?"

Martin did so, feeling the other's body nudging at his feet when they threatened to dig into the sidewalls. He said, "By challenger do you mean a person among you who issues challenges? Do these people influence or control others by means of a greater physical strength or other forms of coercion? Do such individuals indulge in conflict, either directly or by proxy? Do the leaders of your culture achieve their high positions as a result of such conflicts?"

He had almost forgotten that his life could end at any moment, and for that he was deeply grateful to the fat, animated pancake which was following him along the tunnel. It had reminded him of his job.

"We try to coerce people," the burrower replied, "by argument and debate and warnings of impending trouble, but their mental inertia and innate conservatism is such that we have little success. But stranger, are you suggesting that there are beings out there who impose their wills violently on other sentient people? Surely that is inconceivable. It would be the action of an intelligent predator, if that were not a contradiction in terms. Violence must only be offered toward nonsentient animal and vegetable life in the interests of food provision.

"You worry me, Martin," it concluded. "Are there beings out there who practice such insanity?"

And with those words, Martin knew, his preliminary assessment of the burrower culture was complete, and entirely favorable.

Reassuringly, he said, "There are a few such individuals, but they are not allowed to influence normal people. However, if others like myself were to come here, could we talk to the whole population and ask questions of them?"

That would be the final stage of the assessment, the examination of the individual candidates for citizenship.

"Yes, Martin," the burrower replied, "but there is no guarantee that they would listen. My friends took a grave risk in making themselves known to you. Had the outcome been different, we would have been ostracized for life. But the areas of this world which can support my people are fast being eaten out, and if there was the slightest chance of finding an answer to the problem, or of finding someone with the answer, the risk had to be taken. Soil, living space, is our most urgent need."

Martin thought that it was grossly unfair that he had to conduct this discussion while crawling along a low and dangerously unstable tunnel on his stomach, but he tried to choose his words with care.

He said, "Soil can be provided, on another world. There would be no limit to the area or depth you would inhabit, and there would be no predators other than those you might wish to bring along to make you feel at home."

Cromonar was silent for so long that Martin wondered if he had seriously misjudged the situation. Removed from what was literally their native soil, the burrowers might be helplessly disoriented, and Cromonar was intelligent enough to realize that. But still, they dreamed of traveling to the stars.

"Another world?" Cromonar asked finally. "For us? Empty?"

"Not empty," Martin said dryly, thinking of the teeming populations already living within the Federation World. "But there would be more territory than you would ever need if your species lives and grows for a thousand generations. It is difficult to explain while I'm crawling on my—"

"My apologies, Martin," Cromonar broke in. "You do not feel your surroundings as I do, and are unaware of the solid rock above us and that the cavern is but a short distance away."

"Confirmed," Beth said. "I'm sorry, I was too busy listening to tell you."

"Travel in the emptiness above the air was only a theoretical possibility until your first vehicle arrived," Cromonar went on, "and I find it difficult to believe that you have vessels capable of moving an entire planetary population."

"It can be done," Martin said, moving more slowly. "But the people who go must want to go. And they must satisfy my superiors that they would not be disruptive influences, or be capable of deliberately harming any being of their own or any other species they might meet.

Having satisfied these requirements, they can be moved whenever they wish."

"It is probable," the burrower said after another long silence, "that my people are too backward and... unsuitable."

Chapter 17

GENTLY, Martin said, "You must not be over-awed by the size and power of the Federation's mechanisms. They are simply developments of the wheel and the transfer of power along a metal wire, and you should not feel ignorant or inferior because we have had more time to develop and advance. Or do you and your group consider yourselves unsuitable for another reason?"

"We are, or we try to be, disruptive influences," the burrower replied. "I am afraid your Federation would find our group unsuitable."

Martin did not reply at once because they had left the tunnel and he was enjoying the sensation of standing and stretching his arms above his head. As he looked around the wide, low-ceilinged cavern, he said, "My life-mate and I are considered unsuitable, at present, for Citizen status, because we are too restless and inquisitive. Those are some of the qualities needed in our job. Like you, I have to try to convince people, your people in this case, that the course I urge on them is for their own good, that it is in their own best long-term interests to leave this planet."

"I understand," the burrower said. "And because you consider our thinking to be alike, it might be easier to convince our people here, and try to elicit their support, before expending effort on the more conservative element?"

"Correct," Martin said.

Cromonar was moving deeper into the cavern over a floor covered with large heaps of soil from which projected small, irregular pieces of metal. He concentrated his helmet light on one of them and saw that there was a machine of some kind under the pile, with burrowers using the soil heaped around it to position themselves where their stubble could operate the mechanism and feel its indicators.

"People with less adventurous minds," the burrower said suddenly, "are not necessarily stupid. They view situations simply and practically, and can often be influenced by considerations of personal or group advantage. But first, Martin, you must convince me of the advantages. Tell me about this world we should move to. Let me feel its shape and texture and people."

"And how," Beth asked from the hypership, "will we manage that?"

At this stage of a first contact procedure he would normally project tri-di pictures showing the Federation World in space and the incredible immensity of its interior—pictures so awe-inspiring and self-explanatory that the accompanying words were often redundant. It was a beautiful and impressive demonstration, the key element in both the first contact and preliminary assessment procedures, but it was designed to inform and convince beings who could see.

Sophisticated visual aids, Martin thought as he bent down beside a small pool on the cavern floor and scraped up two handfuls of the damp, claylike soil, were no use at all to the blind.

"The new world is shaped like this," he said, when the clay had been molded into a sphere with conical projections at each pole. He placed it on the ground, balanced on one of the points, within a few inches of the burrower and went on, "It is extremely large, hollow, and situated close to the center of the galaxy where the stars are very numerous..."

It was a ridiculous and abysmally inadequate description, Martin thought as Cromonar and several others moved up to the clay model, felt its contours briefly, and moved away again. But how could he convey to them the picture of the Federation World as he had first seen it, and its effect on him?

He went on. "All around this world there are countless billions of suns like your own, with vast distances separating them, but from your position in space they would feel close together, like a great carpet of dense, spiky grass. Closer to you, and negating the feel of the distant suns behind it, is the vast, hollow world of the Federation of Galactic Sentients. It cannot be felt so easily because it does not radiate touchings, except for those needed to enable ships to feel their way to the entry ports.

"It is an unimaginably large world," he continued, "which encloses its own sun. The internal area is such that it will provide more than enough living space for the future projected populations of every intelligent species in the galaxy.

"Even now there are many different species to feel," he went on, "together with their mechanisms, native animal and vegetable life forms, and environments. Or you may prefer, if you are suited to the work, to feel and help operate some of the mechanisms which provide the services for this superworld. For example, you could be trained to—"

"Hold, stranger!" Cromonar broke in. "Surely you exaggerate the importance of the part we would play. And you offer so much. What must we do for you in return? What is the purpose of this superworld, and are you sure that we would be allowed to go there?"

"I cannot promise that you will all be allowed to go there," Martin said. "As to what you will give in return, let me ask instead what reward you receive from your own people for trying to help them against their will? To certain psychological types, the effort is its own reward."

More and more of the burrowers had emerged from the soil enclosing their machines and were gathering closely around him as he went on to describe the tremendous philosophical and technological goals of the World and the Federation contained within it.

"Stranger," one of the burrowers broke in, "is it not a fact that a species contains within itself the seeds of its own destruction? Surely a number of these seeds will take root in your superworld?"

Blind they might be, Martin thought, but they could see a lot farther and faster than many other extraterrestrials he had encountered. He was remembering the shock to the Earth's population when, a little over a decade earlier, they had been contacted by the Federation. But the initial fear and distrust had been quickly overcome because the Federation psychologists were able people who had not tried to lie, diplomatically or otherwise. He should try to do the same.

"Examination and induction procedures will be devised for the special sensory requirements of your species," Martin said. "These will be aimed at identifying, and where necessary excluding, the small minority of candidates who will be unsuitable for citizenship.

"These will be the sentient predators who turn up in nearly every species," he went on, "and who cause disruption and suffering out of all proportion to their number. If there are any such beings on this world, here they will stay."

The burrowers crowding around him had become very still. Perhaps they were worried, or felt insulted and angry at the thought that some of them would not qualify for citizenship. He wondered what he would do, unarmed as he was, if they reacted physically to the insult.

But was he unarmed, when all he had to do to paralyze them with shock was to open his visor and speak loudly?

"There is a third category," he continued, "which comprises the curious, restless, adventure-seeking minority that is in every intelligent species..."

Briefly he went on to describe the advantages and the few, so far as he personally was concerned, disadvantages of non-Citizen status, and when he finished, the silent stillness of his listeners was Teldin in its perfection.

Bypassing the translator, he said worriedly, "I'm not being totally honest with them, half promising things which ... They're blind, dammit! What can they really do?"

"You'd be surprised," Beth said. "The main computer and I have been considering that very question. It seems that their hypersensitivity of touch, and the psycho-sensory matrix which evolved as a result of having one single and unspecialized receptor, gives them a unique advantage over the four- and five-sensed species. They actually feel the world about them and, in time, they will be able to feel the three-dimensional relationships and constituents of space, perhaps time as well. That advantage should enable them to make significant progress toward the complete understanding of the nature and structure of the universe.

"The computer is displaying its equivalent of wild excitement," she went on, "and is making odious comparisons between the long-term potential of the burrowers and Earth-humans. And I thought that thing was a friend of mine."

"These non-Citizens," Martin resumed, knowing that his smile of visible relief was lost on the burrowers, "are the kind of people who might volunteer to go to the Federation World, to experience the hypership journey there and the interesting touch of beings whose shapes they can scarcely imagine; to touch every part of the situation and to report back on it to the main population. I feel that many of your future non-Citizens are here now."

"I understand, Martin," Cromonar said. "But all these matters must be discussed and made known to our people before we can give you our decision about visiting or moving to your Federation World. And you must be anxious to escape from what is for you an unpleasant environment, and to rejoin your life-mate and your vessel. Might I suggest a method which will not bring your violent machine into our research establishment?"

"Please do," Martin said warily. The thought of another slow, claustrophobic crawl back to the digger was making his pulse hammer again. Cromonar was immediately aware of his discomfort.

"Do not be disturbed, Martin," it said. "At the other end of the cavern is a fissure leading to within two of your body lengths of the surface. We can eat a path out for you and ensure that the area remains free of dangerous predators while you are waiting to be retrieved. May we retain your digger for examination?"

Just in time Martin stopped himself from laughing out loud with relief. He said, "You may, with all the other models and devices which we will construct and send down to you, so that you can give a full explanation of the situation to your people."

Cromonar moved closer and briefly touched the side of Martin's leg. It said, "Please follow my friends. I cannot accompany you because I have already eaten much more than was good for me while clearing the tunnel, and must rest. Thank you again, Martin."

As he turned to go Martin gave Cromonar an unseen wave, and was about to say "Be seeing you" when he thought better of it.

"We'll stay in touch," he said.

Chapter 18

IN the eight years since contact had first been established, they revisited the planet of the Blind Ones three times. The visits had not been strictly necessary, but special provision had to be made for the education and subsequent examination for Federation Citizenship of a candidate species who possessed only one sensory channel. While Cromonar's people were not distrustful of the Federation's motives, when situations arose which were particularly delicate or complex, they preferred the personal contact of Martin and Beth to the cold, artificial touchings of induction center robots.

These extended visits had been allowed, the supervisor told them, because there was nothing more urgent or important requiring their attention. In answer to persistent questioning they had been told that first-contact situations were still occurring, but that the physiologies and environments of the life forms concerned were such that the assignments could not be carried out by warm-blooded oxygen-breathers without an unacceptable level of risk.

As a result they had been given a succession of assignments which, however interesting, varied, and demanding, were simply odd-jobs. And this latest one, Martin thought as he stared through the aircraft's nose canopy, involved a trip inside the World itself.

Far below them there unrolled a rich, dark carpet of synthetic soil which stretched endlessly toward the nonexistent horizon until sheer distance, even in this pellucidly clear and cloudless sky, made it disappear into haze. At this latitude it was possible to circumnavigate the globe without seeing any change in the scenery, so widely scattered were the inhabited areas. But if their atmospheric craft's respectable Mach 3 could have been maintained without stopping for the replacement of age-expired components, or crews, circumnavigation would have taken more than two centuries.

In the controlled and utterly calm atmosphere of this world, the airborne seeds and spores from the seven-thousand-miles-distant cultivated area which was their destination did not propagate at anything like Mach 3, and so the soil below remained fallow.

"This place gives me the creeps," Beth said as she stared intently into the incredibly distant haze. "It's too big. I feel much more comfortable in the more confined depths of interstellar space."

Martin laughed sympathetically. "With me, it is a feeling of awe mixed with utter boredom. Knowing our masters, the feelings are being engendered deliberately. They want to remind us of our origin and purpose from time to time, so that when we speak of this place to others it will be with conviction.

"When we say big," he added, laughing, "we will mean *big*."

"And our passengers?" Beth asked.

"Even though they live here as Citizens," Martin replied, "I expect they need to be reminded, too. Especially when they decide to go calling on their neighbors."

Beth sighed and said, "We'll be landing before midday meal tomorrow. Maybe we should go back and try to talk to them again about the difficulties they can expect. Not to frighten or discourage them, of course. We must try to be realistic but reassuring, if that isn't a contradiction in terms."

"It is," Martin replied shortly, then added, "They don't even like us, and don't seem to listen to anything I say. Citizens!"

"Fortunately," she said, smiling, "you're the contact specialist. I'm just the driver. Let's go."

The lounge currently being occupied by the passengers smelled to high Heaven but, because the body odor was alien, it was neither pleasant nor unpleasant. In addition to the smell, the air was filled with an alien gabble which was being processed by his translator into the buzz of excited conversation. The sound faded for a moment as he entered, then continued at a higher level.

Martin tried to control his irritation. From a species which had been Federation Citizens for three generations, he had expected better manners.

When he and Beth had been recalled to the Federation World they had wondered what, if any, work could be found for a hypership captain and a first-contact and assessment specialist to do there. But they had quickly discovered that a Ship Handler One was expected to handle vessels of all sizes down to small atmosphere craft, and a Contactor Three had to do his job whether he was at the outermost edges of the galaxy or at home.

Their assignment instructions had left them in no doubt about that.

A GROUP OF CITIZENS BELONGING TO THE RACE INHABITING AREA BD72355-8 HAVE DECIDED TO BROADEN THEIR SOCIAL AND CULTURAL AWARENESS BY OPENING OTHER-SPECIES CONTACT IN DEPTH. YOU WILL ADVISE AND ASSIST THIS PROJECT AS REQUIRED AND OBSERVE THE INITIAL REACTIONS OF BOTH GROUPS. IF THE CONTACT ATTEMPT IS CLEARLY PREMATURE, YOUR REPORT SHOULD REACH ME BEFORE AN ACT OF VIOLENCE OR OTHER MAJOR INCIVILITY CAN TAKE PLACE.

COMMUNICATION WILL BE BY SIMULTANEOUS VERBAL AND PRINTED TRANSLATION TO FACILITATE LATER REVIEW AND STUDY.

Martin keyed for both audible and visual translations when he spoke to the passengers.

"You will shortly be landing in the principal city of the Surreshon," he said, "and for the first time you will be meeting Citizens of a completely alien species. If you have questions, or require information or assistance of any kind, you have only to request it."

The background conversation continued unabated, but one of the Keidi turned and directed its speaking horn toward Martin to show that its words were for him alone.

"We do not request it, non-Citizen," the being said loudly as its sound focus narrowed onto Martin's head. "Both the Surreshon and the Keidi have studied each other's physiologies and behavior patterns in detail, and contact is desired by both our groups. We are civilized beings, technologically and philosophically advanced, and, for several generations, Federation Citizens. We are grateful for your offer but feel that your presence here is redundant."

"Big-head," Beth said softly, bypassing the translator. Martin smiled, then closed his fist and pointed at the Keidi with a stiffly outstretched arm.

"My orders are to make my experience available to you—" he began.

"Federation Citizens," the other broke in, "do not take orders. We accede to requests if they seem reasonable and in the best interests of ourselves and other Citizens. We most certainly do not obey beings who are non-Citizens, regardless of the orders which they, themselves, must obey."

A species who did not exchange personal information except in circumstances of intimacy, and who communicated with other individuals by pointing and focusing their speaking horns rather than calling them by name, would not be the kind of people to make friends easily. He hoped their behavior toward the Surreshon was better than that shown during the few conversations with their Earth-human crew.

Martin brought up his other arm and pointed both fists briefly at the Keidi, then swung them apart at shoulder

level to indicate that his words were for everyone and
not just the speaker, and tried again.

"There is no problem," he said. "My orders are to
give you advice and assistance when necessary, and I
shall obey these orders. You will receive this advice but,
as Citizens, you are not obliged to take it."

"There are overtones of irritation in your communication," the Keidi said. "This stems, I suspect, from the
widely prevalent attitude of public servants who feel and
act like the masters of those they are supposed to serve."

"Ouch," Beth commented.

Martin reddened, but a change in Earth-human facial
coloration was unlikely to mean anything to the Keidi.
Controlling his temper, he said, "May I make an observation, then, rather than give advice which might be
misconstrued as instructions? The people who make up
your contact group are probably the most advanced, intellectually adventurous, and forward-thinking members
of your species. This is proven by the fact that you have
arranged and are about to make contact with a culture
which is completely alien to your own, and you intend to
deepen this contact in the expectation that both species
will benefit. This expectation is reasonable, but the
wide-ranging cultural exchange which you envisage may
not be as easy and rapid as you expect. Unless you are
very lucky indeed, it might not be completed until several of your generations have passed.

"It is possible," he ended carefully, lowering one arm
to his side and pointing the other at the original Keidi
speaker, "that your natural enthusiasm may have blinded
you to the many problems you will encounter."

The other's horn quivered briefly, then it said, "Is it
your intention, or that of your superiors, to discourage
this project?"

"It is not," Martin said firmly. Before going on, he
glanced at the translation screen where his words appeared side by side in English and the regimented squig-
gles of the Keidi printed language. Carefully, because the
material was available for later study by the Keidi and
his supervisor, he said, "Such projects are to be encouraged and actively supported. They are the ultimate purpose for which the Federation Citizens were chosen and

brought here. Our concern is that you might discourage yourselves by making a premature contact."

There was no observable or audible reaction from the Keidi, and Martin continued. "Like yourselves, the group of scientists you are about to meet are not typical. The majority of the Surreshon population, like their Keidi counterparts, have only a passing interest in inter-species contact, and are much more concerned with the day-to-day business of living, mating, caring for their off-spring. People like these are simply not interested in the long-term future scientific and philosophical develop-ment of their own or another species."

The sound of background conversation had died away and, even though the others were not pointing their horns at him, Martin knew that he had their attention.

"The group you have arranged to meet will be inter-ested in everything you do and say," he went on. "But if the time required for full cultural contact between your species is to be kept as short as possible, it is the interest of the ordinarily disinterested Surreshon which must be aroused, as much and as often as possible. I have no doubt that beings of your level of intelligence and range of abilities will devise ways of achieving this."

"Butter," Beth murmured, again bypassing her trans-lator. "Butter applied with a shovel."

"What are your instructions?" asked the Keidi who was pointing at him, then added, "I mean, of course, what is the advice you were instructed to give us?"

Martin gave a relieved sigh. "I was told that you and your Surreshon counterparts, bearing in mind the serious nature of this project, would prefer a quiet arrival and first meeting with the minimum of outside interference from the population at large. However, it is the general public who are going to be involved ultimately, and it was felt that they should be involved sooner rather than later.

"This could be achieved," he went on, "by arousing their interest in the project as early as possible, and in-creasing that interest by arranging frequent interviews with the media giving your reactions, on a more personal and noncerebral level, to your meetings with ordinary Surreshon citizens. The general public should be influenced by whatever means or activities available to you into desiring wider contact—"

"Are you suggesting," the Keidi broke in, "that we market ourselves like some kind of saleable product? Our group is dedicated solely to the achievement of full understanding and cultural contact. We are not in the business of trading or selling. Your remarks are insulting, and I trust that the insult was unintentional."

"Back off," Beth said softly. Martin shook his head.

"With respect," he went on, "every member of your group is engaged in a marketing project of great complexity and importance, that of selling an idea to people who, with very few exceptions, are not yet ready to buy it. They are like yourselves when you were children, when you were being introduced to the concepts of mathematics, geometry, or written language by tutors who had to devise methods of holding your interest and gradually increasing it within your then limited attention spans. Later, of course, these subterfuges became unnecessary as your interest in the subjects for their own sakes increased, with results which ultimately led to this project and The Builders only know what more besides."

The Keidi's speaking horn remained silent, but the focusing muscles were twitching.

"First impressions are important and longest-lasting," Martin resumed quickly. "You should therefore attract as much attention and interest as early as possible, by putting on a show rather than arriving quietly. I suggest circling their airfield a few times followed by a couple of low-level passes across the landing area. Supersonic, of course, for the benefit of the media and sightseers, but land before the noise becomes irksome. Initially, you should seek out the news gatherers and respond to their questions, rather than to those of your counterparts, because there will be ample time later to—"

"No!" the Keidi broke in sharply. "Repeated overflying at supersonic speed would disconcert and perhaps frighten the young, irritate their parents, and therefore prove counterproductive."

"The airfield is far removed from the densely inhabited area of the city," Martin replied, "and I think that the youthful sightseers accompanying their parents, whose young minds you will be trying to influence, would enjoy such a display."

There was no reply for a few minutes while the Keidi talked quietly among themselves, then the original speaker said, "Thank you, non-Citizen. We are in complete disagreement with you. The suggestion trivializes, sensationalizes, and cheapens a most serious and responsible activity. Our approach will be quiet and dignified, and your approach will be subsonic."

Martin did not trust himself to speak as he turned to follow Beth to the flight deck.

Except for some mild curiosity shown toward them immediately following the landing, Beth and Martin were ignored. The Keidi and Surreshon scientists were Citizens engaged in opening cultural relations with each other, after all, and two non-Citizens of whatever species, who had crewed the visitors' aircraft were of little intrinsic interest to either the Keidi or the Surreshon, who resembled something between an outsize caterpillar and a multi-legged ant.

Enormous efforts were being made by both groups to be polite and understanding and forgiving of each other's mistakes—mistakes which were amusing, embarrassing, and often physically dangerous, but not serious so far as the project was concerned. The errors were, however, frequent enough to keep the few Surreshon news gatherers present very happy indeed.

If their supervisor was capable of feeling such an emotion, it should be pleased with the reports they were sending back. But when it contacted them a few days later, it barely mentioned the project. Plainly it had something much more urgent in mind for them.

WITHDRAW FROM KEIDI-SURRESHON CONTACT ASSIGNMENT WITHOUT DELAY. IN THE SHORT TERM THE PROCESS HAS BECOME SELF-SUSTAINING. PROGRAM THE ATMOSPHERE CRAFT TO RETURN TO KEIDI TERRITORY WHEN REQUIRED AND INFORM THEM ACCORDINGLY. AN INTRAPLANETARY SPACE VEHICLE WILL LAND DI-

RECTLY AND CONVEY YOU TO THE HYPERSHIP
WHERE NEW ASSIGNMENT INSTRUCTIONS WILL
BE ISSUED.

The ship sent to pick them up was small, simple, and
stupid, Beth insisted, because there was no way for her
to modify its orbit or velocity from inside the passenger
observation module. As a master ship handler she was
always a little restless when she had nothing to do but
admire the scenery. The ship was, however, fast.

In spite of its fantastic acceleration they had time to
sleep while their vehicle curved into a path which would
take them into one of the two conical extensions which
grew from the World's north and south medial latitudes
into the polar areas, leaving its totally enclosed sun directly astern of them. When they woke, the ship was
approaching the tip of the north polar cone and only a
few minutes from the five-hundred-mile diameter port
which would enable them to move from intraplanetary to
extraplanetary space.

For a heart-stopping moment the walls of the cone,
the gargantuan ship construction and maintenance docks
lining it like tiny, irregularly shaped metal tiles, rushed in
at them from all sides. He glimpsed other ships, some
distant and others uncomfortably close, moving toward
the huge polar exit port. Then, in an instant too short for
his senses to measure, they were through and on course
for their waiting hypership.

The great exit port shrank into invisibility so that all
around and behind them there stretched out a gigantic
disk of absolute blackness. And above that dark and featureless horizon shone the stars as only they could shine
at the center of the galaxy.

Feeling dwarfed and abysmally insignificant before
such grandeur, Martin said very little during the rest of
the journey to the hypership. No matter how difficult or
dangerous the coming assignment turned out to be, he
almost welcomed it because it would mean dealing with
people like, or completely unlike himself. In that situation he could begin to feel useful and, in however small a
measure, important again.

Chapter 19

GOOD MORNING, read the communications display. ASSIGNMENT INSTRUCTIONS AND ASSOCIATED PHYSIOLOGICAL AND SOCIOPOLITICAL DATA FOLLOW. PLEASE RECORD FOR LATER STUDY.

A pulsating grayness filled the screen as anything up to ten hours of relevant information was transferred in as many seconds, then it steadied again with another message.

SUMMARY OF ASSIGNMENT. YOU WILL PROCEED TO THE SYSTEM AND PLANET LISTED AS FWC/132/88/G3. THE PLANETARY GRAVITY, ATMOSPHERIC PRESSURE, AND CLIMATIC RANGE WILL NOT INCONVENIENCE YOU.

THE PREFIX INDICATES THAT THE PLANET HAS ALREADY BEEN CONTACTED BY US AND THE DOMINANT SPECIES SCREENED FOR SUITABILITY AS CITIZENS. NINETY-SEVEN POINT THREE EIGHT PERCENT OF THE POPULATION SATISFIED THE REQUIREMENTS AND WERE TRANSFERRED TO THE FEDERATION WORLD. THOSE REMAINING ARE AWARE THAT THEY ARE NOT THE ONLY INTELLIGENT RACE IN THE GALAXY. THEY HAVE SEEN TWO-DIMENSIONAL REPRESENTATIONS OF MANY OF THE OTHERS, BUT HAVE NOT EXPERIENCED PERSON-TO-PERSON CONTACT WITH ANY OFF-PLANET SPECIES AND MAY NEVER DO SO IF YOU DECIDE ON A LENGTHY AND COVERT OPERATIONAL PROCEDURE.

Puzzled, Martin said, "We've never been allowed to make that kind of decision on other assignments. Are they hostile? Would a direct approach be dangerous for physiological reasons?"

IT IS THEIR PRESENT LEVELS OF INTELLI-
GENCE, ETHICS, AND INTERPERSONAL BEHAV-
IOR, INCLUDING THEIR DEGREE OF HOSTILITY
TOWARD STRANGERS, WHICH YOU ARE TO IN-
VESTIGATE. OBSERVE.

A rapid succession of still pictures were displayed on
the screen. They showed a species which was bipedal,
bifurcate, bisexual, and in overall appearance utterly
nonhuman, but completely familiar.

"We're being sent to *Keida*?" Martin asked.

CORRECT. INTENSIVE SURVEILLANCE WAS
WITHDRAWN FROM KEIDA WHEN THE TRANS-
PORTERS REMOVED ITS SUCCESSFUL CITIZEN
CANDIDATES TO THE FEDERATION WORLD. THE
FEW UNDESIRABLES REMAINING WERE SO
WIDELY SCATTERED THAT IT WAS THOUGHT THAT
THEY WOULD NOT POSE A THREAT EVEN TO
THEMSELVES. NOW THERE ARE INDICATIONS OF
A VERY LARGE ORGANIZATION EMERGING IN THE
CENTRAL CONTINENT. THE MOTIVATION IS AS YET
UNCLEAR BUT COMBINES MALE PARENT WOR-
SHIP WITH A FORM OF RELIGIOUS MILITARISM.

"That sounds like a nasty combination," Martin said.
"But is it any of our concern? I assumed that, being Undesirables, it no longer mattered what they did to each
other."

YOU SHOULD REEXAMINE THAT ASSUMPTION.
PHILOSOPHICALLY THERE ARE NO SUCH
COLORS AS BLACK AND WHITE. THE DIFFERENCE
BETWEEN AN UNDESIRABLE AND A NON-CITIZEN
LIKE YOURSELF IS LESS THAN YOU THINK.

It was obvious that the words had angered Beth as
much as they had him. Since the completion of their
training they had considered themselves as members, al-
beit not very important members, of the Federation's
elite group of contact specialists. Being told that there
was little difference between themselves and the vicious,
power hungry, or otherwise amoral Undesirables was
deeply wounding to the justifiable pride they had been
taking in their work.

What kind of assignment was it that began with such a

serious attack on their basic convictions and self-respect?

THE CITIZEN ASSESSMENT AND SELECTION PROCEDURE IS EFFICIENT BUT NOT INFALLIBLE. IT IS POSSIBLE THAT AMONG KEIDA'S UNDESIRABLES THERE ARE POTENTIAL CITIZENS AND NON-CITIZENS WHO DO NOT PRESENT THEMSELVES AT THE INDUCTION CENTERS. THESE BEINGS SHOULD BE CONTACTED, INTERROGATED, AND ASSESSED AS PART OF THE ASSIGNMENT. YOU WILL ALSO PROVIDE ASSISTANCE IN WHATEVER FORM IS REQUIRED SHOULD THE KEIDI BE PREPARED TO ACCEPT IT. THEY ARE AN INTENSELY PROUD AND SELF-RELIANT RACE AS YOU ALREADY KNOW. BUT YOUR PRIMARY PURPOSE IS TO INVESTIGATE THE SITUATION WHICH IS DEVELOPING ON KEIDA AND SUGGEST A METHOD OF MEETING AND OVERCOMING THE THREAT.

"We found it hard enough to offer help to Keidi Citizens," Martin commented. "Their Undesirables are likely to be very dangerous and difficult people to investigate openly, and the trouble with a completely covert approach is—"

"Why," Beth asked suddenly, "were we chosen?"

THE ASSIGNMENT IS DIFFICULT BUT MAY NOT BE DANGEROUS. THE KEIDI HAVE ALWAYS BEEN AVERSE TO THE TAKING OF LIFE AND ALTHOUGH MORE SUBTLE FORMS OF VIOLENCE HAVE BEEN PRACTICED THROUGHOUT THEIR HISTORY, THE PRESENT EXTREME RARITY OF INTELLIGENT BEINGS ON THEIR PLANET HAS STRENGTHENED THIS AVERSION. THIS IS THE MOST IMPORTANT ASSIGNMENT YOU HAVE BEEN GIVEN SO FAR, AND FOR THIS REASON YOU WILL BE ALLOWED TO PROCEED WITH MINIMUM DIRECTION AND SUPERVISION. HOWEVER, THERE IS A HIGH PROBABILITY THAT YOUR ASSIGNMENT WILL NOT BE COMPLETED SUCCESSFULLY.

YOU TWO HAVE BEEN SELECTED BECAUSE OF TRAINING, EXPERIENCE, AVAILABILITY, AND PSYCHOLOGICAL FACTORS WHICH I SHALL NOT LIST

BECAUSE YOU WOULD FIND SOME OF THEM UN-
COMPLIMENTARY. YOU HAVE ALSO BEEN RE-
CENTLY IN CONTACT WITH THE KEIDI LIFE FORM.

THERE IS A SERIOUS PROBLEM. THE THREAT
LIES ON KEIDA, BUT IT IS THE FEDERATION
WORLD WHICH WILL ULTIMATELY BE AFFECTED.

Martin opened his mouth to laugh, thinking that the
supervisor was making some kind of alien and utterly
ridiculous joke, then closed it again. For a moment the
closing words continued to light the screen.

During the trip to the Keidi system, Beth and Martin
said very little to each other. When they were not engaged in silently studying the Keidi material they were
arguing bitterly and briefly about operational procedures, which resulted in further lengthy silences. As they
were checking their equipment before boarding the
lander, he made another attempt to reason with her.

"According to the regulations," he said seriously, "the
function of the ship handler is to remain with the hypership and provide support and protection to the contactor
on the surface. We are being allowed a wide degree of
initiative on this one, but that doesn't mean that you can
completely ignore the rule book."

Matching his tone, Beth said, "Don't worry, the ship
has been instructed to furnish whatever protection is
necessary and hold itself ready to respond to verbal signals. These are word combinations not likely to be used
in normal conversation. They're listed on that screen for
you to memorize.

"Besides," she went on, "that regulation was designed
to cover first-contact assignments on planets with hostile
environments and life forms ignorant of who we are and
what we represent. This isn't a completely alien planet."

She smiled and continued, "I know that you don't
want me with you. It stops you from taking the kind of
stupid risks you would have no hesitation in taking if I
wasn't there, because it gives you two people instead of
one to worry about. But that is precisely the reason why
we will be safer together. We have discussed this and
you agreed with me, earlier, but now you want to rele-
gate me to my superscientific kitchen sink again. Next to

a complete family unit with children, an alien and presumably mated couple would be much more reassuring to them, would appear less of a threat, than any individual stranger.

"I can't see this ever becoming a covert operation," she continued when he did not reply. "To understand what is happening here we'll have to get really close to these people, and be accepted and trusted by them. I know I'm right and I know that you, being the kind of person who worries about me, would prefer that I was wrong.

"Have you gone deaf or something?"

Martin forced himself to smile and said, "What did you say?"

"Oh, go terminate," Beth said, and turned her attention to the control console. The lander shot away from its dock and the enormous bulk of the hypership was shrinking behind them before he spoke again.

"We would further reduce our risks," Martin said, "if we took enough time to prepare properly for this operation so that we could go down as a family unit. How many children did you have in mind?"

"You're worried by this job and so am I," she said irritably, without taking her attention from the console. "Don't try to hide it by making stupid jokes."

"I'll try to be serious, then," Martin said.

"Physiologically, our supervisor is a mystery to me, but I've been told that it has a multiple heart system, and I expect they would all arrest if we were to ask for a three- or four-year hold on this operation. However, my suggestion should be considered as a long-term cooperative project in case we're given a similar assignment in the future."

"And you would go to all that trouble," Beth said, turning to look at him, "not to mention putting me to considerable personal inconvenience, simply to prepare us for the kind of assignment we might never again be given?"

"I believe in being prepared for any contingency," Martin said quietly, "even a future resignation from operational service and a joint application for Citizen status.

We would not want to be considered odd by our fellow proliferating Citizens, would we?"

Beth turned back to the console, and even her ears had gone a bright pink. "Is this some kind of proposal, an attempt to legalize an existing arrangement which isn't even illegal? I'm committed to atmosphere entry in eight minutes, dammit. Your sense of timing is weird."

"Relax," Martin said. "It wasn't my intention that we should start a family in the next eight minutes. Take plenty of time to think about it."

"Three," she said.

"Three?"

"And at least one of them," she added firmly, "will have to be a girl."

Only ten of the gigantic matter transmitters remained in Keida orbit, out of the hundreds which had ringed the equator like a tremendous, jeweled necklace prior to the mass transfer of population and property to the Federation World. Outwardly the planet appeared normal, its oceans unchanged and the land hidden by the cloud blanket that was unrolling rapidly below them. Then they ran into the clear sky of a high pressure center and were able to pick out road systems, villages, isolated dwellings, and the raw, green, sharply outlined areas where some of the larger towns and cities had been neatly excised from the landscape and grass had grown in to cover the wounds.

"Someone is shooting at us," Beth said suddenly. "Two surface-to-air missiles with nonnuclear warheads. They are short-range weapons and we are already leaving them behind and, in any case, our meteor shield is deployed. They didn't try to make prior contact on any radio frequency, to ask who we were or to warn us off. That wasn't the act of a nonviolent Keidi."

"It wasn't," Martin agreed. "Maybe it was meant as a warning only because they knew we couldn't be hit. But now we know that this area has a weapons technology and its people are hostile to anything that flies, so we won't land here. Level out at ten thousand and fly below Mach One. We should approach these people slowly, openly, and without making sonic shock waves."

"Approach them where?" Beth asked. "My lander's

computer worries if it isn't given a place to land."

"There," Martin said, leaning forward and tapping his finger against the postion of what had been one of Keida's largest coastal cities. "Just under three hundred miles to the northeast. The sensors indicate very low population and even lower technology levels in and around the old city sites. Any missles launched from there are likely to be hand-thrown."

"But still potentially lethal," Beth said dryly as the lander adopted lateral flight mode and curved onto its new heading.

The entire area once occupied by the towering, thriving, and incredibly beautiful island city—the acknowledged commercial and cultural capital of its world—had been left an almost optically flat expanse of bare rock, tumbled masonry, and muddy brown soil. Tidal pools and a fine, intricate lacework of canals—the collapsed and flooded tunnels of what had been a complex underground transport system—reflected the gray overcast. Tiny squares and rectangles of green showed where the soil had been tilled and planted, and the image enhancers showed tools scattered haphazardly around these areas as if hastily abandoned at the lander's approach.

Incongruously, one of the road and railway bridges had been left in position, probably for the convenience of Undesirables wishing to move between the island and the mainland. It towered, rusting and empty of wheeled or pedestrian traffic, with the absence of all other surrounding structures magnifying the already massive and beautifully proportioned dimensions. At each end of the bridge there were shoulder-high double barricades built from surrounding masonry, presently unmanned.

Beyond the mainland end of the bridge the smooth, partially flooded area extended into what had been the city suburbs where a distant line of buildings marked the limits of the mattran incision. The enhancer showed houses, a small factory, and hangers belonging to a local airfield, most of which had been abandoned, burned, or otherwise vandalized. A few buildings showed signs of occupancy, with clothing hanging out to dry and their outlines blurred by the smoke of external cooking fires.

Standing isolated in what had been a small park, and

dwarfing the dingy and dilapidated structures around it, was the gleaming white cube of the area's Federation examination and induction center.

The lander dropped slowly toward a dry area of rubble in a city which resembled nothing so much as a muddy, two-dimensional map and touched down, rocking gently as its landing struts adjusted to the uneven surface.

"The people are hiding in surface and basement shelters positioned above high tide level," Beth said, "and the body scans show no hand weapons other than gardening impliments and long, wooden staves. The sensors also show a number of small collections of metal, mostly subsurface debris, but a few of them are small-scale power generators which are currently inoperative."

"Civilization is not yet dead," Martin said softly. "They still light their homes at night."

"And notice the perimeters of their gardens," Beth went on. "I'd say that they are having trouble with night visitors who think it easier to steal than to grow food."

They were being watched by a growing number of Keidi, all of them wrapped in cloaks which concealed everything but their heads and all carrying, or armed with, staves. None of them seemed curious enough to want a closer look at the ship.

"The longer we stay here," Martin said, "the more time we give them to worry about who or what is coming out and to get nervous about it. Ready?"

Beth held back for a moment. "These suits are a joke so far as protection is concerned. They're too tight-fitting and are effective only against low-velocity, solid-projectile-firing weapons, provided the shots are not aimed at our heads. A body hit would inflict painful, perhaps disabling injuries. The fabricator could produce a weapon which would outwardly duplicate those staves they all carry and, even though we might never use them, we would have the reassurance of—"

"Exactly," Martin broke in. "We would feel reassured, confident, protected, and unafraid. Those feelings would be reflected, however subtly, in our behavior, which would appear unnatural and suspicious for two people who are apparently unarmed and among strangers. It is better that we go in politely, with our hands empty of weapons and trying to project a high degree of natural caution."

"I won't have to try very hard," Beth said. "Test your watch."

Martin raised one arm and spoke briefly to his wrist-watch, checking that its communication and translation functions were on standby. He said gently, "It might be better, during the initial contact, if you stayed in the lander while I—"

"I'm ready," Beth said.

They emerged together and made an elaborate production or securing the lander's airlock behind them—an unnecessary precaution since the ship had much more effective methods of protecting itself from unauthorized entry or damage. The act was designed to show the distant watchers that their vessel had been left unoccupied, and that they were alone. When they were clear of the lander they stopped, looked all around them, then walked unhurriedly toward the watcher who had moved closest to the ship.

This was Keida, Martin reminded himself firmly, and judging by the contours of the watcher's speaking horn, this is a male Keidi Undesirable. It might be much more difficult to make friendly contact with this being than with an enormous, fierce visaged Teldi or a tiny, soil ingesting, and even more alien Blind One.

The ground underfoot was a thick, lumpy stew composed of dark brown mud in which floated pieces of rotting vegetation and small, soft objects which were probably not what he thought they were. He was glad, nonetheless, that his nose filters were in place.

When they had approached to within speaking distance, Martin raised one arm, fist clenched, to point at the Keidi. Before he could say anything he slipped, lost his balance, and landed on his hands and knees in the mud.

Chapter 20

"I would suggest," the Keidi called, lifting his staff and using it as a pointer, "that you take five paces to the right, where you will feel a section of level foundation just below the surface. Follow it for twenty paces, then turn at right angles to face me, and approach. Unless your species enjoys playing in the muck."

"We don't," Martin said as Beth helped him to his feet. "And thank you."

Close up, the watcher was a large Keidi whose loose-fitting cloak made it difficult to tell whether the garment concealed fat or muscles. His narrow, horn-tipped feet were planted wide apart so as to form a balanced tripod with its staff, which he grasped in a gauntleted hand.

"Are you organic?" the Keidi asked.

"Yes," Martin said.

"I thought so," the Keidi went on, briefly swiveling an eye in the direction of the lander and the silver and black symbol emblazoned on its flank. "A Federation World robot would not be so clumsy. Your species is unfamiliar to me since it is not portrayed in the white building, but you must be one of those all-powerful and all-knowing Federation Citizens. You will excuse me if I don't prostrate myself in abject awe. Why are you here?"

The other's hostility was all too plain. Martin said carefully, "My species is a fairly recent addition to the Federation, but we two are not Citizens, and neither are we all-powerful or all-knowing. It is in an attempt to reduce our lack of knowledge that we have come here."

Always tell the truth. That was the primary rule in other-species contact situations, because to do otherwise and be discovered in a lie could be disastrous so far as future friendly relations were concerned. But there was

166

no need to tell all of the truth, at least not all at once.

"We have been instructed by the Federation to visit a number of your city sites," Martin said, "to report on conditions generally and to find out if you need anything. The fabricators on our mother ship are capable of producing virtually anything you require, excluding weapons, of course. But there is no need to be frightened of us or—"

"I have already implied by my behavior," the other broke in, "that I am not frightened by you. That sanctimonious bunch of other-species do-gooders would never allow you to harm us. But, strangers, the opposite does not hold true."

This conversation was not going well. Not only was this Keidi unafraid and apparently unimpressed by the virtually limitless resources available to them, he was so well-informed that Martin was losing the initiative. It was ridiculous and utterly wrong that an Undesirable should place him at such a disadvantage. He was still trying to think of a reply when Beth broke the lengthening silence.

"Thank you for the warning," she said quietly. "If you think there is danger for us here, we shall leave at once. But is there something we can do for you before we go?"

"Return our city," the Keidi said.

Beth shook her head. "I'm sorry, its inhabitants prefer it where it is. But could we move all this mud, perhaps, or dry it out for you so that—"

"No," the other said sharply.

Martin glared at Beth and tried to send nonverbal signals for her to be silent and leave the communicating to the one who was trained for it. He had not intended that they take unnecessary risks but neither, as she had implied, was he intending to turn tail and run at the first hint of danger—at least, not without knowing what exactly they would be running from. But the silence was lengthening again still he could not think of anything positive to say. And Beth, he saw angrily, was turning to leave.

"No," the Keidi repeated in a quieter tone. "But you are in no immediate danger, and now that you're here you may as well stay for a while. Long enough, at least, for me to find you a couple of sticks." He turned and pointed toward the entrance to a shelter which, until then, they had mistaken for a large heap of rubble. "I'll lead the way. Follow me, exactly."

They did as they were told, but were soon falling further and further behind the more sure-footed Keidi. Martin said quietly, "We nearly lost the contact back there, when you started to turn back. Please let me do the talking from now on."

"Back there," Beth said, "you didn't have anything to say. But the risk was small. I had a strong feeling that it wanted to go on talking to us...he's going into his shelter. Are we supposed to follow or wait outside until we're invited?"

Before Martin could reply, the Keidi emerged carrying three light, stacking chairs which it placed in a line outside the entrance. The red plastic upholstery and armrests were stained and worn, and the metal framework was losing the battle against encroaching rust. They were large for the average Earth-human body, but did not look too uncomfortable. The Keidi disappeared again, this time returning with two staves which he placed carefully across the armrests of the outer chairs before seating himself in the middle one.

"Sit," he said.

The Keidi watched Martin intently as he lifted the wooden staff from the chair, then placed it across his lap as he turned and sat down. It was about two meters long and smelled faintly of some oily preservative. About one-third of the distance from one end it had been tightly wrapped with thin rope to give a secure and comfortable grip to a Keidi hand, and the other end came to a blunt point which was tipped with metal. The Keidi's watchful attitude made him wonder if the staff represented more than a mere aid to travel, and if the gift might be a test of some kind. Slowly, he lifted it from his lap and laid it on the ground at his feet. As he sat back, Beth hesitated then did the same.

"Thank you," he said, leaving it unclear whether he was referring to the invitation to sit or the gift of the staff.

Beth slapped suddenly at the side of her neck and the

Keidi said, "They breed in the mud and are particularly hungry at this time of year. Later I can give you an ointment to repel them, but you may well prefer the insect bites to the smell."

"I'd appreciate that," Beth said.

Martin thought of the variety of chemical and vibratory insect killers available to them on the ship, and forced himself to remain silent. For some reason the Keidi preferred talking to Beth.

"Your offer to dry out our mud was refused," the other went on, "because we do not like or trust Galactics, and will do everything in our power to avoid obligating ourselves to them."

It was time he rejoined the conversation, Martin thought. He said, "This is our first landing on your world. Can you tell us anything about the situation here? If such a question is not deemed to be an impertinence or an intrusion on your privacy, that is, and you are free to talk about it."

"I am free," the Keidi said, "to talk."

But he did not talk again for several minutes, during which Beth and Martin watched him attentively and more and more people came out to watch the three of them. Finally, he widened the focus on his horn to include them both, and spoke.

"I have skills which are important to this community," the Keidi said, "and for that reason I am not completely trusted, and that is why we are sitting out here in the cold. It is to show them that I have nothing to hide, that you are not trying to bribe, threaten, seduce, or otherwise influence me to leave them and not, as you may have thought, because I am ashamed to show you the inside of my home.

"Why did you lay your staff on the ground?" he added, swinging the horn around to bear on Martin. "Your familiarity with the local customs makes me uneasy."

Martin looked down at the staff, then said quietly, "The action wasn't calculated, it was simply that balancing the staff on my lap felt awkward and unnecessary, and the natural thing to do was to place it on the ground."

The horn and the eyes remained focused on him for a long moment, then the Keidi said, "The natural thing for someone like you to do would have been to drive the staff into the ground beside your chair, where it would have been within easy reach in case of sudden attack on you. This action would have symbolized a bloodless attack on our territory and signified to us that, while you were presently unguarded, you had powerful support and any harm or insult offered you would have brought dire retribution. You are Galactics, after all; such power is available to you."

He looked toward the lander and the black and silver emblem prominently displayed on its hull, and went on. "Had you done the natural thing, we would have exchanged a few words about the weather or something equally unimportant, then you would have had to return to your ship because nobody else would have spoken to you. But you did not do the natural thing, you did the right thing. You voluntarily disarmed yourselves as is the custom when one is among family or close friends. It is unusual for complete ignorance and correct behavior to go together."

He paused for a moment to hold both hands palm upward for a moment, then stood up.

"There is nothing I can tell you about this stinking, inhabited swamp we call home," he went on, "that could possibly interest a couple of Galactics. Much more important things are being done in the First's Estate, but special permission is required before overflying his territory—"

"We are not Galactic Citizens," Martin broke in, hiding his disappointment over what seemed to be the sudden end of the meeting while trying desperately to prolong it. "And we would much rather talk to people who did not fire missles at us. And to strangers like us, all news is interesting, and probably important. Besides, we are taught that it is theoretically possible to discover and deduce everything that there is to know about any planetary culture simply by talking to one of its members, given the opportunity and sufficient time."

"Sufficient—" the Keidi began, and made a startled, braying sound. "The few years remaining to me are insufficient for such a project and, forgetful though I have become, I do not remember offering extended hospitality. Quickly, bring your chairs inside."

"Is it all right?" Martin asked anxiously, looking at the distant circle of watchers who were becoming fewer by the moment. "Do they trust us now?"

"No," the Keidi said, "but it's going to rain."

The first large drops were slapping into the mud as they entered the shelter.

They followed him into a small, unlit, outer room, stumbling against what felt like a long, thin table and several chairs similar to the two they were carrying, and through a heavy curtain into what was plainly the Keidi's living quarters. By the light of two wall-mounted candles Martin could make out the dim outlines of a bed, one big, low, thickly padded chair, a few large and small tables, wall cupboards, and many well-filled bookshelves, although not all of them were filled with books. The entire surface of one wall was covered by staves, mounted horizontally and labeled as if they were trophies of some kind. A few of them were decorated with colored bands and carvings and had long, highly polished metal ferrules, while the majority of them had the warped, knobbly look which suggested they had been whittled from the branches of young trees. There were two empty places in the display which, Martin felt sure, their newly acquired staves had occupied.

Although there were no ventilation openings visible, the room smelled fresh and clean except for the faint, acrid odor of the candles. Both the visibility and the smell increased as the Keidi moved around the room lighting more of them.

"An interesting collection," Martin said, nodding toward the wall and trying to find something complimentary to say about the place.

"Most of them were sent to me when their owners died," the Keidi said, "and some are the gifts of important people who felt obligated to me. I like to look at them when, as sometimes happens, I wonder if I am as content here as I expected to be. But I can only use one at a time, so you may keep those two as long as you need them."

Martin, who had been about to replace his staff on the wall, wondered what kind of being this was who would lend his trophies, which occupied pride of place in the room, to a couple of strangers.

"We, too, are obligated to you," Martin said.

"You are," the Keidi said, dropping heavily into his seat and motioning for them to bring their own chairs closer. Even on those totally alien features Martin thought that he could read incredulity as he went on. "If two of you are going to deduce the details of our entire culture by questioning only me, you had better begin."

"The questions," Martin said carefully, "would include asking why some people shoot missles at us while others extend hospitality."

"Some people," the Keidi replied, "maintain themselves in constant readiness for war, and react violently against any threat to their security. A Federation World ship would be seen as the ultimate threat. Then there are other people, some very selfish, unscrupulous, culturally undernourished people, like myself, who might consider the surrender of half a day's time and two well balanced staves a fair exchange for the chance to talk to beings whose background and thought processess are unfamiliar. Will you answer as well as ask questions?"

"Of course," Martin said, relaxing in his chair. By sheer good fortune they had met an elderly, dissatisfied, and very bored Keidi who wanted to talk as badly as they wanted to listen.

"In that case—" he began, when the loud, erratic beating of a drum made him break off. He made a sound which did not translate, and went on. "I'm wanted."

The candlelight paled in the suddenly bright, electrically lit room.

"And the early power switch-on means that I'm wanted urgently, on the radio. It is possible that you will have a long time to consider your questions."

He moved quickly to the radio which, in the candlelight, Martin had mistaken for an incomplete shelf of books, and snapped, "What is the problem?"

"A signal for you from across the river," came the reply. "Relayed from the Estate, coded most urgent, and action immediate—"

"I can't remember a message from the First which wasn't," their Keidi said.

"You are to contact Frontier Camp Eleven direct," the voice went on. "It would be advisable to send your visitors away first."

The Keidi made another untranslatable sound, then bent forward, apparently to change the frequency before going on, "Frontier Eleven, you have an urgent message for me. There are strangers here. What is it?"

There was a moment's hissing silence, then another, harsher voice said, "The dregels take you, our signal went out just after dawn! Why don't you people keep proper radio watch so we wouldn't have to waste time on helio relays? This is an urgent—"

"Why don't you people give us enough fuel to run a generator all day?" the Keidi broke in. "And why don't you stop wasting time talking about wasting time, and tell me what is wrong there?"

"Very well," the voice replied. "But if the channel isn't secure, use voice code . . ."

The message was brief and when the other paused for the reply, their Keidi protested, "But you're nearly three day's journey from here. Can't you use one of your own—"

"The First wants you, and quickly," the voice broke in. "Initial transport will be on a locally owned corsa, which should be saddled and waiting for you on the bridge by now, but a vehicle has been sent out to meet you. Understand this, you will not stop for any reason or any person. This will be a major obligation, a personal three-one on the First. Please, can you leave at once?"

"Yes," the Keidi said, and broke the connection.

Martin stood up quickly. Fingering his wrist unit he looked warningly at Beth, then said, "Plainly we have visited you at an inconvenient time, so we will return to our ship. Thank you for the staves and the hospitality, and if there is anything we can do to help you, it will be done. We hope to meet you again, soon."

The Keidi stared at them for a moment. "My apologies. If you wish to continue this conversation, and if all goes well, I should be back here in twenty days."

"You'll see us," Martin said under his breath, "much sooner than that."

They moved through the outer room, whose equipment and purpose was now clearly revealed by the electric lighting, and onto the slippery ground outside. It was raining heavily, but the staves enabled them to keep their balance and find a way back to the lander without taking another mudbath. Martin glanced back once to see the Keidi, loaded with a heavy backpack, leaving his shelter and heading for the island end of the bridge. By the time they were on board, he was walking quickly along the central span with his staff threaded through the straps of his pack. On the mainland end of the bridge they could see a figure holding the reins of a large, hairy quadruped which had to be the corsa.

Chapter 21

"I have a feeling that we're going to become seriously involved with that being," Beth said when the lander was climbing through the cloud blanket.

"We are," Martin said enthusiastically. "He's just about perfect! An important person, a local medic, with a great many people obligated to him, who is in a tearing hurry and needing but not wanting our help. Are we under radar surveillance?"

"No," Beth said, and added, "The missile they sent after us wasn't radar-directed, either. Looks as though the aimers have to eyeball the targets."

The ground scanner's image showed a picture of the mainland end of the bridge and, about fifteen miles inland, a heavily wooded depression in an area which the sensors declared to be uninhabited. Their Keidi and his mount were a moving black knot on the thin, wet thread of roadway linking the bridge with the woods.

"That looks like a good pickup spot there," Martin said, "where the road runs through these trees."

Half an hour later the lander was in a small clearing about two hundred yards from the edge of the road, and Martin was trying to shelter from the rain which was gusting into the open entry port while he listened for the sound of the Keidi's approach. But when he did hear the corsa's hooves, he realized that for some reason the rider had increased speed. Swearing, he jumped to the ground and ran stumbling and slipping in the darkness under the trees to the edge of the road just as the rider emerged from the curtain of rain.

Too breathless even to speak, he staggered into the middle of the road, waving his staff awkwardly to attract the other's attention.

He succeeded.

The rider leaned sideways in the saddle and swung his staff in a wide arc. Martin dropped to his knees as the metal tip whistled past the top of his head. Then the Keidi checked his mount, turned, and came galloping back to the attack.

"Stop it!" Martin yelled, jumping back to the rougher ground of the roadside. "I mean you no harm."

This time the Keidi did not swing the staff as he went past. Instead, he calmed his mount and returned at a walking pace.

"Oh, it's one of the Galactics," he said in obvious anger, looking from Martin to the dimly seen outlines of the lander. "That was a stupid thing to do. Don't you know that if anyone wanted to take me or my animal, this is the place they'd try to do it? But no, you know nothing. I'm in a hurry. Why did you stop me?"

"I'm sorry," Martin said. "We know you're in a hurry, and the reason for it. We offer you a fast and comfortable ride to the First's Estate."

"So you know," the Keidi said, tightening his grip on the staff. "But in my home you pretended to know nothing. I do not want to know your reasons for lying then or for interfering now. Stand clear!"

"Wait, please," Martin cried, squinting up at the rain-blurred image. It was like trying to hold an important conversation while taking a shower. Carefully, so that the movement would not appear threatening, he raised both arms to shoulder level in front of him and tapped his wrist.

"We didn't lie to you back there," he said, "and we didn't know anything until you began talking on the radio. This is a communications device linked to the mother ship's translation computer. It enables us to understand any kind of intelligence bearing sounds regardless of how they are produced. Since it is programmed to handle every system of other-species communication, it had no trouble changing your simple verbal code so that we received it in clear."

Still the other did not respond. Martin brushed the rain from his face and went on quickly, "The message in voice code was to the effect that a pregnant female directly descended from the First, was overdue by twenty-three days, and that skilled assistance was urgently required because of extreme debilitation and consequent inability to complete the birth process. The First wants you and nobody else. All obligations of time and material incurred during your trip to Frontier Camp Eleven would be personally accepted by the First, and discharged threefold.

"Until I overheard that message and saw your treatment room on the way out," Martin added, "I didn't know that you are a doctor."

"Obstetrician," the Keidi said.

"I guessed as much," Martin said. "And I thought that you would want to reach your patient with minimum delay. So as not to risk compromising you with your people in the city, I thought it better to pick you up where we would not be observed. Our sensors show this area to be inhabited only by small animals."

He gestured towards the lander. "It's a small vessel, so we are unable to take your mount. But you could be attending your patient within the hour."

"Within the hour," the Keidi said, "we could all be blown out of the sky by one of the First's missiles."

Martin shivered in his lightweight suit, thinking that he had never in all his life felt so wet and miserable. Carefully, he said, "I don't think we would be shot at if we matched communications frequency and explained our intentions. Given the circumstances, the First might even feel obligated to us. But if missiles are sent against us, we can take evasive action and land you as close as is safe to the camp so that a ground vehicle can be sent to pick you up. Either way, we'll be safe and you will be there much sooner."

The Keidi was silent for a moment, then said quietly, "Is it your intention, then, to place the First and myself under an obligation to you?"

"Yes, I suppose so," Martin said, trying to stop his teeth chattering. "I mean, it wouldn't do any harm to make friends."

"Always provided you choose them carefully," the Keidi replied, dismounting. He ran a hand through the sodden fur covering the corsa's small, cone-shaped head, and went on, "Very well, I am obligated for the ride with you. And don't worry about Brown Bag, here. I've ridden it many times and it knows its way home a lot better than I do."

Within a very few minutes they were inside the ship with the control deck's air conditioning blow-drying their wet clothing. The lander was already high above the rainclouds and Beth was trying to raise the Estate.

"Frontier Camp Eleven," she was repeating quietly, "this is Federation vessel Three Three Three Nine Five. Come in, please..."

The response, when it came, was harsh and unfriendly.

"This is Camp Eleven. Are you the intruder which violated our airspace earlier today? If so, you will withdraw immediately or risk—"

"We apologize for the intrusion," Beth said pleasantly, "and were unaware of the violation until you fired a warning shot at us—"

"A *warning* shot!..." began the other in an incredulous voice.

"...This is the lander of an orbiting hypership, a small vessel with no offensive armament. We carry a crew of two plus one passenger, the doctor you requested, who is being given rapid transportation to your camp. With your permission we will arrive—"

"Permission denied!" the voice responded sharply. "You will not overfly this area again, and you will be destroyed should you try to do so. Is this understood?"

"It is not understood," Beth replied, in a much less pleasant tone. "We are not hostile and our intention is simply to assist . . ." She broke off because their passenger was waving his hands at her, then added, "The doctor wishes to speak to you."

"Very well," the other said. "Voice code only, please."

The Keidi glanced at Martin's wrist unit and said, "That would be a complete waste of time. I want to speak directly to the First. While you're arranging that, remember that a personal three-to-one obligation was offered to anyone helping me get to the patient quickly. Naturally, we didn't expect a couple of passing Galactics to take up the offer, but they did and they can get me there a hell of a lot faster than a corsa and your clapped-out land vehicles. So check with the First before you say or do anything you might regret.

"In the meantime," he went on, "I want a detailed report on the patient's condition. Has that jumped-up ward attendant you call a medical officer done anything for her and if so, what?"

"Maintain your present position," came the reply.

There was a long, hissing silence from the speaker, broken by Martin who said impatiently, "That isn't necessary. They don't have radar and so won't know if we close to a distance where we can respond quickly if they decide to let us land. What do you say, Doctor?"

"You are a stranger here," the Keidi replied. "The First owns and has civilized the largest stretch of territory on this, our only temperate continent, and he maintains a screen of lookouts well beyond his borders. If they reported sighting you it could make everybody very nervous. The First has a very large, well-disciplined, and personally obligated organization, and has maintained and strengthened it by not taking chances. But he has dreams of continued territorial expansion and the return of the obs owing after his death. In short, he dreams of founding a dynasty and that, because of some as yet undefined prenatal complications, is the reason why I was sent for."

The Keidi was slumped comfortably in the supernumerary's postion, looking relaxed and half-asleep in the warmth of the control deck. Martin reminded himself that this was a very old, tired, and talkative Keidi, and there might never be a better chance to have questions answered.

"It seems to me that the Estate is better organized and has more amenities than your city," Martin commented, "and the First would be glad to have you. Wouldn't you be more gainfully employed, and be able to help many more patients, if you moved to the Estate?"

The doctor opened his eyes and stared at him for a long moment without speaking, then he said, "And it seems that the only thing you people want is information. Now, quite apart from the First's obligations in this matter I, personally, am obligated for what you are trying to do for me. So far you have accepted two staves from me. How many questions must I answer before the remainder of my obligation to you is discharged?"

Martin started to laugh, then changed it quickly to a cough. The Keidi might not be joking. He said carefully, "Is the value of the answer set by the questioner or the questioned? If you were to answer as many questions as there is time for before we land, would that be considered fair? And if the First isn't there, can a subordinate act in his absence?"

"That is four questions," the doctor said. "Do you wish me to begin answering them?"

"Please."

"Very well," the Keidi said. "My reasons not joining the First are ethical and economic. He has obligated a number of self-styled and largely self-trained medics, but their reputations are such that his people try very hard not to return duty and obedience obligations which would involve the risk of serious injury. If he had a fully trained, pre-Exodus surgeon on his establishment, the First would mount, and his people accept, more highrisk operations. By remaining in the city and contracting for special obs like this one, I like to think that his soldiers will take greater care and sustain fewer casualties, so I'm doing everybody a favor. Myself included, since the discomfort, uncertainty, and personal freedom of living in the city far outweigh the tight security and severely limited choices of action offered by the First. The economic advantage is that, as a visiting specialist, I command a greater ob than any member of the First's so-called Family who may already be under a life obligation."

"I begin to understand!" Martin said excitedly. "The tiny fraction of the original population remaining on Keida was too small to support the pre-Exodus financial structures, so you adopted an exchange and barter system. Your own specialist experience is exchanged for the First's fuel oil, out-of-season food, or whatever else you need. But that makes you a very important person back there. Quite apart from the medical service provided to your own people, you are one of the city's prime resources . . ."

The Keidi held up one hand. "You may deduce the answers to your own questions if you wish, but they will still count. Well?"

"Please go on," Martin said.

"The First is certainly there," the doctor went on, "because the mother-to-be is second generation by direct descent, so he would not be anywhere else. Almost certainly the delay is due to his trying to decide whether or not to place himself under an obligation to a couple of Galactics.

"After what the Federation did to Keida," he continued, "they do not like you people. That should not surprise you. They would like nothing better than that you leave this world alone. I'm surprised your offer of help wasn't rejected at once. The condition of the female must be serious."

"But surely they know that we want only to help," Martin protested, "that we won't insist on them honoring their obligation because, well, they have nothing we want."

"They have information," the Keidi reminded him.

Martin was silent. Over the past two decades such blind, unreasoning hostility had become completely foreign to his experience, not only among the Citizens of the Federation World but also on the planets whose intelligent and visually frightful inhabitants he had learned to understand. Some of the Teldins and the Blind Ones had displayed hostility, until the reason for it was understood and the misunderstandings in speech and behavior which had caused it were modified.

But he was forgetting that the tiny remnant of the population left on Keida was not normal people. They were the antisocial elements, the beings who had failed to pass the very liberal requirements for citizenship, the Keidi predators—in short, the wolves who now had only other wolves instead of sheep on which to prey. They were the Undesirables.

But was this aging medic, whose cloak and staff were still dripping rainwater onto the deck at his feet, and who was trying to bring aid to an expectant mother, was *he* an Undesirable? And would the soon-to-be-born offspring of the First's grandchild he was visiting inherit the mother's Undesirability? And what about the descendants of all the other Undesirables on this mutilated planet?

For the first time since he had been given this ill-defined assignment, Martin felt seriously troubled. The Federation, surely the most philosophically and technologically advanced structure conceivable by mortal minds, should not be responsible for a situation which was so grossly unfair and morally wrong. Was the Federation simply the end result of major population surgery, and a refusal to even consider the fate of the Undesirables, discarded and still proliferating on their denuded homeworlds?

The answer, based on his knowledge of the induction procedures used on many worlds, was yes. But then why had he been sent here? Was it to investigate the situation and try to devise a method of separating children and grandchildren from their Undesirable elders, and somehow influence them into induction centers for testing before they became so tainted by environmental and behavioral influences as to be unsalvageable?

Surely not, Martin thought, that would be a cruel and even more undesirable answer.

The Keidi had stopped talking and was waiting for more questions.

Beth, whose thought processess paralleled Martin's so closely that he sometimes wondered if she was tele-

pathic, said, "Judging by your friendly approach to us
and the very laudable work you intend to do after what
should have been a long, uncomfortable, and probably
dangerous journey, I have difficulty in believing that you
are an Undesirable or that—"

She broke off as the muscles around the Keidi's horn
tightened suddenly into spasm. Then they relaxed
slightly and he said, "You will *never* use that word to any
Keidi. You will not use it to me again."

Red-faced with embarrassment, Beth was opening her
mouth to apologise when the speaker came suddenly to
life.

"Intruder, Camp Eleven," the voice said briskly. "You
may proceed. Your passenger will indicate the landing
area on arrival. A vehicle will await him. No others will
leave the ship, nor will they appear at an open exit port.
Is this understood?"

"Understood," Beth responded. "We're on our way."

When Camp Eleven was below them, Martin told the
doctor that the hypership's library included physiological
and clinical data on all Federation World species, and
that the Keida material was instantly available if needed.
But the doctor did not respond other than to point out
the landing area. Plainly he was still angry at being called
an Undesirable, and it seemed that the First's people did
not want to speak to them either because the camp transmitter was also silent.

They were watching the vehicle carrying the doctor as
it was heading toward the perimeter fence, when Beth
said "I'm sorry. I had no intention of hurting his feelings.
But he is old enough to have been one of the original
Undesirables, and must be fully aware of the reasons
why they were left behind, so I don't understand his extreme sensitivity to the use of the word. Have I messed
up your contact?"

Martin thought for a moment, then said, "Don't worry
about it. If you hadn't used the word I would have,
sooner or later, with the same result. But I'm pretty sure
that our friend is not, in fact, one of the original Undesirables."

He could well imagine the tiny minority of Keida's
rejects convincing themselves that they were superior

rather than inferior beings. They had been left to survive as best they could on a virtually empty, scarred, and exhausted world, with only the unwanted scraps of their old technology and culture remaining to them, while their soft, comfort-loving fellows left for the Federation World. They had survived and adapted and reorganized, well enough for the supervisor to assign Beth and Martin to find out what was happening on Keida. So a certain pride in their inferiority, even an intense reverse snobbery and anger toward the soft outsiders who considered *them* to be inferior, was understandable.

But their Keidi doctor did not fit that neat psychological pigeonhole.

He had been the only person in his city to speak to them, and give advice and information. He had not been over friendly, but neither had he been blindly hostile like the First's people, and he had known about many other-species life forms. The mural depicting these life forms could only be seen inside the induction centers, from which Undesirables were automatically excluded.

"You're thinking out loud again," Beth said suddenly. "If he isn't an Undesirable, what is he?"

"A potential Citizen who chose not to go through the induction procedure," Martin replied. "Maybe he had an aversion to following the crowd, or the crowd going to the Federation World contained the usual proportion of medics while the Undesirables who remained had few, if any. I'm beginning to like this Keidi."

As they watched the doctor's vehicle moving along the old, neatly repaired roadways between the rows of long, low buildings, Martin decided that Frontier Camp Eleven was what it had always been, a military base. Such establishments were not needed on the Federation World so they had been left on Keida, untouched and unoccupied except by the warrior Undesirables—as opposed to the civilians temporarily in uniform—who felt at home in them. The taller, windowless buildings grouped around the landing area would once have contained aircraft and surface vehicles, and possibly still did, although the people qualified to maintain them had to be a dying breed.

When the vehicle stopped at what was obviously the

administration center, their Keidi entered quickly and
without any hesitation moved deep inside the building—
obviously he knew his way around—to stop finally in a
large, long room containing a line of beds, only one of
which was occupied. Excluding the doctor, there were
eight other people in the ward.

They could follow his movements because the sensor
display had the doctor tagged, but the others were just
hazy, insubstantial shapes standing deep inside a structure whose corridors, rooms, and walls showed as
ghostly transparencies. As the others were identified in
conversation they, too, would be tagged.

"I'm getting something now," Beth said.

They heard the doctor asking the patient how she felt
and, interspersed with untranslatable sounds of pain, the
female's reply. Another Keidi, a medic judging by the
language, joined the conversation with a fuller, more
clinical description of the case history.

"She's in very bad shape," Beth said. Her concern for
another female at a time like this, regardless of species,
was reflected in her voice.

"That she is," Martin said. "But I think our friend is
talking to the First. He's pointing his horn at that Keidi
who is standing alone halfway down the ward. Listen!"

If it was the First he was addressing, then the doctor
was sounding both insubordinate and very, very angry.

"This patient's condition was described to me with
minimum accuracy and maximum optimism," he was
saying. "Not only was such behavior professionally inex-
cusable, it means that had I come here by the usual
method my journey would have been wasted, because
the patient and unborn would have died long before my
arrival. Distasteful as it is to all of us, the obligation to
the Galactics is truly a major one. Now will all nonmedi-
cal personnel please withdraw."

A bitter argument broke out among the people who
had left the bedside to join the First during which, as is
the way with all eavesdroppers, the listeners heard nothing good about themselves. They were hated, intensely
and bitterly, by all Keidi for no other reason than their
identity.

"The First shows some grandparental concern, at

least," Beth said after one particularly vicious outburst. "I'm trying to tighten the sensor focus on him, but there's some interference which...Oh, no."

Figures and graphics chased each other across the sensor screen for a moment, then she looked up with the color draining from her face. Dully, she said, "The First has been in recent proximity to shielded fissionable material."

"That's impossible!" Martin burst out. "Are you telling me that there are nuclear weapons in the Camp? And if so, why the blazes didn't your sensors spot them at once?"

"Three reasons," Beth replied angrily. "I did not expect to find radiation, so the sensors were not instructed to look for it, and they haven't spotted it now because it isn't here. The original source of contamination is somewhere beyond the range of the lander's sensors. The hypership is scanning for it now."

It was the Federation's policy to forbid all nuclear power sources and weaponry to Undesirables and, long before an Exodus was complete, the supporting technology and fissionable material were invariably dismantled and buried beyond all possibility of recovery by the limited technical resources of those left behind. This was done because of another inflexible rule, that a species which had developed such dreadful and long-acting mass-destruction weapons was required to keep them on-planet as a constant reminder to the Undesirables remaining of the principal reason why they had been rejected as Federation Citizens.

Atomic weapons in the hands of Undesirables was something which just could not happen. But it had somehow happened here.

"The radiation dosage is minimal," Beth went on. "Not enough to have any but very long-term effects. Could that be the reason why the First stayed so far away from the patient? Out of consideration for his unborn great-grandchild."

The possibility that a group of Keidi Undesirables was in possession of nuclear armaments, or even a single device, had driven all thought of the patient from Martin's mind. But before he could reply, the argument which had been raging in the ward died away to be replaced by a single authoritative voice.

The First had reached a decision.

"Degrading and abhorrent as it is to all of us," he began, "I am heavily obligated to these Galactics, and I see no other course than to try to discharge this obligation as quickly as possible." He swung his horn to point at the doctor. "Can a meeting be arranged?"

"Ask them," said the doctor, looking up briefly from his patient. "They seemed quite happy for me to discharge my obligation by supplying information. Now get out of here."

"A meeting with the First," Martin said grimly, "can most certainly be arranged."

Chapter 22

THE First's invitation was not transmitted until more than an hour later—plainly they were dealing with a very cautious Keidi—and within a few minutes there was a convoy of three open vehicles moving toward the lander. The one in the middle contained only the First and his driver while the other two were crowded, presumably with guards. But Beth's attention was concentrated solely on the hypership's sensor data which was being relayed to her screen.

"Look at this," she said excitedly. "Just there, on the inner slope and floor of that inactive volcano."

She enlarged the area to show the piles of recently dug rock and soil which glittered as if they had been seeded with diamonds, large numbers of tents, three tall log buildings which looked like wooden lighthouses, and a high, uneven stockade enclosing everything. The crater walls and floor were overgrown but not wooded, so the timber for those structures must have been brought in from many miles away.

"The records show that to have been the original site of a large underground missile storage facility," she went on, "later encased in a thick shell of fused earth to render it impervious to the limited technology of the natives. But that was before volcanic activity smashed the protective shell and opened the original artificial cavern to the surface. Now the Keidi could dig down to it with their bare hands, but they've brought in some old earth-moving machinery and are—"

"They're moving soil, not earth," Martin said. He felt suddenly afraid of what he was about to hear, and was trying vainly to change the subject. "Remember, this isn't Earth."

"Don't be so pedantic, dammit!" she said angrily. "They've uncovered three long-range missiles, and it looks as though they've salvaged enough of the ancillary equipment and solid fuel boosters to reconstruct a surface launching facility inside those wooden towers. From what I can see, the missiles are ready to launch. It looks as if we've arrived in time to stop a small nuclear war. We'll have to do something about this. Shall I instruct the hypership to knock it out?"

This was what he had not wanted to hear, Martin thought as he stared silently at the screen. Beth was able to abstract more information from sensor displays than he could, but she had not yet noticed or did not remember the significance of the area of cleared ground in the shadow of the stockade, and the matrix of tiny, evenly spaced white dots covering it.

They were graves, each marked in Keidi fashion with a single white stone, and almost certainly radiation casualties of the salvage operations. There must have been hundreds of them.

"Naturally," she went on when Martin did not respond, "a prior warning would be sent to evacuate the area. But these people are *stupid*! There are so few of them left, this is their only temperate and fertile land mass, so why do they want to start a nuclear war?"

"We won't do anything," Martin said firmly, "until after the meeting when we'll know a lot more about the situation here. Officially we know nothing about that place, and knocking it out would not endear us to the First or—"

"It would endear us to the people he intends using those missiles against," Beth said dryly. "But how were they able to do it? The big universities and nuclear laboratories have gone. Surely the building of a launching facility requires specialist knowledge."

Martin sighed and said, "The knowledge was available, from maintenance manuals, test records, drawings. It was the hardware which was withdrawn, not the literature. Probably the First and some of his Undesirable friends helped run the original facility and, with that kind of special knowledge heading the project, it could be done."

He leaned forward and with his index finger traced the outline of the Keidi burial ground, then added quietly, "The First knows enough to direct operations from a distance. They were probably first and second generation and had no previous experience with radiation, and learned the hard way."

It was Beth's turn to be silent. The external mike was picking up the sounds of approaching vehicles and heavy rain.

"This is nasty," Martin went on, "but right now we need information more than anything else. Instruct the hypership to make a planet-wide radiation scan, to check that none of the other storage facilities have been breached, by earthquakes or anything else. I'll take a foodpack in case . . . Quickly, they're here."

The First had left his vehicle and was already walking toward the lander as Martin opened the entry port. He was a smaller and thinner version of the doctor, and the speaking horn which he directed at Martin was discolored and heavily wrinkled with what could have been advanced age or disease.

There was a moment's silence, then the First said, "Plainly your species has physical requirements which differ from ours, so that the hospitality I am offering you will be nonmaterial, and consist only of the satisfaction of our curiosity about each other. The meeting may be a lengthy one, so I thought that you should bring a supply of your food and liquid with you."

"It was a thought shared," Martin said, pointing at his foodpack. Not wanting to sound too eager, he went on, "We thank you for the invitation to exchange information, but we feel that for personal and family reasons this may be a bad time for you. Our vessel is small, with limited endurance, and a visit to the mother ship to replenish our power cells is overdue. We can return at a more convenient time, early tomorrow if you wish it."

The Keidi looked from Martin to Beth, who had just entered the lock, and said, "You show consideration, off-worlders. But now would be the best time, while the memory of our obligation to you is still fresh. And rest assured, your lives, which would not be threatened by any Keidi, will be under the personal protection of the First Father of the Estate."

"Thank you," Martin said. "It is nevertheless reassuring to have such a powerful friend."

"I am deeply obligated to you," the First said, his focusing muscles twitching. "I am not your friend."

A few minutes later they were sharing the hard, rear seat of the First's vehicle, with little to see but rain-soaked pavement and the backs of two Keidi heads.

"I had time to deploy the meteorite shield," she said, holding up her wrist to show that the translator was switched off. "Anyone going too close to the lander will get a bruised speaking horn. There are tracers on our..."

"Better switch on," Martin said dryly, "or they'll think we're talking about them behind their backs."

Beth gave a dutiful laugh and did so, then leaned forward to say, "As a female, I am naturally concerned about the condition of the First's granddaughter. Is there any news?"

The First turned around to face them. "There is indeed news, of a new addition to the family and Estate. A male child, well formed and healthy. The doctor is still working on the patient, but says that the prognosis for both mother and child is good."

"Our congratulations..." Beth began.

"Would you like to accompany me to the Camp hospital," the First continued, "so that you will be able to see the newborn, and judge the extent of my obligation to you and, of course, the quantity of information which must be provided to discharge it?

"Among the females of my species," he went on before they could reply, "a particular pleasure is derived from the close appraisal of a newborn. There are males who do not share this pleasure, and consider a newborn Keidi to be a small, squalling creature of great ugliness, but they are expected to keep such thoughts to themselves and join in the general admiration."

"It is the same among Earth-humans," Beth said, laughing.

The First made an untranslatable sound and said, "I am impressed with the ease with which we speak and understand each other. How is this done?"

Martin unfastened his wrist unit and held it up for the Keidi to see. "This device houses the two-way translator," he said, "and it can also be switched to communications mode if we wish to contact the lander or the mother ship."

There was no harm in letting the Keidi leader know that, while the two off-worlders were unarmed and defenseless, powerful help was available within moments.

"And what is the purpose of the metal tube clipped to your foodpack?" the First asked, obviously worried about concealed weapons.

Martin handed the tube to the other, explaining that while Keidi water was quite safe for them to use provided it contained no substances toxic to Earth-human metabolism, the device was an analyzer which would detect the presence of harmful trace elements.

"Like your timepiece," the First said, handing it back, "I expect it is capable of performing other wonders?"

"No," Martin replied, "this one has no other talents."

Outside the building containing the maternity ward, the vehicles stopped and Martin and Beth were told to wait in the vehicle while the First went, it said, to personally reassure his people about the off-planet visitors. He returned a few minutes later with four large, silent Keidi, who escorted them inside. The First's personal bodyguard's, Martin guessed. But a few minutes later he wondered if he had guessed wrong.

Beth's suddenly worried expression showed that she, too, had realized that they were heading in the wrong direction.

The problem was that they knew that it was the wrong direction, but, because the First did not know of and could not be told about their earlier sensor scan of the building, they were not supposed to know that it was the wrong direction.

It was the Keidi leader who was doing all the talking, keeping up such a continuous flow of conversation that it would have been impolite if not impossible to interrupt. He gave them a lot of very useful information as he described the maintenance work done on the building's heating and lighting systems to provide comfortable accommodation for the people who were joining his family in increasing numbers. Even an off-worlder could see that there was no comparison between the standard of life in the mud city they had visited—or on one of the isolated farming settlements scattered across the continent—and that which was available here and now. And in future years, as the population and security of the Estate increased, the effort now required for border defense would be directed inward so that living standards would further improve.

When they were escorted downstairs and into a dimly lit corridor, Martin had to say something before Beth did. She looked close to panic, which was how he felt.

"Why is your granddaughter being kept below ground level?" he asked quietly. "Is it warmer and more comfortable for her down here, or perhaps cooler?"

The First's horn remained pointed toward the floor while they took several more paces, then he raised it only to say, "We are going into the next room on the left."

As one of the escort opened the door for them, Martin hesitated and looked at Beth. Her face was pale, her lips pressed together and bloodless so that in the dim light her eyes and brows showed in stark contrast, as if drawn in charcoal on gray parchment. They both knew that they were walking into some kind of trap, but had to pretend that they knew nothing and walk right in.

Or did they?

Through the opening door Martin glimpsed the interior of a small compartment containing two of the high Keidi beds placed against opposite walls, a tall cabinet and a low bench or table. The walls were bare of decoration and the beds had mattresses but no bed linen.

"Run!" Martin said quietly.

He spun around and sprinted back the way they had come. But he had gone only three paces before his legs were kicked from under him and two Keidi grabbed his body and rolled him onto his back. One of them knelt on his legs and leaned forward to spread-eagle and immobilize his arms against the floor, the flared speaking horn puffing a sour smell into his face. The other Keidi grabbed him by the hair and banged his head hard against the floor while the fingers of the other hand were clamped tightly around his mouth.

Through pain-misted eyes he saw that Beth was on the floor and being similarly restrained. He tried to call to her, but the Keidi hand pressing against his mouth made it impossible to speak and very difficult to breathe.

Suddenly the First was bending over him and the grip around his left wrist tightened. He felt hard Keidi fingers digging into his wrist, pushing under the strap, tearing off the watch and with it a large piece of skin. His angry reaction was muffled by the Keidi hand.

"Your translation and communication devices have been removed," the First said, "so that neither of you will be able to talk to your mother ship. Your clothing and foodpack will also be removed and examined for concealed information gathering or communication devices, but you may retain the food itself and the liquids analyzer. You would have found this process to be more dignified and comfortable if you had entered the room and it had been performed on the beds. But you became suspicious and your attempt to escape precipitated matters."

The Keidi leader was holding both their translators in his hands as he went on, "Your speaking orifice will be uncovered so that we can talk. But you will talk only to me. If I suspect that you are trying to send a message to the ship, you will be stopped from speaking and possibly damaged. Since the methods of attachment and fastening are strange to us, one of your arms will also be freed so that you can assist with the removal of your clothing. While doing so, if I think that you are trying to activate a device concealed in the clothing, physical damage will result. If you understand and agree, spread out the digits of one hand."

Martin did as instructed and the restraining hands were removed from his hair, mouth, and arm. He turned his head to see that Beth's head and arm were also free. He took several deep, welcome breaths and tried to ignore the throbbing pain in the back of his skull. When he spoke Martin did not even try to be polite, because politeness in his situation would have been suspect.

Angrily, he said, "I became suspicious because I expected to see a ward containing medical attendants, the doctor, and your granddaughter. We came here at your invitation, and under your protection, to see the newborn, not to spy on you. This restraint and body search is totally unnecessary!"

He was pretending to believe that the First's only concern was camp security, in the hope that if he played the outraged innocent, the other would be chivied into revealing more than intended. But if the old adage about attack being the best form of defense had its counterpart on Keida; the First knew exactly how to counterattack.

"You will both assist with the removal of your clothing," the First said calmly, "and you will listen without interrupting while I speak."

Unzipping the front of his one-piece, insulated suit, Martin raised himself to a sitting position while they peeled it down from his shoulders and arms and, knocking him onto his back again, pulled it and the attached boots off inside-out. His undergarment gave them no trouble at all, and he was pinioned once again by the arms and legs with the floor tiles hard and cold against his back.

"Some verbal misdirection is customary during forced negotiations with an enemy to whom one is obligated," the First continued, "or with those whose active support of the family is uncertain. And your intelligence is low indeed if you thought that I had any intention of subjecting my granddaughter, in her present weakened state or ever, to the psychological trauma of a meeting with two of the Keida-destroying Galactics whose species is as visually repellant as the wrongs their hellish world has perpetrated against us are morally repulsive. Let them rise."

The Keidi hands relaxed their hold and he scrambled slowly to his feet, wincing with the pain which exploded in his head. Beth was already standing and glaring at the First. Martin knew that the deep pink color flooding her face and neck was not due to embarrassment.

"You will enter the compartment prepared for you and spend the time there considering your position," the First went on. "In spite of the terrible wrong you Galactics have done to my people, I still feel a personal obligation to you. And it may be possible for you to deepen and extend this obligation, and thereby improve the accommodation's standards of comfort, by cooperating with me in various ways toward the future betterment of my people. I will leave you now to think."

Two large, Keidi hands struck the back of Martin's shoulders, propelling him into the room. He turned in time to keep Beth from falling as she was pushed in behind him. Then the door slammed shut and there was darkness except for the tiny, dim rectangle of light high on the door which was a Keidi eye-level grill.

Chapter 23

"THAT two-faced, long-nosed, hypocritical son of a—" Beth began in an angry undertone, when Martin pulled her close to him with one arm and used his free hand to cover her mouth.

"I feel stupid," Martin said loudly, turning his face toward the door. "When I saw that all of the doors in the corridor had viewing grills I should have realized that it was a detention area. His granddaughter may not even be in this building."

He was reminding her that they were not supposed to know anything about the layout of the building and that their chances of escaping would be increased if the First remained in ignorance of the earlier sensor scan. He felt her nod once to signify that she understood, then she bit his finger to show her disapproval of the manhandling.

"Are you hurt?" Martin asked loudly. They could hear the quiet movements of the Keidi on the other side of the door. They were probably listening to the captured translators, and Martin wanted them to hear what he had to say.

"Only my dignity," Beth said. The voice was steady but her whole body had begun to shake. "What about you? I didn't like the sound your skull made against the floor."

"I think my head is damaged," he replied, and made a loud noise which he knew would not translate. "There is a large swelling, it is bleeding, and my thinking is confused. The medical pouch was removed with the suits. I must speak to the First. Will he be able to hear me on the translator from inside the cell?"

"Yes," she replied, catching the ball neatly. "He can hear everything we say."

Martin winced as he felt exploring fingers on the back of his head, then she stood on tip-toe to put her lips against his ear.

"The translator pickup isn't all that sensitive," she said in a barely audible whisper, "and according to the Keidi physiological data, neither is their hearing. You have a whopping bump growing back there, and you've lost some skin. Do you really have a concussion?"

"No," Martin breathed into her ear, "but act as if I need the doctor, badly."

"You're *bleeding*!" she said loudly. "The skin is broken and the way is open for infection by other-species bacteria, and there may be underlying damage to the bone structure. You—" She broke off, turned her head toward the door and yelled, "My life-mate needs medical attention! Please ask the doctor to come at once."

"Nice," Martin whispered approvingly. "You're scaring even me."

From the other side of the door they could hear soft hissing sounds—the Keidi seemed incapable of breathing quietly—but no other reaction. Martin guessed that the First had left a couple of guards and a translator outside with orders to listen and not speak. No doubt their words would be reported later, but in the meantime the apparent distress of one of the hated Galactics was of complete indifference to them.

Or was it?

"We've been left naked, cold, and in darkness, without external contact or means of measuring elapsed time," he whispered excitedly. "This is classic brainwashing technique designed to reduce our resistance to later—"

"Knowing what is being done to us," Beth said angrily, "isn't any great consolation right now. Dammit, my goose bumps have goose bumps."

"Not so loud," Martin said warningly. He gave another loud, theatrical groan and went on, "It means that the First wants something from us badly enough to go to all this trouble. He has already hinted as much, so we're in no immediate danger. There's a bed just behind you, sit on it so that your feet will be off the cold floor. There was a cabinet against the right wall which might hold blankets."

He gave her a reassuring squeeze and moved in the remembered direction of the cabinet. His eyes were becoming accustomed to the darkness, but the light from the door grill was still too dim for him to see anything clearly. An outstretched hand touched the cold, rough brickwork of the wall, and then the smooth, metal side of the cabinet.

It had a simple lever handle, and the door opened with a metallic screech of long unused hinges. He felt a thin, vertical cylinder which moved toward him as he touched it. He identified it as a brush handle when the stiff bristles scraped across his face. There was a sudden, metallic clatter and immediately the light came on and a Keidi eye appeared at the grill.

Beth slid off the bed and strode angrily toward the

door, where she raised her forearm and placed it across the grill opening. There was the sound of a heavy bolt being drawn and she jumped back quickly as the door slammed open and two Keidi burst in.

One remained in the doorway on guard while the other ran to the cabinet, knocked Martin aside, and began examining the interior. The lower two-thirds contained the bucket, brushes, and cleaning materials Martin had disturbed, and the upper section two blankets and pillows. Then the Keidi moved to a low, boxlike cabinet on the other side of the room, lifted its lid and looked inside before crouching to check under both beds before returning to the door.

One of the translators was suspended from his neck by a thick, woven cord threaded through the unbreakable bracelet. There was no way of retrieving it short of tearing the Keidi's head off. His speaking horn turned to point at Beth.

Harshly, he said, "You will not obscure the viewing grill again."

Beth placed clenched fists on her hips and glared at him. She said coldly, "Then you will not look through the viewing grill at me. In common with many other *civilized* races, my species has a nudity taboo. It is offensive degrading, and intensely embarrassing to have another person, regardless of sex or species, who is not my life-mate looking at my unclothed body. Do you hear and understand that?"

The Keidi continued to regard her for a moment, then he turned to follow the other guard into the corridor. The door was barred again but the lights remained on, and they heard one of them saying, "Females!"

The pillows and blankets raised a cloud of dust when he tossed them onto the bed, making both of them sneeze loudly. A Keidi eye appeared briefly at the grill, no doubt drawn by the strange, new, untranslatable noises, then went away again.

Martin gripped the center of a blanket in both hands and began rubbing the coarse material against the sharp, lower corner of the cabinet's metal door, covering the occasional squeak of hinges with a loud groan. Within a few minutes he had abraded a hole large enough to take his fingers. The material tore easily, and when the tear was large enough he lifted the blanket and pushed his head through the slit.

The humble poncho of Earth had returned to fashion, Martin thought dryly and began making one for Beth, adding slits for their arms. When the lights went out again they were sitting side by side on the edge of a bed with pillows between their feet and the cold floor.

"I never realized that you felt so strongly about nudity," he whispered. "Do you feel more comfortable now?"

"I don't, and I do," she replied. "But when I saw those blankets I thought that if I made a fuss about needing body coverings, and made them believe that it was a sociocultural imperative rather than a need to stay warm, we might stand a better chance of being allowed to keep them when the First comes back."

"I wouldn't have thought of that," Martin said approvingly. "But you're still trembling. One bed is big enough for both of us. We can pool our body heat. I'm worried about Keidi bugs."

"So am I," she whispered. "The mattress is filthy."

"I meant bugging devices," Martin went on. "But the dust in this place was undisturbed and there probably wasn't enough time to install them, so I'm pretty sure a whispered conversation will not be overheard.

"We need to do a lot of talking," he went on, "and we might as well be comfortable doing it. And to be on the safe side we can sandwich our heads between the two pillows and further deaden the sound. The Keidi will think that we always sleep that way. For extra warmth I was thinking that we could share one of our ponchos and . . ."

"I know what you're thinking," Beth whispered. "But for that I really do insist on privacy and freedom from other-species Peeping Toms. No. Besides, you have a headache."

You aren't joking, Martin thought as they lay on their sides with his body pressed tightly against her back, his free arm around her and their legs drawn up inside the blankets. Gradually they began to feel warm, although

Beth still broke into sudden fits of shivering which she said were caused by cold feet.

Martin was not feeling particularly brave himself right then.

Half a mile away, their lander stood, impervious to all external force and unapproachable by anyone but themselves. It represented the simplest means of escape or of summoning assistance, but plainly the First was not going to allow them anywhere near it. And high above Keida, the hypership, which was capable of unleashing forces that their captors could not even dream of in their worst nightmares, orbited in complete ignorance.

"You said that there is a coded message that will bring down big brother," Martin whispered, "and the guards have one of our watches. They will be suspicious if any attempt is made to shout a message through the grill. But I've had a knock on the head, and if I acted delirious and screamed a lot of nonsense words at them, they might not notice when I moved to the grill to shout the real message."

"Sorry," Beth whispered over her shoulder. "You're forgetting that it's set to translate and record. You would have to get your hands on it, undisturbed for about two seconds, to make the change to communication mode."

"Don't worry," Martin said, "we'll think of something."

Even through the double thickness of blanket, Beth's body felt warm and relaxed, and the pain in his head was abating. He made a loud, untranslatable noise that another Earth-human would have recognized as a yawn.

It had been a long day.

They were awakened by the sound of loud hammering on the door. The lights came on and an eye appeared at the grill and remained long enough to see that they were fully conscious, then they were left in darkness and silence again.

"Sleep deprivation," Martin whispered, "is an important part of brainwashing technique."

"Do they also deprive prisoners of sanitary arrangements," Beth asked, "or are we expected to use the bucket you knocked over?"

"Often," Martin replied. "But not this time. That low,

box with the hinged lid is it. I looked inside while the guard was searching the place. Be careful, I've no idea how it works."

Three times they were roused by the switching on of lights and banging on the door without any clear idea of the time that had elapsed between awakenings. The fourth time that the lights came on the only sound from the door was of the bolt being drawn, and suddenly the First and the guard wearing the translator were standing at the bedside staring down at them.

"I shall consider the damage to the blankets a small, additional obligation," he said, "and not a matter for physical chastisement."

They wriggled to the edge of the bed and sat side by side with their legs dangling before Martin said, "Thank you."

"It is customary to stand in my presence," the First said.

"Is it a gesture of respect," Martin asked quietly, "or obedience to authority?"

"Like the torn blankets," the Keidi replied after a long pause, "It is unimportant."

Being allowed to keep the blankets had been a small concession, Martin thought, and this had been another one. Whatever the Keidi leader wanted from them, he wanted it badly enough to ignore this act of insubordination by a prisoner. But now it was time to soft-pedal and not push the First too far.

As if reading his mind, Beth said suddenly, "Are your granddaughter and the newborn well?"

"They are well," the First said. "But henceforth I shall ask the questions and you will answer them."

The Keidi leader wanted to know the exact capabilities of their two ships with a view to possible use in offensive, defensive, and various civilian support roles. Aware of the danger of being caught in a lie, they tried to make their answers truthful but incomplete. The First seemed to believe them, but was becoming increasingly dissatisfied with Martin's answers. When the head injury was mentioned several times as an excuse for a certain confusion of mind, he began to direct more and more of his questions at Beth.

"You tell me that your lander is a low-level observation vehicle," he said, his speaking horn an intimidating few inches from her face, "and that it is the mother ship which holds the power. Under your direction it has the ability to travel between the stars, to fabricate devices, vehicles, and power generation equipment, and to constantly replenish the energies used by absorbing the radiation of any nearby sun. But it seems to me that these capabilities are insufficiently used. I want to know how these vast energies can be utilized and directed toward objectives on the surface of Keida, other than by burying us in a pile of unwanted gadgets?"

Beth did not move or look away from the speaking horn as she said, "You are correct in assuming that the mother ship is not being put to its fullest use on this assignment. That is because it is designed for first contact operations with new intelligent species on strange planets. Keida and its people are not strange to us, your language is already held in our translation computer, and your political and social structures prior to the Exodus are known to us. We were sent here to update that material and help you . . ."

"For now," the First broke in, "I want to know about your mother ship, and how it can be used to help us."

"There are many ways it could be used to help you," Beth replied, "but it was not designed for offensive operations."

"But surely," the Keidi said impatiently, "its power could be so used?"

"Its power," Beth said, speaking part of the truth in a firm voice, "is used primarily in support of first-contact operations. For that reason it is exercised on the non-material level, as a means of disseminating information concerning the Federation World to those whose knowledge of it is incomplete or nonexistent. The methods used to provide this knowledge, which include local demonstrations of weather control, the clearing or drainage of forested or flooded areas, and the projection of three-dimensional instructional pictures on a small or large scale, are both highly sophisticated and extremely power-hungry.

"I will repeat," she went on, "the mother ship has

immense power but no offensive weapons. However, we both realize that many innocent objects can be used for criminal purposes. Even something as harmless as water becomes a weapon if it is forced into the breathing passages of an air-breather."

The First looked across at Martin, who remained holding the back of his head in silence, but kept his speaking horn trained on Beth as he said, "So your ship is not intended to inflict physical destruction. But it might be useful to me, and beneficial to you in your present situation, as a propaganda weapon. Can these demonstrations, and the three-dimensional pictures it projects, be used to warn and perhaps frighten as well as to inform?"

Beth paused to give Martin a chance to answer that one, but he thought she was doing just fine and kept silent.

"Yes," Beth said.

It was obvious that the First had been waiting on that answer, because he gestured to the guard by the door and waited while two large, screw-topped jars of water were brought in and placed on the floor. These were followed by the foodpack and analyzer, four extra blankets, and the most welcome sight of all, their boots!

"I must consider this matter," the First said, moving its horn slowly from one to the other. "It may be that you will be useful to me, and that you will be able to obey your instructions to help the Keida population while at the same time deepening my obligation to you. While you are considering ways in which this can best be achieved, your rest will not be interrupted and your accommodations will be lighted. If you require darkness during periods of rest, or light after a period of darkness, strike the door firmly, twice.

"I leave you," he ended, and turned to go.

"Please wait," Beth said quickly. "My life-mate has a head injury, and the diagnostic equipment is in the ship. Is the doctor—"

The door slammed shut, cutting her off in mid-sentence.

It was not until an indeterminate time later, after the water in the jars had been tested and the food concentrates added to make a bulky as well as a sustaining meal, that they were able to justify signaling for the lights to be switched off so they could go back to bed to discuss the situation.

"You did very well..." Martin began.

"For a ship handler," Beth whispered angrily. "When I asked for the doctor he ignored me and walked out. You might have been badly injured. Or is he smart enough to know that you're pretending?"

"It doesn't matter," Martin said. "Next time we won't ask for the medical attention."

"But we *need* the Doctor!" she broke in fiercely. "He's probably our only chance of getting a message out of here."

Martin tried to laugh reassuringly, and discovered that it was impossible to laugh in a whisper. He said, "The way I see it, the First Father has rewarded us with water, extra blankets, our boots, and a measure of privacy because we have been good, cooperative little children. He has implied that more goodies will be forthcoming if we continue to behave. The only thing he has left to offer is the doctor. So I would say that next time we see him he will begin to tell us exactly what he wants from us, and medical attention is the one thing he can offer which doesn't involve a risk to himself.

"The next meeting will be crucial."

Chapter 24

ON his next visit the First's manner toward them was almost friendly. He began by admitting that they could increase their obligation to his Family and, through him, help the rest of the population if a method could be devised for using that help while ensuring that they could not simply leave the planet once they returned to their mother ship.

Verbal misdirection had been used to bring about their imprisonment, he explained, and it was likely that they would try to use the same method of effecting their escape. He asked them to give long and serious consideration to this problem because, until it was resolved, there could be no real progress toward improving their present unsatisfactory conditions. In the meantime he wanted to discuss some of his long-term plans with them in the hope that they, using the capabilities of their hypership, would suggest methods by which these might be brought to early fruition.

The First was trying very hard to project the image of an aging, careworn, and unselfish leader striving to maintain the order he had created out of the terrible post-Exodus chaos. By offering the close friendship, protection, and spiritual solace of a continent-wide family unit, he had achieved much during those three generations. But there were many, principally among the older Keidi, who would not recognize the value of what he was trying to do, nor realize that the only way to make long-term progress in a world of widely scattered communities was to renounce the individualism of the past and unite into a single family that was planet-wide.

That family would have a single Father, loving, strong, and impartial toward all his children, and he would be the sole authority and arbiter in all matters temporal and spiritual. He would inspire and direct, and when necessary chastise, those who quarreled among themselves or indulged in activities for personal or blood-family gain. And he would constantly remind them of their tremendous common purpose, which was to return Keida to its former glories in spite of the terrible crime committed against them by the hated Galactics.

Martin, who had not spoken since the First's arrival, said carefully, "It is a laudable ambition, but your hatred of the Galactics is undeserved. After all, we were sent here to help you."

It was difficult to know whether the First was annoyed by the interruption or pleased because it enabled him to make another point.

He said, "The crime committed against us was great and any assistance that it is in your power to offer by way of recompense is ridiculously inadequate. Know also that I am the only being on the whole Estate willing to abase myself to the point of accepting your help. The others would spurn such an offer, would insist that we progress, however slowly, unaided. But I am wiser, more realistic, and older than they, and must think and move quickly if I am to ensure the continuance of what I have begun to build ..."

Through his organizational ability the First had amassed personal obligations which would require a thousand lifetimes to discharge, and there were even stronger, nonmaterial bonds of personal loyalty to the First Father and his descendants which would ensure that these obligations would be honored long after his death. But that situation obtained only in the family Estate, whose members had security, shelter, and food proportional to the work performed. When he died there were those who had plans, and had already formed alliances, to break up the Estate and divide it among themselves. If they were successful, the alliances would soon be broken, war would divide and subdivide these unstable groupings. All of the pre-Exodus knowledge would be lost, and Keida's descent into savagery would be rapid and its subsequent rise, if a rise was possible, slow indeed.

"It is to avoid this millennia-long night of barbarism," the First went on, "that I must bring the others into my Family without delay. The Estate is not yet large enough to withstand concerted hostile action against it, but it is large enough for the others to feel threatened by our size and strength. By whatever means becomes available, whether it is force, trade and economic agreements, or psychological pressure exerted with the help of you Galactics, these dissidents must be shown that my long-term plan for Keida is infinitely more important than any short-lived, petty advantages that might be gained through breaking up and dividing my Estate among them.

"Many times I have tried to explain my plan," the Keidi went on, his horn swinging rapidly between Martin and Beth, "by traveling to the estates of other leaders to offer personal security, food, and comfort for the remainder of their days, but they deliberately misunderstood me. I cannot make them realize that we all have major obligations to the unborn of the centuries to come, obligations which must be discharged *now*.

"They are old, fearful, selfish, and stupid," the First ended harshly. "Why will they not trust me?"

The reason is that they, like you, are Undesirables, Martin thought. He was beginning to feel a degree of sympathy for this aging predator who had apparently changed his spots. Perhaps the status of Undesirable was a temporary condition, after all, and the First was beginning to display the level of responsibility and unselfishness required of a Citizen. He said carefully, "As yet you have not explained your plan in detail, but from what little we've heard it shows great wisdom, vision, and unselfishness on your part, and it fully deserves any help that we can provide."

Martin paused for a moment to let that sink in, then went on smoothly, "You are faced with a problem common to many intelligent species. It is that the majority of the older minds are no longer capable of accepting new ideas, however worthy, much less of conceiving them. Have you appealed to the younger people, with offspring, whose stake in the future is much greater?"

"For an off-worlder you understand me well," the First said in a voice which suggested that he was not immune to a well-turned compliment. "Many of the second and third generation Keidi see the wisdom of my plan and give it total support. Many others join my Family but tire of the hard work that is necessary. Or they object to working under my direction, or ignore my teachings and try to leave me, their First Father, for what they believe will be an easier life.

"They are a great disappointment to me."

So interested had Martin become in what the other was saying that he had almost forgotten the continuing pain in his head. He said, "I can understand that labor with no immediate reward is unpleasant, doubly so if there is disbelief in ultimate purpose of the work. Considering the advantages your Estate offers, particularly to those with young families, I don't understand why they leave."

"It shames me to admit it to a stranger, but there is dissatisfaction even among the young people of my own Estate, and strong measures are necessary to check its spread. My population is already dangerously small, and any further reduction would jeopardize the Great Plan, so these malcontents must be prevented from spreading their unsettling ideas or of leaving the Family."

"Leaving it for where?" Martin asked quickly. If there was another Keidi leader offering his people better conditions, he wanted to know about it. The answer came as a total surprise.

"For your accursed white houses!" The First said angrily. "In spite of all warnings that the houses are no longer linked to the Galactics' transportation system, that in all likelihood they will transmit all who enter them to the airlessness of space, or appeals to their pride in their race and constant reminders that we who remain on Keida are the chosen people who will one day surpass the Galactics who have tried to diminish us, our young people still try to enter those white houses. Some cannot pass the outer entrance. Others enter and are never seen again, and the dissidents who remain insist that they have gone, not to instant destruction, but to a better place."

Martin's hand stopped motionless on its way to his head. Beside him Beth had become white-faced and still. Neither of them spoke.

"We cannot afford to lose any more of our young people," the Keidi went on more quietly, "and we consider it a most grievous offense to attempt an escape whether it is to death or some supposedly easier way of life. Those who try are restrained and forced to discharge their criminal obligation by working for the Plan. Now that guards have been posted at every white house on the Estate, the successful escapes are few. Malcontents are easily captured, fortunately, because they insist on trying to take their children and blood relations with them."

Allowing his hand to fall slowly onto his lap, Martin said, "What kind of work do they do?"

"No Keidi will deliberately inflict serious injury or

death on another," the First said. "The lives of these criminals must be made as productive as possible, but the work that they must do is not of the kind which I would assign to a favorite offspring."

Martin put both hands to his head as the thudding pain reached a crescendo, making it nearly impossible to think. He felt nauseous as well, although the words of the First could have been responsible for that.

He had thought for a while that the other had reformed, become a more responsible, farseeing, and altruistic person. But now it was all too plain that this particular Keidi predator had camouflaged, not changed, its spots. Martin was staring into the dry, fissured mouth of the other's speaking horn, but he was seeing the hundreds of grave markers of the so-called dissidents who had been forced to work, quite possibly with no radiation protection, in the old missile arsenal.

"With concerted opposition from without and malcontents burrowing from within," the First went on, "the Great Plan will not long survive my death. There are actions I can take which should quell the opposition, extend and stabilize the Estate to the degree that my children and my children's children may be able to steer my plan to its completion, but the future is still uncertain. It could well be that with your assistance these uncertainties can be removed. Complex negotiations will be necessary, however, and mutual safeguards devised, perhaps a voluntary and alternating hostage system worked out whereby one of you would remain here while the other operates the ship . . ."

He was hearing the Keidi's words clearly but they had become meaningless to him. His head was pounding and he had a terrible need to get out of this place, to get away from the constant yammering of this utterly callous and hypocritical petty tyrant, to find the peace and quiet that would let him think straight. He leaned forward suddenly, elbows on his knees and placed his head between his hands. The untranslatable noise he made was expressive of mental anguish and frustration as much a physical pain.

"What's wrong?" Beth said, looking really concerned. "Is there physical discomfort?" the First asked quickly. "Earlier you asked for the doctor. The request was denied because it seemed at the time that your distress was feigned. But now, as a small and nondischargable obligation between new friends, I am willing to allow the doctor to attend you."

"I don't want him," Martin said without looking up. "He knows nothing of the physiology or treatment of an off-planet patient. I would be in greater danger from the doctor than the disorder. I need the diagnostic and treatment facilities of the mother ship."

"Impossible!" the First said. "Until our negotiations have been completed to my satisfaction, you will remain here."

Beth put a hand on Martin's shoulder and glared at the First. "No," she said fiercely. "He is unwell. Disregard what he says. He does not want the doctor, he *needs* the doctor!"

The Keidi turned toward her, remaining silent.

"It shames me to say this," she went on, "because we are a proud race who dislike showing weakness before others. But there are nonphysical aspects to my life-mate's condition which are becoming more serious than the injury itself. Through pride he wishes these concealed from you. He also knows that during these negotiations, any sign of weakness will be exploited by you, no matter what kind of verbal misdirection you use to suggest the contrary. But I must be practical and forget our pride. There are things which a healer can be told, and forms of nonphysical help which even an other-species doctor can give. Do you understand me?"

Still the First remained silent.

"Speak, damn you!" Beth said. If she was feigning anger, then Martin could not tell it from the real thing. "I know that by making this admission, by revealing my strong personal concern in this matter, I have given you a powerful lever to use against us. But know also that if my life-mate does not receive all the help possible, there will be no advantage to you, no support from the hypership for your Great Plan, nothing. There is no other lever that you can use, no chastisement up to and including ultimate force that you can exert, that will gain my cooperation. Do you understand *that*?"

The First raised a hand and for a moment Martin thought he would strike her, but he used it only to gesture to the guard in the doorway.

One of the Keidi brought in a small, square cage and set it on the bed. Inside the narrowly spaced bars they could see a smaller cage suspended loosely at its center, and inside that one of their wrist units twisted and turned on a narrow cord. There was no way that they could reach it with their fingers, or quickly introduce a narrow instrument, if one had been available, to hold it steady while they made the change from translation to communication mode.

"My plans were made long before you came," said the First quietly. "They will succeed with or without your help. The doctor is already here."

He left, and the doctor entered quickly. Martin stifled a groan and said worriedly, "You weren't exactly respectful toward the most powerful Keidi on the planet."

"I didn't feel respectful . . . " Beth began angrily.

"Let me look at your injury, off-worlder," the doctor said, bending over him. "And rest assured, I shall not poke or pry into an area where my ignorance is total. There is a small abrasion, centered on a large, raised area of bone which looks inflamed. Please begin by describing how the injury was sustained, and its past and present symptoms. Have there been any periods of mental confusion, lapses of memory, dullness of intellect, real or apparent impairment of the senses associated with your episodes of pain?"

The alien features and the bell-mouthed, wrinkled obscenity of a speaking horn which was puffing Keidi breath odors into his face were in all respects identical with those of the First but, strangely, these seemed to radiate sympathy and reassurance rather than barely concealed hostility. Martin began to feel ashamed of himself for exaggerating some of his symptoms and deliberately falsifying others. In spite of the twin gulfs of species and culture which yawned between them, he felt that he was guilty of abusing the trust of a friend. The feeling was so strong that there were times when he told the doctor more than he intended, and had to remind himself to concentrate, to make his sluggish and pain-dulled brain form the words which had to be spoken if they were to stand any chance of escaping from this place. Then suddenly it was over and the First, who had been watching and listening from the doorway, returned to hear the doctor's report.

"There is localized surface damage to the brain casing," the doctor said with the clinical objectivity which seemed to characterize medics, regardless of species. "The effect on the brain itself is uncertain because the Keidi skull is thicker and more complexly structured than that of the patient. There is evidence, however, that the injury has affected the brain function, with intermittent and increasing periods of pain and mental confusion, and partial loss of consciousness which will gradually become total. There is an added, and perhaps more serious, psychological problem which requires immediate attention if the patient's mental capabilities are to be of use to you."

The focusing muscles on the First's speaking horn twitched, but he remained silent as the doctor went on. "You will realize that the patient is not a Keidi, nor does he possess the physical and mental stamina of our species. He is of a more advanced culture, possesses a more sophisticated and delicate sensory network, and is accustomed to a much more comfortable standard of living in which his bodily needs are constantly filled by machines which synthesize his food, fabricate his furniture and clothing, and maintain him in optimum physical health.

"I have also learned," the doctor continued, "that the patient's normal environment is on the planetary surface, in an abode that is warm, spacious, well-lit, and surrounded by open air and distant vegetation. His duty obligations involve extended periods of traveling the awful immensities between the stars. Being confined in this small, comfortless, underground room among what he considers to be hostile beings, and with a tiny supply of food which is unlikely to be replaced is, in combination with the continuing discomfort of his injury, threatening to bring about irreversible psychological damage."

The report, Martin thought, was far more than he could have hoped for. His relief was so intense that it felt like another pain. Beth's fingers tightened on his shoulder as the First made an untranslatable sound, then spoke.

"I agree, Doctor," he said. "His misfortunes are many, and the worst among them is that he came to Keida uninvited. Can you suggest a treatment?"

"None that will guarantee a cure," the doctor replied. "I would not risk a surgical investigation even if he was a Keidi and not the physiological and clinical puzzle that he is, because my specialty is concerned with the other end of the anatomy, and the female anatomy at that. The only treatment I can suggest is pallative; a cold, wet pad might help reduce the local discomfort. Regarding the psychological condition, more positive treatment is possible but a cure is not guaranteed."

"If you were guaranteeing results, Doctor," the First said, "I would be concerned about your own psychological condition. Go on, what can be done for him?"

"In my opinion," the doctor resumed, "the condition will be alleviated by withdrawing the patient, for the longest periods allowable to a prisoner, from the present stressful environment and surrounding him as much as is possible in the present circumstances, with familiar, reassuring objects, and allowing personal contact which is sympathetic rather than that of the hostile Estate people.

"The patient trusts me," he went on. "If I am not his friend, he senses that at least I am not an enemy. He should be allowed to speak to me and I to reassure him, in privacy, without the presence of hostile listeners. His original clothing should be returned to him, he should be given the opportunity to exercise in the open, under my supervision, naturally, and be allowed to see his ship. He should also be allowed . . ."

"To escape?" the First finished for him in a sarcastic voice. "You ask too much!"

"I ask nothing," the doctor said quietly. "It is you who ask how the patient may be rendered more cooperative and mentally coherent, so that your negotiations can proceed. Naturally, I would expect you to post guards, at a distance but close enough to prevent an escape to the ship if, as is doubtful, he is physically and mentally capa-

ble of attempting it. But this is an un
The important thing to understand is tha
had a severe physical and emotional shoc
evidence of increasing mental dysfunction.
wear his own clothing and see his ship, eve
tance which you consider safe, should renew
force his knowledge of who and what he is, and
enable him to adapt to the pressures of imprisonment on
an alien planet.

"If no action is taken," the doctor added, "there is a
serious risk of the patient's knowledge and capabilities
and, I suspect, those of the life-mate and their vessel,
being lost to you."

The First's focusing muscles were bunching like
clumps of yellow seaweed around his horn. "No!" he
said. "Your prescription is too risky for us. We confined
these Galactics, an unprecedented action to take during
the preliminaries of an important negotiation, because
we cannot trust them . . ."

It was the strangest argument that Martin had ever
experienced, and if he had been feeling better he would
have enjoyed it, because the First talked angrily and
continuously while the doctor retained a clinical impassi-
vity and total silence, and won.

"Very well," the First said finally, making no attempt
to hide his displeasure. "You may exercise and talk with
the patient outside. But you will be guarded at a distance, a *short* distance, and you will hold the translation
device in clear sight at all times. If the off-worlder tries
to free it from its cage to call for help, or even looks as if
he might be doing so, or tries physically to escape,
whether or not the attempt is successful, his life-mate
will be severly chastised. Do you both understand that?"

Without waiting for a reply, the Keidi leader added,
"Your clothing will be returned to you," and stamped out
of the cell.

Although he remembered every step of the journey,
the return to the ground-level entrance seemed three
times longer, and the stairs much steeper, than they had
been on the way in. Outside the building they began
walking slowly and silently along the road leading to-

...anding area, while Keidi guards kept their dis-
...head, behind, and on both flanks.

...he rain had stopped some time ago and the ground
...as drying out. The rising, or perhaps setting, sun illuminated the low buildings and the distant hull of the
lander with the warm, orange tones of a theater spotlight. When Martin finally broke the silence, he knew
that he was taking an incredibly stupid risk.

"I am deeply obligated to you for arranging this temporary freedom," he said, "but it shames me to admit
that I was not completely honest with you, and you
should know that the description of some of my symptoms was, well, exaggerated."

The doctor made an untranslatable sound and said, "I
have been long enough in the profession to know when a
patient, regardless of his species, is lying to me. And you
should know, off-worlder, that in spite of the dramatiza-
tion of your symptoms, your condition is worse than you
yourself realize. That is why I argued for you to be allowed out here, so that you would at least have the *opportunity* of escaping, if your condition eventually allows
it. You and your life-mate must try to protract the negotiations with the First until you are feeling better. Also, I
consider myself partly responsible for your involvement
with this fanatical and untrustworthy being. This and my
other personal obligations to you must be discharged."

Martin continued walking, not knowing what to say.

"But I can only give you the opportunity, off-
worlder," the doctor went on, "not actively support any
future escape attempt. The First is unforgiving of those
who oppose him. His triple obligation to me for attending
his granddaughter, and your share of it for bringing me to
her quickly, would be argued away. I have no wish to
spend the rest of my life in the First's labor camp."

Does he *know*? Martin wondered. Is he aware of what
is going on? Aloud, he said, "What is it like in the labor
camp?"

Chapter 25

THEY had reached the perimeter and the lander lay, enclosed by the semicircular halo of its repulsion field, less than a quarter of a mile away. One of the First's ground vehicles, filled with guards, was already positioning itself between them. Nearby there was a cylindrical mass of rust which might once have been a fuel tank. Martin sat down heavily on it, feeling as if he had just run a mile.

The doctor remained standing as he replied, "I don't know what the labor camp is like. Nobody has ever returned to talk about it, and I would rather not find out. You look distressed, and plainly you are in no condition for an escape attempt. We may need a litter to get you back to your cell."

"No, wait," Martin said urgently. "Have you ever treated a patient suffering from radiation sickness?"

"What sort of question is that?" the doctor asked impatiently. "Are you feeling confused again?"

"No," Martin said. "Have you?"

"Never," the doctor replied. "I was an obstetrician, off-worlder, and did not deal with such cases. And after the Exodus all fissionable materials, civil, military, or medical, were taken from us. Thankfully, that particular scourge no longer exists on Keida."

"You are wrong," Martin said.

"And you," the doctor said quietly, "are mentally confused."

"Not about this," Martin said fiercely. "As soon as we put our sensors on the First we knew that he had been exposed to radiation, although the dosage was small. The mother ship was able to detect the original source."

The doctor looked away from him and did not speak.

"You are the only Keidi that I feel I can trust," Martin went on. "From the beginning you did not behave toward us like an—"

"Careful," the doctor said.

"All right," Martin said impatiently, "I will not risk insulting you by using that word. But surely you are not, well, not at all like the First."

The doctor made another untranslatable sound and said, "That is a compliment."

"There must be many others on Keida like yourself," Martin went on. "People who could have gone to the Federation World, but chose to remain because of self-imposed responsibilities, for parents, life-mates or loved ones, or in your case patients. In the city your people were worried, not about losing you to the Estate, but of you leaving them for the Federation World with us. I'm sure that many of the Keidi could qualify for citizenship now and leave, if the First did not guard the induction centers and send them to his labor camp for trying—"

Without giving the other time to react, Martin broke off and quickly described how the sealed underground missile arsenal had been opened by volcanic activity and the First's rebuilding a surface launching facility, adding a rough estimate of the number of grave markers outside the camp stockade.

". . . Earlier the First told us that he could proceed with his plans without our help," Martin went on. "I'm afraid that he intends making a show of force, probably the air detonation of a nuclear device over an uninhabited area, timed so that the fallout would be carried out to sea by the wind. This would demonstrate his power to the independents and force them into his Estate. But winds can change direction suddenly, the contamination lingers and could affect the genetic structure of generations of Keidi to come.

"My guess," Martin continued quickly, "is that the missile project personnel comprises three distinct types. The majority are the slave laborers, who have no control over the situation and are waiting to share the fate of their friends who have died of radiation sickness. There are the guards who are fanatically loyal to the First and, like all fanatics, have minds impervious to the logical

argument. Then there are a few, a very few, aging techni-
cians who may not be as expert at reassembling the old
and perhaps damaged equipment as they would have the
First believe.

"There is a strong probability of a catastrophic accident.

"A lot of this is supposition," he went on, "but only in
the unimportant details. You must agree that the project
has to be stopped, the surviving laborers evacuated and
given treatment that only Federation medical science can
provide, and the launching facility demolished and re-
sealed. To do this I must escape."

The doctor looked toward the lander for a moment,
then said, "If what you say is true, then a great many
people on Keida will be obligated to you. But I am not
convinced. I suspect an inspired and imaginative piece of
verbal misdirection. Your arguments are both cogent,
suggesting that there is little mental confusion in your
mind, and so fantastic as to be the product of hallucina-
tion. Are you using me, applying the nonmaterial pressures which can affect only a doctor, as the First intends
using you."

"Yes," Martin said, "to escape."

"But you're not fit enough to escape," the doctor said
impatiently. "The guards would stop you before you had
staggered ten paces toward your vessel. I cannot go to it
for you because that screen pushed back everyone and
everything else that tries to penetrate it, myself included.
I tried out of curiosity, while taking my morning walk.
Off-worlder, you cannot escape."

Martin shook his head, and gasped at the explosion of
pain. When he could speak again, he said, "You could go
to the screen and speak a certain phrase to the ship.
Even if there are others nearby and you have to speak
quietly, the sound sensors will hear and translate it. The
words are 'I think, therefore I am in trouble.' Can you
memorize that?"

"I think you should return to the cell," the Keidi said.
"Your injury appears to be troubling you."

"No, wait," Martin said desperately, but the could
think of nothing else to say, nor did he rise.

"There have been rumors that the First was guarding

induction centers," the doctor said, "to prevent loss of population. I can understand that even though I disagree with it. But using dissidents to excavate a nuclear weapons arsenal and rebuilding the launching towers . . . No, that is deliberate misdirection. There is no proof that the arsenal exists, or even, with the instruments available to me, that the First was exposed to radioactivity or—"

"But there is indirect proof," Martin broke in. "The First is deeply concerned for his granddaughter and the newborn, and would normally stay as close as possible to them before the birth. Why, then, did he remain far down the ward if he was not afraid that he carried something which might damage the genes of the newborn? . . ."

He broke off, wishing that instead of speaking he had bitten off his tongue. The doctor had swung around and was glaring down at him.

"You know all that happened in the birthing ward," the Keidi said angrily, "yet you concealed the knowledge even from me?"

"Not everything that happened," Martin said, desperately trying to retrieve the situation. "Our instruments were able to show the approximate location of the ward. That was why, when we realized that we were not being taken to see the First's granddaughter, we tried to escape. The people in the ward showed as formless blurs except for the First, whose radioactive contamination made his trace unmistakable. My intention was not to deceive you but to avoid further complicating the situation.

"Please help me," Martin went on, searching vainly for eloquence. "I wish only what is best for Keida."

The doctor grasped Martin's arm and drew him to his feet. "The First makes exactly the same claim," he said. "I will return you to your cell."

On the latitude of Frontier Camp Eleven, darkness fell quickly, and that may have been the reason why Martin fell several times on the way back. Dizziness and nausea were still making it impossible to think, but not to feel sorry for himself. When the Keidi put an arm around his back to support him by both elbows, his reaction was angry and despairing.

"You don't believe me," he said bitterly, "and now you don't believe that I'm unwell. Why are you bothering to help me?"

The Keidi made an untranslatable sound. "If I assisted only the patients who told me the truth, I would have very little work to do."

The doctor took him to the cell, then left to check on the condition of his other patient. Martin fell onto his bed, refusing to allow Beth to remove the warm boots or to give him any of the cold, unappetizing porridge she had made from water and food concentrates. Shortly afterward she spread the extra blankets they had been given over him, positioned the two muffling pillows, and crawled in beside him.

"I'm cold," he said unnecessarily through chattering teeth. "I want to sleep."

"With a bad head injury," she whispered, "is it wise to let yourself sleep? What does the doctor say?"

"Nothing, damn him," Martin replied. "I told him what to do, and everything we know or suspect about the First, but I don't think he believed a word of it."

Her body stiffened in disappointment and her arms tightened around him. She did not speak.

"Don't worry," he said. "We'll think of another way. But later."

He was woken by Beth shaking his shoulder violently. The cell was in darkness but the light outside the grill was brightening and fading erratically, the guards were talking at the tops of their voices, and even louder were the muffled detonations of what sounded like a major thunderstorm.

"Dammit, I think you would sleep through the Crack of Doom!" Beth said fiercely. "Just *listen* to that! It could be natural, a freak storm, even though it seems to be scaring the hell out of the guards. Or then again, our darling main computer likes to show off, and maybe it thinks we might need a diversion as well as a rescue. We haven't checked it for some time now; it may be planning something."

"We'll soon find out," Martin said excitedly. He swung his feet to the floor, and wondered if his head was going to explode or just fall off. "Start shouting for the doctor. Try to find out if he's come back from his morning walk."

"Right," Beth said, and took a deep breath.

The lights came on at her first shout and the doctor who had evidently been on the way to see them, arrived before the guards could send for him. He stood in the open doorway, breathing heavily, his focusing muscles twitching silently and with pale areas of discoloration showing on the dark, Keidi features.

Beth went over to him and gently took his arm, then led him to the bedside where she sat him down between Martin and herself. The caged translator he was gripping in the other hand carried her words, but the guards were too busy trying to reassure each other to listen.

"Don't be afraid," she said. "It is only very bright lights and noise, a projection, and nobody will be harmed. But in case the First holds you responsible for it and wants to chastise you..."

There was a silent flare of blue light, and their rusting bed was standing incongruously on the polished metal deck of the hypership's matter transmitter module.

"...We thought it better to bring you along," she went on, sliding off the bed and walking quickly to the module's computer terminal.

"First, I have to arrange for medical attention for our patient," she said, while her fingers moved over the input keys, "and cancel all the melodramatic meteorological effects down there. Then later I'll bring up the lander on automatic. It's needed to return you to the city, or back to Camp Eleven if you prefer it. Unfortunately, we can't send you back the way we brought you, because there is the risk that you might materialize inside a wall or something. Then, when my life-mate's brain is functioning normally again, we'll have to decide what to do about the First."

"I understand," the doctor said. "If I can assist you with local information or advice, I shall be pleased to do so. As for my other patient, she and her newborn will

the near future—and they spoke volumes even to a
Keidi who could not understand the figures but was experiencing tri-di images for the first time. The patches of
discoloration had returned to cover his face and speaking
horn.

"You will have urgent duty obligations to discharge,"
the doctor said suddenly. "But if it is possible, I should
like to return to my people at once."

"That wouldn't help them or you . . ." Martin began,
when Beth held up her hand.

"Doctor, yours is a coastal city," she said quietly.
"The prevailing winds are off the ocean, so that your
people will have longer than those living inland on the
Estate, perhaps as much as five days, before they are
seriously affected. Your underground shelters are probably more effective than any other dwellings on Keida,
and will give protection until the air and food becomes
increasingly contaminated. By then nothing you or they
can do will—"

"No," Martin said, "there are better shelters."

Beth gave him a puzzled look, but before she could
reply the doctor said, "My people are of the second and
third generations. They know nothing of pre-Exodus nuclear weapons and their effects, and they will be fearful
and confused. I have a strong duty obligation to speak to
them."

"You can speak to them from here," Beth said. "We
can match frequencies with your radio in the city, so long
as it is switched on and someone is listening."

"They will be listening," the doctor said.

Beth indicated the sound pickup at the doctor's
elbow. "Whenever you're ready."

"And while you're talking to them," Martin said
quickly, "we'll have to find a way of making the other
Keidi listen as well. The First might be slow to warn
everyone about the full extent of the danger because that
would mean admitting blame for it. He is aware of the
danger, as are most of the other Undes—I mean, others
of the same age group, and will know what a large-scale
nuclear fallout will entail. But for the younger adults, a
warning will not be enough, we'll have to include a crash
course in post nuclear disaster survival. I . . . I'm having

second thoughts. Maybe we should swallow our pride and scream for Federation assistance."

Beth did not reply. The doctor was watching silently, plainly more interested in what they were saying than contacting his people. Martin sighed.

"I know that look," he said. "It means you don't agree."

"This is a Federation hypership," Beth said quietly. "A very potent hunk of machinery, if I do say so myself. If we call for help, they will send, quickly but with a time lapse of at least four days, another hypership that is equally capable but with a ship handler and contact specialist on board who are unfamiliar with the situation here. We will have to take additional time to explain it to them before they can even start to help us. We don't have that much time to waste. So wouldn't it be better if you decided exactly what kind of help is needed, then I will tell you if my ship can deliver it?"

There was a moment's silence, during which the doctor's speaking horn moved slowly from the sound pickup to point at Martin.

"I had assumed," the Keidi said, "that my people were beyond help, that the radioactivity would kill all of them sooner or later, and that anything you or they could do would merely delay the end and make it, at best, only more lingering and unpleasant for the offspring of the survivors, or is there something of lasting benefit that you can do for us? Do not misdirect me. On your answer depends what I must say to my people."

Beth was looking at him as well, her expression puzzled but hopeful. He sighed again. "Don't expect miracles."

"From Galactics," the Keidi said gravely, "I don't know what to expect. Answer me."

"Very well," Martin said. "Whatever we decide to do, it must be done quickly. The Keidi, all of the Keidi, must be contacted at once and the situation explained to them, and they must be made to believe the explanation. That will be difficult because of what they've been told about Galactics. But if you, Doctor, were to expand the message to the people in your city so that it would apply to everyone, so that it contains the information, advice, and instructions which all the Keidi will need, we could beam it to every operating receiver on the planet. Coming from you the message would be believed. As for the small or isolated families and settlements without receivers, the ship's fabricators should be able to produce the required number of audio broadcast devices, which will be dropped on them so that they, too, will receive their instructions."

"No problem," Beth said.

"What instructions?" the doctor asked.

"To go to the nearest shelter as quickly as possible," Martin replied. "I know that some of them, those far beyond the borders of the Estate, will be quite safe for a few days or even weeks. But a warning that is hedged around with qualifiers loses urgency. Once they are safe, for a while, at least, we will have time to think about what is to happen next. My species has a proverb, 'Where there's life, there's hope,' and—"

"If there is no hope," the doctor broke in harshly, "why needlessly prolong life?"

"We haven't time for a philosophical discussion, Doctor," Martin said. "Your Keidi must be instructed to go quickly to places of safety. The only safe, guaranteed radiation-proof shelters on Keida are the Federation's induction centers. There will be a minor food supply problem there, since the reception areas have only the Keidi equivalent of coffee and sandwich dispensors, but if the price of safety is—"

"There is a major problem," the doctor said. "Entrance to those centers was barred to many Keidi, even when they were able to elude the First's guards. You are asking that they go to these places of safety when some of them will be forbidden entry. The movement into your shelters would not be a smooth one. There would be deep mental anguish at the thought of separating barred and eligible friends, or parents and offspring. I know my Keidi, off-worlder. They would not accept your offer of shelter under those conditions."

Martin took a deep breath. To Beth he said, "The induction center computers are small and relatively simple. I expect, rather I hope, that the ship's computer can instruct them to open the induction center doors, to everyone."

Beth nodded. "A hypership main computer has the rank," she said. "But do you realize what you're doing?"

Suddenly she was looking frightened.

"Yes," Martin said reassuringly, "I'm gaining time to think of a longer-term solution. First we move the Keidi under cover. There may be overcrowding in some of the centers, but they have their own, short-range matter transmitters. During my interrogations I can remember being transferred from center to center all over Earth. Here we can relieve local congestion by moving the people to areas on Keida not likely to be affected by radiation. But now we must contact them quickly and—"

"Hold!" the doctor broke in angrily. "These radiation-free areas, are they in the northern and southern latitudes, the areas which were abandoned after the Exodus for the central continent because of the climate and poor cultivation? Would you protect the Keidi from radiation poisoning only to let them die of exposure and starvation?"

"No," Martin replied. "This vessel is powerful and versatile, so much so that there are times when it frightens even us. Shelters and warm clothing can be fabricated, sufficient food synthesized, and dropped to take care of their short-term needs, and in time a satisfactory solution will be worked out. While you prepare your message, Doctor, I will contact the First."

"Wait," Beth said anxiously. "That is Keida's complete induction center network we're opening up, to all comers."

He knew that and she knew that he knew it. Without replying he turned to the doctor and said, "The ship can give us everything we need, except time. Do you understand enough now to be able to speak to your people?"

"No," the doctor said, "but I shall do it anyway."

"There is another question, however," the Keidi went on, turning to Beth. "Is the plan that your life-mate has devized one that will be approved by your superiors?"

"No," said Beth, "but he will do it anyway."

As the pale blue glow that was the hush field dropped around the Keidi, Martin tried to tell himself that his offense might be considered a venial one. But one of the first directives given to a trainee contactor was that a Federation Examination and Induction Center was a highly sophisticated and sensitive assemblage of equipment which must remain inviolate. Impregnable though it was from external forces, the interior contained equipment and material which should be used only for the interrogation, instruction, and processing of potential Citizens and non-Citizens. Now he was deliberately withdrawing the primary safeguards, the first and most effective line of defense, and throwing the centers open to everyone.

Undesirables included.

That, he was very much afraid, would not be considered a venial offense.

"You understand that the centers will be used only as temporary radiation shelters?" he said to Beth. "The doors will open and the reception areas and matter transmitters continue to function, but everything else is to be powered down. In the present circumstances there's no point in allowing the refugees to be tested for citizenship. The ones who qualified might not be allowed to leave by those who didn't, and if fighting started inside the shelters... Can you shut down the interrogators?"

"Yes," Beth answered. "Are you having second thoughts again, I hope?"

"No," he lied.

"In that case," Beth said in the toneless voice which indicated extreme disapproval, "you can speak to Camp Eleven whenever you like. The doctor has already begun talking to his people. The first audio units are on the way down and your messages will be recorded for later rebroadcasting. Is there anything else?"

"No."

The Camp's radio room was an alien bedlam, with too many voices shouting at once for Martin's translator to separate them. But the Keidi leader was there, and within a few seconds the clamor died so that only his words were heard against a muted background of the other incoming signals.

"Out of this terrible catastrophe," the First said bitterly, "we thought that some good had been achieved, that we had succeeded in destroying you and your landing vessel. But now it is clear that, having brought about the destruction of my Estate, you have escaped ultimate chastisement."

"Be glad that we did," Martin said, controlling his anger, "and that we are still willing to help your people. I will ignore your attempt to make us appear responsible in any way for the nuclear detonations, since the devices and the decision to launch them were yours, and I will assume that your words are for the benefit of those around you who do not as yet know the truth. So stop wasting valuable time and listen to me. We knew about your missile site and the frightful toll of radiation casualties among the dissidents forced to work there. We do not believe—"

"This is sensitive material," the First broke in angrily. "Only a few of my most trusted family members know of it. Do not speak of it further or I shall break contact."

"At present I am speaking only to Camp Eleven," Martin said, "but I can just as easily address every Keidi on the planet. If you don't want to save your lives, there are others who do. Now listen to me.

"We do not believe," he went on quickly, "that you intended to loose a multiple warhead weapon over your own territory, but the mistakes of frightened or overzealous subordinates remain your responsibility. The underground detonation in the missile arsenal was undoubtedly an accident, for which you also bear ultimate responsibility for uncovering the facility in the first place. You are old enough to have learned the effects of these air and ground bursts, and know that very soon the radioactive contamination will poison the air and lands of your Estate, and beyond. The criminal obligation you have incurred in this matter is so enormous that it can only be discharged by—"

"Off-worlder," the Keidi leader broke in, "I will not listen if you speak to me in this manner!"

"You will listen," Martin said fiercely, "because you are the First Father of your Estate, the one person above all others on this continent with the authority and the organization to move large numbers of Keidi quickly to places of safety..."

Martin quickly outlined his plan, and when he finished speaking there was a long silence from Camp Eleven, but the sound of quiet, urgent conversations in the background indicated that they remained in contact. Martin pointed at the ship status displays and said, "I'm worried. We're fabricating thousands of soft-landed audio units, sensors, high altitude flares, and three two hundred seat transports. The logistical computations alone... Are you sure the ship can handle all this?"

"My ship," Beth responded, "hasn't had so much to do since it got between that Teldi city and a meteor storm during our first assignment, and on that occasion it had had to use its muscles rather than its brains. This time it has to use both and, well, let's say we have a very busy and happy ship.

"I'm worried, too," she ended, "but not about that."

"Off-worlder," the First said before Martin could reply, "I have considered all that you have said, but I will not accept the entire responsibility for what has happened. You know of my plan to unify Keida into one family, and I believe this would have succeeded without your help, or interference, by using those missiles solely as a threat. Your coming here precipitated this disaster..."

"He has a point," Beth said softly.

"...But for the good of my people," the First went on, "I will accept your offer of assistance. Are you sure the white houses will open to us?"

"They will open," Martin said dryly, "even to you."

"That," Beth said, "is what worries me."

Martin wanted to steer her away from that subject. As soon as the First broke contact, he said, "Have you been monitoring the doctor?"

Beth looked angry for a moment, then she said, "Yes, the doctor is doing fine. He didn't tell us that, as well as being their medic, he is the city's Negotiator of Obligations, a sort of non-family Father, who is respected all over the continent for his fairness in arbitration. No wonder the people are listening to him. A few of them are still arguing. As soon as he's finished, bring him to the surveillance module. Very soon we shall be dealing with a large number of simultaneous events, and the screens here are too small to show everything we'll need to see."

Chapter 27

FROM the observation platform at the center of the surveillance module, the small, equatorial land mass and the sparsely populated coastal strips on the north and south continents lay spread out below them at an apparent distance of one hundred miles. The vast image might have been mistaken for a view from space, until the eye and mind realized that it was strangely distorted, concave, so that the observer had a clear, vertical view of every part of the picture; and the hundreds of multicolored diagrams and figures constantly drawing and erasing themselves across the surface left no doubt regarding its unreality. But its effect on the doctor, who was gripping the guard rail tightly with both hands and pressing his feet hard against the metal platform, seemed to be a total paralysis of body and mind.

"It is only a tool," Martin said gently. "A tool to extend vision, a tool whose use can be easily learned even though its operating principles are beyond our understanding. There is no reason to be afraid of it."

The doctor made an untranslatable noise. "*Only* a tool! There is misdirection here, through kindness, and I thank you for it. But these are the tools of gods."

"No," Martin said. "They are the tools of two Earth-humans and 79 Keidi, and we are expected to use them. Are you ready to begin?"

The reference numbers and positions of nearly eighteen hundred centers were shown in white, and the numbers assigned to refugee groups displayed in shades ranging from yellow to red, depending on their current level of risk, together with those of their destination centers. Fortunately, the entire Keidi population numbered just under one million, and every center could easily accommodate up to six hundred refugees—but only if everything went according to plan and everybody did exactly as they were told.

As expected, the people of the Estate were the first to begin a concerted movement toward the centers, which was fortunate because many of them were in areas of high risk. Martin listened to the instructions going out to the First's people, but, apart from relaying them via the soft-landed audio units to those who otherwise might not have heard them, he did not interfere. The Keidi leader had a large, well-disciplined organization and he was using it much more effectively than Martin could ever have hoped to do. The doctor was becoming less timorous about requesting local information and visual displays, and the desolate, muddy scenes of his own home city were appearing less frequently on his personal screen.

The last picture Martin had seen showed a steady trickle of refugees, carrying children and possessions in their arms or dragging them behind them on carts, crossing the rusting hulk of the bridge from which the barricades had been removed. They would all reach the ten-miles' distant center several days before the radiation would reach their city, but the doctor had been made to understand that if *everyone* hurried to shelter, more attention and resources could be devoted to those with less time.

"I am guilty of a shameful misdirection," the doctor said when he saw Martin looking at his screen. "Only my city people know of the presence of a Federation ship, but do not as yet associate it with the rescue operation. They, and everyone else outside the Estate, believe that my words come through one of the First's transmitters. I am doing nothing to remedy this error, because to do so would cause argument and delay, but this omission is a most serious ingratitude toward the true benefactors."

"Don't worry about it," Martin said. "Your presence and active cooperation discharges any unknowing obligations owed by your people. Besides, the First is taking all the credit, too, and we want it to stay that way for as long as possible. Sooner or later direct intervention will necessary, and then things will become really complicated."

"It will be sooner," the doctor said, using both hands to point simultaneously toward a spot on the main surveillance screen and the enlarged view on his own. "If my reading of your displays is correct, the population of Group Seventy-one, two hundred plus refugees in all, is heading toward center Eleven-eighty instead of Eleven-seventy-nine as directed. Eleven-eighty is much closer but is in the path of the fallout from Burst Three. Heavy rain is predicted which will bring down the fallout and seriously contaminate the intervening ground before they can reach shelter. The village First knows which induction center is closer and he refuses to go to the farther one because of the number of aged, unwell, or very young Keidi in his family. They have not actually seen a burst, so they consider my verbal description an overly dramatic misdirection, and my attempts to make them take the longer journey have been unsuccessful."

And if they did not begin moving toward Eleven-seventy-nine at once, Martin saw from the display, it, too, would be affected before they could reach it.

To Beth he said, "Are you seeing this? Can you whip up some really foul weather between Group Seventy-one and Center Eleven-eighty? Bad enough to make them want to take the longer trip?"

Beth looked doubtful. She said, "A day's march, maybe thirty to forty miles, doesn't give me much elbow room. A really bad weather system is difficult to position with accuracy and some of it will spill over onto the refugees and slow them down. Even the hypership can't make rain on one side of the street and sunshine on the other."

"We need something quick and simple," Martin said. "How about a simulated ground level nuclear burst, with the projection scaled down to fit, between them and Eleven-eighty? Did you record the missile site detonation?"

"From all angles," Beth said. "But won't that be a bit drastic on the refugees? There must be a gentler way."

Martin looked at the doctor, who had resumed his

vain attempt to make Group Seventy-one change direction, and said quietly, "Not in the time we have. My responsibility. Do it, now."

When it happened the doctor's screen was displaying sharply defined, wide-angle views with sound which were being relayed from the sensor pickups hovering above Group Seventy-one. For one terrifying instant the Keidi old and young, their packs and litters, even the dark leafed trees around them became an incredibly bleached picture in shades of white and palest gray. But it was a still and silent picture whose subjects were paralyzed by shock and fear, until a low, rumbling sound began which mounted rapidly in volume to become the shriek of a thousand hurricanes. Then there was movement, the uncoordinated scurryings of a nest of disturbed insects. But the shouts of despair and panic, and the high-pitched, pitiful squeakings coming from infant speaking horns, could not be heard until the roaring died into silence and the even more fearful specter of a massive, misshapen, nuclear mushroom could be seen climbing and darkening the sky above their destination.

"Don't worry, Doctor," Martin said quickly, "they're all right. It was only light and sound; a harmless, three-dimensional projection. There is no radiation, no heat, and the leaves on the trees didn't even stir when the sound of that shock wave went through. But now they will listen to you and go in the right direction without argument."

"There are injuries among the old and young," the doctor exclaimed angrily. "Fortunately, none appear serious enough to slow the evacuation. And there is general fear and mental distress. That was a cruel act, off-worlder!"

"It was a necessary act," Martin replied firmly. "It was for their own ultimate good."

"The First uses those same words of excuse," the Keidi said, and returned his attention to the screen.

Beth did not speak. Perhaps, Teldi fashion, her silence denoted the absence of dissent, but Martin doubted that. He wondered what the Masters of Teldi, who were no strangers to major catastrophe, would think about his recent behavior.

The sunset line moved steadily across the continental land mass, leaving the Estate and the outlying settlements in darkness except for the scattering of bright, fuzzy stars that were the flares suspended above the refugee groups forced by the inexorable approach of radioactive fallout to travel at night. On their first appearance, the flares had caused nearly as much panic as the projection of the nuclear detonation. But the doctor, in words which were becoming slower and more slurred by the minute, explained that the tiny suns hanging in their night sky were harmless and had been sent by the Galactics to guide them. Then his speaking horn had dropped limply onto his chest and he collapsed over his console.

The medical computer scanned its clinical data on the Keidi life form and stated that aging members of his species lacked stamina and often lost consciousness after lengthy periods of physical or mental stress, that the condition was temporary and there was no reason for concern. Martin pushed the doctor back into a more comfortable position and replaced the hush field because the weird, discordant noises emanating from the Keidi's speaking horn made it impossible to talk or catch up on their own sleep.

An irate call from the First kept them from doing either.

"I have been listening to some of the doctor's broadcasts," he said angrily, "and you must tell him to stop undermining my authority! He is trying to make our people trust you, and is as good as telling everyone that the disaster is my fault, while the truth is that it was precipitated by your escape..."

"They were your missiles," Martin said tiredly, "and it was trusted but stupid members of your family who launched them. Lie to yourself if you must, but don't try to—"

"...And stop filling up the sky with your flares," the First raged on. "My people are capable of lighting torches and my vehicles have headlamps. Apart from providing temporary fallout shelters, we didn't ask for and do not want your help. I am the First Father of the Estate, I have the organization to lead my Family to safety without interference from you!"

Once again the First must be talking for the benefit of the people around him, Martin thought. Diplomatically, he said, "Your organization and movement of the refugees has been exemplary, but we thought that the flares might expedite matters. However, there are a number of groups which are moving in the wrong directions. We count eight of them, all headed toward one induction center which is not the nearest to their present positions. This is time wasting and dangerous for the people concerned, and they should be redirected at once. Also, our sensors show three settlements in the mountain region seventy miles west and presently upwind of the missile arsenal, who seem to be totally unaware of what has been going on. If you have no radio contact with them, we can soft-land the necessary equipment and—"

"No," the First said sharply. "They are small, widely scattered groups who will not be affected for many days. They are not easily accessible to my vehicles which, at the present time, are being more productively employed elsewhere. There is no need to worry them at this stage and, in the present situation, a certain number of casualties must be accepted."

"There is no acceptable number of casualties," Martin replied firmly. "I'll ask the doctor to explain what is happening, and get them moving toward the nearest centers. If necessary we can provide transport."

"No," the First said angrily. "I will do what is necessary."

"Very well," Martin said. "Will you also instruct the eight groups who are converging on the same induction center to sort themselves out? Five of them have much less distant shelters available."

There was a moment's silence, then the First said, "The convergence is deliberate. They are special members of my Family, trusted and able, who I wish to have around me for protection against dissidents and as a nucleus of the organization which will restore order after the present emergency is past. They are well-trained and capable of moving quickly enough to escape the fallout.

"To avoid overcrowding," he added, "no other groups are being directed to that center."

"Wait," Martin said.

He asked Beth to display close-range aerial views of the groups concerned, which included a very large one containing the First himself. The Keidi leader shared a vehicle with what were presumably his granddaughter, her life-mate and the newborn, but everyone else was on foot. They were all mature young Keidi, fit and fast-moving in spite of being heavily armed. The older and very young members of their settlements, he saw, had been left behind with a few vehicles and had just enough time to reach the nearer induction centers.

"That is the nucleus of a *military* organization," Beth said suddenly. "Those groups are composed of his trusted guards and handpicked bullboys who are going to turn their center into a fort. If those groups join the First, well, there'll be long-term trouble. You've got to divert them to other centers, quickly."

"No," Martin said. He wanted to explain that forcing the groups to go to other centers would require direct intervention on a large scale, of a type which would cause fear, conflict, and a considerable loss of time and therefore of life. And there was also a strong probability that they would not be diverted, that the Keidi leader knew that Martin would not kill any of them by forbidding entry to any center when the fallout radiation reached lethal levels, and that the First would simply call his bluff. But there was no time for explanations and the arguments which would follow them. Instead he went on, "No, but we'll let him know that we know what he's up to, and pull his teeth."

To the First he said, "We can see that all the members of your eight special groups are heavily armed. Weapons may not be taken inside an induction center, and the entrance sensors and protective devices will make no exceptions. The weapon carrier will also be excluded until the weapon is discarded. Is this understood?"

"But a person in my position needs guards," the First protested. "A few, at least, for personal protection. Your interference, and the things the doctor is saying about the detonations, have placed my life in danger."

"You will be surrounded only by friends," Martin said dryly, "since you have already arranged that potential enemies be directed away from your center. But they will be unarmed friends, and I suggest that your people discard their weapons now rather than carry them to be left outside the center."

Angrily, the First shouted, "So you would exclude my family and friends, and sentence to a lingering death the Keidi who love and wish only to protect me?"

"Your armed friends exclude themselves," Martin said quietly, and broke the connection.

Beth's attention was divided between her console and the big sensor screen, but there was enough of it free to tell Martin what she thought of him.

"I don't understand you," she said vehemently. "You should have split up the First's guards, destroyed his organization before it could take shape. Disarming them won't do any permanent good because, to adapt the old Earth expression, there are no dangerous weapons, only dangerous Keidi. Now you're putting all the bad eggs into one stinking basket, and the smell will eventually cover the whole planet as it was beginning to do before we arrived, except that it will be one of the First's heirs setting up a military dictatorship instead of him. You should have split them up, dammit, in the hope that the other, more normal Keidi would have absorbed and perhaps had a civilizing influence on them. Instead you've gone for a sick compromise!"

"Have you finished?" Martin asked.

"No," Beth replied angrily, "but the doctor is waking up."

The Keidi medic wakened complaining of hunger. Beth ordered a large helping of synthesized and nutritionally balanced food tailored to the Keidi metabolism, which drew high praise from the doctor. He asked her if it could be supplied in bulk to some of the refugee groups who were being forced to sacrifice the weight of food supplies for speed of movement.

It could and it was.

By the end of the second day the majority of the groups within and beyond the borders of the Estate were safe or looked as though they would reach safety in time, barring accidents. The First's convoy, closely followed by two more groups of his special followers, reached their induction center but milled about outside the en-

trance for more than an hour before disarming themselves and going inside. Subsequent groups disarmed
themselves and entered without delay.

For the first time since the escape from Camp Eleven,
Martin and the Keidi leader were able to see as well as
hear each other.

"I have urgent questions," the First said angrily. "As
you can see we have entered one of your white houses
but, far from finding it a place of shelter, we find ourselves in a large, rooftop area apparently open to the sky.
We cannot find an exit much less a way down to the
entrance. Many of us feel that we have been tricked,
captured, and are to be left to die from radiation sickness
in this unprotected place. Before I signal the other Keidi
to turn back and avoid entering all white houses, and to
ignore and refuse anything you may say or offer to do for
them, I must have answers. Is this an isolated act of
vengeance against my Family and myself for my earlier
capture of your life-mate and yourself, or do you intend
to treat all Keidi refugees in this utterly ruthless fashion?
I would hear your words, off-worlder, even though I am
unlikely to believe them."

Martin was silent for a moment. The threat to turn his
own and perhaps some of the non-Estate refugees away
from the induction centers was a development he had not
foreseen, and it worried him. He could blank the other's
radio signals easily enough and allow the doctor or
themselves to do all the talking, but at this stage a sudden silence from their leader would be suspicious and
would probably have the same disruptive effect. He desperately needed the First's active cooperation.

"This is not the time for vengeance or misdirection,"
he said finally. "The entrance to the induction center is a
short-range matter transmitter which immediately transports candidates to the uppermost floor."

"Scientific tricks," the First broke in, "do not impress
me."

Martin recalled his first visit to the local induction
center on Earth, and remembered that it had impressed
him out of about five year's growth.

". . . Which is the only level within the building not
occupied by interview compartments or equipment," he

went on. "The roof and three walls of the reception area are transparent but completely impervious to radiation, and will enable you to watch the approach of the rest of your people. Around the three walls are pictures, more than two hundred of them, showing all the different species who make up the Federation of Galactic Sentients. By pressing the sensor plate that is under each picture you will be given a brief summary of the physiology, environment, and culture of the species concerned. Your people might find this material instructive . . ."

"I have no wish to learn anything about Galactics," the First said.

". . . Or an amusing means of occupying your waiting time," Martin went on. "But there is an area which you should avoid, the desks lining the fourth wall and the doors behind them. These doors must not be forced open. They form part of the Citizen examination and matter transmission network which would move the person entering to a compartment in a different part of this or another building, and time would be wasted finding and getting them back again."

"My people are not barbarians, off-worlder," the First said angrily. "They will not damage your equipment. In any case, none of them would be passed by your examination machines, they are warriors."

"Don't be too sure," Martin said quietly. "It depends on their reasons for becoming warriors. Did they feel an obligation to protect their friends and families from harm, to provide them with food and shelter? Or did they simply enjoy the power of killing, hurting, or frightening others? A warrior does not necessarily make a bad Citizen."

"Off-worlder," the First said coldly, "we are surrounded by pictures of the horrifying creatures which you say are Federation Citizens. We cannot sit at a table without three-dimensional displays appearing on it, and literature printed in the principal written languages of Keidi is everywhere. Are you trying to influence, seduce, and divide my family?"

That was exactly what Martin was trying to do, but this was not the time to say so. Instead, he went on, en overcrowding or other factors make it necessary to move your Family, or when we have accurately charted the future progress of the contamination, you will be told which doors to use so that you can be transported to induction centers in safe areas. These will probably be on the north or south continents, where you will be given supplies, shelters, and assistance to resettle.

"When we are not using it to communicate," Martin continued, "this projection will be enlarged to reproduce the master display of the hypership, so that you will be able to watch and give advice on the overall progress of the evacuation. Have you other questions?"

The Keidi leader was silent for a moment, then he said, "I have many questions which concern the ultimate fate of my people, but I cannot ask them until I have a clearer idea of what is happening. If I were to study your master display for a time, I might learn enough to ask the right questions."

Whatever else the First was, Martin thought as he broke contact, he was not stupid.

Chapter 28

ANOTHER day of frenetic activity passed. Beyond the borders of the Estate, in spite of the urgings, pleadings, and repeated descriptions of the effects of radiation poisoning, there were areas where the evacuations were not going smoothly. Instead of *the* First there were many Firsts who, while possessing the authority, were more used to government by committee.

There was little that the doctor could do about this. He had been obeyed without question by his own people. In the towns and settlements where he was known and respected, they obeyed him, reluctantly and with much argument. But in the outlying districts he was just a Keidi voice warning of dreadful things to come—a voice which inspired fear but not always belief.

When Martin tried to intervene in support of the doctor, that caused even more arguments, dissension, and delays. The dislike and distrust felt for Galactics all over Keidi came close to being a planet-wide psychosis. And the dissension was beginning to spread to the hypership.

"Group Eighty-eight has wasted too much time," said Martin impatiently. "That cloud, as you can see from the figures, is a particularly dirty one. It will cross their path half a day before they are able to reach shelter, enough time to give the very young Keidi a lethal dose and render the adults sterile. They must be redirected to Center Twelve-twenty-seven, now. Even then it will be a very close thing."

The doctor's speaking horn swung round angrily. "Off-worlder, I have only just succeeded in getting that group moving, and now you want me to tell them to move in what is nearly the opposite direction! There will be disorganization, argument, and more delay. Twelve-twenty-seven is being threatened by fallout from Burst Five, and the delay will mean that they face the same danger going there."

"Not if they decide quickly and turn back at once," Martin said. "I think another nonmaterial show of force is indicated, to help concentrate their thinking."

"No!" the doctor said. "Give me credit for understanding my people's thinking better than a meddling off-worlder. Sudden terror could just as easily cause them to scatter in all directions, or not move at all."

Trying hard to control his anger and impatience, Martin said, "There are five other groups in much the same position as Eighty-eight, but for different reasons. We could lift them out, if the transports are ready."

He looked at Beth, but before she could reply the doctor said, "Off-worlder, the First tried to explain it to you and now I will try. We do not want, but we are forced to accept, your help. But we must also be allowed to help ourselves. Since the Exodus took away our population and skimmed off the finest layers of our culture, the Keidi who remained have become a backward, angry, and very proud people. Any attempt, however well meant, to force all but the minimum of assistance on them, or to impress them with the scientific marvels of the Federation, will have negative results. This, the First's dreams of conquest and unification, the premature detonation of his nuclear devices, and everything that has occurred as a result, is our problem. Do you understand that, off-worlder?"

The Keidi sat within arms reach, but he seemed suddenly to be miles away.

Beth looked worriedly from the doctor to Martin and said, "The first transport is ready to launch. It is untested, but testing is a formality because the fabrication module's self-inspection system is . . ."

"But you are a healer," Martin said, ignoring her. "Surely it is your duty to save lives?"

"Yes," said the Doctor, "that is why I wanted to help you. But I have found that a patient who wants to survive will aid the healing process, and live longer, than one who has no incentive for continued survival. The loss of pride and self-respect destroys the will to benefit from the healing."

"I don't accept that," Martin said, "especially in the present situation. Pride is no protection against radiation poisoning, and what about your people who are too young to have learned about pride?"

"Don't be stupid, off-worlder," the Keidi said. "There are exceptions, naturally. I was simply making the point that too much help can be worse than . . ."

Beth pointed at the attention light blinking unnoticed on Martin's console and said, "The First is calling you."

The Keidi leader was staring out of the screen at him, his speaking horn twitching with impatience. The First began speaking without giving Martin time to talk. "Offworlder, we must negotiate. We have duties and obligations which must be exchanged without delay or misdirection on either side. I shall bind myself, by the continuing respect of my people and by the parental duty of a First Father to his Family, to discharge my obligations fully, without omission or deliberate misunderstanding, to your satisfaction. You must bind yourself and the members of your organization by whatever personal, legal, or nonmaterial authority that you honor, to do likewise."

"What—" began Martin. "This is not the time for complex negotiations. We're very busy here right now, as you can see from your repeater screen. If you're worried about something, don't be. You are in no danger and the remaining groups of your special family are making good progress toward your center. Please, let's discuss this later."

"We will discuss it now," said the First, "or my remaining family will not join me, and few indeed will be the other Keidi who reach any of their designated centers."

Beth and the doctor had swung around to stare at the screen. Martin wet his lips and said quietly, "Explain."

There were many Keidi crowded around and behind the First, but none of them made a sound as he said, "Off-worlder, I have been considering your earlier words to me about overcrowding and your means of relieving it, and the real meaning of these words so far as my Family and myself are concerned. I have decided that you intend to use the center's matter transmitters to split up my family and organization and scatter it to centers all over the north and south continents."

Too quietly for the doctor to hear her, Beth said, "So that's why you weren't worried about letting his special people into one center. A neat, but nasty, solution."

"The idea had occurred to me," Martin said softly.

Concentrating Keida's proven Undesirables—they had been unknowingly nominated as such by the First—into one center, then scattering them so thinly among the more normal Keidi that their ability to reorganize and regain control would have been lost, had been a very attractive idea. After all, on a planetary scale that had been the primary purpose of the induction centers, as well as to filter out potential non-Citizens like Beth and himself. But it had been a nice, simple, and too uncertain solution which he had been reluctantly obliged to discard.

To the First he said, "I do not intend to split your family. Your fears are groundless."

"That," the First said harshly, "is the expected reply,

a piece of verbal misdirection aimed at rendering my people more amenable until the treachery is accomplished. You must bind yourself to those words, completely and without any possibility of later argument or modification, as I have bound myself to mine. You must do this now."

"Or else?" asked Martin.

"Your evacuation," the First replied, "will become an ever greater shambles than it is now."

"Explain," Martin said again.

In order to allay his people's distrust and suspicions regarding the Galactics' intentions, the First explained, he had told them that they should proceed toward their assigned centers only so long as he was able to report it safe to do so. He was in constant communication with them and they with each other, and if he signaled that the centers were not, in fact, radiation shelters but a cunning trap devised by the off-worlders to gather them together for easy execution, few indeed were the refugee groups who would not immediately halt or go somewhere, anywhere, else. If advanced technology was used to blank out or otherwise interfere with the First's continuing signals of reassurance, his people would then know that the off-worlder's treachery was a fact and act accordingly, by spreading the news to the other, non-Family groups.

"If you were to blank all Keidi-operated radio transmitters," the First added, "I suspect that your own ship-directed rescue plans would be seriously hampered. Is this not so?"

For a moment Martin was too angry to speak, then he said, "Those nuclear detonations were a fact, not an off-worlder trick. You know the effects of massive radiation exposure on unprotected people. Will you risk killing a large proportion of your present and future population for selfish, political gain? And for a personal reassurance which you have already received?"

"The majority of my people are post-Exodus second and third generation," the First said slowly, "and have no understanding of nuclear fallout. They treat the stories about the terrible things which may happen to them with disbelief. Unless, of course, it is a trusted person and not the hated off-worlders or a Keidi healer who has apparently sided with the Galactics, who is telling the stories. It is possible that I would not risk killing so many of my people but you, off-worlder, cannot be sure of that. And the political gain I seek is not selfish, it is for the future of a people who want to live, no matter how difficult that life may be, without the help of off-worlders. As yet your reassurances have no substance."

"But such threats are unnecessary," Martin said angrily. "Wait."

"Had your response been immediate, off-worlder," the First said, "I would have suspected a total misdirection. I shall wait as long as you can afford to wait."

That would not be for long, Martin thought. Beth and the doctor were staring at him, ignoring the master screen where the sensor displays and attention lights which were flickering into the colors denoting third-level emergencies. He swore and tried to think.

Plainly the First was frightened by a situation which would not occur, so badly that he was overreacting. Was the Keidi leader so old and selfish and power hungry that even the thought of losing control of his Family Estate was worse than death to him? Martin did not think so. Perhaps the First really believed that he was being unselfish, that he was acting for the ultimate good of his race, the Keidi equivalent of death or glory.

"I don't understand," he said in quiet desperation. "Why is this promise so important to him? He is an old Keidi, after all. Why doesn't he let go?"

"I don't know what overall strategy, if any, you had in mind," Beth said sympathetically, "but this particular battle you've lost."

Martin shook his head. To the First he said, "For my promise you offered a return which would be equally binding. Please specify."

"I offer active and total cooperation in the evacuation and movement of refugees," the First said. "From the situation reflected on my screen it is obvious that the operation is being mishandled by a couple of ignorant if well-meaning off-worlders no Keidi trusts, and a healer who is good at his job but sadly inadequate in other areas. I will take charge of this operation, which is essentially a military one, and complete it, if not to your satisfaction, at least with a degree of success many times greater than you could achieve unaided.

"All Keida knows the First Father of the Estate," he ended proudly. "When I speak they will listen, believe, and obey."

The attention lights on the status and prediction panel were proliferating like tiny, fast-growing flowers which blossomed yellow and orange and, in a few places, bright red. More and more refugee groups were either not moving or moving too slowly to reach safety. Martin stared at the wrinkled, age-discolored features on his screen and reached for the transmit stud.

"Off-worlder," the Doctor warned. "Take time to think."

"Yes, dammit," said Beth. "He made fools of us once already. Now he wants to take all the credit for saving, not only the people of his Estate, but the entire population from the disaster he caused, while maintaining his precious military dictatorship intact as well. It means giving him what he has always wanted, the leadership of all the Keidi, and what he could never have expected, their life-long gratitude for saving them as well. Surely we can't let him get away with that!"

Martin nodded toward the status board and the immediate attention lights that were winking urgently all over it, and sighed. "I have no choice."

To the waiting First he went on, "Very well. In return for the services specified, I most solemnly bind myself and my life-mate to this obligation. To the best of our ability, and without any misdirection or omission of effort, we will ensure that you, your blood family and the special members of your Family Estate whom you wish to remain with you will so remain. All of the relevant facts and circumstances governing this situation are being recorded for later study and assessment by our superior, who will..."

"Have our bloody guts for garters," Beth said with quiet intensity. "This is exactly what we aren't supposed to do."

"... Who will be obliged to follow our recommendations and be similarly bound by them," Martin went on, "since we have been given responsibility for the Keida assignment. This obligation will be honored and may not be abrogated, nor amended in any particular, until you and your chosen Family, even to its youngest present member, have died by accident, at the hands of other Keidi, or from old age . . ."

"There was no need to go that far," Beth protested.

". . . And no future agency," he continued, "direct or indirect, will be used to separate your group or hasten the death of any member covered by this binding. Are we agreed?"

"Have you the power to do that?" asked the Keidi leader. He sounded impressed.

"As the Federation's representative on Keida," Martin replied, "I have the responsibility."

The First regarded Martin silently for a moment, then said, "We are agreed, off-worlder. The primary responsibility for the movement of the refugees is now mine. Henceforth you will provide information and additional communication channels when required and will not, by any word, act, omission, or implication try to undermine or criticize in any way my personal authority or that of my organization. You will not interfere verbally in any situation nor provide material assistance of any kind unless requested by me to do so. Is this also agreed?"

Beth seemed ready to go into spontaneous combustion.

"Yes," Martin said quickly, "unless we are able to provide forms of assistance which you cannot."

When the First spoke it was obvious that he had been testing Martin, trying to see just how far the off-worlder could be pushed, because there was no argument. He said, "We and our organizations are agreed, then. I shall begin by speaking to Group Eleven-twenty-seven," he went on, "which is progressing like a beheaded cretsil with one leg . . ."

During the three hours which followed Beth and Martin had nothing to do but watch the sensor data flashing onto the big surveillance screen and listen while the First did all the talking with, occasionally, a little help from the doctor. In the time they saw, with very mixed feelings, an increasing number of the Immediate Attention lights flicker from red to orange, and the orange down-

grade to the yellow or green denoting refugee groups
which, barring accidents, would make it to their assigned
centers in time or had already reached them. A few of
the lights persisted in burning red, but the Keidi leader
was working hard on those groups, in turn bullying,
threatening, encouraging, and, wherever possible, sending Estate vehicles and draught animals to speed them
along. Much as Martin hated to admit it, the First was
doing a fine job.

Beth's angry voice made him realize that he had been
thinking aloud again.

"I can admire the job he's doing," she said, "but I
most definitely do not admire *him*! He deserves to be
lynched for what he did, and instead he's going to end up
as the apparent savior of all Keida. You've handed him
exactly what he's always wanted, the whole damned
planet, and without even trying to reduce his demands."

Martin looked from her to the main screen and said
quietly, "Bargaining might have satisfied my pride,
wasted time, and lost a lot of Keidi lives which the First
is busy saving. In the circumstances I couldn't afford to
be proud.

"Pride, independence, self-reliance," he went on, "are
considered more important among the Keidi than I had
realized, even though there were clear indications of
how they felt during that Keidi-Surreshon contact in the
World. They'll need Federation help, food, fuel, insulated housing and so on, to resettle, but they don't want
too much outside help. The First is saving their pride as
well as their lives, and, even though the motive is self-
aggrandizement, I think he also has the ultimate good of
the Keidi at heart."

"If he has one," Beth said. "But what bothers me is
that there is nothing we can do to save people like the
doctor, potential Federation Citizens, from people like
the First. I can't see him allowing anyone to try for citizenship under the new set up...Oh, no, this is all we
need!"

"What is it?" Martin asked.

"Seismic activity along a fault line which runs thirty
miles south of the missile arsenal," she said. "A delayed

reaction to that subsurface detonation in the crater, I should think. The shockwaves are moving in both directions along the line, which diagonally bisects the continent. Our sound sensors are beginning to pick it up and within a few minutes the nearest refugee groups will feel as well as hear it. I'm flagging the areas at immediate risk on the screen. We'd better tell the First what's happening..."

The Keidi leader reacted quickly, rerouting his groups where necessary to avoid them having to travel through forested areas where the severe shocks would be certain to bring down trees with consequent death, injury, and reduced mobility. Martin was still talking to the First when Beth interrupted him.

"More bad news," she said quickly. "This isn't a simple plate movement along a fault line. The sensors in the crater have been reporting the levels of radioactive dust expected after a large, subsurface detonation. But now they are showing increasing amounts of steam, hydrogen sulphide, and other sulphur combinations indicative of an active volcano. The deep probes show a massive pressure buildup centered under the arsenal site where the old lava plug sealing the conduit which opens the crater to the underlying magma has been fractured and severely weakened by the detonation. We can expect a major eruption as well as earthquakes which are, in fact, the advance warning of the volcanic activity to come. The computer is predicting severe and continuing shocks all along the fault line, and it keeps reminding me that the induction centers are not proof against major earthquakes and that their matter transmission equipment is delicately tuned, sensitive, and susceptible to vibration damage.

"The good news," she added dryly, "is that the matter transmitters should remain operative for at least two hours after the last few groups are due to reach shelter, but it would be safer to transport all refugees to centers on the north and south continents as soon as they come in."

While she was speaking Martin had kept his eyes on

the Keidi leader. He said, "Did you hear that?"

"I heard, off-worlder," said the First. "The Keidi are a stubborn race. The more obstacles are placed in our path, the harder we try to surmount them. They will reach your centers in time. My obligation will be discharged. I remind you of yours."

"I have not forgotten," Martin said angrily. "But surely you are being overconfident? We still have red lights on groups Seven-eighteen and Twelve-twenty-one. Both are large, widely scattered groups. What are you doing for them?"

"Seven-eighteen will go orange very soon and will reach shelter in time," the First replied. "The other group is encamped in thickly forested mountains on my western border and would have been difficult to move even without this latest complication. I am particularly sorry about them, but in an operation of this magnitude and complexity a certain level of casualties must be accepted."

"There is no acceptable level of casualties," Martin said firmly. "If you can't help them, maybe I can."

Not for the first time Martin wished that he was able to read those alien features as the First said, "It is a large training establishment, staffed by aged Keidi who make their experience available to very young trainees. The isolation and hostile environment aids the development of strong character. The camp instructors know of you and will not listen to or accept help from a Galactic, and the trainees will follow without question the orders of their superiors, whose minds lack the flexibility to adapt to the present situation.

"The loss of this group saddens me, off-worlder," the Keidi ended, "but this part of my obligation, you must agree, is impossible for me to discharge."

"If they won't accept help from an off-worlder," Martin persisted, "they might listen to you or the doctor. Can you spare him if he will come with me?"

"I will come," the doctor said. The First remained silent.

"Don't worry," Martin said impatiently, "we won't

criticize you in any way. I won't even mention your name."

"In that camp," said the First, "your words of criticism would not be believed. You may have the doctor, off-worlder, and I wish you success."

Chapter 29

THE two newly fabricated transports, which had the capacity to evacuate all of the training camp personnel in a single trip, were ready to leave within the hour. The delay had been due to the special equipment which had to be taken along: remote-controlled vehicles, life sensors, restraints and handling devices for injured, unconscious, or actively uncooperative refugees, as well as the external PA and translation systems. Ever since the original detonations, Beth had foreseen a probable need for a wide range of disaster medication tailored to the Keidi life form, and this had been synthesized in quantity—including, in case of dire need, enough anesthetic gas to stop a small war.

"I may be too old for this kind of work," the doctor said in a worried voice as they were about to leave for the launching bay. "I'm stiff in the mind as well as the joints. What can I possibly do, alone in an enormous transport vessel I cannot understand or control, if something goes wrong? You have already said that these vessels are untested. In the old days I couldn't even repair my grandchild's play cart."

Reassuringly, Beth said, "One of the transports will be remotely controlled by the other, which will contain you and my life-mate. If necessary I can control both vessels from here. And this is a hypership, Doctor. Its fabricator module does not produce substandard equipment. You will be quite safe."

The doctor did not speak until the hypership had shrunk to a blob of light behind them and their transport was encountering the buffeting characteristic of hypersonic flight through the upper atmosphere.

"Your life-mate," he commented sourly to Martin, "is not riding in this thing."

Storm-force winds and heavy rain were sweeping the area when the transports arrived above the camp. It was a collection of low, log buildings whose uniformity of structure and precise positioning made it plain that this was a military establishment and not a settlement of civilians. In no sense was it a covert approach as they dropped slowly below the level of the high, thickly wooded mountains surrounding the camp. Maximum external lighting on both ships brightened the noon overcast and brilliantly flashing communications probes shot ahead of them to spear the ground outside the buildings.

With the volume controls set on high because he was competing against the sounds of the wind and rain, the doctor began to speak—to only a handful of Keidi who opened up on them with small-arms fire.

From the scraps of translated conversation being picked up by the sound sensors, Beth was able to piece together the reasons for the hostility. Even in ideal weather conditions the surrounding mountains made radio communications with the rest of the Estate uncertain, she explained, and the last coherent signal to come through had been the news that a ship of the Galactics had violated Estate air space. Since then they had heard only incomplete messages, rendered almost unintelligible by radiation interference, ordering evacuations from many areas, and they had assumed that the Federation ship which had triggered the initial warning had been the forerunner of an invasion fleet. The manner of the transports' approach had supported that assumption.

"We haven't time to argue," Martin said. "Patch the First through and let him explain it to them, but quickly."

"There's worse to come," Beth said. "The trainees have been scattered in small groups all over the valley, out of radio contact with the camp and each other. This seems to be common practice with them, aimed at instilling self-reliance, initiative, and character. The problem is . . ."

"That we have an unknown number of Keidi boy scout patrols to rescue," Martin finished for her.

"Not quite," she replied. "After the lander was first sighted, they were sent out with orders to disperse and conceal themselves as part of what could have been turned into a war situation. They had solid-projectile–firing weapons, and when they see you their response will be extremely hostile."

Martin swore but under his breath so as not to confuse the doctor's translator, and said, "We'll hold back until the First has tried to straighten them out. We need a reassuring message, couched in very general terms, which we can record and rebroadcast to all the trainee groups. Tell him to do it quickly."

"I'd better *ask* him to do it quickly," Beth said. "He's very busy just now."

"Who isn't?" Martin replied shortly.

He was already guiding the transports toward the nearest group of young Keidi. But the ships had been hovering silently, and Martin had been waiting impatiently, for nearly ten minutes in the rainclouds above them before the First came through.

"Off-worlder," he said briskly. "If I am to reassure the young people sufficiently to make them board your vessels, I must know something about them. Tell me their size, shape, the sounds they make, the method of boarding and their interior accommodation. Tell me quickly..."

In a surprisingly short time the First's message was blaring out of the soft-landed speakers, and the Keidi on the ground had overcome their natural suspicion and were obeying their leader's instructions. The unmanned transport dropped silently through the cloud layer and onto the wooded mountainside, where the sound of thunderously snapping tree trunks and branches stopped the trainees dead in their tracks. It took several additional minutes of reassurance from the First Father, delivered in a manner which would have been the envy of an Earth drill sergeant, before they boarded the transport.

"I could not have done that," the doctor said quietly.

"Nor I," Martin said.

Inside the transport there was more reassurance in
the form of external view-screens which would enable
them to see the takeoff and subsequent evacuations,
comfortable seating, and the pleasant but authoritative
voice of Beth speaking through the translator in the
manner of one of the pre-Exodus air hostesses that they
had been born too late to remember. She was telling
them to move away from the entry hatches so as not to
hamper later boarders who might be injured or in a
greater hurry than they had been.

They did as they were told, and without the First having to reinforce her request. Within a few minutes the
hatches closed and the transport was on the way to the
next group.

The repeater in the manned transport was showing
induction centers already covered by the fallout symbol
and others where the angry red markers were moving
dangerously close. But at all those centers the people
were either already under cover or would reach it in
time. Martin could not say the same for the groups of
Keidi scattered all over this mountain valley.

In all, the sensors had located eleven groups of
trainees, averaging twenty to a group. While Martin and
the doctor went after those which were most likely to
contain injured Keidi, Beth and her remote-controlled
transport had been assigned the more simple and accessible pickups, and had done very well.

While she was boarding her seventh group and the
doctor and Martin their third, the area was shaken by
two severe, closely spaced ground tremors. Trees all
around the last party of trainees uprooted themselves
and toppled onto their sides. The situation was further
complicated by a minor avalanche.

From the sound sensors which had survived the devastation came terrified appeals for help and the untranslatable and even more urgent cries of pain. Martin
dropped the transport onto the bed of fallen timber as
close to the trainees as possible, and the fear and confusion in the young Keidi voices increased. Many of them
were assuming that the quake, landslide, falling trees,
and the transport's sudden arrival were, in spite of the
reassurance of their First, an attack on them by the off-

world ship. Martin climbed quickly into a medium-weight excursion suit.

"You are wearing armor," the doctor said accusingly, "and a weapon."

"It fires bulbs of anesthetic gas which explode on contact," Martin said.

He opened the entry ports and despatched the first of the ground vehicles, half of which had been converted to the casualty evacuation configuration.

"The young Keidi will think it is a weapon," the doctor said.

"You tell them it isn't," Martin said impatiently, "if I ever get close enough to use the thing. Take this mask. It won't fit over your head but, if you need to use it, press the filter tightly against your speaking horn."

Three-dimensional traffic jams had formed outside the ports as the vehicles tried to push through or rise above the tangle of branches which now sprouted vertically from the fallen tree trunks. The time wasted extricating them, Martin thought, would be doubled as they pushed through a similar barrier above the trainees, and then they would have to do it all again, fully loaded, on the return ship.

"They're less than two hundred meters away," Martin said. "We can climb between the branches and get there quicker on foot. Coming?"

The doctor followed without replying as Martin led the way, swinging around the larger branches and steadying himself on the smaller as he jumped from trunk to trunk or moved along those which by chance had fallen in his direction of travel. He had to be careful not to fall into the tangle between the trunks and the ground, where the broken stumps of smaller trees bristled like the stakes in an old-time tiger trap. In spite of the obstacles he was making good progress, but the doctor was not.

Martin stopped and tried to curb his impatience by reminding himself that the doctor was a very old Keidi who might not have enjoyed climbing trees even as a child.

Beth used the delay to report.

"I have you spotted," she said briskly, "about halfway to the trainee group. The other transport is loaded up and headed for the First's center. He wants the young Keidi sent to him there because most of them are the offspring of his special group. It's going to be pretty crowded in that center, but he insisted so I agreed. There was no need to worry you with it.

"But there is something you should be worrying about," she went on. "The crater sensor readings don't look good. There is a steady buildup of pressure on that weakened lava plug, and they are predicting an increase in the severity and frequency of earthquake activity..."

He lost her then as both the transmission and the noise of the wind and rain were drowned out by a roaring, crackling tidal wave of sound that swept toward and then around them. The tree trunk twisted alarmingly beneath his feet, and he wrapped one arm around a branch to steady himself. The doctor, who had almost caught up with him, had no handholds and was falling. Martin stretched out his free arm and felt the Keidi's fingers lock around his wrist in a grip so tight that he grunted with pain.

For the longest few seconds of his life Martin held on with the branch digging painfully into the crook of his elbow and his arms feeling that they would tear off at the shoulders. From all around them came the deafening crepitation of the fallen trees and branches grinding against each other. Then suddenly it was quiet again except for the almost comforting sounds of the wind and rain. The pull of the doctor's weight on his arms was relieved as the other found a hand-hold and climbed up beside him.

"I lost you," Martin said. "We were having an earthquake."

"Oh, very droll," Beth said, her voice angry with relief. She went on, "The seismic activity is incidental, it's that volcano we have to worry about. An accurate prediction is impossible, but the computer thinks it could go any time between three to five hours from now. We should start transferring refugees to the north and south continent centers as soon as possible. Shall I ask the First to advise on the best locations?"

Martin shook his head, not in negation but in an effort to stir his brain into constructive thought. He looked at his helmet status display. Many of the rescue vehicles had become hopelessly entangled in the shifting branches and were in need of rescuing themselves, so much so that it could take the rest of the day rather than a few hours to move the trainees—more if some of them were badly injured. It was a time for not wasting time.

"Send the loaded transport on automatic to the First's center," he said quickly. "Tell him to ready his people for moving out, explain the matter transmitter linkups and tell him again, if he is still worrying about it, that he and all of his special group will be sent to the same location.

"While you're doing that," he went on, "bring the hypership down to, say, half a mile above the valley. I know it's tricky handling that monster in atmosphere, but you did something like this on Teldi, and this area has to be cleared quickly if we are to do anything for these people."

Quickly and carefully, he added under his breath. There were a lot of valuable and fragile organic objects, himself included, buried by the fallen trees she was about to clear.

"Twenty-three minutes," she said.

Once again they began climbing and crawling through the branches in the general direction of the trainees. Martin told the doctor to speak to them about the giant space vessel that was coming to help with their rescue, and try to describe its shape and size, and tell them that they had nothing to fear from it. But when the hypership broke through the clouds to darken the sky above them like some gargantuan, metal overcast, even Martin and the doctor, who knew it for what it was, had an instinctive urge to run and get from underneath before it could fall and smash them flat.

There was a sudden, unnatural stillness as it deployed its force shield and the wind and rain ceased. The voices of the young Keidi sounded loud and very close. Martin pointed to a tiny clear area of ground below them.

"Climb down there and lie flat," he said urgently. "Don't move no matter what happens. And tell your people they have nothing to fear."

"I will try, off-worlder," the doctor said. "But I am fearful myself."

For a few minutes nothing moved except for the small, irregular tremors which were shaking the ground on which they lay. Then the invisible, immaterial cylinders that were the hypership's tractor beams speared out, came to a focus, and whole trees were lifted gently into the air and, when it was clear that nothing was entangled in their branches, tossed away. The sound of discarded trees crashing onto the lower slopes became continuous.

Beth began by clearing the area outside the transport's entry locks. Martin watched admiringly, marveling at her precision of control as she raised one particular tree into the air and shook it gently to dislodge a vehicle which had trapped itself in the branches. Plainly she wanted to gain experience rescuing inanimate objects before trusting herself to extricate the living. But very soon her confidence and speed increased and the splintered tree trunks and branches were lifted from above them so that they were able to stand again.

A broad pathway of tumbled soil and small branches lay between the transport and the Keidi trainees along which the rescue vehicles were already moving.

"Oh, nice *work*!" Martin said enthusiastically. The doctor did not speak. He was already hurrying toward the group of young Keidi who were lying in their newly created clearing. Some of them were moving and trying to crawl away.

"It was just like weeding a big garden," she said modestly, "except that the object was to rescue the creepy crawlies as well as remove the weeds.

"But you have another problem," she went on seriously. "All of the trainees who are able to move have taken to the woods. When I tried to lift the trees off one of them he just took off in a different direction. Talk to them, dammit, we haven't time to play hide and seek!"

"The doctor will talk to them," Martin said.

But the doctor had time only for a few hasty and general words of reassurance because he had casualties lying on the ground all around him awaiting attention. Most of them were young Keidi who had suffered limb fractures, heavy bruising, and lacerations from the treefalls. But there were two older trainees in very bad shape indeed. They had been trying to protect a couple of their smaller charges with their bodies—successfully, because the young Keidi had been seen wriggling from under them and running away.

When Martin tried to lift one of them onto a vehicle, the doctor told him to please go away because his presence was distressing the still-conscious patients.

"I'm just an off-world bogeyman," Martin said bitterly. "But there's something I can do. Point me at the nearest escapee."

Beth did so and reminded him, unnecessarily, that his gas bulbs exploded on contact, that he would have to get close enough to hit his target so as not to waste them on any intervening foliage, and that he should be very careful because the sensors showed most of the escapees to be armed.

Martin was too busy forcing his way under fallen branches to reply. In the unnatural stillness he must have sounded like the Keidi equivalent of a rampaging elephant, which would have done nothing at all to reassure the people he was trying to help.

Suddenly he caught sight of a small Keidi crawling slowly under the branches, dragging one leg stiffly behind him. Martin waited until he had a clear shot and fired. The gas bulb plopped wetly against the back of the target's head and the Keidi went limp. As he went forward to check on the other's condition, there was movement in the leaves of a thick bush about twenty meters to his right. Since the arrival of the hypership there had been no wind in the valley.

He swung his gas-gun to bear and fired twice at a tree stump close behind the suspect bush, then dropped flat. There was the sharp crack of a solid-projectile–firing weapon, but the bullet went nowhere near him. Probably the Keidi had pulled the trigger instinctively as the anesthetic took effect.

By the time he had the two sleeping forms draped one over each arm, Beth had cleared a path back to the other casualties. As he placed them in one of the vehicles he announced loudly that they were asleep and uninjured, but it was plain that only the doctor believed him.

Although they had scattered at the arrival of the hypership, Beth reported, the remaining trainees had joined up again in a small ravine which ran up the mountainside before dividing into three. When he reached it Martin saw that the rock walls were so narrow that the fallen trees formed a roof over their heads rather than an obstruction. The runaways were climbing fast, much faster than he could manage hampered as he was by the protective suit.

"Can you squeeze a vehicle in here?" Martin asked quickly. "I might as well climb fast and in comfort. And can you block the top end of the ravine before it divides, to keep our friends from scattering all over the mountain. How long do you need?"

"In order:" Beth said, "just barely, but you'll have to keep your head down if you don't want it knocked off; can do; and three minutes."

With its gravity repulsers whining in protest at the steep gradient, his vehicle rounded a bend in the ravine in time to see the log roof ahead of the Keidi collapse into a solid plug of splintered wood, soil, and loose rock —the hypership's tractors could push just as hard as they could pull. He was still at extreme range for the gas-gun, but there was so much dust and noise up ahead that he doubted if any of the Keidi could hear or see his approach. When he was certain of maximum effect, he loosed off a short burst. In the confined space it did not matter whether he hit his targets or not.

A few minutes later the dust had settled, the fog of anesthetic gas had dispersed, and the four sleeping runaways were in the vehicle.

"There should be five of them," Beth said. "Wait, I see him! About thirty meters behind you, on the left top edge of the ravine behind a stump. He isn't moving, but that doesn't mean he's unconscious. Be care—"

Martin jumped quickly to one side as he turned, only to be knocked to the ground by two savage, irresistible blows to his chest and shoulder. He blinked the tears from his eyes as a third shot buried itself in the soil a few inches from his helmet.

There seemed to be a small patch of haze, which dispersed before he could be sure it was really there, high on one side of the ravine. It could have been smoke from the Keidi's weapon. He swung his gas-gun to bear, grunting with the pain which the movement caused in his chest and shoulder. His eyes were watering so badly that he could scarcely see. He fired in the remembered direction and kept on firing until his weapon was empty, then rolled painfully onto one hand and his knees, wondering if he could reach the cover of his vehicle before another bullet found him.

Chapter 30

"YOUR target is unconscious," Beth said. "I heard shooting. Are you all right?"

Martin grunted again as he climbed awkwardly to his feet. "Yes," he said.

"My ears and the bio-sensors are calling you a liar," she said worriedly. "What happened to—"

"I'm all right," Martin said.

He could not incline the helmet far enough forward to see, but with his fingers he could feel the two long, deep trenches that the bullets had cut in the suit's chest and shoulder section. He could not move his left arm or inhale without pain, and he thought he had been very lucky indeed to escape with what felt like a broken collarbone and a couple of cracked ribs. But he could not afford to waste his breath on a verbal self-diagnosis—he might need all of it if he was going to recover the last runaway.

A few minutes later as he was struggling to lift the Keidi one-handed into the vehicle, Beth said, "Get in the back with the others and lie flat. I'll bring you in on remote. Your bio-sensor display worries me, and I don't want you to pass out, not now. There is another problem..."

It had been a mistake to show the young Keidi everything that was happening outside their transport, she said, because the sight of Martin knocking over their friends with his weapon had made their immature minds jump to a wrong conclusion—that the evil off-worlder's intention was to kill and ultimately eat all of them. She had tried to reason with them, and had played back the original words of reassurance spoken by their First, but they were too frightened to listen to anyone. She had been forced then to seal the entry ports to keep them from escaping again.

". . . Now they're taking the interior of the transport apart," she went on quickly. "The doctor has the others loaded onto vehicles and is waiting outside, but if I open up the ones inside will escape. Gas?"

"Gas," Martin agreed.

On the way back the vehicle lurched and bumped several times, rolling one of the Keidi against his damaged shoulder. He mentioned it to Beth, who said crossly that gravity repulsion vehicles were designed to maintain a fixed distance above the land or road surface, and that it was the ground that was lurching. A few minutes later he heard her telling the doctor that there wasn't time to unload his casualties and that, with the exception of her life-mate, they should remain in their vehicles until they were off-loaded at the nearest safe induction center.

The First, who was still on the transport's frequency, did not agree.

"They must be brought *here*!" the Keidi leader said firmly. "Many of their parents are with me and it is wrong to separate them. I insist."

"But the radiation level in your area is dangerously high," Beth protested, "and they are young people. They are anesthetized, unable to move, and many of them are injured, and this will complicate and delay the transfer. Unprotected and in the open, they could take only a few minutes exposure without the probability of serious gene damage."

The First did not reply for a moment, during which Martin was being lifted and pushed through the personnel entry port. When he reached his control console, he saw that Beth was already lifting their transport with one of the hypership's tractors. The direct vision panels showed only the receding top of the cloud layer.

Around them the Keidi trainees were asleep amid the self-created wreckage of the furniture. The doctor glared at Martin disapprovingly, but could not say anything because of the mask pressed tightly against his speaking horn.

"Land your vessel as close as possible to the entrance of my building," the First went on suddenly, "and open all entry points. Older members of my Family, those who are too old to worry about further offspring, must be transmitted back to the entrance. They will remove the other casualties from inside your vessel. My own medics will attend the injured, but the doctor may advise if there are special cases. During the transfer the doctor and your life-mate will not try to assist my people in any way and will remain out of sight at all times.

"It is for their own safety," the First explained harshly. "The feelings of Keidi parents for their offspring are strong and not always logical, and the way the young trainees were rescued has given rise to intense anger and hostility toward both of them. Do you understand your instructions?"

"Do *you* understand," Beth said angrily, "that your young Keidi, the ones you feel so strongly and illogically about, will still be at risk. We can take them to another center and send them to you later when—"

"Do as he says," Martin broke in sharply. "We must think of our obligations."

He had been thinking about little else since returning to the transport, and hoping that the pain he felt with every breath would not affect his clarity of thought. He had even more time to think as he watched the screen showing the small, limp, and strangely, no longer alien bodies of the trainees being off-loaded. The operation was so fast and well-organized that he doubted whether any of the children were placed at risk, although the same could not be said for the elderly adults who had volunteered, or been told, to make several return trips. Was it a display of bravery and selfless devotion to the children, or of blind obedience to their First Father?

The Keidi leader had influenced the conduct of this assignment from the time, a few minutes after entering

planetary atmosphere, his people had fired on their
lander. Because of their desire to obtain information and
be helpful both to the doctor and the First in the medical
emergency involving his granddaughter, they had become personally involved with him and had come off a
very bad second best. They had regained the initiative,
briefly, during the escape from Camp Eleven, but since
then the First had quickly regained control of the situation by maneuvering them into a position where he was
running things—the two off-worlders as well as the
whole population of his soon to be contaminated and
desperately endangered planet—exactly as he pleased.

Although Martin had never been quite sure of what
constituted evil in a human being much less an extraterrestrial, he did not think that the First was a completely
bad person. He was a brilliant politician, organizer, and
tactician, an inspiring leader who had a great dream for
the future of his people, and he had the ability combined
with the ruthlessness to make that dream come true even
after his death. But now, because of the coming of the
off-worlders, the entire population would forget their
earlier fear and distrust of him and would instead look on
him as the greatest benefactor in their history, never considering that for the majority of them—those who were
not of his inner Family—the dream would become a
nightmare, a future of near slavery.

He was also, as were many of the people he had gathered around him, completely and utterly Undesirable.

More than anything else, Martin wished that his
friend Skorta, the Master of Education, and the other
Masters of Teldi were here to advise and support him.
The Keidi people, the old and very young, the Undesirables and the potential Citizens alike, were not his property in the Teldin sense of the word, but the time had
come to grasp his Master's sword and assume ultimate
responsibility.

The time had come, Martin thought sadly, to stop the
First from doing even more damage, to end the playing
of his planetary power game by removing him and his
group of handpicked Undesirable followers from the
board.

"I am troubled, off-worlder," the doctor said suddenly.

Having made a decision which he would probably regret for the rest of his life, not because he thought it wrong but because others with influence over his future career would think so, Martin welcomed the interruption. By giving him something else to think about it decreased the temptation to change his mind.

"The First does not like me and no longer wants me in his Estate," the Keidi went on. "This does not trouble me because the feeling is mutual. But I hear your lifemate telling the people in the centers that the doors of the matter transmitter rooms are now open, and that they should prepare themselves for transfer to the north and south continents. The people of my city will be confused and frightened by this and worried about what is to come. Will you be able to send me back to them?"

"Yes, Doctor," Martin said, thinking that the subject had not changed after all. "But not until we know their new location. You may have to wait a few days."

"I am obligated beyond the possibility of discharge," the doctor said, "and I have come to realize that the whole of Keida is obligated to your life-mate and yourself. The First will doubtless try to misdirect the discharges toward himself, but my people will be told the truth.

"However," he went on, "I have had sufficient experience as a healer to know when another person is troubled, even when he is a being of another and visually repugnant species, and I would like, if it is possible, to discharge a small part of my obligation to you. I think that you are troubled. Is there a burden other than your recent hurts that you would like to share with me?"

This is ridiculous, Martin thought wildly as he stared at the leathery, alien features and into the puckering, widely flared mouth of the other's speaking horn. He had always had a clear idea of what a concerned and trusted psychiatrist or a father confessor should look like, but this was certainly not it.

He surprised himself by saying, "There is a burden, Doctor. I am about to do something very wrong for what

I believe are the right reasons. That is what troubles me."

For a moment the old Keidi was silent, then he said, "The First has the same belief and I do not think it troubles him. But you are not the First. What is the wrong that you are about to do?"

The docking signal interrupted him at that point, followed by the voice of Beth. Either she had been too busy or was pretending not to have heard their conversation.

"Can you come to Control at once," she said briskly, "or do you have to visit the medical module first?"

"Yes," Martin said, "and no."

The moment for confession had passed.

When they arrived Beth looked at his face, the bullet furrows in his suit, and at the slow, careful way he took his seat, but did not comment. Instead, she nodded toward the main screen and said, "The seismic activity is increasing all over the continent. Most of the centers are feeling it now and the refugees can't get out and are close to panic... In an earthquake situation their natural instinct is to get outside before the building falls on them and to treat the radiation, which they can neither see nor feel, as the lesser danger. There will be serious casualties if they aren't moved out quickly. The transmitter rooms are waiting for the destination instructions. So am I."

Plainly she was still annoyed at him, and he should take a few minutes to apologize and explain.

"Sorry about the way I cut short your argument with the First," he said, "but there wasn't time for a debate. I thought that the radiation risk was acceptable, the First certainly thought so, and we both wanted the trainees with him because my idea was to separate—"

"It doesn't matter," she broke in angrily, "whether they receive a sublethal dose now or slowly over the next five generations. I called up the Keida pre-Exodus data and the missile arsenal the First opened up contains virtually all of the fissionable material on the planet. That volcano was dormant and would have remained so for thousands of years if the subsurface detonation hadn't... When it erupts it will make Kratatoa look like a hiccup. All that radioactive filth will be distributed by stratospheric winds all over Keida, and five generations is how long it will take for the radiation to fall to a safe level.

"During that time," Beth went on, "the race will probably not die out, but there will be a high incidence of cancers, sterility, mutant births, and drastically reduced resistance to disease and wound infection. They may never be able to rise again, and if that wasn't bad enough, they'll have the descendants of the First's bullboys riding on their backs if they even try. They don't deserve any of this, especially not the First's plan for them.

"You should disperse his organization to centers all over Keida," she ended vehemently, "not allow him to keep it intact. Break your promise to him, dammit. In these circumstances no sane, ethical being would think any the less of you."

"No," Martin said quietly. "I have special plans for the First and his organization. They will no longer be able to affect, or infect, the other Keidi."

It was the doctor who spoke first.

"You disappoint me, off-worlder," he said. "Is this the great wrong whose doing so troubled you?"

"Yes," Martin said, still looking at Beth. "I want you to prepare the transmitters for the immediate transfer—"

"I've already done that," she said impatiently.

"I mean," he said quietly, "the orbital transmitters."

It was obvious from her deathly pallor and the sudden fear in her eyes that she had already guessed what was in his mind but, for the benefit of the recorders, he went on to tell her exactly what he wanted done so that there would be no possibility of misunderstanding.

The doctor, sensing that something was wrong, moved his horn uncertainly from one to the other but did not speak.

"You're *mad*," she said angrily, "if you're not joking. You're breaking every rule in the book. Worse, you're breaking rules that are so basic that they didn't even think it necessary to write them! Opening all the induction centers to Undesirables was bad enough, but *this*! I don't think there is a precedent, or a punishment, for what you're doing. Demotion and loss of non-Citizen

status, psychological reconstruction, maybe even reclas-
sification as Undesirables. I just can't imagine what they
will do to us."

"To me," Martin corrected.

"To us," she said firmly. "I have no better answer to
the problem. Maybe the hypership will refuse to transmit
an illegal instruction like this, I hope."

"Try," Martin said.

Beth swung around, played a brief, silent composition
on her console and said, "Federation hypership One
Seven Zero Zero Six requesting immediate reactivation
of circum-Keida matter transmission network, all units."

The intership communication screen lit at once with
the reply.

STATE PURPOSE AND AUTHORITY.

She looked at Martin, giving him a last chance to
change his mind, then said firmly, "The emergency evacuation of remaining Keida planetary population, currently awaiting transfer from equatorial continent
induction centers, to the Federation World. Authority,
non-Citizen Contact Specialist MJC/221/5501, Level
Three and non-Citizen Ship Handler ECM/221/4977,
Level One."

REQUEST REFUSED. AUTHORITY INSUFFI-
CIENT.

The reply did not seem to surprise her. She changed
her approach and said carefully, "Information requested.
Am I correct in thinking that a high level of computer
mentation is necessary to coordinate the dematerializa-
tion, transmission over interstellar distances, and reas-
sembly without distortion of the individual atomic
particles which comprise a planetary population, food
and draught animals, selected artifacts, and vegetation?
All data on the present emergency will be transmitted. Is
the level of mentation sufficiently high to evaluate and
check present planetary geophysical data, current and
predicted long-term radiation effects on the population
concerned, and the nonmaterial factors involved, specifi-
cally the political, ethical, and emotional considerations
peculiar to intelligence bearing organic life forms?"

FOR YOUR INFORMATION THE LEVEL OF MEN-
TATION IS AT LEAST THE EQUAL OF THAT OF A

HYPERSHIP MASTER COMPUTER. PRESENT THE DATA.

The reply appeared in supposedly unemotional white characters on a black screen, but Martin could imagine icicles forming under each and every letter. Beth had told him on several occasions that the more highly evolved the computer, the more susceptible it became to the human or other-species influences such as flattery, criticism, or a professional challenge.

For a very few seconds the hypership spoke in its highly compressed language and the mattran coordination computer listened, and Martin held his breath.

DATA EVALUATED. PROPOSED SOLUTION CONTRAVENES CITIZEN EXAMINATION AND INDUCTION PROCEDURE. REFER REGULATIONS 1, 4, 7 THROUGH 18, AND 145A. COUNTER INSTRUCTIONS ARE ACCEPTABLE ONLY FROM A SUPERVISOR LEVEL ONE OR ABOVE. REQUEST REFUSED. INSUFFICIENT AUTHORITY.

Beth looked briefly at the master screen, where the sensors were reporting increasing levels of seismic activity and of mental distress among the Keidi inside their quaking centers. The most optimistic forecast for the eruption was only a few hours away, but it could happen at any time. With a visible effort she curbed her impatience and spoke as one highly intelligent, responsible, but utterly emotionless computer to another.

She said, "The data supplied was intended simply to inform you of the complexity of the problem. A solution was not requested since many of the factors involved, the sometimes illogical and emotion-based thinking associated with the nonmaterial aspects of their lives, place it beyond your level of competence. The problem can be fully appreciated, and a solution provided, only by another organically constructed computer or computers of Supervisor or Planner level empowered to modify or temporarily rescind the regulations being contravened. This is an emergency situation with insufficient time to seek the advice or permission of organic superiors. The solution must therefore be provided immediately by subordinates assuming full responsibility and temporary authority. Activate the orbital transmitters forthwith."

The reply did not appear for nearly three seconds, which was a very long time for such a high-level computer to consider its response.

WARNING. REGULATIONS 1 AND 4 SPECIFI-CALLY FORBID THE INTRODUCTION OF ANY IN-TELLIGENT LIFE FORM OR FORMS INTO THE FEDERATION WORLD WHO HAVE NOT BEEN CLEARED BY THE INDUCTION CENTERS, AND WITH PARTICULAR REFERENCE TO BEINGS CLASSIFIED AS UNDESIRABLE. ACTUAL OR ATTEMPTED CONTRAVENTION OF THESE REGU-LATIONS AND ALL ATTENDANT CIRCUMSTANCES WILL BE REPORTED TO SUPERVISOR LEVEL FOR INVESTIGATION, EVALUATION, AND DECISION RE-GARDING DISCIPLINARY ACTION TOWARD THE BEING OR BEINGS RESPONSIBLE. IN THIS IN-STANCE THE REPORT WILL NOT BE TRANSMIT-TED UNLESS OR UNTIL THE INSTRUCTION TO CONTRAVENE THESE REGULATIONS IS CON-FIRMED.

"A nice, considerate computer," Beth said softly. "It's offering to let us off the hook, giving us time for second thoughts. Maybe we should—"

Martin shook his head.

"Your original instruction," Beth said, in a human and very frightened voice, "is confirmed."

REACTIVATING ALL UNITS. PLANETARY MAT-TRAN NETWORK OVERRIDE ON. INTERSTELLAR MATTRAN INTERFACING WITH INDUCTION CENTER TRANSMISSION ROOMS. AWAITING DES-TINATION COORDINATES.

Chapter 31

THE interstellar matter transmitters, which had remained dark and inactive while three generations of Keidi had grown to maturity on the planet below them, blazed suddenly with light. During the Exodus hundreds of them had encircled Keida like a dazzling string of jewels which shone so brightly that night had become a soft, gray twilight.

Now there were only the ten which had remained in orbit, to accommodate those Keidi who were expected to try for Federation citizenship from time to time. A combination of pride, independence, hostility, and, in recent years, the guards and labor camp of the First Father had kept them inactive, but ten of them were more than enough to handle the transfer of the present Keidi population.

Martin said, "They'll have to go to one of the areas allocated to warm-blooded oxygen breathers with similar gravity and atmosphere requirements, but with enough distance separating them to avoid premature contact with—"

"Do I understand you correctly?" the doctor broke in harshly. "Are you going to move my people from this, our home planet, to an alien and dangerous world? One that is already populated by strange, frightening, and perhaps hostile creatures whose effect on the Keidi is unknowable. And you would do this without asking their permission or giving prior warning? You are doing a great wrong, off-worlder."

"You don't know the half of it," Beth said tiredly. "But there is nothing to threaten you on the Federation World, unless it is some of your own people. And yes,

273

that is what he intends unless you can make him change his mind."

To Martin she went on pleadingly, "We are considering contravening Rule One, but we haven't actually done anything yet. If we changed our minds even now, the supervisor might consider this a temporary aberration in a couple of otherwise responsible non-Citizens. It was bad enough letting the First blackmail you into keeping his organization intact, so that his particular form of poison could reinfect all of Keida. But now you're going to infect the Federation World itself with that same poison. I can't even imagine what they will do to us for that. Think, *please*. There must be another answer."

"We both know that this is the only answer," Martin said quietly. To the doctor he went on, "The Keidi will be told exactly why and where they are going and what to expect when they get there. We owe them that much, at least, for precipitating this disaster..."

"But Regulation One..." Beth began.

"I know, I know," Martin said impatiently. "It states that no intelligent being who has not passed through an induction center and qualified as a Federation Citizen or non-Citizen in Federation service may be transferred to the Federation World, nor may he, she, or it be given information about the World. I think the last part was probably included so as not to make the Undesirables feel too bad about what they were missing, it being considered kinder not to tell the damned too much about heaven."

Beth shook her head. "Couldn't we move them temporarily to the north and south continents? It would be rough on them, especially on the very old and young, but only for the time necessary to explain the situation to the supervisor and get permission to—"

"If permission was not given," Martin broke in, "and we, through a combination of moral cowardice and inaction, had to leave the Keidi here to degenerate physically and culturally on their contaminated planet, I don't think we would feel very proud of ourselves.

"While I'm talking to the refugees, let them see what is happening to their planet right now," he went on, "and be ready to project the Federation World visuals to all centers."

"Except the First's?" Beth asked.

"All centers," Martin said. "I have a promise to keep."

He talked slowly and simply and without making any attempt at verbal dramatics, letting the inputs from the visual sensors do that for him as he described the present plight and the probable fate of the Keidi people should they remain on their home world. While he spoke Beth projected the terrifying, three-dimensional pictures of the great chasms that were beginning to open up in their forests and fields, splitting or swallowing up or demolishing newly built shelters and the old, pre-Exodus buildings alike.

He spoke of the north and south continents which were free of earthquakes but, because Keida did not have the axial tilt which would have given seasonal changes, remained cold and virtually barren, requiring pre-Exodus levels of population and technology to make them habitable. This was the reason why the Keidi had gravitated to the now doomed equatorial continent and the Estate of the First. He reminded them of the words of the First and the doctor when they had been describing the short- and long-term effects of radiation exposure. He told them that Keida was no longer a suitable home for its people, and that when they moved into the matter transmitter compartments they would be transferred to another world.

It was a world where the soil was fertile, the temperature and climate mild, and the territory available to them and their descendants unlimited. It was the world where the pre-Exodus Keidi who had qualified for citizenship and their descendants now lived and flourished. In centers all over Keida the interior lighting dimmed, and he showed it to them.

Beth said softly, "Just let the First try to take the credit for *that*!" The doctor made an untranslatable noise so high-pitched that it might have come from one of the First's child trainees, and Martin had to stop talking for a moment because the sight, although familiar to him, was still enough to take his breath away.

In all the projection screens there blazed a picture of the countless suns which crowded the center of the galaxy, except, that was, for the one place in the middle of the picture where there hung a featureless, black diamond shape which absorbed the light all around it like a gigantic, three-dimensional shadow.

"This," Martin said, "is the Federation World..."

He went on, trying to word the explanations of what the World was and how it was made, so that even the younger Keidi, untutored as they were in astronomy and astrophysics would understand.

As the view from interstellar space was replaced by sharply detailed pictures of the interior, Martin tried to describe its topography and environmental variations, its incredibly advanced technology, and, most importantly, its reason for being.

"... The primary purpose of the Federation is to seek out the intelligent races of the galaxy and bring them to this place of safety before they perish in some natural catastrophe or in some unnatural manner devised by themselves. In this world they will grow in knowledge and in numbers and, in the fullness of time, they will intermingle and share the fruits of their respective cultures. Ultimately they will be capable of achievements unimaginable to the most advanced minds among its present-day Citizens.

"But it will be a slow, natural process," he continued, "free of any kind of physical force or mental coercion. While the Citizens are climbing to the technological, philosophical, and cultural heights, they must be protected from those who, like a slow growing, insidious malignancy, would warp and weaken and ultimately destroy them from within. That is why the examination and induction centers were set up on all the inhabited worlds discovered by the Federation, to exclude the troublemakers, the power seekers, the intelligent predators who prey on their own kind, and so it was on Keida."

Martin paused for a moment to let his words sink in. Beth was staring at him, her face looking white and pinched. The doctor's eyes were on the screen. Neither of them moved.

"After the Exodus," he resumed, "the only people remaining on Keida were these Undesirables and those Keidi who would have qualified for citizenship but for reasons of their own elected to stay. Since then two generations of Keidi have been born, many of whom would have qualified for citizenship had they not been prevented by force or misinformation from visiting the induction centers. But now the Keidi who remain are in danger and there is no time for the usual examination and selection process. It had been decided that, rather than allow the potential Citizens to share the fate of the Undesirables, everyone who chooses to do so will be moved to the Federation World."

He had to give them a choice because the Keidi were proud and independent to a fault, but they were not stupid. Martin sighed and took the final, irrevocable step.

He said briskly, "Will everyone who has chosen to go please form into groups of twenty persons or less and move with your possessions into the matter transmitter compartments. Don't worry about being separated, everyone who is presently occupying a center will be sent to the same destination. Shelters and basic needs will be fabricated and supplied shortly after your arrival..."

He ignored the attention signal winking impatiently on the comm panel. The First was trying to talk to him.

"...Since you have not been accepted as Federation Citizens," he went on, "you will be placed at a sufficient distance from the descendants of the Keidi who preceded you so that you will not be able to meet or influence them until such contact is mutually desired. But the distances separating your new towns and settlements will be similar to those you are accustomed to on Keida, that is, within a few days' or weeks' journey by land. The sole exception to this will be the First, his Family, and the specially chosen members of his Estate. They, for the reasons I have already outlined, will be placed together at a very great distance from everyone else."

He pressed his accept button and said, "Speak, First Father."

"There has been gross misdirection, off-worlder!" the

First said angrily. "For my help with the evacuation you are obligated to allow me to stay with my people, with *all* of my people!"

"My obligation," Martin said firmly, "was to allow you to keep your Family and your organization intact wherever I sent you. That obligation will be discharged."

"Listen to me, you treacherous off-worlder," the First said in a voice that was so calm and controlled that it made Martin shiver. "My people need me on this new, safe, comfortable world. More than ever they must be organized, disciplined, toughened, welded together into one tight family unit that will be the fear and envy of the countless millions of soft, spineless Federation creatures all around them. Be warned, off-worlder, my Estate will cover even your great Federation World. Mere distance will not keep me from my Keidi, and from fulfilling my destiny."

"Mere distance . . ." Martin began, and stopped.

The First had not realized the awful size of the super-world—nobody, himself included, could. A diameter in excess of two hundred and eighty million miles and a useable surface area of nearly two hundred fifty quadrillion square miles, or well over one billion times the entire surface area of Keida. He would place the First one million miles, or maybe more, from the other Keidi settlements. It would be a very long walk, over fallow, synthesized soil or the as yet uncovered metal shell of the world itself, to reach them—if he knew which direction to take. But suddenly Martin felt sorry for this fanatical old Keidi Undesirable who honestly believed that he knew what was best for his people, and he resisted the temptation to gloat.

Instead, he said, "It is possible that, without your influence, the Keidi will become full Citizens in time. And it is possible that the descendants of your organization, with nobody but themselves to organize and order around, will also grow to maturity and sanity and become eligible. That is my belief and my hope.

"The other centers are emptying quickly," he went on. "Your building's foundations have been severely weakened and it may collapse at the next shock. You must leave with your people at once.

"We will not meet or speak again."

Even though it seemed that a couple of the centers were disintegrating around the last few Keidi to leave them, the evacuation was completed without injuries or loss of life. With the planet emptied of potential Citizens requiring transport, the great, orbiting matter transmitters disappeared one by one as they began the long hyper-jump back to their Federation World maintenance docks. The doctor had been delighted to learn that he would be able to rejoin his city people in their new home, but not for several days because he would have to travel back on the hypership. There was no need for them to wait for the eruption, but under the circumstances neither Martin nor Beth were in any hurry to return.

"Volcanic activity is always difficult to predict with accuracy," Beth said, trying to make conversation with a life-mate who had seemingly taken a vow of silence. "Even with our deep probes it isn't possible to be sure of the exact timing or size of the energy release. But it will be a big one."

After another lengthy silence the doctor, for the first time, called him by name.

"Now I believe that my understanding of your situation is complete, friend Martin," he said. "When you spoke of your concern over a great wrong you were about to commit, I assumed that it would be a serious misdirection against the First for imprisoning both of you. That would have been understandable if not praiseworthy. But now I realize that the wrong is directed against your superior, your own First Father, for the benefit of the Keidi, and that the offense is both unprecedented and so serious that chastisement of an unimaginable kind is likely to result."

The strange puckerings which briefly distorted the alien features must be an expression of deep, personal concern, Martin thought. He sighed and said, "That's true. Whatever is decided it is certain to come as a surprise. But don't worry, they might not be too hard on us."

The old Keidi rose to his feet and unfolded his long, strangely jointed arms until one hand rested gently on Beth's head and the other on Martin's. He did not point his speaking horn at them as he said, "Please turn off your recorders, this knowledge is for you alone. My name is Thretagartha. You are my Family."

Martin swallowed but did not speak. Beth said, "You honor us, Thretagartha."

"Martin and Beth," the old Keidi went on, "as your advisor, assistant, and Father on Keida, the responsibility for what has happened is partly mine. I shall speak, therefore, to the horrendous, highly intelligent but morally confused off-worlder who is your supervisor, and explain that—"

He broke off. Beth was pointing wordlessly at the main screen.

A great, black flower flecked with the bright red streaks of molten lava, rooted in the site of the buried arsenal, was growing out and upward into the stratosphere. For hundreds of miles around the eruption the central continent was behaving, not as land surface but as a sea on which there rolled long, green, forested waves. As they watched the original fault line opened up in both directions like an enormous, ragged-edged wound oozing with the angry red sores of secondary eruptions, widening and lengthening until the land mass was split open from coast to coast.

The ocean poured in to fill the wound, exploding into steam as the water met the molten core stuff and setting off further eruptions. Then gradually the violently dying continent was covered by a streaked and dirty shroud of smoke and steam and stratospheric dust. And radiating from its devastated coastline came the tidal waves, mountainous and irresistible as they thundered toward the habitable coastal strips of the north and south continents.

"And we," Beth said numbly, "were worried about the effects of residual radiation."

"Martin," the doctor said. "No Keidi could have survived this, and no wrong has been done here."

A few minutes later they left the Keida system, and except for the persistency of mental vision which projected the events of the last few hours onto the flickering gray blur that was hyperspace, there was nothing to see or say because nobody wanted to talk. Martin's chest and shoulder began paining him again, and he decided to pay an overdue visit to the medical module.

As he climbed into the treatment cabinet he still could not rid himself of those ghastly mind-pictures of Keida's destruction. But now they were interspersed with those of the First interrogating them in the cell at Camp Eleven; and organizing, directing, bullying, and encouraging the Keidi refugees like the military officer he once had been; and his words and manner as he had boasted that his Family Estate would one day include the entire Keidi species, and even the Federation World itself. Then just before the anesthetic took effect there was the picture of Thretagartha and the last words that the Doctor had spoken to him.

No wrong has been done here.
But had there been?

The doctor was returned to his people by a robot spacecraft and the hypership was instructed to remain Outside, where it hung between the black metal of the superworld and the breathtaking starshine of the galactic core. In the past such an order had meant an early reassignment, but this time it could mean anything.

Their supervisor did not keep them waiting.

RECORDINGS OF ALL SENSOR DATA, VISUALS, AND CONVERSATIONS PERTINENT TO THE CURRENT ASSIGNMENT HAVE BEEN STUDIED AND EVALUATED. ADDITIONAL INFORMATION IS REQUIRED REGARDING THE THOUGHT PROCESSES LEADING TO THE DECISION TO TRANSFER KEIDI UNDESIRABLES, PARTICULARLY THE ENTITY KNOWN AS FIRST FATHER, TO THE FEDERATION WORLD. DO YOU REQUIRE TIME TO CONSIDER YOUR ANSWER?

"No," Martin said. Beth gripped his hand tightly but did not speak, so he went on quickly, "Investigations showed that the majority of the Keidi were not Undesirables, but were being prevented by physical and psychological coercion from presenting themselves for candidate examination at the induction centers. In the situation which developed it seemed inherently wrong that potential Citizens should suffer because of the power seeking Undesirables among them. The children of Undesirable parents were also potential Citizens, so the decision was taken to—"

THE CIRCUMSTANCES AND YOUR DECISION ARE KNOWN TO ME. WHY WERE BEINGS WHOSE UNDESIRABLE STATUS WAS NOT IN DOUBT TRANSFERRED TO THE FEDERATION WORLD?

Martin took a deep breath before continuing. "It seemed to me that I was continuing the Citizen selection process which preceded the Exodus. On Keida, had the planet not been rendered uninhabitable, the people would never have been free of the military rule of the Estate. The First, by insisting that those he had chosen to form his present and future military organization should stay together, made the isolation of the confirmed Undesirables a simple matter. The progress of both groups, potential Citizens and Undesirables, can be monitored more easily here than on Keida.

"It is my hope," he went on, "that among the descendants of the First's people an increasing number of Citizens will arise until, in time, the Undesirables among the Keidi will become extinct."

IS YOUR ANSWER COMPLETE?

"Not quite," Martin said. "It also seemed to me that Undesirables, regardless of their planet of origin, are analogous to a wasting disease which can ultimately bring about the death of many species. Federation Citizens are protected, isolated, from this disease. This is not necessarily a good thing because soon they will have no understanding of this cultural malady, and no defense should they encounter it when, in the distant future, our people emerge from this overprotected womb to go out among the other galaxies. So it occurred to me that our Citizens might be immunized against this disease by exposing them for short periods, inoculating them, with its dead or inactive germs, as is done during the vaccination process.

"That is all," he ended bitterly, "except that I consider it grossly unfair that a Contactor Three should be faced with such a damnable and unique dilemma, between the breaking of the First Rule and the saving of so many lives."

YOUR DILEMMA WAS NOT UNIQUE.

Martin felt an angry surprise, and deep sympathy, for his predecessor or predecessors who had been caught in the same trap. He wondered what the sentence for such an offense had been, and knew that he would shortly find out.

NOTIFICATION OF CHANGE IN STATUS.

"Here it comes," Martin said grimly. Beth's grip on his hand tightened.

EFFECTIVE IMMEDIATE. NON-CITIZEN MJC/ 221/5501 CONTACT SPECIALIST PROMOTED LEVEL TWO. ASSIGNMENT INSTRUCTIONS FOL- LOW.

"Wha-*what*?..." Martin began incredulously. Beth was laughing and beating her fists against his chest, unmindful of his recently cracked ribs. Intense relief, he thought, was a very effective painkiller.

SUMMARY OF ASSIGNMENT. SITUATION SIMI- LAR TO THAT FOUND ON KEIDA WITHOUT THE COMPLICATIONS OF RADIATION POISONING, IN- STABILITY OF PLANETARY CRUST, OR RE- STRICTED OPERATIONAL TIME LIMIT. OBSERVE, EVALUATE, MAKE RECOMMENDATIONS REGARD- ING ACTIVITIES OF FIRST GENERATION UNDESIR- ABLES AND NON-CITIZENS WITH SPECIAL REGARD TO IMMINENT SO-CALLED HOLY WAR THREAT BY MAJORITY GROUP, WHO ARE ALSO PREDOMINANTLY UNDESIRABLE, AND INCREAS- ING INFANT POPULATION. PRINCIPAL DIFFICULTY FORESEEN WILL BE EMOTIONAL INVOLVEMENT WITH SUBJECTS.

PROCEED AT ONCE TO FWC/139/92/G3. ENVI- RONMENTAL PROTECTION AND SPECIES PHYSIO- LOGICAL DATA UNNECESSARY. YOUR NAME FOR THE PLANET IS EARTH.

About the Author

JAMES WHITE was born in Belfast, Northern Ireland, and resided there until 1984 when he moved to Portstewart on the North coast. His first story was printed in 1953. He has since published well-received short stories, novellas, and novels, but he is best known for the Sector General series, which deals with the difficulties involved in running a hospital that caters to many radically different life-forms.